THE WIDOW WALTZ

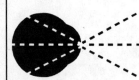

This Large Print Book carries the
Seal of Approval of N.A.V.H.

THE WIDOW WALTZ

SALLY KOSLOW

THORNDIKE PRESS

A part of Gale, Cengage Learning

GALE
CENGAGE Learning®

Detroit • New York • San Francisco • New Haven, Conn • Waterville, Maine • London

LIBRARY OF CONGRESS CATALOGING-IN-PUBLICATION DATA

Koslow, Sally.
  The widow waltz / by Sally Koslow. — Large print edition.
    pages ; cm. — (Thorndike Press large print peer picks)
    ISBN 978-1-4104-6105-6 (hardcover) — ISBN 1-4104-6105-X (hardcover) 1.
Widows—Fiction. 2. Mothers and daughters—Fiction. 3. Adult children—Fiction. 4. Loss (Psychology)—Fiction. 5. Adjustment (Psychology)—Fiction. 6. Domestic fiction. 7. Large type books. I. Title.
PS3611.O74919W53 2013b
813'.6—dc23   2013023962

Published in 2013 by arrangement with Viking, a division of Penguin Group (USA)

Printed in the United States of America
1 2 3 4 5 6 7 17 16 15 14 13

To Helen Davis Koslow Sweig,
whose love of life inspires me

Fortune helps those who dare.

— VIRGIL

People are just about as happy
as they make up their minds to be.

— ABRAHAM LINCOLN

1.

Benjamin Theodore Silver wasn't the youngest runner at the track, not by thirty years, but he was a quietly humming machine with a rare grace that turned your head: long legs, fluid movement, a stride that spoke of confidence. Most men his age galumphed around the track — oxen, winded, and hairy. If you passed them, you heard them gasp like a pair of old bellows as they cursed their knees. Ben ran without sound effects, a dancer, barely sweating. His hair was well-cut and graying at the sideburns; his jaw, still strong. Ten years ago, someone once said he resembled a young Jeremy Irons. He liked that.

Today Ben was wearing broken-in shoes and plain black running clothes. He was opposed to logos, although he made an exception for Apple. Ben looked open and approachable, a man you'd cast in a Cialis commercial even if he needed no such drug in real life — nor, according to his doctor, statins. Ben Silver took sweet pride in his cholesterol number.

He was a guy who knew a little about a lot. If you were a stranger who sat next to him on a flight to, say, New Zealand, where he traveled last year with his family, his conversation wouldn't be too frequent, too dull, or too lengthy. You'd chat about whatever sport was in season, the latest rumble in the Middle East, the play he saw and no one else knew about that would be sold out in three weeks, about where to buy leather in Milan, and whether or not you should drink barrel-aged bourbon with oysters. Then he'd bury his head in a biography or a civil war history. The year he and Georgia married, he was the best man in six other weddings. Today he was the emergency contact on nine phones, not just Georgia's and the family-plan phones he covered for Nicola and Louisa, daughters on whom he doted as much as Rhett worshipped Bonnie Blue.

Most people didn't begrudge Ben Silver his enviable life — the law practice, the apartment on Central Park South, the house at the beach, the club memberships, even the urban hedonist's wardrobe of suits and electronics. He had a lot, but not so much that you felt disgust for an avaricious nature, which wasn't the first trait, or even the eighth or ninth, that came to mind when you got to know Ben — to the degree that was possible. He worked hard for his money, some of which he donated to obscure microfinance programs and worthy candidates' campaigns. He was a solid A-minus/B-plus attorney practicing independently — corporate, criminal, matrimonial law. Ben had degrees behind him, educated at Brown on a scholarship rounded out by tending bar at a Providence saloon beloved by the pols, after which a state senator pulled strings to get him into Columbia School of Law, where he graduated with honors. Ben seemed like the last man in the world who'd ever need to cheat at poker, or anything else.

Other men loved Ben, with the exception of Georgia's brother, Stephan Waltz. He had his suspicions, which Ben reciprocated. Dogs loved Ben. Cats? Not so much, but women especially loved Ben, and the woman who loved him the most was his wife. Georgia Waltz clung to her maiden name as some women do to the hairstyle they wore at the time of their beauty's peak. Georgia was just fifty and adverse to needles and scalpels, so there was the faintest, softest droop to her face, which hung on fine trestlework. Over the years, at least one close friend had brought a picture of Georgia's genetically sculpted nose to their surgeon, saying, "I want what she's got." In Georgia's battle for that comely face and a tiny butt, her face was winning, and this upped her appeal. Women like a woman who has at least as much padding as they do.

Georgia hadn't gone aggressively blonde. Her hair was the color of clover honey, almost the brown of years ago. Ben was tall; Georgia was tall enough. A nearsighted nurse once recorded her height at five foot five. Ever after, Georgia respected this error and exaggerated by three-fourths of an inch. That was all she lied about, and this quality attracted people whom, after scrutiny, she'd allow one by one past her velvet rope. Georgia had countless acquaintances and admirers — more than she knew — gathered from heading up school and volunteer committees and years as a docent at the Met. She had buddies from her gym, and women friends with whom she took current affairs classes at NYU and Italian at the New School. Of course, there was an obligatory book club. But the role of First Friend was reserved for Ben, who took greedy pride in the honor. His understudy was Daniel Russianoff, the partner of Georgia's brother, Stephan.

The New York City marathon was on Sunday, three days from now. For Ben, a Philadelphia native, this would be the first in his adopted hometown, though he'd run the twenty-six-mile endurance test in Boston, Chicago, and, most memorably, Honolulu. For next year, he was flipping a coin between Amsterdam and London. Running emptied his soul of the trivial. As soon as he started, he felt an internal engine turn over, and solutions to problems appeared in boldface, anxiety sluiced away.

Today was one of Ben's favorite times of the year to run — to be *alive,* damnit — because by now the international runners had gathered in Central Park for warm-up sprints. The sun cast a copper glint and the November air hummed with Japanese, Italian, French, Swedish, and tongues that Ben couldn't identify. They blended in a universal language of goodwill: in this gathering of outsize fitness, nothing bad could happen.

Yet, something did. Ben had finished the third of what he had planned to be four laps around the reservoir, a well-groomed path jogged, back in the day, by Jackie O. He had passed the sign bearing her name, pacing himself behind a round-rumped redhead

13

whose ponytail bounced with every footfall. As he ran by the steps of Engineer's Gate he started to pant. His first emotion was embarrassment. Unless he was having sex, Ben never panted. Was he pushing too hard? He hadn't planned on getting old.

He slowed a bit, and then considerably, letting runners from a Korean team pass. By the time he'd reached the north side of the path, he halted and swiveled to take in the midtown skyline and catch his breath. In the haze, the fountain, equidistant between east and west, looked a mile away.

That's when a blistering pain crept from his chest like a hot poker heading for his neck. Ben grabbed his left shoulder and started to crumple. When he opened his eyes, two of the Koreans hovered above him. One looked as if he could be his daughter Nicola's twin brother. He thought of the day he and Georgia met their Mi Cha, whom they renamed for his mother. His mind bounced to Louisa coming home a year later, how full and happy he and Georgia were in that Mount Sinai delivery room. He pictured his wife, a beauty at twenty and a beauty now. *My God,* Ben thought, *I am a lucky man, albeit one who at this moment is having one helluva panic attack.*

He was beyond mortified, skidding toward terrified. The sun was in his eyes and as he shut them, he heard, *"Appelez un auxilliaire médical!"* He damn well hoped that meant, "Call a paramedic."

But who would call *her*? He reached into his pocket. There was his iPhone, but his smaller phone was missing, most likely gone flying when he fell, probably resting now among the weeds beyond the iron fence or sunk to the bottom of the reservoir.

A minute passed, or it could have been ten. A gurney arrived. The Frenchman and the Koreans stepped aside for the husky, red-blooded American EMTs, full of kindness and McDonald's. They loaded him fast but gently, taking his pulse, asking questions he was too out of it to answer.

His last thought was of how she looked in Hawaii. Like a woman half her age . . .

2.

What is the proper attire for the reading of your father's will? I'm certain it isn't the orange yoga pants that hang below my daughter's slightly convex middle. "Luey," I bark. "Please change into something decent."

"Nothing fits," she snivels. Louisa's colic has continued for twenty years. Her nettling ways penetrate my thinner hide as she shimmies out of the pants, wagging her behind. On flamingo legs — identical to mine, minus my lattice of spider veins — I see my own behind from fifteen pounds and years ago. On one sharp hip bone a Rolling Stones tongue tattoo taunts me.

"What about these?" Luey presents two pair of jeans, one in each hand. I shake my head. "Or would you prefer a burka?"

Luey may have inherited my lower torso and face, but in almost every other way she is Ben. Though my daughter's nose is sharp and her gums more evident than she'd prefer, her jigsaw of imperfection works. She has large, round eyes of a color people call hazel by default; lips that are full, pouty, and raspberry tinged.

"Where's the black suit you wore last week?" I ask, weary. Following even our limpest confrontations, battle fatigue does me in.

"In the pile."

For any degree of efficiency with which the Silver-Waltz family may operate we should thank, more often than we do, the unmatched competence of Opal Owens who, had she gotten the chance to have gone to college, could have led a Fortune 500 company. She will see that Luey's suit is transformed into crisply dry-cleaned garments, as well as dispose of her ossified Thai food and trampled magazines. You can depend on Opal to not only unearth the thick biography of Colette that was due back to the Stanford University library four months ago, but to see to it that the book is FedEx'd with a polite apology.

"Skirt?" my daughter says, offering up a tube of brown spandex.

"Better." Barely.

My daughter hoists the hanger like a Grammy and blows me a kiss. "With thanks to my savior, I will proceed. You are dismissed, Mommy dearest."

With pleasure. I pad barefoot back to our — my — bedroom and escape into the dressing room. It smells faintly of cedar and Ben's aftershave, a mossy scent that when mingled with his sweat, I consider the ultimate aphrodisiac. His suits, size 42 long, fill one wall. Blindingly white sneakers are waiting to be broken in after the marathon he missed by one heart attack. The Zappos Web site, the source of this footwear, promises "Happiness in a box." Ben would appreciate the irony.

I twist the safe's combination — two, fourteen, eighty-one, our wedding day — open the velvet-lined drawer, and reach for the ruby brooch, a modest posy on a gold stem given to my mother fifty years ago by my father when I was born. Today I need a piece of Camille Waltz with me, though I am grateful that through her veil of increasing dementia she may have forgotten that I have raised a brat. When we visit Mother, she fixates on Louisa and sees a younger version of me, albeit with hair spiked through the artful use of shiny goop. Despite her histrionics, Louisa Silver-Waltz makes her grandmother smile, and in those fleeting moments I forgive my younger daughter because she returns the mother I have lost, the mother I could use right now as a crutch and a crucible for my wobbly emotions.

I pin the talisman to my proper charcoal lapel and stare at Ben's photo. Salt-and-pepper hair, cropped close to his well-shaped head; lines bracketing his blue eyes; and the tiniest sag under a sharp chin are the only clues that he is not still my Benjy, whom I started loving before I was a woman. I see the college senior in the man, press two fingers to my lips and gently caress his grin. Ben brought a swagger to every task — making love, money, or mischief, to which he devoted equal time.

A massive coronary? Ben, you were the healthiest person I know, a study in egg-white omelets and soy, although you might have liked your flashy demise, surrounded by a United Nations of marathon runners gathered with their Smartphones to capture the shining city. Seven people dialed 911. I'm told that, until the medics arrived, dozens of runners circled the tall guy clutching his chest, sprawled on the dirt, who was making jokes before he passed out. By the time a stranger called and told me to meet the ambulance at Lenox Hill Hospital, you were gone. A marriage of twenty-nine years, *poof,* over, done.

"Though lovers be lost, love shall not; and death shall have no dominion." I have taken to reading my treasured Dylan Thomas. This morning, I am determined not to cry. I open a drawer filled with wraps and am ready to choose one, as much for its cashmere cheer as for its defending warmth. And then I hear Nicola.

"Mother?" she says in her satiny voice. "We need to leave in five minutes."

"Come on in, darling," I say, turning toward the door. "I'd like your opinion." As if it matters what I wear, though my own mother believes it does. *Look the part you want to play,* I can hear her say.

Nicola's dressed in a dark plum wool sheath, the capped sleeves offsetting its severity; her father's bulky steel sports watch, which she borrowed so regularly there's no question that it now belongs to her; and chunky beads she most likely fished from a jumble at the Paris flea. Her chignon is loose enough not to look prim. On the outside — only the outside — she is as pulled together as her sister Lucy will never be. Were it not for Nicola's Buddy Holly eyeglasses, worn today instead of her contacts, you might never guess that she, like all of us, has spent the better part of the last few weeks in tears.

20

Two months after we adopted Nicola, who began her life in a Korean orphanage, I discovered I was pregnant. My daughters are one year and a universe apart. Biology is the least of it. Where Nicola cooed from the moment she settled in my arms, Luey has challenged me since she could talk, the message as audacious as skywriting. *Why did you bring home that other little girl first? Cola's the phony. I'm the real deal.* Luey may be my blood, but in Nicola I see myself.

Embracing, we meet as equals. "When we're finished, I think we should have lunch," she says. "The three of us."

The three of us: a fractured family and trio of females who have always depended on Big Ben, a man a bit too ready to whip out a credit card to solve a problem. A daddy ready to spoil his girls — and that would include me — three lap dogs in an estrogen-soaked Mary Cassatt reverie. Ben adored his harem and served up unassailable opinions on genteel, feminine rituals. I had to convince him that it was inappropriate for a father to buy teenage daughters skimpy teddies and thongs. How perspicacious of God to give my husband daughters: Litigator Silver would have obliterated sons as surely as if they were opposing counsel.

From a pile on my closest shelf I pluck a

lilac shawl and turn for Nicola's approval, which she bestows with a nod. "I'll be glad when this meeting is over." My voice shakes. "Today is the first day of the rest of my life and all that."

"Who's this lawyer we're seeing?" My daughter averts her eyes from Ben's archived rows of belts and ties.

"The attorney who handled your father's private affairs." In the mirror, I am positive I see my daughter wince. Shall I clarify: his *business* affairs? I will let it pass. There were rumors. I'd hoped they had escaped my girls.

"Name?"

"Walter Fleigelman." Wally is boorish, brilliant, and remarkably kind, a Muppet shark among the hundreds at Ben's memorial, as well as one of the more welcomed faces at the house during the week. I cannot remember which monument of fruit he sent or which evening he stopped by, only that he took me aside, held both of my hands, and after heartfelt condolences, murmured, "Georgia, we need to talk. I'd be happy to make a house call." When he saw my reaction, his face beaded with perspiration and turned even redder than usual, and I knew that Walter Fleigelman Esq.'s proposition was strictly professional. This made me blush as well.

"Is there some sort of hurry?" I asked.

"Of course not," he said. "I didn't mean to rush you." But the following morning someone from his firm called to arrange an appointment, which, when I awoke this morning, I was nonetheless ready to postpone. After weeks of outlying cousins and acquaintances oozing sympathy, I wanted to do nothing today but nap, walk Sadie, and spend the afternoon and evening watching Diane Keaton movies that I could now lip-synch. Then I thought of Nicola and Luey: the mother-love chip implanted in my heart was activated and I realized I had to at least try to behave like the dignified woman I never expected to be.

What did the rabbi say of "the mourning process"? Beats me. I know we spoke for forty-five minutes but I remember nothing more than that he should clip his ear hair.

"Mother, are you there?" Nicola says gently.

I look up, startled. "Make sure your sister hasn't punked out and decided to wear a nightgown."

"Exactly what Luey wants, another prison matron."

"For me, darling." I stop short of begging. "Please." Nicola turns to leave. I know she

23

will do as I ask.

Before I go public, I need a minute. Gray roots are winning against my dark blond. Buck up, Georgia, I tell the mirror with its hollow eyes and puffy lids. You're a more fortunate woman than most. You've known long-lasting love. You have children. You want for little — the city apartment, the house on the beach, the trips, the cars, and an overload of possessions. And we've been philanthropic, though the donations are also the quid pro quo that has won me committee memberships. Pay to play, New York City's bumper sticker.

"Georgia!" I hear Luey yell. "You coming?"

"I'm Mom, Mother, or Mama — I will even accept Ma," I shout back. "Extend me that small courtesy, please."

"Sorry, Ma." She sounds surprisingly contrite.

The three of us wait, unspeaking, for the elevator. As we exit our building I link arms with my daughters and walk to the car. For better or worse, we will need one another. "Good morning," I say as I slide into the back, after Nicola. Fred has been our driver for five years. I suspect he knows more about my private life than I do. He shuts the door after Luey.

"Fine day, Ms. W," he says, taking his seat. I hadn't noticed that it's oddly warm for this late in the fall. I picture a polar bear stranded on a dwindling iceberg. "Where to?"

"One hundred twenty Broadway, please."

"Tell me again what's happening today," Luey says.

"A formality," I say, as I have, twice. "A lawyer will explain your father's will."

Luey knows that Nicola came into the first third of her trust fund at twenty-one. The big bang will occur when Second Daughter discovers that I will be her guardian until she is thirty. This is what Ben and I decided three years ago when, without consulting us, she dropped out of Stanford in the middle of her first semester to go work at an elephant camp in Zimbabwe with a boyfriend, now long gone.

Whenever I consider the august responsibility of being a solo parent, especially Luey Silver-Waltz's, I retreat a bit more into myself. Ben weighed in on every decision for the girls. Not just Stanford or Duke, but matters most mothers and daughters resolved by themselves. Gymnastics or horseback riding? Short hair or long? Red dress or blue? Ben had a viewpoint on everything. I allowed my thirty-year friendship with my

25

college roommate to expire when she said she couldn't stand to see me "act like a weak cup of tea." I never talked to Jill again until last week, one of many at Ben's funeral, because I liked the way my marriage worked. Ben Silver had an aptitude for happiness. No matter what he said or did, he could wheedle his way back into my heart.

"Here we are," Fred says, pulling in front of a grand tower. "How long do you think you'll be?"

"I'm guessing an hour." I fish a twenty out of my alligator handbag. "Please get yourself some lunch and I'll call when we're ready."

"Yes, ma'am," he says, accepting the bill, then gets out, comes around, and gives me his arm as I climb out of the black Lincoln.

Six heels clack up the steps and shoot straight through the marble lobby. A man in his thirties rubbernecks in our direction, though surely I am invisible next to my daughters. Once, I had a phalanx of admirers. Then along came Ben. When we met, I was less polished and far prettier. As I walked the sidewalks of Providence, I, too, turned heads, and even when I was with friends, I knew and they knew the stares were for me. My hair, with its shaggy bangs and layers, fell obediently into place to reflect the sun. My teacup breasts were round and high, which was enough, this being decades before implants inflated bosoms and expectations. My hips were slender, as were my legs; my skin, the creamy sort that you have no idea will crinkle with faint crow's-feet before twenty-nine, and beyond forty, betray you with a crush of wrinkles.

Time is history's bulldozer. I am no longer a glorious bloom in the ecosystem. I can almost hear people saying behind my back, *You should have seen her in college — Georgia Waltz . . . a knockout.* I try to evaluate my daughters as the rubbernecker must, gliding with the posture of ballerinas. "Stand up straight, shoulders back." Every time I said it, I heard my mother's voice. At least Nicola and Luey listened, though they're tall enough to get away with a little slouch. When you're like me, every quarter inch counts.

At the end of the lobby, a concierge asks for identification. "Luey, do you have yours?" My tone is freighted with impatience. She scowls at me as she presents her driver's license and the three of us ride an elevator to the thirty-fourth floor, which, along with the floor below, is occupied by Fleigelman, Kelly, Rodriguez and Roth.

I expect to have to wait — we are early —

but when I check with the receptionist, I'm told that Mr. Fleigelman is ready. She escorts us to a corner office with windows facing north and west. As we cross its threshold, Wally marches toward me on slightly bowed legs. He is wearing a somber dark suit and a white shirt. As I notice his stubby arms, I see a penguin.

"Georgia," he says, pulling me toward his barrel chest. Wally Fleigelman must shower in eau de toilette. I fight the reflex to squinch my nose. He can't see the gesture, but Nicola and Luey can; I respect Wally and want them to as well. "You brought your daughters?" He seems surprised.

"Of course," I say, as I allow him to lead me to a black leather couch under the window. Nicola sits by my side, Luey on an Eames chair facing the taller wooden armchair where Wally takes a seat. "We have no secrets." How can I make such a disingenuous remark? By not letting my glance drift toward the girls. "This is Nicola," I say, and the two shake hands. "And Louisa." She only nods and Wally doesn't press it.

"Pleased to meet you, ladies. Coffee?" he asks. "Fiji water? Scone? Berries? Help yourself." He gestures toward a platter on the coffee table as well as a bar against the wall.

Luey slathers what looks like cherry preserves on half of a scone as I say, "No thanks."

Let the fun commence.

"So, Georgia, girls," he says, puncturing the anticipation. "We'll talk *tachlis.*"

My daughters look baffled.

"Getting down to brass tacks," Wally, the portable Yiddish dictionary, explains. "And let me say, this is hard."

Shame on me. I am forgetting that my loss extends to Wally, who also adored Ben. In his way, Wally, too, must be grieving. This time it is I who lean forward and put a hand on an arm, which feels far meatier than the sinewy male limb I am used to touching. Tufts of dark hair creep out from Wally's pristine, monogrammed cuff.

He clears his throat. "What I mean is that this is going to be tough for you, Georgia." Wally stares into my eyes. "Very tough. And I'm deeply sorry about that. I am."

I shudder. There is finality to this protocol like nothing I have yet experienced. I have been so thoroughly focused on putting one foot in front of the other, day by endless day, I haven't considered the future. I have no close contemporaries who are widows, only never-marrieds or divorcees, women who despite their careful, chirpy behavior, are marked by a *bindi* establishing that they are of a lesser caste of the lonely and needy, or so we think in condescending moments, as they walk amid the wedded. The thought of joining their ranks brings on the tears. My eyes fill and nose drips.

Wally is fast with a tissue. "Go ahead. Don't mind me." I succeed in smiling.

"Georgia, dear," he says. "I'm so sorry, so truly sorry, but, well, here it is." He takes a deep, audible breath. "I've found an account that contains, as of yesterday, $38,392."

"Yes," I say, waiting for the rest.

"And that's it. From what I can tell, virtually all of the money — your money — is gone." He spreads his palms.

Wally is speaking a language I do not understand. I say nothing.

"Georgia." His tone as gentle as fingers caressing an infant's skin.

"Excuse me?" I ask.

"Sweetheart," he says, moving to the couch, wedging himself between me and Nicola, who leans away. Wally puts his arm on my shoulder and speaks slowly, as if I am deaf or dumb. "Let me explain this as simply as I can. I'm having a hell of a time finding assets. Your accounts appear to have been emptied."

That can't be. I know Ben's will like I

know *The Owl and the Pussycat*. "They took some honey and plenty of money / Wrapped up in a five-pound note." We reviewed the document every year, on the day before our anniversary. Ben always said that if he died first, he wanted me, the merry widow, to take a few years to travel, maybe sell the beach house and buy something cozy with shutters and an herb garden in the Berkshires, where I used to go to summer camp, a location that made him snore. "I'm going to provide for you, so promise me you'll have some fun before you settle down with some other lucky schmuck," he said. "But remember, I'm leaving you plenty. You won't have to remarry unless you want to." Half the point of his generosity was to make sure I never loved another man.

"I don't understand," I say to Wally. "This has to be a mistake."

"Georgia," he murmurs. "I wish it were."

My tongue turns to cotton but my speech speeds up. "Was Ben losing cases? I thought things were going well at his firm. Did he make a bad investment?"

With each burst of words, my voice gets higher and Wally shakes his head *no.*

"Is something happening Ben thought I was too fragile or ignorant to understand?" Was my husband going through a hell from which he thought I needed to be protected? Darling Ben.

"None of that, from what I can tell." Wally, too bulky to squirm, shifts uncomfortably in his seat.

Ben was a softie. "Did my husband give everything away?" Before Wally can answer that question, I zing another. "Where did all the money go?" Tough customers brought out Ben's machismo, but maybe the last laugh was on Ben, who had tried to play in leagues where a code was spoken that he couldn't understand.

Wally extends his hands and shakes his head. "Georgia, Jesus. I don't know. I've been on the trail for weeks. God knows I hope I'm wrong, but I didn't think it was ethical for me to keep this to myself any longer." The edges of his mouth tremble and his inflection is that of a dentist saying, *You may feel some slight discomfort,* before he yanks a tooth without Novocain.

"I just can't believe it. I can't, I can't. This is impossible. You can't be telling the truth."

I hide my eyes. I am whimpering, not unlike Sadie when I refuse to give her a third treat. What about life insurance? Ben had two policies, both borrowed against, Wally informs me. The accounts receivable at his firm? Not much there.

"Ma, don't worry." I glance up. Luey is streaming tears. "There's my trust fund. I'll take care of you."

Wally turns in her direction. "Are you Louisa or Nicola?"

"Louisa." She glares. "We met five minutes ago."

"Sweetheart, I'm afraid your future portfolio is also, at the moment, compromised. You, too, Nicola. Your father managed your accounts, you see."

"But Daddy said I'd be getting stipends until I'm thirty-five," a peevish Nicola answers.

"That was then." This is now.

Luey balls up her cloth napkin and shoots it across the room "So Daddy was just another dick?" Her face curdles into a grimace. "Why should he be different? Why didn't I see this coming?"

Why didn't *I*? But I snap, "Nicola! Louisa! Hush! I forbid you to defame your father this way. We'll get to the bottom of this. There must be some grievous errors." Please, please, please. I search Wally's face. *That was then, this is now.* Maybe all I need is a different lawyer.

I feel like a moth batting against a wall. *That was then. This is now.* But I am no fool. The investments may be gone, but we have other income. Surely, I cannot be poor. I have never been poor.

"What about our apartment. I could sell it. We own that free and clear."

"Mortgaged — to the hilt. Though, of course, you'd still get a little if you sell."

"The beach house?"

"Sorry. Same."

"The cars?" Besides the Lincoln, we drive an SUV to the country, where we keep a Jeep.

"Leased. But the furniture, the antiques, your art, your silver, your furs, your jewelry — all that you still own." He says this brightly, as if I could live in an armoire and auction off an earring at Sotheby's whenever my stomach growled.

"The property I inherited from my father?" When Ben and I moved Mother to a nursing home, we sold her house in Chestnut Hill, but there's a small office building in Philadelphia.

"Ben unloaded that last year. He forged your signature, I'm afraid."

I pictured Ben signing my name, with a long, swishy tale on the uppercase G of *Georgia.* You can be sent to jail for that — if you're alive. "Where did all this money go?" I could have asked the question fifty times, shrinking smaller as I repeated each word.

"At this point, I don't know," Wally says. "It's going to take some heavy lifting to find out. This is a long story, with footnotes."

To my surprise, I don't want to kill the messenger. I sense that if Wally Fleigelman could have stopped Ben, he would have. What could Wally truly know?

Then a second Georgia rises within me, ready to blow. Am I simply transferring my naïveté to a different man? I search the room for a steady focal point, but the painting on the wall across the room, with its scramble of angry reds, taunts me. I am afraid that if I get up I'll stumble, yet I find the courage to speak. "For today, Wally, just tell me what I absolutely have to know. What's the next step?"

He returns to confident sage. "If you're careful and conservative, you have enough to live on for a couple of months. Providing you can pay your debt service, you won't be foreclosed, and of course, in the worst-case scenario, you could eventually file bankruptcy. But none of this needs to or will happen instantly. I'm not saying you don't have plenty to sort out, but for now, Georgia, as your attorney and your friend, what I want you to do is take a deep breath."

You tell someone tottering on the edge of a cliff to take a deep breath?

35

"I wonder if I could have a minute . . . alone?" His eyes bounce from daughter to daughter.

All I have to say is, "Girls," and the two of them flee the room, and perhaps the country.

After the door is shut behind them, Wally says, "Your daughters are young, with their own concerns. They might not be your best confidantes. Do you have a sister you can speak to?"

"Only a brother. Stephan. Perhaps Ben has mentioned him. We aren't close."

"Right, Stephan Waltz." When Wally sees me shaking my head at the mention of Stephan's name, he continues, "How about a parent?"

"My father is dead, my mother isn't well."

"A trusted woman friend?"

I have a phone loaded with email addresses and numbers. Yet among the first- and second-tier of women I see with regularity at meetings, the gym, or lunch, did I have any genuine cozy-beyond-cordial, for-richer-for-poorer friends? I'd ordered four hundred notes in delicate ivory — which read, *Your thoughtful presence and kindness have touched our family deeply and will always be remembered with love. The family of Benjamin T. Silver* — and planned to send them to the hordes who'd shown up to mourn. Many people had made contributions. A shame they hadn't started the Georgia Waltz discretionary fund.

Suddenly I'm emptied of emotion, milk poured down a drain. My posture caves, but somehow I am standing, and moving toward the door.

Wally blocks my way. He kisses me on the cheek, saying, "I know this is a lot to take in. We'll talk. Next week is soon enough. Get some rest."

I say nothing, as ghost-Georgia floats past the receptionist and finds her daughters, who are sitting demurely. "Ma —" Luey starts.

"Not now," I say, surprised to see my own child.

"Shall we still have lunch?" Nicola asks. "Fred's downstairs."

I hadn't yet thought about him, or Opal, virtual family members. Fred is young and could probably find another job, but Opal is five years older than I am. How do I explain? I pull my daughters close. I do not want to release them.

"We need to go home," is all I can say.

In the sun, I feel illuminated as if by the light a bad detective has shined into the eyes of a crook. What is my crime? Trusting my husband while I played the dilettante? I slip into the car. Luey rests her head on my right shoulder, and on the other side, Nicola holds my hand. No one speaks for the length of the ride.

When we arrive, Opal takes my coat. I give her a hug and head straight to my bedroom and into my dressing room.

"Ben," I say to his photograph. "Explain yourself, please. How could you do this to me? What were you thinking?"

The man I love has left me naked and exposed. My first impulse it to hurl his picture across the room. My second is to hope for an explanation, a flotation device I can hold on to because I don't want to hate him, this boy who became my husband, this man I have loved for more than half my life.

I bury Ben's picture under a mound of his sweaters, out of sight.

3.

Nicola Silver-Waltz never knew when Luey would be as soft and yielding as a freshly baked sugar cookie or when she'd bubble into a blistering pot of crazy. "Put on a bra!" Nicola had shouted this morning at the closed door of Luey's bedroom. "If you own one. The lawyer doesn't need to size up your nipples."

Luey had been blasting *Super Freak*. When this song had been hot, they were little girls in leotards doing crooked arabesques at ballet recitals or shaking their small, saucy booties for their parents, who thought everything they did or said was adorable. Their mother had gotten over this fiction, though they used to be able to count on their dad. If they'd shared their thoughts — which Nicola and Luey had done little of for the last decade — they'd both admit that they expected Ben Silver to sail through the door and swoop to spin them around in his long, strong arms. How could he be . . . Neither sister could get to *deceased,* let alone *dead.*

Luey had ultimately worn her most reactionary garment, a brown jersey skirt, knee-length but clingy. Still, Luey barked at Nicola as if she had admonished her choice. "We don't all have trust funds and get to shop in Europe," Luey said, as if that had anything to do with her clothing selection.

When Nicola turned twenty-one two years ago, she had achieved financial emancipation through no effort of her own. Luey continued on the parental dole and was often groveling for extra cash. She regretted that she and Nicola weren't tightly braided, like some sisters.

Nicola had a nauseating feeling that Daddy was as tapped out as the lawyer claimed. She would have dismissed the story he told them about their dad's money, had the lawyer not been so gaga over her mom. It was apparent to Nicola, who trusted her intuition on such matters, that Walter Fleigelman was smitten with Georgia Waltz. During the meeting, each time her mother glanced at the artwork assaulting the walls — garish paintings that Nicola guessed had been selected all at once by an interior decorator — the man feasted his beetle eyes on Mother as if she were a candy bar. Nicola had stopped telling her mom that men were always doing a looky-loo, because Georgia never noticed. If only she had half the appeal her mother had.

Not that Nicola lacked for admirers. Men of all kinds, she had discovered in high school, were drawn to Asian women, even if that woman had visited her native land only once on a teen tour. Just last month in Paris, she was juggling the attention of an understudy acrobat with Cirque du Soleil and, in the top position, a sous-chef who may or may not still be married whom she'd met in culinary school. He had helped her get a temporary job as a prep cook, coming in early to cut vegetables, break down meats, and fillet fish — culinary grunt work. Neither man was on this side of the Atlantic or, Nicola was certain, the One. She'd been holding out for a love like that of her parents, who were as drawn to each other as a bee to a rose, though she softly regretted that since she'd returned to the United States for her father's funeral, she'd yet to hear from the chef, Emile. Not an email, not a text. She blinked away the image of him pulling her into one of the restaurant's walk-in freezers, the act's heat heightened by the possibility of discovery.

When they came home after a silent ride, she, their mother, and Luey each decamped to their respective bedroom and collapsed. Nicola sobbed. She thought first about how her father was her mother's center of gravity, an indubitable fact, and that to lose him young and suddenly — this wasn't fair. Then, like a swiftly moving weather system, her mind shifted squarely to herself, especially to how she'd gotten to love Paris and the small furnished flat she'd let not far from the Picasso Museum on the Place du Marché Sainte-Catherine. The city felt like one giant block party, as if the spirits of the world's creative elite haunted the cobblestone streets and she belonged next to them, soaking up inspiration, stopping for a coffee at random cafés in the city's misty mornings; reading in parks during the afternoon; drinking wine in the amethyst twilight. Paris might be her answer. But would she ever be able to make another deposit to the account she'd opened at Crédit Lyonnais — or even return? She chided herself for thinking this, but there it was.

4.

"Sadie," is all I have to say, holding up her leash. My goddess, whose coat I ask my hairdresser to match, trots toward me on sturdy corgi legs. I believe she is grinning.

For Sadie, Ben's death has turned into Mardi Gras. I have lifted the ban on night-long cuddling, her warm back bookending mine where his used to be. Sadie's monogrammed bed waits on the carpeted floor, but I may as well dump that sucker — there's no going back for either of us. The bigger bonus is that for the last three days I've walked her every four hours. Who needs a personal trainer when you have heartbreak? Some days we find ourselves heading south, once as far as the Village, another time east toward Chinatown, whose layers of pungent odors drive Sadie mad, and on to what remains of Little Italy and over to the East Village. This is where the half of Nicola's friends who don't live in Brooklyn's Park Slope or Williamsburg have settled, a neighborhood that even ten years ago was known mostly for its drug dealers, or so I, in my cloister, believed. Currently, one-bedrooms cost more than those uptown by Gracie Mansion, where Ben and I began our life together in a white brick box devoid of architectural integrity but armed with doormen, on which my mother insisted.

"Going out again, Georgia?" Opal says. We long ago dropped formalities, though Opal never felt at ease addressing Ben with anything less than "Mr. S."

"I need some air." From the concern on Opal's dusky Modigliani face, I know I'm not fooling her. "It's the only time I can think," I offer, inching toward the truth.

For the last two days, with Opal's help, I've been ripping apart my home. I've claimed that we're looking for insurance records, though I'm sure my poorly disguised anguish suggests a greater apocalypse. Together we've burrowed into at least half of the closets, drawers, and cupboards. As my life has turned out to be a sanctum of secrets, there are ample opportunities for concealment within my rambling apartment: I'm convinced that I'll find if not a pot of gold, at least a clue to the Sudoku that has become my MIA inheritance. I refuse to let myself slow for a cry or accept my daughters' help. I can breathe only if I steer clear of Nicola and Luey's beseeching looks and reasonable paranoia. But a few hours of ransacking at a time are all I'm able to bear. It is Sadie who benefits when I need a break.

"Come on, girl." I snap her red wool coat under her belly. As she wags her stubby tail, I grab Ben's old trench, tighten the belt, and slip into Luey's rain boots. Sadie is better dressed than I am. I hold the leash in one hand and a golf umbrella in the other and we're off.

Sadie tugs when we pass the doughnut shop on Sixth Avenue. "Forget it," I say. Today we're traveling south, as I replay the moment when Wally ripped the scab off the truth. He looked at me as if I were Joannie, our beloved cocker who preceded Sadie. Joannie had received a steroid injection the day before her death, which allowed her to prance to the gallows on her own four paws. She gave the vet a sloppy kiss, never suspecting she was going to be put down. I lit out of the room. Ben handled it.

I refuse to be Joannie. No one is going to wind a pink bandage around my flank, stab me with a hypodermic needle, and kick me out of the game. I'm going to find the money. Ben couldn't pass a homeless person without dipping into his pockets. He was always big-hearted and princely, never parsimonious. The husband I know and love would not be capable of leaving me almost stone-broke.

It came to me in a dream that he cashed in every investment and packed away neatly bundled bills, somewhere. So far the results of my dig have yielded only the ragged ephemera of four sloppy lives: given-up-for-dead sunglasses, crumpled receipts for restaurants that have gone AWOL and keys to doors that have vanished from memory.

"Georgia?" someone says as I plod along, eyes down. The face I see lacks a name my brain is willing to cough up. "Franny Wilson?" the woman says. "From the Met."

I must be staring dumbly because she adds, "Nicola and Lisa were together in grade school."

"Of course." I remember to say, "Congratulations on Lisa and Todd." Not long ago the *Times* ran Lisa Wilson's wedding photo, her face as round as a pizza, her fiancé a boy who went to camp with Nicola. I sent the clip off to her in Paris.

"They've been programmed like robots," Nicola scoffed in a later conversation, reciting the names of the investment banking firms where the bride and groom worked. I resisted pointing out that at least the two had graduated from college in the standard four years and completed their MBAs. It did not take them five years and three academic institutions to get their bachelor's degree, after which they moved three times to three continents with little more to show for it beyond culinary skills, Japanese knives to execute every recipe, and an enviable wardrobe. Nicola may be my even-keeled daughter, but no one can accuse her of following a straight path toward success. At least she can mince a Bermuda onion faster than I can brush my teeth.

Franny grasps my hand. "I read about your husband's passing. I'm so sorry. The way Ben always ran the auction — he was such a terrific father, such a great guy."

I'll be the judge of that, I think, but answer, "You're very kind," eager to escape her stilted pity.

"Will I be seeing you back at the Met soon, I hope?"

I know my life must be reinvented. That I have to go forward. But I can't picture myself leading groups of high school students through the American wing, then catching up on gossip with other docents while we pick at salads in the cafeteria.

Since Ben's death, however, I have discovered that when I meet people, if I say almost nothing, they cut the compassion and move on, which is what this woman does, with, "Well, bye — please call me if there's anything I can ever do."

Within a few steps, Franny Wilson's offer is forgotten. I keep going, and an hour later Sadie and I are in the Meatpacking District. It used to be that on those rare occasions when Ben and I walked along this dark armpit of a street, I worried we'd be robbed by a transvestite hooker. Now, I force myself not to gawk at the windows of stores and restaurants that I most likely can no longer afford. I am near Daniel's gallery and look for my watch, which I have forgotten to wear. Then I consider, does it matter what time it is, since I've cancelled every lunch, meeting, and appointment for this week and the next? The drizzle has stopped and Daniel won't mind callers, even if one reeks of wet dog.

Twentieth off Tenth is on the southern fringe of the Chelsea art scene. Sadie and I move to the middle of this gritty industrial stretch to avoid two yacht-sized trucks unloading their rarefied cargo in delivery bays. We arrive at 529, which is respectable if drab, and greet the concierge before we take the elevator to the sixth floor. A layer of anxiety melts as soon as I see the thin black logo quietly proclaiming: DANIEL RUSSIANOFF GALLERY. I breathe deeply before I push open the glass door and enter the modest space with its requisite sludge-brown concrete floor, alabaster walls, soaring ceilings, and track lighting. There are grander galleries on ground floors a few blocks away, but this one belongs to Daniel, my closest friend.

Half the walls are empty. Daniel's recent show, a copse of muted Zhivago-esque landscapes, ended last week. I had coveted a triptych of lonely birches on backgrounds that faded from a dawn gray to the faintest violet, but I couldn't persuade Ben to buy the piece. Now I'm grateful, because had Ben indulged me, I would see these works as Nicola, Luey, and me, swaying in the breeze, ready to topple. I stare at the space where the paintings hung.

"She who snoozes, loses," says Daniel, black-haired with a closely trimmed beard and mustache. He has broad shoulders and stands only a few inches taller than I do, his bulk rendered elegant by the fine tailoring of his tweed jacket woven in the grays of cobblestones. Dark curls I have to resist touching tumble over his forehead and collar. His nose is a beautiful, bumpy beak.

"Did they at least go to a good home?" I ask Daniel as he plants kisses on both my cheeks. He smells of the woods and a spice that recalls Thanksgiving, a holiday that last Thursday I celebrated with my imploded family over margaritas and take-out enchiladas.

"I'm guessing it's an anniversary present for the Mrs. or the first acquisition of newlyweds," he says, down on his knee, rubbing Sadie's back. She turns over and exposes her stomach for equal treatment. "I restrained myself from sinking the deal with too many questions. You'd have been proud."

"Good boy," I say.

Daniel is as loquacious as his partner, my brother, is not, and he gives new meaning to the term *better half.* It's worth putting up with Stephan's superiority to enjoy the gift of Daniel, nine years my brother's junior. Around Stephan, I see myself as a bore simply for having been born heterosexual. Next to him, I feel ungainly, although I am pleased that I'm not like many of my friends, overly proud of ropy, hard-won bodies mismatched to faces that may as well display logos advertising cosmetic surgeons and dermatologists. Daniel, however, never

50

makes me feel like a fool. Rather, in his company I see myself as attractive, lively, and, most important, almost woozy with happiness. His energy is a helium that inflates every depleted cell.

Daniel not only visits my mother more often than Stephan does, but through one degree of separation to him, my life has been blessed. There's Kieran Shanahan, the designer of our apartment; Howard Hansen, an art consultant; Andreas Kimmel, a florist of impeccable talent; and Jimmy Lopez, a personal shopper who has refused to allow me to look as "dowdy as the rich bitch you are." Since Stephan is a jeweler, Daniel likes to point out that with my team of dedicated professionals, augmented by a skilled hair colorist — Josie, Jimmy's twin — I require no taste of my own and need a hetero male in my life strictly for bill-paying and sex.

"Let's go in the back and have a coffee. I've made a fresh pot."

"I'm way over my caffeine limit," I say, "but I can never turn you down." To my ears, my laugh sounds as shrill as Sadie's bark when someone stomps on her paw.

"You don't say no because whatever I offer is always sublime. Like today. Biscotti with dried cranberries and hazelnuts. I'll make you eat two — you look too thin."

As I said, an angel.

We sit in the tiny office, Daniel at his desk, Sadie under it, and me in a leather folding chair the color of good scotch. From a small refrigerator he raises a glass bottle of organic whole milk as if it's a scepter. "Sorry. No one percent. If I'd known you were coming . . ." He finds white porcelain cups and saucers. Daniel considers mugs plebian, one of the few ways in which he's adopted Stephan's affectations.

Before I lose my nerve, I hit him with the question I've never dared to ask. "Why didn't Stephan like Ben?"

Daniel doesn't respond. He may be protective of me, but he has my brother's back.

"Why, exactly?" I repeat. "I'm going somewhere with this."

He leans away as far as he can, which isn't far. "I heard you."

"Did he think Ben wasn't as smart as he is," I offer, "because I wouldn't want to live on the difference between those IQs?"

"Don't be ridiculous, George." From anyone other than Ben or Daniel, I hate this nickname.

"Was he jealous of Ben's success?" Big Brother once called my life "one endless soft-focus French toast brunch," though he has plenty of his own high-thread-count details to envy — a fussed-over Brooklyn Heights brownstone; Liberty Farm, which isn't a farm but a two-hundred-year-old stone house in Pennsylvania with a greenhouse and an empty horse barn; and a willow green 1972 Jaguar that he protects from inclement weather as if it were the queen of England. "I've always sensed that in the Ben department, Stephan felt loathing and contempt."

I see that Daniel is debating whether to say anything.

"Some sort of a trust thing," he offers.

"What do you mean?" I pretend to be offended that the reputation of the husband who has left me high and dry has been impugned. It throws everything off to think that my brother is perceptive.

"Stephan sometimes thought Ben was full of . . ." Daniel is too polite to damn the dead. "Bluster."

"I'm mystified."

My tone is coy and loaded, yet Daniel is gentle. "Stephan worried about you," he says. "Worries about you."

"And he shows this how, by telling me I'm spoiling Nicola or riding roughshod on Luey or simply avoiding my calls and invitations?"

"Oh, come on," Daniel says, affectionately.

"Cut the indignity."

"Even if it's earned?"

"Especially if it's true."

It's an open secret that to our mother, Stephan is Gregory Peck meets Hugh Jackman, her final pre-Alzheimer crush on the tall, dark, and handsome continuum. Since Stephan developed a thing for scarves, she has referred to him as "debonair," her highest praise for a man. Now Daniel and I are both chuckling, until I find myself starting to unspool. "Will you please tell my brother 'Point, Stephan,' " I say. "He did have absolutely every reason to think Ben was a . . ." I fish for a word. "A liar." Only when I say it do I hear how derisive it sounds.

"George, no." Daniel gets up from his chair to rub my shoulders. The motion wakes Sadie, who starts to bark as he croons, "Better days ahead, darling. Better days. Calm down, please. Tell Danny. What can I do?"

"Nothing." Truly pathetic, I lose it. "You can't do a fucking thing. The poor dead schmuck's left me . . ." I gasp. Daniel hands me tissue after tissue, though the snot drips faster than I can mop it up. "He's left me penniless. I don't know what I'm going to do."

His face contorts. I know Daniel well

enough to see that he is trying to decide to what degree I am exaggerating "But I thought you hadn't had the reading of the will yet — or do they call it that only in B movies?"

"I lied." Sadie jumps upright, disturbed by my racket, and hustles for attention. "Ben's lawyer met with us last week. Unless there's been some cosmic bungle, in a few months you'll be looking at a bag lady." I stretch open my hands in front of me, then pet Sadie's head. She's not buying it, and whines.

"Georgia, it's beneath you to dramatize."

"I assure you, I'm not, if this lawyer is right, which I can't believe he is." More for my own sake than Daniel's, I am trying to keep myself together, because if I release my emotions — anger, anxiety, humiliation, worthlessness, and sheer terror — there will be a flood.

"Christ. Crap. Nothing?"

"If I listen to the attorney, every one of my illusions has been dismantled. But I don't believe him. I can't. Ben would never do anything like this."

"You probably haven't slept in weeks, poor baby. Anyone would be a wreck." He opens a drawer and from a small vial counts out six white, pea-sized pills. "Ambien?"

"Stop mothering me, Daniel. I don't need better living through chemistry. Sleeping isn't the problem." For the last two nights, I've almost been in a coma. "Did you hear me? Virtually zero, that's what the lawyer says."

"This is seismic. This is impossible." Daniel rifles through the drawers again. Everyone needs one bad habit and cigarettes are his. He lights up and adds, "Do you mind?"

"Do I look like a woman so flushed with her own importance she's going to object to secondhand smoke?"

"What happened?" he asks as he exhales. "George, honey, what the fuck? This is madness."

I shrug, smoothing Sadie's back in long, slow strokes that match Daniel's puffs. "I don't know yet. The lawyer and I spoke this morning, and he reminded me it could take weeks — maybe months — to sort through every record. That's for the ones he can find."

I am still trying for cool nonchalance, so Daniel responds with, "Are the lovelies aware of this puzzle?" He takes my measure.

"They got the news bulletin but do they believe it? I doubt it. And who can blame them? I don't believe it. When they're around, I try to remember to act normal, whatever that is. Last night they went out together, to a club, so at least there's that." Luey might resent that Nicola was the first leaf on the family tree, but for the moment my daughters are a unified front. In Luey's algebra I am still the X for which she solves in the extra-credit equation of her lifelong resentment.

"What can we do?" Daniel's voice trembles.

"Is Stephan in this royal 'we'?"

"Come on, he'll want to help, and you know I hate keeping secrets from him."

"Can this stay between us? Please? I have to work myself up to Stephan."

I stand, hug Daniel tightly, and turn to leave.

"Forgive me if I sound disingenuous," Daniel says as Sadie follows me. "I'm sure this lawyer will come through for you and in weeks you'll have answers you can live with."

"Daniel, that's not the kind of b.s. that's going to be helpful."

"Then let's start over," he says. As his powerful hug begins, so do my tears. "I think you're in shock. Whatever Ben did is crazy."

"Crazy," I repeat. "Awful. Frightening."

"Unbelievable."

"Unbelievable."

I am eight years older than Daniel but he holds me like a father, patting my back, murmuring nonsense words that don't make sense and don't need to, because what counts is that he is there for me, as a friend, a true friend.

5.

Luey wanted to turn on music, loud, but out of consideration for her mother she opted for earphones. In the last few weeks she'd been immeasurably sad, but today she felt angry and terrified, her body prickling. She, too, had secrets, so why wouldn't Daddy? She'd always believed they were much alike, yet the possibility of concealment on his part felt like a betrayal.

Last week, when they'd gotten back from the lawyer — a lamentable reptile pimped out down to his super-shined oxfords, which Nicola admired and said were John Lobb, English, and obscenely expensive — she wanted to go to her mother's room and crawl into bed like she did the morning she flew back from Palo Alto. Georgia was the one Luey depended on for comfort, even when Luey rejected the notion. Luey wished she could turn back the clock to when everything was simpler, though she hadn't realized it at the time.

Her door opened. "Okay if I come in?" Nicola whispered.

Her sister had no respect for boundaries, Luey thought. *What's hers is hers and what's mine is hers.* Cola sat on the edge of the bed, pushing aside a pair of leggings in a way that suggested they might be infectious. Her eyes were swollen, Luey noticed as she thought how this made them even more deep set than usual, adding to Nicola's striptease exoticism. Say what you want about her, she grew up to be a lot prettier than Luey predicted.

"I saw your light on." It was close to two a.m.

If Nicola got chummy, Luey got wary. When Luey was seven, the big thrill was having a sleepover in Nicola's bedroom. Luey would be the one to knock on her sister's door, shouting, "Hola, Cola." Daddy would tell stories starring pigeons named Loofa and Mazola. Mommy would call them the giggle queens and bring breakfast in bed, cinnamon toast and grape jelly. Talk about the sweet life. Things were still good when they were eleven and twelve; often, Luey remembered, they'd go into the kitchen and make popcorn or fudge. But now Nicola had turned into the sort of woman Luey would never strike up a conversation with, even at a party: overly groomed, overly careful.

"What's on your mind?" Luey asked.

As the words slipped out, Luey realized they were asinine. In this home, what could be on anyone's mind?

"I'm scared," Nicola said. "And nervous." She held her hands to show nails gnawed to the quick. "I'm worried about Mother, mostly."

Boo-hoo — it's yourself you're stressed out about, Bad Luey thought. *You might have to actually get a permanent job.* Then Good Luey came out like a tornado on the Fujita scale and thought the same of herself. Plenty of Luey's friends earned money — in Stanford's video labs or libraries, tutoring, babysitting, or offering themselves up as research guinea pigs. Their own father had tended bar. Luey had never earned a dime. Summers had been R & R disguised as line items for her college applications.

"I'm worried about Mommy, too." She knew it annoyed Nicola when she called her Mommy.

"It would help to get through this if we were together," Nicola said. Luey nodded in agreement. "You think the money will turn up?"

"Definitely," Luey said. "I don't trust that lawyer. Daddy was too smart to fuck up totally."

Then Luey thought of two years ago when their father had hung out with them one night and smoked grass, which is what he called it. He started telling a story — he always took you right there, made you practically pee in your pants — about how he was a dealer in Providence and scored close to a hundred bucks a week, which he explained was a lot of money back then. The evening turned into a bad *Saturday Night Live* sketch. Her father hadn't realized their mother was right outside the door, seeing and smelling everything. She went ballistic, called him a child — and that was the civil term. Her father had paid for his sin by sleeping on the couch. She hated to think of her father as a fool then and she hated it now.

That night, in a sororal cease-fire, Nicola slept on Luey's floor. In the morning when Luey checked Twitter, she'd been retweeted: RT @feralkitty: *Every woman has a dark side she never shows to anybody.*

6.

Watching my daughters eat breakfast, I see them twenty years ago, Nicola in Pippi Longstocking braids and school kilt, Louisa all glitter and glow, a baby rock star.

While Nicola is leaning against the counter, sipping sensible green tea, Luey is downing sugary cereal, a brand I did not buy. "What?" she says when she catches my glance. "I'm eating it with Greek yogurt."

"Don't forget we're seeing Nana today," I say as I measure coffee. "At noon."

Twice a week, I visit my mother in a groomed, green enclave midway between her former Philadelphia home and mine, a spot of New Jersey under the radar of comedians, Soprano aficionados, and Springsteen fans. Although Camille Waltz's grasp of time has become so tentative that I am willing to believe she has not noticed my absence, my guilt is encroaching. I need to be with my mother, though I will require every minute of the hour-long ride to warm up to the assault of seeing the faux mother who occupies her sarcophagus.

"I'd like you two to join me," I tell Luey and Nicola.

"I have cardio jazz at one." Cereal crunches as Luey speaks.

"I was meeting Jamie but I guess I can change it," Nicola replies.

"I'd be grateful, Cola," I say, and hope the statement isn't edged with the sarcasm I feel. "And who's Jamie?"

"No one special."

"Male or female?"

"Like I said. Not special."

Luey swats her sister on the derriere as she dumps her soggy cereal into the trash. "That's not how it sounded the other night."

Nicola tosses a napkin in her direction. "Skank," she hisses, in the not altogether unkind way sisters can shoot an arrow.

"I'll take the class another day," Luey's back says.

She is doing this for her nana, not me. In the presence of her grandmother I see the best of Luey. *Camille and Luey, separated at birth,* Ben would say. Separated by me.

"Please be ready in forty-five minutes." I page through the newspaper, going straight to the obits — my new fixation — then take my coffee along to prepare for today's persecution. Camille Waltz is still able to spot a pill in a sweater at twenty paces. I dress accordingly.

The three of us are standing where we park our car, in the costly but convenient dungeon beneath our building. Today is Fred's day off. Tomorrow I will give him a severance check, a gushing reference letter, and a "Oh how we will all miss you!" note that is waiting in my desk drawer, knowing it is insufficient compensation for losing his job.

"Can I drive?" Luey asks, as I unlock the door.

I relinquish the keys as a peace offering, though I am always happy getting behind the wheel and becoming a rolling body in a simple right-left-straight-reverse universe of navigation, acceleration, and stops. "Be my guest," I say and climb into the passenger's seat. I hand each daughter a bottle of water and put my own in its designated receptacle.

Nicola reaches forward from the back to nuzzle me around the neck. "Georgia Waltz, always prepared," she says.

If only. And then I say it aloud. Both girls laugh, and Nicola adds, "It's going to be okay." I do not want to know if she is referring to today's excursion or the rest of my life.

Whoever's in the driver's seat chooses the music — our Silver-Waltz rule. If Luey goes with hip-hop, I will tell her that I've grown to like the poetry and cadence, not to appease her but because it's true. She turns, however, to Frank Sinatra, who starts crooning a ballad as mellow as cognac in a sidecar. "Nana's day," she says. "Nana's songs."

We drive without conversation, I for one, thanking God for Mr. Sinatra. Maybe this afternoon will be different, which is a wish I make before each visit. The familiar yearning simmers with the hope that my only living parent will feel sufficient and appropriate outrage at the injustice done to her daughter. No husband drops dead and stiffs Camille Waltz's child! No son-in-law does that to *her* baby! My mother will fold me into her arms and, while smoothing my hair, drop pearls of wisdom I will use to pave my way to a safer place. I allow myself to float on crazy thoughts as I ignore ugly Jersey, with entire stores devoted to laminate kitchen tables and cheesy party goods, until we turn into a residential area zoned for acreage generous enough for polo games. With its circular drive and meticulously

66

raked grounds, you'd expect The Oaks to be studded with lacrosse sticks, not walkers. Daniel refers to the institution as "the finishing school." Which it is.

For five years after the death of my father, my mother stayed on in Philadelphia, eventually tended to by a round-the-clock entourage. When it became too hard to manage the moving parts of this puzzle — unannounced journeys, mysterious no-shows, outrage when a previous shift left behind an unwashed dish — Stephan and I, in a rare show of filial togetherness, searched for a "facility," hoping to find one jauntier than that word suggests.

Only Daniel wondered aloud why neither of us invited our mother to live in our own home. "Easy for the orphan boy to say," Stephan responded. Daniel's parents were killed in a head-on collision when he was fourteen. He was raised by an aunt and uncle.

"Beast," Daniel responded.

"If I'm a beast, I'd happily be a satyr," Stephan replied.

"Stay on point," I said. I could have invited my mother to take over one of the girls' bedrooms if I had not known that in one month's time I'd be devoured by Camille's custom brand of rebuke. It's no coincidence that on the Monday following every Thanksgiving, where she was always present, I escaped to ski or hike, after which I allowed myself to be pummeled with hot stones and swaddled with herb-scented towels. I felt I had earned the indulgence.

Camille Waltz's current residence comes with exorbitant fees because the place doesn't reek of urine and sadness. The Oaks is a cruise ship docked on dry, well-tended Garden State soil where you can join a choir, study French, prattle on in a book club, paint your portrait, fox-trot, or play eight hours of daily duplicate bridge until the others boot you out of the game. You can do any of these things if your mind isn't now frayed wires mated with missed connections. My mother can sit in a chair, sway grandly down the hall, feed herself, and stare at a television. Some days she knows me for as long as twenty minutes.

At least it is Mallomars season. Today I'm bringing six boxes, realizing that even in this swankiest of joints, I'll be lucky if one winds up staying in my mother's room. It's not the staff I'm accusing of theft but residents who, in the argot of The Oaks, are "ambulatory," trolling for treats they liberate from other residents.

Nicola grabs the cookies. I carry a tote

with a new flannel nightgown and six pairs of fuzzy socks that my mother would loudly reject if she realized that the feet that would soon wear them were her own. Under my arm is a nosegay of ranunculus, each blossom like a vest-pocket peony. Luey carries gifts for the staff, fancy teas and dozens of doughnuts gaudy with sprinkles. As we enter, we resemble well-dressed peddlers.

"Hello, Jessie."

"Mizz Waltz," she answers. "You here to see Mom? You go on back now, you and your beautiful girls. What a sight you are."

We greet residents who are well enough to roam, turn right at the fake Cezanne and the locked door, and get buzzed into dementiaville, where yesterday is more present than today. Here you can be a once-haughty woman of seventy-seven and yet the epitaph on the door to your room will announce: CAMILLE WALTZ OF PHILADELPHIA. MOTHER AND GRANDMOTHER. LOVES KNITTING, POLITICS, AGATHA CHRISTIE AND RED ROSES. The anonymous author of that living obituary might have added vodka gimlets, golf, and her granddaughter Louisa. Then Stephan. Then Ben. Then me.

"Nana!" Nicola crosses into the dim room. My mother is dozing in an armchair brought from home, while chintz butterflies circle cottage posies on scarlet fabric faded to rose. Her feet, still narrow and elegant, shod in black velvet slippers, are daintily crossed at the ankles, propped on an ottoman. She ignores Nicola, who gently places a hand on her grandmother's arm. Once well-toned, a star tennis player, my mother looks as though she's been put in the washing machine on a steam cycle and has emerged shrunken, creased, and limp.

"We've brought you your Mallomars," Luey says. Perhaps it's her younger granddaughter's songlike voice, a version of my own untouched by an early decade of cigarettes, that does it. My mother opens her eyes and, in a gesture I have seen thousands of times, brings her hand to her forehead to brush away locks that might have escaped from her disciplined coiffure. That hair used to be thick, lustrous, and sable brown, inflated and lacquered into a bouffant inspired by Jackie Kennedy, her muse. As Jackie morphed into Jackie O, Camille changed, too, allowing her hair to grow longer and looser. When Jackie died, so did my mother's imagination. For the last fifteen years she's been stuck with Editor Jackie, the version with blazers, trousers, and Hermès scarves, squired by Maurice Templeton, who, my mother never failed to point out with pride, was Jewish. Her kind: not *too*.

In Mother's first year at The Oaks, I booked her appointments at the hair salon, but as she grew increasingly rattled, the exercise seemed cruel. Now I keep her Jackie hair shorn. With the dye grown out, silvery whirls shine like well-used cutlery. When Mother looks in a mirror, I doubt she can place the woman with the wide-set brown eyes and broad smile, but I like this rebranded version with slightly less ability to lacerate.

"Mother," I say, stepping out of the shadows. "It's Georgia." I pause for station identification. "Your daughter."

The woman in the chair lifts her head. "Oh, hello, dear." She delivers the line with the courteous, one-size-fits-all neutrality that allows her to be one of the residents whom caregivers here actually like.

"I've brought Nicola and Luey," I add. "Your granddaughters."

"Not just granddaughters," Luey says, stepping forward. "Granddaughters with Mallomars." She rips open a box and hands her grandmother one of the chocolate mounds. My mother stares at it as if it's a turd. "It's something sweet to eat, Nana." To illustrate, Luey pulls another cookie

71

from the box and gobbles it in two bites. Mother mimics the behavior, and as I watch, a tear slides down my cheek, which I quickly brush away. I possess a finite amount of fortitude at present, and I can't allow myself to squander too much of it here.

Nicola reaches forward to pluck a crumb from her grandmother's chin. "We brought you socks, Nana."

"Who are you?" my mother, on alert, asks.

"Nicola," she says. "Your oldest grand-daughter."

She narrows her eyes. "The Chink."

Nicola looks as if she's been mugged. "Yes, I'm that little girl. All grown up. Part of your family since I was a baby."

My mother sniffs. "Why don't you go back to China? To your own kind. We don't need you."

"Now Mother." I put my arm around Nicola, who is shuddering. "That's not nice. You love Nicola."

"Don't worry," Nicola says to me. "I know Nana doesn't mean it."

I have always been afraid that she does. "I have a new nightgown for you, Mother." I hold the gown aloft, swinging its soft coral fabric. "See? I sewed a label with your name in it." She may as well be a camper. "Jackie

Onassis had one just like it," I lie. "You're going to look gorgeous in this. Like when you and Daddy went to nightclubs."

"Papa?"

"Not your papa. Your husband, my father." No reaction. "You once went to Cuba," I add. "Tell me about Havana. I remember you wore a flowered cocktail dress with a big skirt and a little waist."

"Who took me to Cuba?" She sounds genuinely curious.

From the bureau, I remove the 1955 wedding photo and place it in her hands. I point to my father, dark and chiseled in the same way Stephan is. "Martin Waltz."

"Gorgeous couple," she says. "I went to their wedding. He kissed me, that man. At his own wedding. But I was a stunner." Almost six sentences. The month's record.

I open a drawer in the bureau to tuck away the nightgown and see a tangle of polyester clothing. "Cola, why don't you sort through all this?" I ask. "Whatever isn't Nana's we'll give to the nurses and they can figure it out." The task will keep Nicola safely away from the line of fire.

"Do you want me to give you a pedicure, Nana?" From her backpack Luey removes opalescent enamel, its blue shade last seen in *Finding Nemo.* "See, I have it on my own toes." She pulls off a boot to illustrate. Her grandmother stares at Luey's feet and chuckles. "Let's take off these slippers first."

For the next twenty minutes, Nicola straightens the bureau and Luey performs her footsie juju while I lie on my mother's bed and wonder what to say. *Ben left me with nothing, Mother,* I rehearse. Too abrupt, and I risk that she might say, *That's what you deserve.* Perhaps, *The strangest thing happened, but the attorney can't find Ben's money. What should I do?* I worry with such intensity that I expect my mother to hear me and react. I am wishing she could, because Camille Waltz would know what to do. Nothing like this would ever have happened to her.

After Nicola and I give Luey's work its due respect, I say, "Why don't you hand out the gifts? I'd like a minute with Nana." My daughters troop out of the room, most likely relieved. I pull over a Queen Anne dining chair, also from our home in Philadelphia, park it next to my mother, and squeeze her hand. "Aren't the girls lovely?" I say.

"Love-ly," she repeats, as if she's learning a word. "Love-ly."

"It's been wonderful to have them around" — which isn't wholly true, but my

mother believed in protective artifice —
"because, well, Mother, I'm going through
a very bad patch." There is no response.
"Did you hear me?"

"Patch," she says. "I heard you."

"You remember Ben." Ben flirted with
Camille and Camille flirted back, verbal
ping-pong at which they were fairly
matched. She asked him to call her Mother.
He laughed it off and suggested The Count-
ess, which stuck. I'm fairly sure my mother
thought Ben was more in love with her than
with me. "Ben died, Mother. It was sudden.
A heart attack. He was only fifty-two." I pull
out a picture from my tote — Ben and I at
our wedding, a frothy extravagance twenty-
eight years ago at my parents' country club.
I am carrying an enormous bouquet of
cream roses. The whole wedding was in
shades of ivory, as befits an almost-virgin
bride convinced by her mother that she was
plain vanilla.

"Poor Ben," my mother says, touching his
face.

"Yes, Benjamin Silver."

It's then that a clear, sentient tone bores
through the dementia. My refined and arrogant mama spits. "You never should have
married that *mamzer.*" This is uttered in

the voice that's launched a thousand lectures.

"Mother, why not?" I plead. "What about Ben?" She turns and smiles. Does she see me? I want another volley of conversation. I want a damn filibuster. But she says nothing. "You were talking about Ben!"

"I know Ben," she says, indignant. "Ben married my daughter."

"Yes. I'm your daughter."

She looks full at me. "I'll say not," she insists. "Georgia is my daughter. My daughter is young and beautiful. She has a twenty-four-inch waist and dark hair. My daughter looks like Natalie Wood. You aren't my Georgia."

"You're right — Georgia is your daughter." I hear my own weariness. "Why should Georgia not have married Ben?" My voice trails off as I ask, but I don't want my mother's spastic beam of lucidity to simply dissolve into her batty sea like a splash.

"Cheater."

"Did Ben cheat on Georgia?" I ask this silver-haired stranger.

"Cheater."

"Yes, but how did he cheat? Who did he cheat?"

"Whom."

"*Whom.* Fuck it. Whom did he cheat?"

Mother closes her eyes. When she opens them, she says, "Nurse," sweetly. "Be a dear. Might I have help with my makeup, please?" She reaches for a Mallomar.

"Lipstick?" I ask, proffering a tube of Chanel Fire that she keeps in her top drawer.

She expertly reddens her lips, accepts a tissue to blot them with a kiss, mascaras her eyes, dusts her nose with powder, and runs a comb through her cropped curls before she sprays three bursts of Joy — clavicle, right wrist, left wrist — and admires the reflection of a handsome, albeit unfamiliar, woman. I hear a tap-tap-tap.

"Maurice," she says as she turns. "Darling."

"Jacque-leen," says a man in a velvet smoking jacket. Leaning only slightly on a cane, he remains tall and upright as he walks toward her, extending his other arm, which she accepts. "Shall we?"

"Yes, my love. I've missed you." With that, my mother and Morris Blumstein proceed down the hall, and I behind them. I have met Morris. He is a gentleman indeed, like Papa, who'd also come from Antwerp. Both men made their fortune in the diamond trade, Papa as a master stonecutter in Europe and here, before he opened a shop, and Morris as a gem broker.

Harry Connick Jr.'s voice wafts from The Oaks's dining room,

"There goes Jackie O with her Maurice Tempelsman," a resident cackles loudly as they pass. "And I am the queen of Rumania."

Camille glides past the woman. "Vera Levine, you were homely as a spider when we were in sixth grade, and even more *mieskeit* now."

7.

I doze in the backseat of the car, burrowing to escape, and wake with a start as we pull into the garage, each of us wasted and unhappy in her own sour way. Luey and Nicola clomp away without explaining where they're headed. I am looking forward to solitude. I take the elevator to the lobby, pick up my mail — bills that I won't open, just yet, and a trickle of condolence notes that I will — and head to the top floor. I am greeted by Sadie, starved for affection as much as for dinner. We do our kissy-face routine then, without removing my coat, I rip open an envelope with a New Mexico postmark.

"Ben and I were fraternity brothers at Penn," writes David Someone. "I just learned of his death from Josh Adelman and the two of us were remembering that time . . ." I read two paragraphs in praise of my husband's high jinks and humanity and toss the missive into a basket, already full. One of these days I will address the hotsy-totsy engraved cards that await for me to express appreciation to Ben's bereavement club. But not tonight. My plan is to watch whatever movie is playing on television and devour leftover chili.

"Okay, Sadie, your turn, doll face," I say, walking to the closet where I hang her leash. That's when I see him, a cartoon rat in black calmly poised on my living room chaise, long legs stretched in front of him, his chin resting on slender crossed fingers, his face wearing the slightest smile. I scream so loudly that Sadie echoes with her own screech and hides under the kitchen table.

"Good God, Georgia." His voice is calm, followed by a low laugh.

"Why did you scare me like that?"

"I'm just being your Byronic brother, melodramatic and melancholy, the Waltz with the highest disregard for society's norms."

My chest continues to pound. "Stephan, shut up. You flatter yourself." I catch my breath enough to say, "If it's you being gay, I've had plenty of time to adjust. How many Bar Mitzvah boys demanded an Oscar Wilde theme for their damn party?"

"How many mothers agreed?"

"How many Camilles are there? Only one, fortunately." I bend to stroke Sadie, who has returned and is cheerfully wagging. "I saw her today. That shrew needs a muzzle. You wouldn't believe what she —"

Stephan raises his hand. "Spare me. 'Children begin by loving their parents; as they grow older they judge them; sometimes they forgive them.' You've got to move on."

"Forgive her? Easy for you to say — she spoiled you rotten."

"You've been pretty spoiled yourself, little sister."

" 'The truth is rarely pure and never simple.' "

"Ah, an Oscar pissing match. 'Experience is the name everyone gives to their mistakes.' "

Fair enough, but instead I say, "Is this why you're here? To torment me? And did you bribe the doorman to get in?"

Stephan jangles a set of keys. "Did you forget you gave me these after Ben died — and that we have dinner plans?" I vaguely recall his invitation, thinking at the time that Daniel put him up to it. "I'm also betting you're sorely in need of my excellent advice."

"Ah, a mercy mission."

"This is getting tiresome," he groans. "Go

make yourself look like my gorgeous sister while I let your poor beast relieve herself."

Every time I see my brother I am struck by how his deportment clashes with his run-for-office looks. Someone as handsome as Stephan should be blessed with an exquisite soul, but his benevolence is a campaign pledge on which you know the candidate will never deliver — yet you'd vote for him anyway. In my spine I feel a paralysis of hard feelings. I force myself to accept the brush of his lips on my cheek.

"The reservation is for seven," he says, picking up his black wool flannel coat. It has a detachable cape. I wonder when Stephan will buy a bowler hat.

"Someplace quiet, at least?"

"You underestimate me, Georgia. You always do."

No house Chianti for my big brother. In a tiny Italian restaurant with a stoked fireplace and matching wine cellar we are on our second perfect Manhattan, nibbling olive tapenade, while he warms me up with tales from the front. "This Mrs. Mob-type came in and groused about how a ten-carat stone wasn't quite large enough." He takes a sip. "It looked like a cocktail onion" — with a hand more carefully manicured than my own he measures an inch — "but she apparently wanted at least a good-sized shallot."

"And it kills you to sell vulgarity so you refused and directed her to a tasteful stone? Three carats in an oval cut?"

Stephan throws back his head and laughs, a sound both rakish and cosmopolitan that he perfected long ago, perhaps by working with a coach. "I told her if I have to go to Belgium myself, I'll find her that stone."

"Mr. Waltz, always the gentleman."

Stephan himself wears only knotted gold cuff links, a simple sapphire ring, and, on ceremonial occasions, discreet diamond studs that belonged to our father. My brother's taste is exquisitely expensive, perhaps determined by a sartorial focus group who believes that even paisley is left wing. If it weren't for Daniel, their home wouldn't have a spot of color. A caramel suede pillow required a negotiation, and Stephan drew the line at purple. Whenever I visit, I taunt him by bringing jelly beans, parrot tulips, and, the last time, months ago, monogrammed magenta cocktail napkins.

He picks up the menu and begins to read. "Ready for dinner, sis?"

Worrying is a better way to lose weight

than hiring a personal trainer. I am wearing pants I haven't been able to button for years. But as the server delivers gnocchi to the next table, the promise of pasta taunts.

"Yes," I say. "Famished."

"Excellent, and now it's your turn to talk." It sounds like a command. "How are the little women?" he asks after we order.

My daughters adore Uncle Stephan and consistently defend him against slurs that cross my lips. Thanks to Stephan, Nicola appreciates Charles Aznavour and Luther Vandross, Luey has seen every Hepburn and Tracy movie, and on Mother's Day one will give me a Diptyque candle — tuberose or gardenia — and the other a bouquet of peonies. In a show of solidarity, on my fiftieth birthday I received a first edition of *Wuthering Heights,* a gift from both daughters surely prompted by Stephan and Daniel.

What my daughters don't know is that Stephan links their shabbiest behavior to every misstep I've taken as a mother. "You let Nicola get away with procrastination because she's adopted and punish Luey for having all the spit you lack," he says, feeling free to don his pointy shrink hat.

"You offer me this observation based on your many years of fatherhood?" I invariably respond. Accusations fly.

"The girls are sad and fussy," I say, "and flash-frozen. Nicola keeps postponing her return to Europe — though I can't figure out quite what she'd be going back to or what she ever did there beyond peel carrots and parsnips — and Luey's on hiatus from school." In my day we called that dropping out. "They have way too much time on their hands. They're aimless as chickens, going out late, staying in bed until noon."

As soon as I stop yammering, I regret my candor because I've opened myself up for Stephan to say, rightfully, "Does any of this surprise you? You've never set limits." And yet he adds, "Want one of them to work with me?"

Immediately, my mind jumps to Luey making hundreds of thousands of dollars' worth of precious gems disappear. *I borrowed those hoops and one fell off at the club. I flushed the bracelet down the toilet.* Or, worse, an indignant lie, *I resent that look. I have no idea what became of that sapphire pendant and why are you accusing me?*

"You can't be serious," I say, when *Thank you* would have been a better response.

"I'm not promising tenure," he says. "But when my assistant gets married next month, she's taking a long wedding trip and I'd

85

rather not hire an unknown temp."

His is a discreet upstairs jeweler — the kind that doesn't have to advertise, be it in Basel, Düsseldorf, or Paris — or in S. Waltz and Company's case, tucked into a hushed Fifth Avenue suite, literally looking down on neighboring street-level emporiums: Harry Winston, Tiffany, Cartier, Van Cleef & Arpels, H. Stern, and Bulgari. Stephan sells impeccable riffs on their wares as well as fine estate pieces. Customers reach him through recommendations, whispering the language of money in their native tongue, be it Arabic, Spanish, or Staten Island English. Nobody shouts. Nobody sweats. The customer is always right, because Mr. Waltz has asserted his subliminal yet strategic influence — Buy this stone, not that; Go with the platinum over the gold; Do not allow this one-of-a-kind ruby bracelet to leave the shop on a lesser woman's arm.

Stephan James Waltz inspires confidence. He is highly regarded within a coterie of elite jewelers, many of whom have been trying to hire him away for years. This amuses anyone acquainted with my sibling, who could never have a boss. That included our father, whom Stephan deserted when he was twenty-six, abandoning Philadelphia — a city he'd never call Philly — along with cheesesteaks and Eagles season tickets, for an apprenticeship in London. Before he was thirty, albeit a very old thirty, he opened his own small New York operation. Stephan was never Steve, Stevie, or Steph, never easy and never young.

"For the sake of argument," I say, "let's say Nicola came to work with you. What would she do?"

"Besides track the inventory on Excel? Greet customers, answer the phone, serve cappuccino, polish the goods, look absolutely splendid, model jewelry, make people feel good about spending fifty-thousand dollars in fifteen minutes."

I take in the restaurant's tiny white lights, inhaling the fragrance of evergreens.

"It might work." It might.

"She won't be bored and quit after a week?" Stephan asks.

My brother's eyes, which are my eyes — almond shaped, charcoal, deeply set — are sharp upon me. There it is, the rusty nail waiting for my bare foot. Is he going to remind me that Cola left her first job, in the fashion department at *Elle,* when she was asked to come in on a Saturday to pack eleven trunks? "You know my daughter," I say. "She's got her virtues, but if you don't want to be disappointed, you better find someone else."

"I see you're not suggesting Luey."

"I've only lost my husband, not my mind."

"All right, have Nicola call." He finishes his martini. "How is Luey?"

"Distant."

"Aha," he says. "And you. Holding up?"

I was able to confide in Daniel because I knew he wouldn't suggest that I was responsible for getting screwed. But now I face a higher judge who may or may not have been informed by Daniel. I drain the last few drops of my cocktail, shifting in my seat.

"You look like hell," Stephan adds. At least he has noticed. I read this as a term of endearment.

"Do you know anything about Ben cheating?" I ask, emboldened by the drink.

His eyes hold me. "On you?"

"That's a good place to start."

Stephan brushes back a lock of his black hair, his temples distinguished by a feathering of silver. "Couples have their indiscretions," he says. "Look at our parents."

"I'd rather not." I'm bleeding enough without reliving the six months after my father packed his stalwart leather luggage, leaving us to minister to our mother cursing in a dark room, complaining of a migraine. Not that much changed when they reunited.

88

More migraines, more moaning.

"Why do you care about cheating now?" he asks. "The poor bastard's buried."

"It matters because I may have been left with next to nothing."

He frowns. "Georgia, don't play the thespian."

"You're allowed showmanship and I'm not?"

"Cut the accusations, too. You're one exasperating, prevaricating woman. Just the facts, please."

"This is what you need to know." Although I wish I didn't have to repeat them, I tell him. "The worst-case scenario safety net Ben assured me was in place — well, there is no net. He's sold stock, drained accounts, borrowed on his life insurance, and taken out second mortgages. We owe money everywhere. I'm not down to nothing, but I'm getting there fast." I see my brother trying to decide where hyperbole seeps into truth. "I've been all over it six ways to Sunday with Wally Fleigelman —"

"Fleigelman! What a clown. He's your first mistake."

"Who says I've made a 'mistake'?" I've allowed myself to stumble into what feels like a trap and I need to wriggle myself free, even if it means gnawing off a toe. "Wally may not be your style," I say, pulling myself tall in my seat, "but he's the attorney handling the estate and I happen to like and trust him. If there's any money anywhere, he'll find it." I look at the sharp knife that the waiter puts down next to Stephan's plate and picture myself sticking it into my brother's hand. I am horrified by this image, yet grateful for the two cocktails that have helped me achieve it.

"From what Ben reported of your finances," Stephan says with an edge, fully intended, a trenchancy that implies bragging and lying, "it wasn't an insignificant amount that's missing. How's Attorney Fleigelman doing?"

"He's investigating — and I'm tearing my place apart, actually, trying to find God knows what. I had Ben's secretary send me all his canceled checks, cell phone records, the works. I'm going over them like Nora Charles."

The snapshot of myself that I am offering is not, I realize, flattering or dignified, and I am relieved to be rescued by my pasta. Steam rises from the bowl. I close my eyes and breathe in the savory aroma of the three herb kings: sage, oregano, and tarragon. When I look again at Stephan, I believe I see sympathy, that or the fear that I will beg him for money.

"Shall I go with you to see Fleigelman?" he asks.

Smart, competent brothers like Stephan produce two kinds of sisters: those who look up to their sibling, craving fatherly guidance and protection; and my kind, who run the other way, knowing that if they allow themselves to be in their brother's debt, the interest will compound for eternity, bankrupting them of independence, of pride, of any wisdom gained from making their own decisions and mistakes.

"That's not necessary. I can handle it," I say, though I doubt I can. This morning it was as hard for me to get out of bed as it would be to swan dive into an icy ocean. "But down the line, I may need your help in a different way."

Holding his steak knife and fork as if he had been raised by British aristocracy, not first-generation American suburbanites, Stephan cuts one small piece of filet, then another. Silence hangs between us. I stare at the gravy forming a fjord between his pureed peas and delicate mound of mashed potatoes.

"I may ask you to sell my jewelry." The fireplace blazes, but I feel chilled. To take this step would mean that my circumstances are real.

"Not the pieces from Mother, I hope," he says immediately.

Except for the small ruby pin and a sly, amethyst-eyed lizard, the unworn lady-who-lunches collection would be the first to unload — elaborate brooches shaped like nosegays and starbursts, a diamond evening watch that stopped telling time at ten past midnight in another century, studded bangles suitable for a belly dancer, and a pink sapphire necklace shaped like a horse-shoe. "Not Mother's wedding jewelry," I say, although I have never put on the dagger-shaped marquise solitaire or the thick matching band. "I always thought one of the girls might want them."

"I see." I imagine Stephan compiling a list and wonder if he would charge me commission. "Maybe *you* should come and work with me, not Nicola."

I manage to laugh. "Within a day one of us would wind up in a maximum security prison."

"I take your point," he says. "But have you thought about working again?"

"Only day and night."

"Would you return to teaching?"

My résumé is one paragraph long and twenty-four years stale, rendering me underqualified yet shopworn. Until we adopted Nicola, I taught English at a small girls' high school. I loved my work, but felt that if another woman had sacrificed her child so I could have one, I needed to give up my job. As the years passed and the girls were in school all day, I considered returning to teaching, but by that time Ben's law firm had prospered and I'd gotten the kind of rich-lady lazy that passes for busy, earnestly volunteering, often chairing committees. I wasn't just a museum docent but one of the Central Park Conservancy's star flowerbed weeders, and I have the T-shirt to prove it. But I never again worked for a salary, even when I was chloroformed by boredom.

"I've sent out letters — nobody's jumping," I say. Stephan seems to expect more, so I go on, my hackles up and ego bruised. "I keep cycling through all the obvious choices for women my age who haven't had a job since the Clinton administration. Does the city require another residential real estate broker or personal shopper? I don't cook well enough to cater. I'd rather eat nuclear waste than be a wedding planner, choking on other people's stress, and opening a store or going back to school to get another degree costs a fortune. I've put out feelers to tutor in English and" — heaven help me — "help kids write their college application essays." I feel out of breath and pathetic from my speech.

"So I guess you'll have to be a high-priced escort."

"If only I hadn't aged out of that one. Maybe a madam. I'm not creative enough for phone sex."

Stephan sits back in his chair and looks as if he were seeing me for the first time in a decade, maybe more. "You may truly be in a pickle, yes?"

Unwanted pity is embedded in that statement. "Don't cry for me, Argentina," I say. "Not yet. I have a little money, and in this town you shouldn't underestimate the pressure of getting in to college. Plus, if you'll turn my baubles into cash when I ask, I'd buy me time."

"I assume that includes your own treasure chest?"

Over the years, Ben gave me gifts that I'd always imagined he had chosen with exquisite care. Each carried history, and when I put them on, I wore more than bracelets, rings, pins, necklaces, earrings, and watches. I wore the day when Nicola arrived, the morning when after thirty-eight hours of labor I gave birth to Luey, the time when Ben won his first big case. I wore every anniversary and exotic vacation, each year together, which I viewed as twelve more months of good fortune. Well-deserved good fortune, if I'm being honest, because who considers an accidental advantage unserved? Find me a rich person and I'll show you someone who in her heart feels she's been exempted from pain and poverty because God has noticed and rewarded her unique goodness, vaccinating her against bad luck. Gratitude is often a forgotten postscript.

Not only has the statute of limitations on my utopia expired, I feel itchy with guilt for having taken it for granted all these years. With a shadow cast on Ben, I also feel robbed of my past. I wish my glowing memories had come with warranties. This is why I say, "I'm not going to be sentimental. If I have to get rid of things, I will."

"I've never seen you wear much, anyway." It is true that for the daughter and sister of jewelers, I am a heretic, a walking white cotton shirt.

"Most of it doesn't work with yoga pants."

"Your watch?"

I love that watch, circled by diamonds, but I say, "I can give that up. My phone tells time just fine." I shovel the last squiggle of fusilli into my mouth.

"And that epic Art Deco ring with the emerald and diamonds I got a glimpse of? I thought I'd see it on your hand tonight."

The server approaches our table with a tray of desserts. Lemon tart is the centerpiece of the selection. I am tempted.

"What ring?"

"Your birthday present, I thought."

"My birthday present was a trip to Japan we were supposed to take in January. After I pleaded sympathy, the travel agent gave me a full refund." Almost.

"Georgia, are you daft?"

"Did you just say 'daft'? Are you?"

He leans back and cocks his head. "I would suggest that you look very hard for a diamond and emerald ring, probably from the 1920s, a real showstopper. I've seen few like it. Ben brought it to me for appraisal — he was hoping I'd sell it for him — and led me to believe he was accepting it as collateral or payment from a client."

During our marriage Ben often repeated this practice, one I protested on the grounds that it was as sleazy as it was risky. Why couldn't he be paid in money like every other decent lawyer? What would be next, sacks of grain?

"Ben was told the ring would go for close to a million. In my opinion, your husband was taken. It's a fine old piece but would fetch maybe half of that. This did not make my dear brother-in-law happy and he left with the ring, accusing me of low-balling him, ranting about how he'd take his business elsewhere. 'Be my guest,' I told him." In the tone of a university provost my brother continues. "This was the last conversation I had with your husband."

With that, I lose my appetite for dessert.

8.

"Nicola, my sweet," Stephan said over early morning croissants on Madison Avenue. "You appear to be nonplussed. I'd like your answer."

Nicola couldn't decide if being employed by S. Waltz would be the beginning of the resplendent opportunity on which her mother was trying to sell her or plain and simple martyrdom. She pictured herself modeling pave diamond cuffs, fingering precious gems (or semiprecious, she wasn't picky), and helping design shoulder-grazing opal and platinum filigree earrings like the ones she'd coveted in Paris. Then she remembered how imperious Uncle Stephan could be. Around him, she felt lumpy, bone-headed, and twelve.

"Thanks for the vote of confidence" — if the offer was that, or her uncle's version of pity — "but I don't have much office experience. I wouldn't want to disappoint you,"

Nicola said, though this was the one aspect of the job she felt she could fulfill.

"What I need, mostly, is common sense," Stephan said, not that he'd ever given Nicola the impression that he considered either her, Luey, or her mother, for that matter, to be endowed with that quality. "Beyond that, the primary qualification is trust."

"Oh, I am absolutely trustworthy," Nicola replied with dead earnestness, though a few minutes earlier she'd exaggerated her office experience. She had none. The moment the statement sailed from her lips she knew, from the smile Uncle Stephan was failing to suppress, that the specious answer was wrong. Luey would have responded with something half clever. She took herself for Dorothy Parker, aiming for intellectual flirtation. Repartee was not Nicola's strong suit, with her uncle least of all, and when he said something like, "A man's face is his autobiography; a woman's is her work of fiction," Nicola suspected that he was testing or insulting her. To compound her irritation, in his case that particular quote wasn't even true. She'd bet good money — if she had any — that Uncle Stephan had had surgery on his neck and eyes, which looked a lot tighter than before she left for

Europe. And those silver sideburns? C'mon. He could thank the hair colorist who left in a bit of gray to add authenticity to his dye job.

What, however, were her job options? Despite her culinary skills, she'd had only one brief job in a restaurant, in another country, at the bottom of the line — not experience she could leverage or for which she even obtained a reference letter when she walked away — and she could not see herself trying to sell cupcakes or organic baby food at the Brooklyn Flea or sweating in food trucks. She'd like to return to Paris, but at the moment she didn't have enough saved even for a plane ticket. The best part of the job at S. Waltz would be that it would come with a salary — nothing major, but a step up from tying on an apron to become a barista, and she'd already been turned down for two bar-tending spots. As one employer plainly said when he reviewed her résumé, "Liking martinis and looking hot at a party don't count as qualifications."

"If you apply yourself, I could teach you a great deal about our family business," Stephan said, stirring his double espresso, which she noticed he drank unsweetened. "There's a lot more to it than baubles and trinkets."

The word Nicola liked best in that sentence was *family.* For all his shortcomings, Uncle Stephan had never once suggested that Nicola was anything but a Waltz. That territory was exclusively inhabited by his mother. She looked up over her café au lait. The restaurant Uncle Stephan had chosen was small and winsome without being coy. He spoke to the waitress in French, and to Nicola's ear his accent sounded authentic. This would have made Luey laugh, though Nicola took it as a sign. She needed a sign.

"When would you like me to start?"

9.

Wally has found nothing — I check with him every other day — and I am running out of places in the apartment to look. In my waking hours, I'm blurry around the edges yet keeping it together, trying not to act as if I am subsisting on a diet of cottage cheese and opprobrium. I stumble through my routines, reminding myself to floss, to take Vitamin D, to stock up on dog food, and to care for my plants — the bromeliads, the flowering maple, the hopelessly retro Boston ferns that wick away the humidity of my bathrooms, and the mistletoe fig and prayer plants that line my kitchen window. Other people can get their cardio workout hauling mulch and fertilizer as they grow organic vegetables. Except for my sometime servitude in Central Park, I am an indolent gardener. In the country we employ a landscape service, and in the city I exploit the advantage of my apartment's enormous west- and north-facing windows.

Since I have neither strength nor inclination to lift a blow-dryer, my hair shambles around my face in an animated halo — frizzy in spots, strangely lank in others, a mirror of my soul. When my standing salon appointment came do, I canceled it, and with Nicola assisting, I have tried hair coloring at home. My shade now hovers between margarine and mustard.

It's after dark when Ben rolls in like fog, crowding me, teasing me. His night shift begins after I turn off whatever Turner Classic has dished out, the warm milk that puts me into a coma. Tonight, Clark Gable was in zany pursuit of Myrna Loy.

"Ben!" I groan in my sleep, as he thrusts, hard and demanding. My mate knows the history lessons of my anatomy and places his hands confidently on my hips as he pushes deeper. "Ben! I love you, Ben. Love you, love you, Oh . . ." I arch to meet him, luxuriating in the warmth that runs its intimate course between my thighs.

I call out his name again and jolt awake to find that there is no Ben. At the foot of the bed, Sadie rolls over, snorts, and kicks a back leg reflexively as she wrestles with her own dream. I freeze into stillness for minutes, or maybe an hour, ultimately forcing myself to open my eyes. On television Myrna has become Claudette Colbert, and Clark, a long-faced, soft-jawed boy-next-door type. The pair is raising chickens in some godforsaken bump on a log. An actor is muttering about eggs. I see that I am wearing a T-shirt from a charity walk, not one of my Jordan almond–hued wisps of lingerie nestled in a drawer I haven't opened in weeks.

I remember: Ben is gone, yet I feel him in the room as I do every night, embracing me with arms kept strong by endless push-ups — my husband, the invincible gladiator who expected to live past one hundred. Some nights I cry or curse or simply lie like a corpse myself, eyes open to the sooty darkness, and other nights are like this one — Ben and I make love, after which I pummel away his image with my fists.

I kick off the duvet, which feels as heavy as a lead apron, and look at the clock. It is already tomorrow, three in the morning, that war zone infested by workaholics, parents of fretful infants, and, my own demographic, the freshly bereaved. I want to shout at Ben, but this might convince Cola and Luey to cart me off to some public snake pit of a mental institution, since the private, leafy variety is a luxury we can no longer afford. I keep my voice low, my whisper more plaintive than sneering, because I have not fully committed to anger or husband hatred.

Perhaps animosity is what Ben deserves, but my heart argues for a postponement of sentencing, even an ultimate reprieve. Since my dinner two nights ago with Stephan, I've doubled my search efforts. "Give me a clue," I say to the man who cannot reply. "Darling, you owe me an explanation. What is this insanity about a ring? And why did you empty our accounts?"

I am answered by the wind whistling beyond the window, which is open, blowing a chilling mist into the room. I move one foot and then another, feeling a cramp in my lower back as I force myself out of bed. Floors below, a couple is letting it rip, and words carry into the still night. "Why the fuck did you do that?" a woman screeches. "Again! Every goddamn time!"

Get away now, when you're young, I am tempted to shout back. Stick around and in twenty years you'll be wondering if ghosts are real. I try to convince myself that this is fatigue talking, pull on Ben's plaid robe and a pair of his warmest socks coiled on the floor where I let them fall last night, and wander into the hallway. A light shines. God forbid anyone in this family should flick off a switch.

Nicola's door is closed, as is her sister's, but when I reach the kitchen, there is Luey, scrunched into the corner of the banquette, her back toward me, idly yanking a spike of hair with one hand, the other cradling her phone. She is speaking in a heated, breathy voice, saying, "I'm not kidding."

If I turn to leave, I may make a noise and she will surely accuse me of eavesdropping. I stop dead until she speaks again. "That's a help." This is followed by a lengthy silence, after which Luey slams down the phone so hard that she spills a mug of cocoa sitting on the table. She doesn't mop it up.

Except for when she visits the dentist, of whom she is terrified, Luey is not a crier. As a child, she would bite her lip to staunch the tears that any other small girl might shed as she would swallow a verbal clobber from a kid who was an even bigger bully than she. But in the lamplight, my daughter holds her knees to her chest and rocks, after which the sobbing comes in gasps. This is Luey very angry or very scared.

I would not hesitate to run to Nicola's side, but Luey keeps me at a remove. A minute passes. "Honey?" I whisper hoarsely.

She looks up, though her arms stay in

place. "You're sneaking up on me now?" I expect a glower, but her face is open for business.

"Can I help?" I ask.

Crisis intervention is not my specialty. I've never gotten beyond offering balm for elementary boy trouble, if that's what's on the table. As far as I know, however, neither of my daughters currently has a boy, least of all a man, in her life. Luey releases romantic information on a need-to-know basis, pointing out that I have no need to know, and when Nicola's last beau that I knew of started a PhD program in Iowa City, she paid the young brainiac exactly one visit. "Imagine, a college town where you can't find crème fraîche," she griped. "Not even a decent baguette." A week later, she'd enrolled in Berlitz and bought tickets to Paris. Nicola has a way with foreign languages and American Express.

After a sustained glare, Luey gathers her cell phone, grabs a container of yesterday's pad thai from the refrigerator, and stomps out of the room. The statement, "You can help by not asking questions," trails in her wake.

I picture my daughter pulling noodles out of the box like so many worms and hope she keeps a fork, even an unwashed one, in her bedroom. I fill the teapot, turn on the flame, and search the cupboard for the plastic honey bear and Sleepytime tea. While I wait for the water to boil, my head does a one eighty, hoping for any distraction. I will force myself not to think about Luey.

The kitchen is a shiny, tidy room, though Opal is now coming in only once a week. "This schedule is temporary," I stressed when we had our conversation. Opal graciously accepted my lie, saying she'd make up the days by working for the young mother of twins who lives downstairs. I felt grateful that an unknown neighbor has absorbed a portion of my contrition.

I used to love to read cookbooks at night, planning imaginary parties. But now cooking is almost the last thing I want to do. The last thing is to face my finances. On the desk in the kitchen, un-opened mail is stacked in toxic clumps. Somber envelopes, thick and thin, hit the mailbox every day, some for accounts that I've never realized we had. *Over here! Overdue! The Silver-Waltz National Debt, climbing by the nanosecond!*

For years after Ben and I married, we kept up a financial ritual so precise we might have been Swiss watch parts. The second Sunday afternoon of each month we would write out checks, address envelopes, affix whatever jaunty commemorative stamps I'd selected, and drop the bills in the mailbox as we walked to a theater to reward ourselves with a movie, after which we would eat Chinese. I balanced our joint checkbook down to the penny, and if pop quizzed, I could recite the bottom line of our account as accurately as my daughters' birthdays.

Then Ben bought a toy, a personal computer, and became an early adaptor to a genius program that allowed him to manage all our banking, down to printing every check, which he stopped showing me when the novelty diminished. The movies continued, but around the time Szechwan turned to Thai, my attention to fiscal minutia faded away. Every month, my husband direct-deposited a sum into an account he established for me. "The money's yours — I don't need to know how you spend it," he said, with the understanding that I would use this fund for Opal, household expenses, clothes, and other spoils of being in a high-tax bracket. In a glorious spike of upward mobility, I downshifted to the role of a child, though I threw around words like *liberation* to describe this era when my sense of financial responsibility ended.

I eye the stack of envelopes as if they

might spill out anthrax. *Dare you,* says a chunky one with the return address of Bank of America. There's no way I'm going to fall back asleep. I'm up to the threat.

I use a letter opener to carefully remove the statement. No surprise: the last infusion into my account was seven weeks ago. Since then, there are withdrawals every few days — I have been hitting the ATM like a mother whose children enjoy a bottle of eight-dollar Shiraz with a square meal. I brew my tea and settle in, ripping open envelopes, dividing the big bills from the small. Utility company; telephones; car rentals; mortgages; insurance; mini-storage; dry cleaning; dues to four gyms — everyone in the family had a favorite; doctors; and credit cards — Nicola's, Luey's, and my own. I sort the bills right, left, right, left, picking up speed like a cardsharp dealing in a high-stakes game. I toss each subscription renewal in the trash, along with course catalogs from NYU and the New School, but when I see a solicitation for a worthy cause — when did every other friend start supporting a school in Africa, and could the globe please stop cracking with earthquakes? — I flinch. For all their flaws, my parents were charitable, and I've prided myself on carrying that torch. It hurts to think of myself as a skinflint.

Once more, I study the bank statement. In a few months I'll be underwater.

I had a life. Now I have a situation. Perhaps I, too, should open a chicken farm and start selling eggs. Isn't this one of Martha Stewart's ninety-nine sidelines?

Suddenly I am too beat to wash my mug or wipe up cocoa, and I tell myself I will think about this tomorrow, though it is tomorrow. I heave myself out of the chair, pull Ben's robe tightly, and begin to stumble back to my bedroom for a shower. As I pass Luey's door, the light is creeping through. I think about knocking but keep going, a mother incapable of either wisdom or common sense. Then I hear a voice.

"Ma?"

I turn. Luey is standing in the doorway, looking barely fifteen. "Sweetie, you're still up," I say, feeling a love rush so strong that my knees wobble.

"Want to come in?"

I cross into Lueyland, which smells of bubblegum and patchouli and hasn't changed in ten years. My daughter climbs under her covers and looks at me with solemn eyes. I am being sized up. I sit at the foot of the bed, longing to reach forward and brush the hair out of my Luey's face, but I am fearful of overstepping, of rejection.

"What's going on?" I try to sound less tentative than I feel. Luey cocoons herself deeper into her lavender polka-dot linens and says nothing. "Did you have a fight with a friend?"

This evokes a laugh. "Oh, yeah."

I name every friend I can recall — Emily, Sheena, Amanda, Miso, Madison, Katy and Katie, and Caitlin.

"Cold, colder, much colder," she says.

I wonder if I'm being teased, and my fatigue sucks me into irritability. This is why I say, "Does this have to be a game?"

"I wish."

I'm not going to take another risk, so I offer nothing and wait.

"It's a guy thing," she says.

"You're going to have to help me out here," I say, "because I wasn't aware you had a boyfriend."

"I don't." She laughs. "I had a fuck buddy."

"Charming." I regret my sarcasm.

"It doesn't matter one way or another. He's out of the picture."

"You broke up?"

"We were never really together."

I want to say, *Then why does it matter?* But

clearly this boy or man counts for something. "Is there anything you *can* tell me?"
Luey doesn't respond. My nose finds the
pad thai, upended into the wastebasket.

"Yes," she says. "I'm pregnant."

10.

Louisa, you asshole, how could you? That's what Luey wished her mother had said, along with *Didn't you use protection? Have you never heard of contraception? This is going to ruin your life. I'm only glad your dad isn't here to witness your latest dumbass stunt.* Instead, Luey could see thought bubbles effervescing above her mother's head. "Honey bunny, you aren't the first girl this has happened to. I will support you in this decision. If you want an abortion, I will find a clinic. If you want to keep the baby, I will feed you chicken soup and vitamins. I'd have the baby myself if I could. In fact, let me look into that. I read an article in *Good Housekeeping* when I was at the doctor's office . . ."

Luey stared at her phone, willing him to call. From his Web site, she knew he was in Sydney.

The thought that within her was human

life the size of a sesame seed left her feeling as if she were living in a sci-fi movie. *A living thing.* Part of her wanted to say, *Ew, get it out,* yet the rest of her was curious. An online test said her IQ score was 135, not genius but pretty high. What if this child would go on to cure cancer? Invent a new kind of music? Be God's way of bringing back Daddy? What if?

Luey clutched her stomach, ran to the bathroom, and threw up.

11.

"Sorry for calling this early, but I'm selling the house," I say.

"But you love that place." Daniel's voice is still tamped with sleep.

This used to be true. The house at the beach is not fashionably old, fashionably new, or fashionably located. What it has going for it is a sweep of bay view from a broad roof deck where Ben would read a thriller each weekend. There is also a widow's walk, his idea. What the hell was he thinking?

From this perch I adored the endless tent of blue sky and the faraway fireworks we watched with the girls and their friends every Fourth of July. But I'm no longer seeing lazy meringue clouds or jeweled bursts against an inky sky. I'm reliving every grain of sand that followed me from the beach into my butt crack and kitchen, every mildewed towel, every gridlocked mile as my car crept to the village to buy a forgotten quart of overpriced milk, every artificially serene face at yoga, and every disturbing freckle on my chest from hours sprawled under the pounding sun. Mostly, however, I'm seeing every mortgage payment coming at me like a breaking wave.

I can live without this house, which Ben always felt more affection for than I did.

"Get your tenses right, my friend," I tell Daniel as I sip lukewarm coffee. "I *loved* that house." It is seven-thirty, though I have been up for hours. "But now that I'm done with it, the place may not necessarily be easy to sell."

"Weren't you going to try and rent?"

"That was last week."

"I hope you've slept on this decision."

I did. It was the backache with which I woke up that convinced me there was no reason to be a halfhearted homeowner whose problem will boomerang the first weekend after Labor Day when renters departed, leaving behind their worn-thin flip-flops and cheap, crusty grill.

"I'm good with the decision. Except I don't know a broker."

"I can make some calls," Daniel says, as I hoped he would.

That was last week.

Today he and I are on the Long Island

Expressway. It's not a scenic drive, unless you count the car itself, Stephan's Jaguar. I am dressed in layers of silk underwear topped by wool and puffy down. I look round as a Botero and don't care.

The last trip I made here was in October, when Ben ran fifteen miles on the beach and I grilled veal chops with Swiss chard and ridiculously expensive Italian ricotta. That evening I pushed aside the photography books — Annie Leibovitz's nudes, Bruce Weber's Newfoundlands — and set two places on the coffee table in front of the hearth. Ben built a fire. I lit my fattest white candles. He poured Prosecco. I wore a moth-eaten Shetland turtleneck and my most sacred, broken-in jeans. After dinner we ate coffee ice cream dripping with hot fudge and had each other as an after-dinner delicacy.

This is the kind of memory I try to bat away as if I'm taking a broomstick to a spider web. I am entangled in it until, as we slow down and turn onto Route 27, Daniel's voice erupts with, "What sayeth Fleigelman?"

"Want a direct quote?" I offer up in my most dulcet Brooklyn-meets-Great-Neck tone, " 'Bubkus, my dear.' " I smile at Daniel. "He promises he's looking 'with all due haste,' but I need to start living as if nothing will come from his efforts."

Daniel and I already know that so far Stephan hasn't found any sign of the storied emerald-and-diamond ring, though he has sent out an all-points bulletin to jewelers to alert him if the ring surfaces. He assured me that if the ring isn't on someone's hand, he will find it.

Daniel turns up the country and western station that Stephan forbids and warbles along with the radio. Stephan's patron saint is Bach; Daniel's is Johnny Cash. "I can't believe that's true, darlin'," he says, and when I don't respond, he adds, "Come on, y'all. Sing it, sister."

"If you promise not to sing, I won't either." Ben, who searched for karaoke bars wherever we vacationed, could carry a tune. My repertoire is limited to the blessings over the Hanukkah candles, which the whole class learned at my private Quaker elementary school.

"In that case, get out the directions, will you please? We're getting close. I can smell money."

I put on my glasses and call out street names until we arrive at an East Hampton realty office in a Hansel and Gretel clapboard cottage. " 'Chip Sharkey' sounds like a bookie. How do you know this broker?" I ask, as Daniel gently slows and parks Stephan's Jag like the elderly, pampered child it is.

"Like I find everyone. He's Pedro's ex and registered in the official gay underground."

"Why is it when men break up, they turn one another into friends? I don't see that happening with women."

"Because men are bigger people, inherently kinder and more beneficent?"

I think of Ben. "Nah, that can't be it."

We've been in the car for two hours. I am glad to stretch. Like a good husband, Daniel puts his arm around my shoulder as we maneuver the icy path to the realtor's door. Inside, where the temperature is barely warmer than outside, a noisy electric heater glows like a menacing jack-o'-lantern. A receptionist instructs us to wait on a hard bench. Daniel makes phone calls while I page through an oversized magazine from last September.

I'm wondering why Chip Sharkey, he of the flawless reputation, is late for an appointment on a slow Friday morning. This gives me time to consider if I've made a mistake. The house I want to heartlessly offload is rife with Silver-Waltz history. Clam bakes, post-prom parties, barbecues for Ben and Luey's August birthdays — our family has taken its measure here in corn on the cob, fresh basil, and ripe tomatoes; in bottles of chardonnay and tiny bikinis; in guests who've arrived for the night and stayed a week. This is where I learned to roll out pie crusts and parse the difference between UVA and UVB. I'm time-traveling back to the summer when Nicola lost her virginity to a riding instructor with a Holden Caulfieldish name — Montgomery Ward? Ward Montgomery? — when a man who looks to be in his forties, with buttery, meticulously parted hair and round tortoise-shell eyeglasses, who seems to have walked out of a J.Crew catalog, comes through the door. Despite the frost, he wears only a navy blue blazer and a spiffily striped scarf.

"Chip Sharkey," he says, extending a hand gloved in tobacco-colored leather. His jeans are pristine but not ironed, his boots too fine for this weather. Under his other arm, he carries a cardboard tray. "Sorry I'm late — made a coffee run."

We exchange introductions and follow the broker to a small office in the back fitted with a desk faced by Windsor chairs. Vintage maps of the island cover the walls.

"I did a drive-by," he begins. "Your land-scaping is excellent. Enough greenery so the house should show well even in this season. Good that the walks are shoveled and the driveway plowed."

While I tally how much this required service continues to cost, Chip Sharkey swivels his chair to retrieve a folder, which he opens and places carefully on his desk, then reaches for a fountain pen. He leads me through a checklist. How many bedrooms? *four;* kitchen? *renovated six years ago, soapstone counters, white wood cabinets, Sub-Zero fridge, Viking stove;* bathrooms? *three and a half;* security system? *of course . . . ;* and on and on.

Chip lifts his key. "So, two cars or one?"

No way is Daniel going to abandon the Jag. "We'll follow," he answers. We wander out and I take my seat. Before we can gossip — *What man that old has hair as yellow as Tweety?* — Daniel says, "You don't have to go through with this, George," concern creasing his forehead. "We can go home and forget we were here."

I reach over and pat his hand. "You're more worried about me than I am," I lie. "Let's at least see what kind of price Chip Sharkey" — I try not to snicker when I say the name — "comes up with after he cases the place."

We drive past the sites of out-of-season

farm stands and follow along the back roads where next summer another round of inebriated celebrities and teenagers will most assuredly collide with trees. I think that unless Chip suggests that I give away my house for a bargain-basement price, I need to finish this chapter of my autobiography. As soon as I unlock the back door of the house, however, I feel that *E*A*S*Y* is a password my life no longer accepts. This place is so damn Ben. Hanging on pegs are his faded baseball caps with logos from every resort where he's ever parasailed or golfed. Against the wall are a row of size-eleven men's sneakers. On the kitchen counter is an empty bowl. I see it filled with ripe peaches and Ben grabbing the most succulent one, as he took everything and anything he wanted.

Chip follows me, with Daniel behind, as I open appliance and pantry doors, grateful for the absence of mice, and then lead the men into the open room furnished with overstuffed parchment-pale couches that circle a tall fieldstone fireplace. ("Why are there only three?" Luey wanted to know when they arrived, as if my choice in seating was intended to exclude her.) There are back-to-back hearths, the flip side facing a dining room furnished with a rough, round table and ten mismatched wooden chairs acquired at auctions and flea markets. Each has been lacquered a different color, the only touch that's strictly my own.

Chip sizes up the nothing-special view while I stare at the birch logs in the fireplace. I move closer. These are the remains of the logs I kept in place all summer but never burned, the East Hampton equivalent of plastic slipcovers. Now, charred like five babies in an apocalypse, they are the calling card of someone who wasn't me.

I was cold. Now I am colder. I have to remind myself to smile when Chip praises the putty-white of the walls, the floor-to-ceiling bookshelves, the rugs walked to silkiness.

"Would you sell it furnished?" he asks.

"Why not?" I answer, as I pass a mirror and instead of my own reflection, see Ben. I would like to gauge out his eyes, but I find myself leading two men upstairs. We enter Luey's bedroom, then Nicola's, one electric green, the other carnation pink. A guest bedroom, two bathrooms. Nothing is garish or amiss.

Chip nods. "And where's the master?" he asks.

The master is in hell. And then another channel of my bifurcated inner workings wakes up to hush me, saying, Georgia, you have no proof that Ben did anything wrong — his loss of money might be an idiot blunder he was trying like hell to reverse.

"The master bedroom?" the broker repeats.

Daniel senses that I am out to sea. "C'mon, buddy," he says, guiding Chip down the hall. "You're going to love it."

I did, once. A stark four-poster faces the window with its lulling, watery vista. Four pillows lean against the headboard, and a pale gray mohair blanket awaits over a thick comforter. It is folded precisely, but its form is not my folding, which I have taught my weekly summer housecleaner to duplicate. I stare at the mohair throw and see an origami of deception.

Chip is opening closet doors and pacing off square footage. "Aren't I lucky?" he asks. "Each of my feet is exactly twelve inches long!"

Anxiety snakes from my gut to my gullet. I expect it to stick out its tongue. We wander here and there, to the small attic with camp trunks, to the basement where lawn furniture waits out winter, to the patio with its empty stone planters, to the laundry room, and to the garage. Chip scribbles while I tell myself that everything can be explained;

any chicanery is purely in my imagination. Maybe Nicola or Luey made a secret trip out here. Or the cleaning woman's sister and her boyfriend might have had a fling. Burnt birch logs and an oddly folded mohair throw — neither are evidence on which to build even a screenplay, much less a legal argument. Yet it's as if I can smell Ben, though when I breathe I inhale only the cold, the damp, and the loneliness of a summer house in winter.

"That about does it," Chip says. "Very marketable. Though of course we'd need to stage the place" — remove family pictures — "except for one of a dog — people like dogs in the country" and paint the girls' bedrooms Decorator White. I zone out as he continues, ending with, "An orchid delivered every Friday."

Daniel takes over, because evidently it's polite to answer a question. "I'm sure Georgia will think about the staging, won't you?" I can tell from his face that mine has all the intelligence of a grapefruit. "Thank you very much. This is good to know."

"I'll get back to you later with a suggested listing price," Chip Sharkey says. "I need to check the comps. Traffic may be slow in the winter, but it should pick up by March. Buyers want to make a deal by late spring and settle in before the summer."

Settle. Imagine. A gracious impersonator of the Widow Waltz thanks Chip Sharkey for his time and trouble. *We'll be in touch. We'll talk. We'll see.* He leaves and it is only Daniel and me, standing across from each other with a kitchen island between us.

"What do you think?" he asks.

My urge to discuss Chip's grooming habits has vanished. "He seems thoroughly competent."

"About selling?"

Without hesitation, I reply, "No problem there. Get rid of the place."

"I don't want you to rush and regret this. I'm sure I can find some friends who'd rent for a season, maybe even long term."

"Daniel," I say, skipping over kindness. "I've got to do it. Nothing will ever make me feel Ben's not going to race through that door, throw down his tennis racket, and go for a Corona."

He narrows his eyelids slightly, sending a message that asks, *You think you're fooling me?*, zips his jacket higher, and says, "In that case, I refuse to return to the city without a lobster roll."

"Sorry, Danny, out of season."

"Ah, then other sustenance will have to do. Lunch, George?"

Twenty minutes later we're watching seagulls strut outside the window and listening to the Atlantic slap against the shore. A fire is blazing in the seaside bar where we're tucked into a booth, letting chowder steam warm our faces. Daniel tells a story about an artist he's signed; twenty-seven years old, a prodigy. Which reminds me. "What does Stephan say about Cola?" It's been one full week since Nicola reported for duty, leaving every morning promptly at eight-fifteen. I have been impressed.

"He insisted she lose the vampire nail varnish."

"She's not acting loopy?"

"Actually, 'smart' and 'efficient' were in his lexicon. She convinced a nervous bridegroom to go with the square instead of the cushion cut. Said it was her favorite."

Who knew? "This is a relief." My brother isn't ready to terminate Nicola's employment with some withering remark that will cost me thousands in therapy I can't afford. "I've been worried and she's telling me nothing. Acting almost like Luey."

Naturally, then, Daniel asks, "How is my favorite malcontent?"

I let it sail. "Pregnant."

He gulps and coughs up soup. "Little Luey? Mother of God!"

"No, just pregnant."

"Is she going to . . . you know . . . do something about it?"

My face twitches into the kind of half-smile you see on a stroke victim.

"I don't know."

12.

My heart is calling me back to the bat cave. After lunch I tried to persuade Daniel to take me to a supermarket and then return me to the house.

"George," he said, "I know you're climbing the worry wall, but how much can you accomplish alone, without a car? Wait a week — I'll come out here and we'll do it together, with cocktail breaks. The girls should —"

I growled, "I shouldn't be inflicting myself on anyone just now," *now* having commenced two hours ago.

"I don't want you to throw out your back excavating closets. If I have to endure one more friend's play-by-play about physical therapy . . ."

I lean forward to stroke Daniel's cleanly shaven chin. "Daniel obviously needs younger friends. I give you my word — I'll behave like a matron properly respectful of her joints and tendons."

I have. Getting out of bed today, my third morning here, I quickly assessed the damage from the previous evening's banshee storm — branches littered the yard. I stood straight and made the bed, folding the mohair throw a la Georgia, with thorough disgust and lapidary precision, brushed my teeth, ran a brush through my unwashed hair, and got down to business.

I had already tackled each bedroom. The evidence stands by the front door, as piles of clothing await their next stop down the food chain: the chichi village consignment store, an Internet auction, or the local dump. Thus far, I have found nothing more incriminating than a Costco-sized condom assortment in Luey's room. Where was this stash when she got pregnant? There has been a sensation close to satisfaction in my mindless sorting and deciding, as if by putting my house in order I am doing the same for my head. This illusion winks at me while I stay the course.

Today I will attack the kitchen, which I intend to clean as thoroughly as did my mother's rabbinic grandfather who before every Passover rooted out offending crumbs with the help of a feather and a candle. It is astonishing and disgraceful how much food a family of four can stockpile. Friday and Saturday I boiled up half-filled boxes of spinach lasagna and a member of the penne family the color of a bruise, creating sauces from sardines, anchovies, fennel seeds, tomato paste, and smoked oysters that would have made my great-grandfather curse and gag. Tonight I will move on to quinoa, and for tomorrow I have my eye on some kernels that resemble shriveled caviar, a delicacy that thanks to my reduced circumstances, I no longer need to pretend to like. When I return to the city, I plan to find my mother-of-pearl caviar spoons and learn how to sell them on eBay. Will this switch from buyer to seller feel oddly unnatural, like trying to write with my left hand instead of the right?

I begin to evaluate the cereal, stopping to consider whether Ben's devotion to steel-cut oatmeal puts his death in the same subset of irony as a vegetarian being gobbled by a wolf, when I hear someone pull into the driveway. I carefully straighten my knees, walk to the back door, and peer through the window. A dark green, mud-spattered van is discharging what appears to be a tall, thin teenager wearing work boots and, on this overcast Monday, sunglasses, with a hank of blondish hair peeking out from a cap that says, ADAM AND EVE.

The very expensive gardening service — I've seen those triple-digit bills — has arrived, although not in the form of the squat Ecuadorians with which I am familiar. This must be the out-of-season brigade. Adam, I suppose, deposits a cache of tools on the edge of the driveway and walks toward the outdoor shower, then the shed, bending to gather branches blown down in the storm.

What would it be like to have a brisk job in fresh air? To dress every day in gently worn overalls and wear nothing more on my face than sunscreen and Chapstick, my shorn hair squashed under a hat, to become a twenty-first-century Emily Dickinson, raising flowers instead of children, allowing weather to dictate my life.

I surrender to the romance of the notion until I remind myself that I loathe Emily Dickinson; I am more of an Edna St. Vincent Millay "My candle burns at both ends" sort of gal. My Emily Dickinson animus is not simply because I cannot weed unless under expert supervision. I'm strictly an indoor gardener, a fact confirmed when I ordered two hundred bulbs from a mail-order catalog and planted every last one upside down, providing fast food for rodents. The following spring a grand total of seventeen tulips rose from the earth to give me the finger. Everything Emily represents — her *me-shugas* with the white dresses, her fanatical virginity, and yes, her deranged midnight gardening — appeals to me only slightly more than, say, pro-wrestling. If Emily had been my freshman roommate, I would have demanded a single. Becoming even an elegant landscape architect would be, for me, too earthy and exhausting. I sigh and am ready to return to my cupboards when the visiting gardener stops before he enters the sheds, turns toward the house, squints, and waves.

I wave back but he is no longer in sight and I return to toss opened packages of flaccid potato chips into an industrial-sized black plastic bag. On the radio, an announcer is giving top-of-the-hour news, delivered with the calm, peculiar cadence exclusive to NPR, as if there is a subtext about a bombing in Syria that I should get.

I progress to canned goods, looking for dents and leaks that, given my recent track record, I am positive will breed botulism — baked beans; pineapple, sliced and crushed; garbanzos; beets; yams in sweet, heavy syrup; and enough pumpkin to bake a pie for every Pilgrim. When I'm back here with a car, I'll make a hefty donation to a food pantry, I am thinking, as I hear a soft knock. I get up from my crouch, go to the back door.

The gardener is here but he is not Adam. She is Eve, aggressively wholesome and most definitely cold, with a small, pointy nose that is slightly runny, and rough lips. She's also no teenager, but not much older — Nicola's age, at the most.

"Mrs. Silver?" she asks.

It never was, officially. I have been steadfast to Waltz.

"Yes?" I've spoken to both daughters and Daniel every day and to Wally Nothing-to-report-I'm-so-sorry-Georgia Fleigelman on Friday. Nevertheless, my voice sounds as if it's been greased with an unguent, and before I continue I clear my throat. In those seconds the face comes into focus. This Eve looks familiar. I might know her from valet parking at a party or standing behind a cash register ringing up insect repellant at the drugstore. She belongs to the tribe that makes the Hamptons hum and who I assume, if I think about it — which I haven't, until now — must despise my kind, the second-home crowd. Now that I'm staring at her, I realized I have misjudged this girl, who is actually far more attractive than most of the summer people with their three-thousand-dollar watches and spray tans. Despite her lanky frame and slender limbs our gardener is blessed with what Ben referred to as a rack. Unlike most of the women at the beach similarly endowed, I am going to guess her set is God given.

"Excuse me," she says. I realize that I must be gawking. Expecting condolences, I prepare my stock response, gratitude encased in stoicism. *Yes, a heart attack. You're right, way too young. Hanging on, thanks for asking. The girls? It's tough.* But what the gardener says is, "Pardon my asking, but could I please use your phone? My battery is dead."

"Certainly," I say. "The phone's over on the counter." I return to my task at hand while I eavesdrop.

"I'm finished here. . . . Okay, I'll wait til he wakes up then. . . . See ya in a bit." She replaces the phone in its cradle, thanks me, and heads toward the back door, pulling a tissue from her pocket to blow into it with a thoroughly unladylike blast.

"Can I offer you some tea?" I find myself asking. If my life was measured by tea bags, I have discovered that I would still be wealthy. Organic cranberry green, lemon chamomile, Earl Grey, et cetera.

"Thanks. I have to wait awhile for my mom to pick me up. This is nice of you, Mrs. Silver."

"It's Waltz, Georgia Waltz," I offer.

"I'm Clem," she says. "Clementine DeAngelo." She surveys the scrambled objects around the room. "Doing some cleaning?"

"Major purge. I'm putting the house on the market."

"Really?" I think I catch chagrin. "Why? It's such a beautiful property, and the perennials are going to be great this year. We just put in those rhododendrons and forsythia a few springs ago. This year they'll come into their own."

I never cease to be amazed at how every human being views the world through her personal lens, and how even the shy among us are prepared to chat up their angle. The historian observes a moment in time — how New York at the dawn of the twenty-first century is not so unlike Vienna in 1890, let's say. The writer keeps an eye out for material, the psychiatrist, problems. Daniel looks at life as if it were a painting he might buy — is the composition balanced and original? Stephan evaluates in carats and profits. This Clementine looks at my life and apparently sees beyond scrawny privets, stunted shrubs, and a broken trellis to picture ruby red phlox, blue clematis climbing the wall, and herbs that I, proud hausfrau, will hang to dry.

Or maybe she just doesn't want to lose a customer. "The house is too big for me," I half lie as I sit opposite her at the table. "And, well, you probably heard about my husband."

"Ben?"

I'm "Mrs. Silver." He's "Ben"? Clementine DeAngelo hooks me with a steady look as I hear a loud, angry noise. To my ears it's like a gunshot, and I startle like Sadie roused from a dream.

"I think your water is boiling," she says evenly.

"Right!" I get up awkwardly and have to grab the counter not to trip.

"Are you okay?"

In the lingua franca of Luey, I am so not okay. "Don't mind me," I answer as I pour water into mugs. I have already placed an assortment of tea on the table next to the sugar. "I don't have fresh lemon, but there's lemon juice in the fridge. And milk."

Why did I invite this Ben-knowing stranger into my home? I want her gone. I want her to never have been born.

"Just sugar is fine."

I rip open a Splenda and swirl it into my

tea, happy to not have to look at her.

"You were saying?" she asks.

I have not forgotten. "Yes, my husband."

"I know him. From the pro shop."

"You knew him?"

A pause hangs in the air like a grenade. I believe she may have caught the tense I used. I search her tone and come up blank while a second Georgia realizes that she will have to phone the private golf course ten miles from here and cancel Ben's membership. This Georgia has forgotten he belonged there and she hadn't seen a notice for yearly dues.

"I see," I say wearily. "Then I guess you haven't heard." I feel hollow and shivery. "My husband has passed away."

Clementine DeAngelo takes in a breath as sharp as a scythe. Freckles stand out on her ashen face. I'm almost ready to reach forward and comfort her when she turns back toward me and says, with complete composure, "Excuse me. That's horrible. I'm so sorry, Mrs. Silver. What — when did this happen?"

"Beginning of last month."

She shakes her head. The cheeks that looked chapped when she entered my kitchen are drained of color. "I had no idea."

"It was sudden." And none of your business.

"I wonder if my mom knows, and if she did, why she never mentioned it," she says in barely a whisper. I can hear the wall clock ticking and outside, the wind continuing to blow, as if the weather is angry. Clementine DeAngelo stands, her mug in hand, and glides toward the sink, where she pours the tea down the drain. "I think I better go. Thank you."

"But your mother isn't here yet. And it's started to drizzle."

"Thanks again." She slips her jacket. There is grace in her simple movement. "I'll be back to finish."

To finish what, I am unsure, but I tell Clementine DeAngelo that tomorrow is fine. I return to the table to drink my tea. That damn ticking is louder than I have ever noticed.

It is fifteen minutes later when I hear a vehicle come up our driveway. I watch as the girl standing in the hard rain bolts to the car. I crane to see the driver, but all I can make out is a baby in the back, strapped into a car seat, a child who Clementine DeAngelo reaches to hug.

13.

Buffalo Bob r u out there? @feralkitty pressed Tweet. The last time Luey had been at this bar, she'd downed four dirty martinis and was wearing her shirt unbuttoned to flash a lacy black pushup bra. Today she was in the same jeans she'd had on every day for the last week and the only thing good she could say about her underwear was that it was clean.

She had never sat alone at a bar in the afternoon, an act of slutty defiance that Luey could have gotten off on if demons hadn't been line dancing in her belly, announcing either morning sickness or garden-variety panic. As she sipped a second ginger ale, she wished she could puke. Or at least make up her mind.

Luey would have liked to dissect her quandary with a female that she felt bonded to beyond all others — her mother, a best friend, her sister — and arrive at a reasonable resolution. But this wasn't, unfortunately, a YA novel, so instead she had called several crisis hotlines, and hung up each time she heard the overly solicitous purr on the other end. Luey decided it would be better to simply walk into Planned Parenthood, which was nearby, and try to trick herself into believing that if she was facing a live body, she wouldn't have the nerve to bolt. From going through this drill with her college roommate, Luey knew it was early enough for her to swallow a pill. In a few days she, too, could be sitting on the toilet, doubled over with cramps, wailing for her mother or God, while trying to pretend she was enduring a natural miscarriage of a pregnancy that wasn't meant to be. And this was considered the easy solution.

The soft ding of her phone broke her thought. A text: *Hey Miz Kitty when can I see u again?* Luey could understand why second-rate writers talked about leaping hearts. She could text back, maybe even call, and tell him everything. Or not. If she laid this on him, she'd probably never hear from the guy, and the problem was that Luey liked this one. No thank you, she decided. At least no thank you for now. She allowed herself the privilege to change her mind. Wasn't that part of a woman's right

142

to choose? If it wasn't, it should be.

"Is this seat free?"

Luey hadn't noticed the curly-haired type who was parking his beer next to her glass. Of course it was free, she thought, as was every other seat at the bar.

"I don't feel like being alone today," Curly said.

I do, Luey thought, and fixed her face in outta-my-space mode.

"Don't judge a man by his come-on."

How could you not? she wondered, as he extended his hand for an actual shake. "I'm Marc."

Mark's trying to make his mark. Mark drinks Brooklyn Lager, not Maker's Mark. Mark starts with the same letter as mnemonic. *That's how I'd remember his name if I wanted to, which I don't,* Luey thought, because karma had failed to take into account that this was a highly inauspicious moment to meet a guy with broad shoulders, which topped her list of nonnegotiable requirements. "Mark with a K?" she asked. She wasn't ready to write him off just yet.

"M.A.R.C. You?"

"Caroline."

"With a K?"

"How did you know? Call me Karo. Like the syrup."

"Because you're sweet?"

"Not at all."

"Whew."

"Why the suit?" He looked like he'd come from court. Lawyer or plaintiff, she couldn't say.

"Job interview." Marc pulled a tie out of his pocket.

"How'd it go?" Luey approved of the tie, Rat Pack skinny.

"I got an offer, but it would mean I have to move."

"From where?"

"Bay Area."

The door of the bar opened, blowing in a gust of cold. "Why would anyone move to New York who could be living there?" Luey asked. What, for example, was she doing here in New York when she should be in Palo Alto this minute, improvising a scene in her sketch comedy class? "Whereabouts?"

"You know San Francisco?"

"A little." Enough to love it. She thought of learning to drive a stick shift and chugging up and down the hills, her heart in her throat; biking the Marin Headlands; bowling at Lucky Strike; and Japantown's cherry blossoms in the spring.

"I've got my own place in the Mission between a Burmese restaurant and a used-book store," he said.

Maybe he wasn't as old as she'd thought.

"How about you?" Marc asked.

"Paris." She went on to describe the apartment where she'd visited Cola, on the sixth floor of a Belle Epoque walk-up with a rooftop view straight from *Gigi,* Nana's favorite movie.

"I was hoping you'd say 'here.' " He smiled — his teeth were endearingly crooked — and took a business card from his pocket.

Luey was touched by his complete lack of cool and, hormones be damned, felt dangerously close to tears. "Maybe you'll hear from me, @notanarcmarc."

She scribbled *@feralkitty* on a napkin. "I'm leaving tonight, but here."

"So, bye," he said, helping Luey into her jacket.

She left the bartender a five-dollar tip, and thought about giving Marc a kiss on the cheek. "Bye," she said, and walked out the door toward the clinic.

14.

I consider it a triumph that my family of three has dodged Christmas — yesterday — which neither Ben nor I was raised to celebrate. That is why, perhaps, it became his fetish, no goose or Norway spruce too large, no holly sprig or tinsel wisp too slight. Every year I sent out six dozen cards engraved with a carefully chosen religious-neutral greeting featuring a black-and-white photograph of the Silver-Waltz family. Our clan became a vision of orthodontic splendor grinning from mantels across the land. I squeeze my eyes tight against the memory. It horrifies me to think of the spectacle, the expense.

This year there were no festivities. I sent regrets to invitations and quashed our own born-again tradition, as well. On the Sunday night before Christmas one hundred of our closest friends used to crowd the apartment for Ben's glogg, my Kansas City chili, and

Opal's bûche de noël, a cavalcade of marzipan and rummy buttercream guaranteed to fatten our gang for the winter. The presents? I am trying not to think of either the gifts or the orgy I made of wrapping them with a cascade of organdy ribbons and my navy blue paper, starchy stiff. Yes, I had a signature paper, ordered in bulk from Charleston, South Carolina.

Truly, I was a risible creature, hostage to a religious holiday to which I had no claim. With Ben gone, I've done a pretty fair job of leaping right past it. Except for Fred and Opal's checks, I have pushed my Scroogeness to a craggy low, even taking a pass on the ritual that Ben and I instituted when Nicola and Luey were in middle school: volunteering on Christmas Eve at a homeless shelter. I signed us up this year, but when the moment arrived. I was too forlorn to go. The girls came through, at least, making me proud but shamed by my absence as well as my paltry donation. Lady Bountiful gone frugal.

"Mother," Luey says. Her voice is shrill, which is what it takes to rouse me from my funk. "If you sit for one minute more with that crab face, I'm suing you for maternal malpractice."

She has an open-and-shut case. In a rare

show of solidarity, Cola and Luey had pleaded for a tree, a wreath, or at least a lone poinsettia. Perhaps I was wrong to deny them. Self-righteousness used to top my chart of most despised traits, but self-pity is gaining and the current me has become a bore.

"Luey, what do you say we take our stroll tonight?" I ask, since there'd also been no window gazing this year.

I had always looked forward to our walk-about where we sized up the city's holiday displays. We'd start with the flashy commerciality of Macy's, proceed to the prim sweetness of Lord & Taylor, then hike north to the Rockefeller Center skating rink before we scoped out Saks. There, one of the girls would say, reliably, "This sucks" or, "I'm freezing," but I never allowed family members to break ranks. Not that the weather wasn't chilling and the crowds weren't thick. I, for one, got a second wind as we progressed to the peacock opulence of Bergdorf, where I scrutinized each diorama as if it were priceless art. Those windows were my secret blankie and my family indulged me as I *ooh*ed and *aah*ed over every feather, dripping crystal, vintage leather suitcase, velvety gown, and taxi-dermy ostrich. Only after a good twenty minutes of adulation would I give our group the green light to hike east to the painful cleverness of Barney's.

"Yes, I am definitely in the mood for a long walk," I say, putting on a smile and noticing that I have devoured two slices of a gift sent by Wally, fruitcake, which I don't even like.

I am enjoying the grin that flashes on Luey's face when Nicola joins us. Had daily exposure to her Uncle Stephan terrified her into skipping meals? Cheekbones have emerged in her rounded face and her stomach appears to be ironed flat, though maybe it's the contrast to her sister that makes this apparent. Luey isn't showing yet — by her calculation, she is only seven weeks pregnant — but I see a softness that becomes her, though I am keeping that observation to myself, waiting for my opening. All I know is that Luey has been "weighing her options," and that I found a drugstore bag that contained prenatal vitamins. The profound explanation for my daughter's rosy glow tops a lengthy list of untouchable topics: their father, our dashed security, the fact that by mid-January our apartment is going on the market along with the house in the country, Fred's termination and Opal's vastly reduced hours, how long Nicola will work for Stephan, whether Luey will be returning to Stanford next semester, and how, if she does, I will find the tuition.

We can't talk so we may as well walk.

"Did I hear you say you want to check out the windows?" Nicola asks, balancing on the edge of an armchair.

Within the carefully cultivated voice of this woman in her twenties I hear the child. I can see an eight-year-old Cola in flannel pajamas eating cookies after we finish decorating the tree. Ben is lifting her to the top, the angel in her hand. Where is that angel? In tearing apart the apartment I don't recall seeing any of the yuletide trappings, but trying to solve this peculiar mystery is a distraction that tonight I will force myself to deny.

Maybe I need a little Christmas after all. "Get your coats before I come to my senses," I say. "I am having a spasm of cheer."

"I'm in!" Luey shouts. She pulls on her Uggs, sleeping like lazy puppies beneath the coffee table, and saunters to the closet, where she stuffs her hair under a peaked knit cap and slips into Ben's black down jacket. Nicola bundles herself into a red toggle coat that I haven't seen in years. As she artfully winds an orange scarf around her neck, I grab the worn shearling jacket I use for Sadie's outings. I consider taking her along and decide against it, in case my mood lasts long enough for us to toast this terrifying year at a real bar. I am eager to leave before I change my mind.

"That's what you're wearing?" Nicola chides in a tone I recognize, same as that which I suspect I inherited from my own mother.

"Take me as you get me."

"Where's your sheared mink?"

"Keep up, Cola," Luey says. "Georgia took that beast to the Ritz Thrift Shop three weeks ago."

"No!"

"Yes," I say, with no regrets. After I returned from the beach, I went on a tear, ditching the furs and bringing baubles to Stephan. It felt strangely liberating to begin stripping away, although it might be weeks or months or never before I see a dime from the consignments.

"Nana's black broadtail, too?" Nicola asks, her jaw dropping.

"No, darling, I saved that one for you." Only Nicola fits into this fanciful garment with its bracelet sleeves and tricky frog closures, a coat strictly for show, not warmth, not unlike my mother.

"Well, then," she says, half smiling.

"Well, then," I say, reaching for my key.

Two hours later, we have completed our rounds, ending at Barney's, which we declare to be even more arch than ever. The air has the damp smell of snow. I find myself telling my daughters, "I'm glad you talked me into this." This is true. "And I'm not in the mood to go home yet."

"Neither am I," Nicola says. I see her hesitate. "We could stop at the Pierre."

"Definitely not dressed for the Pierre," I counter.

In unison, both daughters sigh, and say, "Not the Plaza," which has renovated away its *Eloise*-esque appeal to resemble any upscale condo complex from Atlanta to Santa Barbara.

"There's the hamburger joint at the hotel on Fifty-seventh Street," I say, despite the fact that Ben considered it our neighborhood diner, a no-name, grease-spattered rec room knockoff tucked behind thick red curtains, the Parker Meridien's idea of caprice. Ben said it reminded him of the places he went to as a kid in Philadelphia.

"Okay with me," Nicola says.

"I have a much, much better idea," Luey says.

"Not a hansom cab, please." A weary

horse would make me weep.

"Or beer," Nicola adds.

"St. Patrick's," Luey announces, pleased.

"The cathedral?" her sister asks.

"Is there a bar by that name?"

"Why?" Nicola wants to know.

"I like the place," Luey says. "I find it soothing."

The things you don't know about your children. It touches me that my prickly girl wants soothing. Which is why I say, "Let's go."

In ten minutes we find ourselves entering the Gothic, marble-clad oasis, and I am sorry the word *awesome* has been co-opted and forever tarnished. The grand cathedral is quietly swelled with visitors. Many are marveling at the soaring arches and vaulted ceiling, the dozens of red-ribboned wreaths hung high, marching toward the distant nave, and the jewel-hued stained glass, the vastness of it all. Others kneel or sit in pews, one by one or in small groups. I hear the echo of a soft sob, and from somewhere far off, holiday music. I am not sure what to do or where to go within this holy, humbling place of worship that I don't wish to treat as if it were a hasty pit stop on a traveler's agenda.

"Mother, I'm going to light a candle,"

Luey says. She gestures toward banks of burning lights. In the dark, they look like a distant village illuminated against a midnight sky.

"Honey, really. I don't think that's right." It's one thing to appropriate Santa, another to brazenly trespass on the hallowed. But my daughter has already moved toward the candles.

"Who do you think she's going to pray for?" Nicola whispers.

"Your father, I suppose," I say and shrug. My gut tells me that Luey has confided nothing in her sister, and that she will be praying for the decision she apparently hasn't made.

"I'm going to light a candle for him, too," Nicola says after a minute of silence.

I put my hand on her sleeve. She removes it, and half a minute later Nicola is standing next to Luey. My daughters glance to their right and left to size up the protocol before they each kindle a white taper. *No harm done,* I hear Ben say to me. *No harm done.*

Everyone seeking refuge within this fatherly enclosure must have a story of grief and loneliness, but I am thinking only of mine. Plain and simple, I miss Ben. He is gone, my husband who has left me trembling with fear. I hate that he can't respond when I cry out to him at night, both sleeping and awake. I want explanations and ledgers, anecdotes and apologies. As much as I worry about what has happened to me, in my heart I cannot wholly despise Ben, a man whose absent laughter and touch is more powerful than my beseeching and animosity.

I am taking the steps that a responsible woman must to swim upstream and reconstitute her life, if my state is in fact permanent. But I remain in shock, encased in an icy carapace of disbelief, and as bad as it has been, I am only now realizing it has been worse in this season of false merriment, where every ho-ho-ho feels like a jab. In a few days, the calendar will turn over to a new year. That is something for which I can honestly thank God and do, mouthing a silent prayer that ends with, *I will not cry,* which I repeat like a mantra. But the enormity of the cathedral has swallowed my self-control. I feel a tear run down my cheek, paving a salty path to the corner of my mouth.

"Georgia?"

My knees buckle and shoulders shudder. I stumble as a strong hand catches my arm.

"I thought that was you," he says.

The face is remotely familiar.

155

"Chip. Chip Sharkey."

"Ah, excuse me," I say, spooked, as I flick away the tear. The broker and J.Crew disciple. "Of course."

He grins. "I do the same whenever I see people out of context, which, for a salesman, is unforgivable."

I am at a loss for a polite response, but he continues. I'd like to think this is because Chip is a kind soul who realizes he has caught me off guard. As I try to turn myself into a sociable human being, he says, "This place overcomes me, too. I always stop here this week. You?"

"Never," slips out. "I know the cathedral mostly from my daughters renting *Spider-Man.*" I feel myself blush, sorry for my remark until a man who has appeared at Chip's side laughs.

"I'm not a regular either," he says. "I only know it from that James Patterson novel. Chip dragged me here."

"Georgia, Nat. Nat, Georgia," Chip says. As he turns his head from side to side, Chip's glossy blond hair — expensively colored, definitely — reflects a spotlight. "Georgia owns a house I'm positive I'm going to sell once we're past the holidays, and clients get real."

"Happy to meet you." I extend my hand.

"Season's greetings." What English-speaking person says *Season's greetings*? I may as well whip out a Star of David.

Had I ever considered what Chip Sharkey's partner might look like, it wouldn't have been someone this rumpled, in cords with shaggy salt-and-pepper hair and the sort of thick, black glasses I associate with serial killers. That my real estate broker has attached himself to such an unmade bed of a guy makes me actually notice Chip, who up until now has been merely a functional widget in my life. It also makes me like him.

"Are you in the city for the week?" I direct the remark at Chip.

"I'm the city guy," Ned-or-Nick answers. "Chip's the houseguest."

"The guest who makes the party happen, I might add."

"This is true. Without Chip's intervention I'd spend the holidays —"

How, I'll never know, because Chip interrupts with, "Say, why don't you join us on New Year's Eve? Come early or come late, but be there to watch the fireworks." He recites a Central Park West address. I know the building, where Luey used to see a shrink named Dr. Heckler. "We look east, tenth floor."

"Thank you — that's so kind, but I

couldn't." I mean that.

"Of course," Chip says. "Why would a woman like you be free on New Year's?"

"That's not it. . . ." I trail off. I haven't let myself think about New Year's, an evening that Ben and I reserved for ourselves and — when they were willing — the girls. After our family graduated from lasagna and ginger ale to pâté and champagne, Ben and I went full circle, back to a solo celebration crowned by oysters we gorged on when our daughters abandoned us for better company. While the clock struck twelve, we'd dance to "Sea of Love," our bodies melting together as we saw out one year and greeted another. Then we'd toast our good fortune, a cocktail of health, devotion, and privilege. I'd thank Ben for giving me everything and he'd say the same to me. I wonder, what part of this was true?

"What's not it?" Luey asks. She and Nicola have appeared at my side.

"Ah," I say, "these are my daughters, Louisa and Nicola. And this is Chip Sharkey and . . . I am so sorry, I'm an idiot with names."

"Nathan Ross," he offers. "Nat."

"Nat Ross," I echo. "Chip is trying to sell the house in the country."

"Ouch," Luey says, although this is not

news to her. "Please don't."

Luey loves Fortress Hampton as Ben did, playing tennis, flambéing herself on the beach, and once she could drive, scaring the bejesus out of us as she navigated the winding, wooded streets late at night.

"Would you be the daughter with the pink bedroom?" Chip asks.

"Would you be the guy who insisted it be painted white?"

"Both of you are invited, too," he says to my daughters, and reels off details.

I make a show of checking my watch. "My dog," I say, invoking Sadie, the all-purpose excuse. "She's waiting for a walk." We offer polite good-byes and Nicola, Luey, and I weave our way through the crowd, which has doubled, out through the wide front doors. Since we entered St. Patrick's the city has been set to mute. Flakes have begun to stick, frosting Fifth Avenue, slowing traffic. I feel as if I have stepped inside a snow globe.

"Do we really have to head home?" Nicola asks, linking her arm in mine as if we were promenading on a Warsaw boulevard, circa 1932.

"Honestly? I'm exhausted." What has worn me out most is faking a normal, five-minute conversation with strangers. "But you two have fun without me."

Luey and Nicola exchange the look that tells me I have been Topic A. "No, let's get home," Luey says. "Cola can make us hot chocolate."

"You should go to that party, Ma," Luey says, when we are almost there.

"Don't be nuts. Anyway, I think I'll drive out to the country. Seeing that broker reminds me of all the work I have to do" — and the young woman and baby, I'm *sure* there was a baby, I'd like to forget. My mind has run an endless race, imagining the baby's face as Luey's. Or Ben's.

"I like him," Cola says.

"Chip? You don't think he comes on a little strong?"

"The other guy. His smile reminds me of Dad."

"Your father was a God next to that guy," I say, surprised by my stern defense.

"Maybe I just liked him because he liked you."

"He didn't 'like' me. He simply has good manners, which you see too seldom to recognize." He's probably gay, and if not, too young, early forties.

"We should all go to the party," Luey says.

"Can't — I have plans," Nicola says. "In Boston."

"So you're leaving me all alone in the city?" Luey asks me. "Imagine the damage I'll do. I might trash the place. And in my delicate condition —"

"What delicate condition?" Nicola swoops in to ask.

"I am always in a delicate condition," her sister snaps.

"Isn't that the truth," Nicola says.

"Silence, please," I say.

There are times when I wonder what it would be like to have had sons. Surely they would have simply adored me, and been less demanding and intrusive than daughters, for whom I feel destined to never measure up as we tramp through life side by side, each girl always making me feel as if I've done her wrong or favored the other. Ben had it easy. All his daughters required was love and approval, which they reciprocated without question.

Back home, I escape to my bedroom, Sadie at my side. In the morning, I get up early and drive our one remaining car to the beach. For two days straight I sort, box, donate, or ditch whatever is left from my earlier assault on the house, scrubbing it clean of family history. But this is not all. In the phonebook, I search unsuccessfully for Clementine DeAngelo's phone number and

161

address.

What would I do if I'd found it? Call and hang up? Stalk the girl? I tell myself I've gone mad to think what I think, but in every parking lot and on every trip to the dump, the thrift shop, or the grocery store I search for her mother's van and a baby tucked into a car seat with arms outstretched, twenty pounds of swaddled evidence. I look up the address for Adam and Eve and drive by, seeing only an austere metal building surrounded by cold, lonely shrubs.

15.

At first Nicola didn't recognize him. He'd grown taller and filled out since high school. "Michael T. Kim?" she said, dropping the black turtleneck for which they'd both reached at Uniqlo.

"Nicola Silver-Waltz?" His smile told her he wasn't going to hold their last conversation against her. "What the fuck? I thought you were living in Europe."

How did he know that? "I came back. My father died." *Why are you shopping? in that case,* is what he's probably saying to himself, she thought.

But he responded with, "My God. That's horrible. I'm so sorry."

Nicola had dated men who were Indian, African American, Chinese, Japanese, a guy who claimed to belong to the Cherokee nation, and dozens of Caucasians. But Michael T. Kim was the only Korean. That was her senior year at Stuyvesant, the city's most

163

selective public high school, overrun by arrogant geeks consumed with grade-point averages, others' as much as their own. Most of the students took themselves far more seriously than Nicola did, leading them to the glory of colleges better than SUNY New Paltz, the only college where Nicola was accepted.

At Stuy, it was hard not to wind up with a Korean boyfriend. Sixty percent of the population was male and almost that big a wedge was not merely Asian but Korean, though not Nicola's kind. These were children of immigrants — doctors, midwives, and pharmacists now slaving as dry cleaners, manicurists, and owners of twenty-four-hour delis — hard-driving parents who treated their kids like lumps of Play-Doh to be molded into scholarship winners who'd restore the family honor as surgeons, investment bankers, and hedge fund managers. On the evenings of teacher conferences, many classmates accompanied their parents to translate. The Korean students had strict curfews, unrelenting pressure, and dire consequences if they earned less than an A or talked smack to their mother and father.

Nicola had met no other Korean girl adopted by Caucasians who considered their daughter a perfect Asian rose. The

Korean girls got up at five in the morning to practice their figure skating or violin and commuted by subway from solidly middle-class Queens, not an apartment with a Central Park view. Those girls stuck together, often jabbering in a language as foreign to her as Flemish. When she'd started high school, a few of them made chummy overtures. Nicola could never relax around these supremely self-confident creatures, however. They had little in common beyond the products they preferred for their silky black hair. The Korean crowd hadn't spent the previous summers at camps in Maine, didn't commute to school by taxi, and they certainly hadn't had a Bat Mitzvah, after which they celebrated at a disco with a hundred classmates.

None of the friendships stuck. Which was why Nicola was surprised when the boy who sat behind her in AP French asked her to go to the prom. She didn't immediately accept Michael T., the initial to distinguish him from the four other Michael Kims in their grade. She said she'd think about it — she might have even thanked him — and then told her best friend, Ashley, that she'd go to the prom with Michael T. Kim when pigs fly. To start, she hardly knew the guy. He'd tried on two unsuccessful occasions to explain the subjunctive tense to her, but in the cafeteria he sat with the Koreans. She sat with the hot girls who were anything but Korean. Furthermore, Nicola expected to go to the prom with Ari Klein, captain of the tennis team.

Ari wound up asking that twat Ashley, to whom she never spoke again. The next day, Michael T. unleashed fifty pig-shaped balloons at the end of French class — Ashley had obviously repeated Nicola's remark — then kneeled at Nicola's feet and asked her to prom in front of the whole class, all thirty-two students chanting *"Oui, oui, allez avec lui!"* in unison.

Nicola did.

On prom night, Michael T. swung by the apartment, decked out in a tuxedo with a black silk shirt, looking surprisingly handsome and impressing her parents with his politeness. Downstairs a party bus was packed with his friends and dates, all Korean, and not of Nicola's ersatz variety. The booze was flowing, the laughter loud.

Before that evening, all Nicola had thought about was her dress. No knockoff gown from a prom magazine for Nicola Silver-Waltz. Mother had let her splurge on a Narciso Rodriguez, and shoes that cost almost as much. So when Michael T. had moves on the Waldorf dance floor and even better ones at the after-party at a suite in a W hotel, Nicola was surprised. She didn't have sex with him, not even a blow job, because she wasn't sure if a legit Korean girl would on a first date, but they made out on the bus, and wound up wrapped around each other all night long in one of the suite's many beds. He slept. She didn't.

The next weekend, they went to see "The Hangover," and later to a karaoke bar in Koreatown, a few dingy streets of restaurants and stores selling tchotchkes and flimsy handbags in the shadow of the Empire State Building. Over Stella Artoises, they quoted lines from the movie and were working up the nerve to sing. Nicola was thinking how she might be able to take a relationship with Michael T. Kim to the next level — she'd started seeing him as a guy, not a Korean — when at the third beer he said, "Why do you behave like a white girl?"

"Excuse me?"

"Like you're not proud of your heritage?"

What heritage would that be, Nicola wondered. She'd spent two weeks of her life in Korea, not nearly as long as, say, Israel, where she visited for an entire summer on a Hadassah tour with a gang of hormonal American teenagers, exactly as her mother had some thirty-five years earlier. Luey would go the following summer. That was her family's tradition.

"My background isn't like yours," she offered.

"What's that supposed to mean?" Michael T. asked. "Because my family lives in Flushing we're a subspecies?"

"Don't be so defensive," she said, though while she'd never been to Flushing, she was grateful that she didn't live in a neighborhood that doubled as a punch line to a scatological joke.

"I find it pathetic that a smart, full-blooded Korean girl could be utterly clueless about her DNA," he chided.

Nicola liked the "smart" part. Next to Luey she generally felt like a dolt. When Nicola had scored high enough to get into Stuyvesant, she and her parents could barely conceal their shock, though Nicola had lived up to expectations by being in the bottom third of the class all four years.

"I am what I am, not some guy's rehab project," she snapped.

"I never implied that," Michael T. said. "But I thought you might evince some curiosity."

"*Evince?* Learn that at an SAT prep course? How about evincing some curiosity

168

about my life?" Her voice was shrill. "Where's it written that the way your family does things is the gold standard?"

Nicola didn't wait for an answer. Bristling with resentment, she found her way home, and never spoke to Michael T. Kim again until she ran into him today. When he asked her what she'd been doing since college, she kept turning the conversation back to him. Michael T. had graduated from Yale. Now he was at Harvard med school, sharing an apartment with guys — she could tell from their names that they were all Korean — who'd also gone to Stuyvesant. She pretended to remember them.

"We're having a New Year's Eve party," he said. "Why don't you come up? I could give you a ride."

16.

At noon on December thirty-first, driving back to the city, traffic is sluggish. By the time I arrive, Nicola has already left.

Late in the afternoon, Daniel and Stephan swing by with fine cheese, Greek olives, and two bottles of champagne, which Luey doesn't touch, along with the soft cheeses. I, however, drink two glasses. Stephan, at his most priestly, offers a cool kiss on both of my cheeks. We call our mother, who thinks Stephan is our father and I am Mildred, her dead sister. When Luey excuses herself to prepare for a night out with high school friends, I ask Stephan, "Any sign of the mystery ring?"

"Not as yet," he says. "None of the jewelers who handle this quality of stone have seen or heard about it. Keep in mind that Ben may have palmed off the ring to another jeweler in October, after he brought it to me for appraisal. Or parked it in a safe deposit box, as your forensic wizard will discover."

Or Ben may have given away the ring or sold it in a private transaction. I'm sure the same thought has crossed my brother's mind.

"Try not to be downcast, little sister," Stephan says in what for him is a landslide of affection. "Despondency does nothing for a woman's face. And don't forget — this is the fabled holiday season. Perhaps the gentlemen I've been pestering have given my request short shrift because they're too busy selling the crown jewels."

After an hour, Daniel and Stephan leave for dinner at home, where I imagine my brother dandied in velvet smoking slippers, holding two snifters of brandy, while Daniel lights Cuban cigars. They are in matching leather wing chairs in a secret eating club fit for Hogwarts. While I clear and wash the dishes, Luey emerges from her bedroom wearing black leggings, a long, tulle ballerina skirt, and a tight silver sweater which shows off her newly voluptuous breasts. Looking as if she has stepped out of *The Rocky Horror Picture Show,* she grabs her coat and leaves.

Sadie and I trot up and down Central Park South. At the Ritz Carlton, couples in evening dress are coming and going, wishing the world a happy new year. I return home and crack open a P. D. James, but I am restless and switch to channel surfing. Every movie is maudlin or vacuous. I miss Ben, who was supposed to be my permanent New Year's date, and without a daughter or two, the fragrance of a scented candle, or a sumptuous spread, the apartment is too big and too empty.

I will not cry. I will not cry. Crying is for cowards and I am trying to hardwire myself for moxie.

I put the second bottle of champagne in a black velvet pouch I unearth from a drawer and I head out to Chip and Nat's party.

It's going to be a new year. What the hell.

17.

"Greetings, stranger."

"Shots! C'mon!"

"Hey, everyone. It's Loo-ey."

Luey knew this pig call was meant to be affectionate. It had never bothered her, until now.

From the time Luey Silver-Waltz started nursery school, she was the person friends counted on to get the party started, or at least keep it alive beyond its natural life span. She still chafed from the injustice of fourth grade, when Miss O'Leary insisted she be sent to a shrink when she had merely conducted a poll on how many blackheads dotted the teacher's nose. It was math, after all, and despite what Miss O'Leary told her parents, Luey *did* have compassion. By seventh grade, Luey earned the ignominious distinction of being the first girl to show a boy her boobs. In all fairness, there was a limited pool of contenders since most classmates hadn't yet grown a set and hers went to B right out of the gate.

Did it bother her that a group of mothers in the school called a meeting to discuss "mean girls," and by "girls" they meant "girl" and by "girl," Luey Silver-Waltz? In retrospect, yes. Was she for-a-good-time-call-Luey? Throughout high school, probably, but people could change. She was sure of that, too.

On New Year's Eve, when Luey met up with her friends, it was past ten o'clock and her appetite for revelry had slithered away. The bar was in Williamsburg — her old crowd venerated the L train that connected Manhattan to Brooklyn as if it were the Orient Express. Before she stepped off the subway, Luey checked her reflection in the window. Her burgundy lip gloss now struck her as sadly Blanche Dubois.

When she got to the bar, the DJ was spinning "I Just Died in Your Arms Tonight," a hit she'd considered overdramatic even before she'd had, as any one of her psychiatrists might have put it, issues. Christmas decorations hung limply, recycled for one too many seasons.

"Not wine — cocktails!" someone shouted.

"Not cocktails, flights of cocktails," another voice said, as Whitney Kantor yanked her by the arm. She and Whitney used to spend whole weekends playing board games in the blood orange wing of Whitney's Park Avenue apartment, with its colossal acrylic sculptures and birds of paradise poised to devour lesser flowers. By senior year she and Whitney had drifted apart. They hadn't spoken since last summer, not counting shiva after her father's funeral.

Whitney was a beauty, until she spoke. "C'mon, hang your coat. Time for karaoke!" she screamed in her nasal voice over the uproar, swinging her satiny red hair, keeping time with the beat. "We've been waiting for you, Lady Gaga."

"Not in the mood!" Luey yelled back.

"But we always do a duet." Whitney started to sing "The Fame." What she lacked in subtlety she made up in volume. "Your line next!" she shouted, throwing her toned arm over Luey's shoulder, pulling her toward the stage. Luey could smell Whitney's tea rose perfume. She'd never liked it. Yet Luey found herself singing, and then Whitney chimed in, "All we care about is runway models / Cadillacs and liquor bottles."

Ain't that the truth, Luey thought?

"Okay, you got it. We're good to go," Whitney said, and dragged her to the mike. Luey stared into blackness. As she harmonized with Whitney, she could see only dust floating in the smoky air, for which she was grateful. When Whitney pretended to lick the mike between lines, the room detonated with applause.

Mercifully, the song ended. Whitney and Luey were replaced by one of the former water polo players from their school. Luey wasn't sure which team member he was. When she watched the meets, the players looked like identical action figures in Speedos, their broad shoulders and hairless chests tapering to narrow waists, their pinheads covered by sleek, black bathing caps featuring padded ears.

"Got to pee," Whitney said. "I'll be back in a minute." This allowed Luey to do a one eighty and spot Harrison Taylor, her former chemistry lab partner. She climbed onto the bar stool next to him.

"Luey," Harrison said, and kissed her cheek. Unlike Whitney, he smelled clean and worthy, like a new book.

"Harrison," she answered.

"Happy New Year," he said.

"In ninety minutes."

"Let me buy you a drink," he offered. "What'll it be?"

"Seltzer with lime."

He raised his eyebrows. They were bushy, like his hair. Luey always had the urge to pet Harrison as if he were a rescue dog.

"AA," she said.

"Ah." He nodded, as if he wasn't surprised. "How long you been sober?"

"Three weeks," Luey said.

He turned toward the bartender and snapped his fingers. "My good man, a seltzer with lime for the lady, please."

Did he mistake himself for F. Scott Fitzgerald? Pretension and irony aren't the same, my good man, Luey considered saying.

"To sobriety!" He handed Luey her seltzer, then hoisted his own beer. Their glasses clicked.

"On Wisconsin!" Luey cheered. "That's where you go, right?"

Harrison scowled. "Michigan!" he said, pumping his arm. "Premed."

Luey's friends at college in Ann Arbor thought they were of a higher stratum than those in Madison, while Wisconsin students dismissed the Michigan crowd as tight-assed grinds. "Sincere apologies," she said.

"You?"

"Stanford."

"Always too smart for your own good."

Luey disregarded what may or may not have been a compliment. "I'm taking a break," she added. He was the first friend to whom she'd admitted this.

"Internship?" He was shouting over the music, which the DJ had cranked to an eardrum-splitting decibel. "I'm off to Bangkok. How about you?"

She chased her lime with a straw. "Not allowed to announce it yet."

They sipped their drinks for a minute before Harrison said, "What do you say we get out of here?" He smiled. "Go someplace where we can hear ourselves think?"

She'd always liked Harrison, and not just because she'd gotten an A in chemistry thanks to his lab skills. "Let me hit the bathroom first."

As she slid off the stool, something sticky trickled down her leg. Could this evening suck worse?

When Luey got to the bathroom and turned on the light, she realized the answer to that question was yes. She was bleeding — not a gush, but her tights were soaked. She sat on the toilet for a minute or two, but it seemed as if the blood flow was increasing and she felt a dull ache. She grabbed a wad of paper towels, shoved them into her underpants, and waddled back to the bar. Harrison had paid the tab and slipped on his coat.

She clutched her stomach with one hand and put the other on his arm. "I'm feeling a little dizzy." It was true, and now the ache was a cramp. "I'm so sorry, but could you put me in a taxi?"

"Really?" He made no effort to disguise his disappointment.

She was glad her tights were black, as was her coat, which she threw on. "I'm not shitting you, and I am sorry. Another time."

Harrison shrugged, led her out to the cold night air, and whistled for a taxi.

"And can I borrow some money?" Luey asked, as he opened the door and she slid into the cab. Now he'd really hate her, but all she had was twenty bucks. She knew enough to realize she had to get herself to a hospital, and hadn't a clue where she'd find one in Brooklyn.

Harrison handed over three twenties. He'd always been able to blow through two hundred dollars in an evening, between food, cover charges, concert tickets, drinks, and taxis. "Thanks. I'll call you!" she shouted as the cab pulled away.

She did a quick search on her phone and gave the driver the address. "Beth Israel Hospital."

Luey closed her eyes and started to cry. *Bye-bye, baby,* she said to herself.

18.

By the time I reach Central Park West in the seventies, my sense of derring-do has drifted away. But here I am, at one of the grand dowager buildings. I won't let myself turn back.

"Mr. Ross?" I ask the doorman. If he tells me no one lived there by that name, I would flee, relieved. But he says, "The penthouse, miss," nodding toward an elevator at the end of a deep, chilly lobby.

Miss. The title underscores how juvenile I feel and that tonight, and possibly every night ahead, I may be one more woman alone in head-to-toe black hoping that choice will render her invisible. I am very likely underdressed or overdressed, New Year's Eve being an occasion when half the country stays loyal to sweats and the other breaks out skin-tight spangles.

When the elevator arrives, two men exit, their arms bound around each other's narrow waist. They rush by without as much as a glance, and I wonder if I register as flesh and blood. As I step inside, I say, "Penthouse, please," liking the way it sounds.

"Hope you brought earplugs," a uniformed attendant says as the door closes. He smiles, and as I absorb his humanity, in some remote bodily cell I sense encouragement. One foot in front of the other, I remind myself, as if it's a fight song. You have widow-worries, not Asperger's.

When the elevator opens, I see a rack bowing under a crush of wintry garments, and squeeze my coat between a sleek vacuna and a parka engineered to defend against Arctic temperatures. Music assaults me from the opened door at the end of the hall. All I see ahead is a tunnel thick with people.

I have never been anything close to a party animal, not in high school, not in college. I saved my truest, unwound self for Ben and Daniel. Whenever I'd be with other women over a bottle of wine and a bowl of cashews, our shoes kicked off, I would have no comic material to add to their howling histories of the dating front or their husbands' jolly 3-D flaws. By the time I would feel ready to reveal myself, others would have filled their friendship quotas elsewhere. I was that endangered species, a faithful wife whose story started and ended with her husband. I sensed that women found my social currency lacking, and me unimaginatively monogamous.

This is not to say that after I became Mrs. Someone, men didn't approach me. Once Ben had staked his claim, other husbands gave me a closer look. I let them, knowing that nothing would come of the game, whose rules had changed now that I wore a gold band, the one I'd recently buried in a drawer. The promotion from wallflower allowed me to see party posturing as married-lady tennis, an innocent sport punctuated by the graze of a male hand or a man leaning in as he talked, sending a message in no way subliminal.

I laughed. I smiled. But I didn't encourage. I didn't tease, and even after more than two decades, I never morphed into a wife curious to know what it would feel like to meet another man for a cocktail, or more. When fingers lingered or a face hovered close, I disengaged.

Can I say the same for Ben? Most likely not. But I remind myself that in ninety minutes it will be a new year, a dreary moment for rumination on this dreary subject, especially when I've gotten over the first hurdle — walking through the door — and

a waiter is sticking a glass in my hand, saying "Chocolatini?"

That's 342 calories for 4.5-ounces, I
think, recalling a stat Nicola recited to me
last week. I accept the beverage and clutching the champagne I've brought, try to
nudge through the throng, where between
taller, broader bodies I spot air. I head
toward the bubble of light like a miner
trapped in a shaft.

When I reach beyond the entry gallery,
however, the crowd closes in around me.
They are young and old, comely and not.
No one looks familiar among these couples
and small clusters, each individual his own
self-important branch on a stalk. In a city
where I have lived for more than twenty-
five years, I am continually shocked by how
frequently I find myself among strangers.

I square my shoulders, pretending I have
a destination, and pummel forward in
search of a face I might recognize from one
of my own small circles — another parent
or docent, a neighbor or an adult ed student,
a fellow subscriber to the ballet or Central
Park weeder, a pal of Ben's or Daniel's or
Stephan's, an acquaintance from an organi-
zation or the gym where I used to belong,
anyone — and in particular, the hosts. If I
could find Chip Sharkey or his boyfriend,

Nat, I could thank them for their hospitality, hand them the bottle, and escape.

I feel a promising tap on my back and turn. A plump woman in her sixties or beyond faces me, her red hair swirled into a crowning froth, rhinestone glasses glinting like fish eyes on a small, pointy face. Her lips, stained as purple as eggplant, break into a grin showing large, chalky capped teeth. She is wearing a feathery blue boa and seems to have toddled off a stage for a curtain call.

"Lila Kent!" she says, and throws her arms around me in a tight embrace. "It's been years! How's Milton?"

Tonight I could be anyone. I consider impersonating Lila, but lacking the hubris to give that approach a whirl, I say, "Sorry," and pull away. "I'm not Lila." Though maybe I wish I were. "Georgia Waltz."

"Really?" she says, squinting with suspicion. "I could have sworn."

"Not Lila. I promise." I force a smile.

"Harriet Ross," she says. "Nathan's sister-in-law."

"Nathan?"

"Our host," she says, in a tone generally accompanied by an eye roll. "The one who doesn't believe in fire safety codes. There must be two hundred people here. The shrimp ran out hours ago. Nathan invites everyone he's ever met." Harriet Ross sounds indignant. As she shakes her head, a hank of red hair falls from her coiffure. She brushes it away and I stare at her dagger nails lacquered the purplish black of a nasturtium.

"I'm afraid I fall into that category. I just met Nat — Nathan — the other night. I know Chip." The woman's doubt reappears. "Chip Sharkey?" I say.

"Ah, yes. The dizzy blond. Nathan's stepbrother."

So, stepbrother. Daniel always did tell me I needed a remedial seminar in gaydar.

"Chip's my real estate broker," I feel disloyal to the harmless Chip, which makes me add, "He's a great broker." Not that I have, as yet, any proof.

"Well, Happy New Year," the woman says, most likely bored and disappointed that I am not Lila Kent. As she swishes her boa around her neck it tickles me in the face.

"Happy New Year," I say to her back, as I wriggle between dancing couples. I feel the beat of the music vibrate in my chest and need to get away. I beg-your-pardon myself into the next room, where tiny white lights shine on a Christmas tree hung with homey, mismatched ornaments. There is a crowd here, too, surrounding a table groaning under the weight of cured meats, pigs in blankets, crudités with a green dip of indeterminate provenance, and yes, a bowl in whose melting ice four lonely shrimp are doing the dead man's float.

"Georgia Waltz, you came!" Chip is walking through another door, wearing a tartan jacket, holly in his buttonhole, and a Santa cap. He reaches me in three long strides and lands a peck on my cheek. "Happy New Year."

I am suddenly so delighted to hear my name, I am afraid I may cry. "What a party!" I say with shaky enthusiasm.

"Nat's ready to murder me. He thinks I put up a flyer on a street corner. Have you seen him?" Chip looks left then right.

"Not yet," I say. "I just arrived."

"Party hopping, are we?"

"Not exactly," I say, as a tall man with a shiny shaved head swoops down on Chip and kisses him on the lips.

"Bongo! You slut!" Chip shrieks. "Georgia, I'll be back in a minute." He is swallowed by the crowd.

As I get pushed aside, a tear starts. I need an escape hatch, if only for a few minutes, and then I will try again to impersonate a mature social butterfly. I find a hallway. On either side are bedrooms piled with coats, mostly furs valued too highly by owners to leave in the hall, and in room a couple on an iron bed. From behind another door I smell marijuana. I open two more doors that lead to closets, but a third is, fortunately, a bathroom, where a woman not much older than my daughters is enthroned. Her sequined skirt is pushed up around her hips, and I hear her tinkling. "Excuse me!" I say, horrified.

"No biggie," she says. "And say, could you grab me some tissue? The TP's all gone."

I hand over a fistful of tissue and I bolt. I am finished with this party. The celebration feels like a diorama of revelers working too hard to have fun. My desire to be here is officially extinct. Retracing my steps, I reach the end of the dark hall. I hope to find the dining room, but emerge instead in a paneled library where the redhead and others are gathered around a piano, blasting "I Wanna Hold Your Hand."

"Lila," she shouts. "Join us!"

In my family, Ben and Luey were the singers, his baritone blending with her throaty alto. The Beatles featured prominently in their repertoire, too. My range is a half-octave with a voice that's reedy and flat, and I remember only the first line or two of most lyrics. Yet this is the best invitation I've had all night, as long as no one expects me to sing. I park the champagne, which I am still carrying, on a table and hoof it to the piano, a baby grand with a menorah as ornate as Liberace's candelabra. Guests are three-deep.

"I Wanna Hold Your Hand" turns into "All You Need Is Love," followed by "Back in the USSR." But when some depressive asks for "Eleanor Rigby," another voice shouts, "Give us a break — let's at least hear some Billy Joel, for God's sake." The pianist, an elf in skinny black jeans seamlessly breaks into "Uptown Girl," garnished with trills.

As I glance at my watch, a low voice shouts out my name. I look up and see my host Nat with a leash in his hand that leads to a black standard poodle so elderly its face has turned white. "You made it."

"Wonderful party," I mouth over the singing.

"Great to see you — hope you've gotten something to eat," Nat says, then joins the singing, shaking the dog's leash as if it were a maraca.

From here, the pianist goes to "Only the Good Die Young," the song I was afraid he might play. I feel myself stiffen. This, I decide, is my cue to leave. I turn to Nat, salute him with my empty glass, and say, "I better go — but thanks for everything."

"But you'll miss the fireworks — and they're the point."

The pianist tilts his head toward Nat. "Duet?" he says.

"You got it," Nat answers, and slides next to the younger man, handing me the leash. "But not this," Nat says, and begins "Through the Years," which the crowd breaks into with gusto.

Ben sang this to me at our twentieth anniversary party. *Don't cry, don't cry, don't cry,* I tell myself. The dog drops her body down to the floor with a sigh and I'd like to do the same. When the song is over, Nat returns to my side.

"You can sing," I say, and find a smile that I believe will pass for genuine.

"Desperate measure to make a lady stick around."

I am trying to think of a response when I hear the ping of my phone. It's Nicola, I'm guessing, with New Year's greetings. She and Luey used to call from wherever they were; I guess it's come to this, a text. I find the phone but can't see the small print without my glasses, which I've left at home. I don't have a choice and hand Nat the phone. "Could you read this for me, please?"

"Pleasure," he says, squinting into the phone. When he looks up, his face has darkened. "It's from someone name Lou who's in the hospital and wants you to call ASAP."

"No! It's my — never mind. I better call back." I do, trying to make out what Luey's is saying through the din, though all I can know for sure is the name of the hospital, and shout, "I'll be there as fast as I can!"

Nat hears me, and in a scramble, helps me find my coat on the rack, moving with efficiency and asking no questions beyond wondering which coat is mine. Outside, he hails a taxi and I clamber into it. As it pulls away from the curb and I call Luey, he waves. Minutes later, the sky explodes with the colors I see when I have a migraine. The *pow* of the fireworks matches the thunder-clap of my heart.

19.

I push back the curtain in the ER and Luey shouts "Mommy!" in a voice of an eleven-year-old. I am relieved yet terrified. Mascara has run down my daughter's cheeks; she resembles an exhausted mime. Her party clothes are heaped on a plastic chair, though the tulle skirt has fallen on the linoleum floor. As I cover her legs with a thin blanket, I see that the sheet below is stained with blood.

"Sweetie, what happened?" I am remembering my own hospital visits before we adopted Nicola.

Gulps and tears meet my question. "I . . . can't talk." An animal keening interrupts each word. I pull Luey's shivering body toward me and pat her matted hair, the same way I had done less than two months ago, when she took the red-eye home the morning after Ben died, arriving in the colorless dawn. The preceding evening,

Daniel had put me to bed with a fusty hot water bottle, which he magically produced along with a sleeping pill. At four-thirty in the morning, I woke up to take a second pill he'd left by my bedside, but in my blur I reached for Luey, who crawled under the covers fully dressed. We slept until past ten that morning. When Nicola tiptoed into the room and found us, we became three women joined in grief.

"When I got to the bathroom, there was all this. . . ." She points beneath her. Again, sobs.

A miscarriage is never a blessed event, but I see tonight's drama as a merciful conclusion to the latest turn in the biopic of Luey, child-woman, feckless female, and, apparently, birth control abstainer. God, in his infinite wisdom, giveth and God taketh away. Maybe He hath recognized that Louisa Silver-Waltz is as ready to be someone's mother as I am of giving another human being financial — and possibly equally misguided, marital — advice.

"Don't talk, honey," I say, and continue the rocking motion. I will be grateful if Luey doesn't speak, because I won't know what to say, but she whispers, "Mom, I'm scared."

Me, too. "Hospitals are always scary." I know this isn't what she needs. "No one wants to be here. Try to sleep." I attempt to quiet her moans with a *shush-shush* that emanates courtesy of some backup generator of maternal response.

"You're wearing your good perfume," Luey murmurs as she closes her eyes. "Where were you tonight?"

"Nowhere," I say. "Not important. Sleep. Luey. Sleep." After a few minutes her hand releases the blanket that she had clasped tightly. I gentle her onto the bed and speed-walk to the public area of the emergency room to find whoever is in charge.

I may as well be in a mosh pit. Every bed is filled. Hovering outside each one are boisterous groups that bump into one another. I stand as still as a hoary old beagle, trying to make myself invisible while I catch a scent, but if someone is directing this chaos, I detect nothing.

A woman in a smock silly with candy canes scurries by, clipboard in hand. "Excuse me," I sputter, but she races to the end of the room, escaping into a tiny glass-walled office. I follow her, stand outside, and glare as she speaks on the phone. Am I being rude? So what? I'm a mother doing her job. When the woman gets off the phone, she catches my eye and leaves the enclosure.

"Yes?" she asks, as I rush toward her.

"Can you please tell me what's going on with Louisa Silver-Waltz, the girl at the end?" I point toward her cubicle.

The woman, thickset with many small gold earrings and dark waves caught in a butterfly barrette, checks her clipboard. "And you are?"

"Her mother."

She flips back a form and reads without looking up. "Your daughter is past twenty-one. I'm not allowed to reveal any information without her consent. You know, HIPAA laws." She hesitates and meets my abject gaze. "If you wait by your daughter's bed, a doctor will be by." She has the grace to add, "I'm sorry."

I sense that she is. Back by Luey's side, I fold her ruined finery piled on the floor next to the plastic chair, where I sit, shifting my hips in a futile attempt to find comfort. While I wait I rest my eyes and evidently I doze, because I startle to Luey's voice.

"Mother," she's whispering hoarsely. "Can I have some water, please?"

Spittle has run from the corner of her mouth. I lean toward her, wipe it away, and wince. An ogre has made a grab for my neck, but I manage to say, "Of course, honey," and stand. "I'll find some," I add, because not only is there no pitcher of water next to the bed, there is no glass and no sink.

I check my watch. It's past three a.m. The ER no longer resembles a balloon ready to burst. Before I go searching for water, I walk to the glass booth, where a thin young Indian or Pakistani man with wire-framed glasses has replaced the dark-haired woman. When he sees me approach, he slides open a panel. "May I help you?" he asks, leaning forward.

"My daughter is Louisa Silver-Waltz, in the bed at the end. I'd like some information, please. She was brought in earlier tonight. She lost her baby."

"Let me check," he says. He thumbs through a stack of papers. "Ah, yes," he clucks. "She'll be examined again first thing in the morning."

And so we wait. I walk Luey to the bathroom. Her hair is sticking to her forehead, and I don't need a mirror to know I can't look much better. I would barter my watch for a breath mint and suddenly a headache is levitating my scalp. If I don't have a cup of coffee, I will pass out.

"Lu," I say. "Hungry?"

She groans, dramatically. "I suppose."

"That settles it. Hold on — I'll be back

soon." I leave the ER, weave through serpentine halls the chartreuse of a sinus infection, wait and wait for an elevator, push through a set of doors that appears to be designed to defend against nuclear waste, find the cafeteria, and buy two coffees along with a hermetically sealed cinnamon bun, most likely stale. I find my way back to the ER and enter just as a tall young man wearing a lab coat and a stethoscope is leaving Luey's bedside. I nab him before he disappears behind the next curtain.

"Excuse me. Can you tell me what's going on with my daughter?"

"Certainly," he says. "I'm Dr. Pandit." So young he has acne, he looks ready to shake my hand, were I not carrying a cardboard tray. "You have nothing to worry about. Your daughter is fine."

My heart is a drumbeat. "Doctor, I am aware that my daughter was pregnant."

"You can relax." He draws a deep breath and smiles. "Your daughter hasn't lost the baby . . . at least not yet."

I stare at him, harebrained.

"I've recommended bed rest. The next forty-eight hours will be crucial, but there's quite possibly good news ahead."

He grasps my arm, as if shaking me awake. "Relax. Grandma," he says. "I'm fairly sure the worst is over." He pulls away. "Now, if you'll excuse me. . . ."

I'd like to find a chapel and have a word with God, but not because Doogie Howser here has promoted me a generation. I feel a landslide of guilt for being dumbstruck by this news when another mother might rejoice. But there it is. I cannot even count the reasons, rational and not, why this pregnancy fills me with dread. I am paralyzed, and if when I leave this hospital, I should see a street lined with red-faced placard-carriers hissing my name, reviling me for my irreverence toward human life, so be it.

"Mother, *vamanos,*" Luey says, however, pushing back the curtain. Her tights are ripped but her face looks gloriously relieved, as the ill and injured are when discharged from a hospital. "You ready to roll? We're outta here."

But we aren't. It takes more than an hour for paperwork to be executed. Only then do we leave, and after twenty minutes in the deserted streets finally manage to hail a taxi. Although its windows are cracked open to the cold, the vehicle reeks of last night's vomit. I lean back, again aware of the literal pain in my neck, and close my eyes. I pray for strength and a sense of humor.

Luey and I have just enough money to cover the fare. When I open the door to the apartment, Sadie greets me with gusto while my daughter heads for the couch, kicks off her four-inch platform heels and collapses. "Shit," she says. "It's good to be home."

"Go rest," I say. It is a command, and I am grateful that Camille Waltz's titanium tone has come to my defense.

Slowly, Luey pushes herself up from the couch and makes her way down the hall, leaving garments in her wake. After she disappears into her bedroom, I gather each piece of clothing, head for the back hall, and deposit the heap in the garbage. I give Sadie a serviceable walk and then, without even washing my face — for me, a stress sign as blatant as hives — strip off my clothes, throw on a T-shirt, and burrow under my covers.

It could be noon or it could be four when a voice sings out, "Anybody home?" I am mid-dream, screeching at Ben for winding up in an Iraqi jail because he neglected to pay taxes throughout our whole marriage. This reminds me that, for the first time, I will need to complete my returns single-handedly, which sends me straight to the thought that tomorrow is a workday. Wally should be back and hot on the trail of my worldly assets, leading to an ice cream sundae of money with a ring on top.

"Happy New Year!" Nicola trills as she knocks on my door.

"Nicola . . . c'mon in," I say.

Her gleaming black hair is smoothly braided, hanging down her back. She is dressed in a narrow rose satin tunic, her legs in tight jeans tucked into narrow leather boots that reach her knees. My older daughter resembles an elegant branch of quince.

"Napping?" she asks.

"Long story." I stifle a groan. "How was Boston?" I pat the bed next to me. "Tell me everything."

I need a dose of normal, a daughter reporting prosaic details — who she saw and kissed, what she ate and wore, where she danced and slept, and why she's very glad to be home. Which is exactly what I hear for a good ten minutes. If anyone demanded that I repeat the particulars, I would fail, but having Cola next to me is like listening to a mixed tape of beloved show tunes.

"Where's Luey?" she asks when she's finished with her headlines.

"Sleeping."

"Not anymore," Luey says, joining us. She is wearing one of my robes. Her hair is freshly washed, hanging in tousles. She smells like citrus and almonds. "Happy New Year, sister." Luey grabs Nicola in a tight embrace that I see less often than I wish.

"Back at you," Nicola says. "How was your night?"

"Big and ugly."

"Do tell."

"Not now."

"How about you?" Nicola pivots toward me.

"You'd have been proud. I went to the party given by the broker and his friend."

"The smokin' broker," Luey says in a droll voice that she didn't bring to the hospital. "And his boyfriend."

"Stepbrother, as it turns out."

"Did you mingle with the beautiful and the damned?" Nicola asks.

I present Harriet Ross and the bald slut as exhibits A and B.

"Did you know anyone?" Luey asks.

"Not a soul except the hosts" — whom I know barely.

"I love a party when I know no one," Luey says.

I hope she knows the father of her child.

"I'm starving," Nicola says. "How does pizza sound?"

Like a beautiful Band-Aid for our problems. "If you're cooking, I'm helping. Luey?" Again, an order.

The three of us improvise, grating cheese, rolling dough, slicing, dicing, and perfecting. We do pizza well. Thirty minutes later I've busted out the Wedgewood that's mid-auction on eBay, courtesy of Luey, getting bid up by hopeful brides. I light some half burnt candles and we sit. If I were a more traditionally religious woman, I would repeat the prayer in my mind: *Thank you, God, for keeping my daughters safe and healthy. Grant us a new year of peace.*

Nicola produces a bottle of Chianti. She pours one glass, then a second, and is onto the third when Luey intercepts. "Nothing for me," she says.

"Hung over?" Nicola asks.

Luey places her hand on her stomach. "No, Cola. Pregnant."

Cola groans. "Jesus, who put you in charge of bad jokes?"

"Point taken," Luey says. My daughters simply stare at each other for a moment too long, in a silence — not a good silence — I am desperate to shatter.

"Say, do either of you know a Clementine DeAngelo?" I ask.

Now I have their attention.

20.

"What's up with Clementine?" Nicola asked. She could picture Clementine, with cheekbones jutting like parentheses while her own appeared to be merely embossed. If the girl got a decent haircut, she could model, she'd thought.

"She sent her condolences. I ran into her in the country," her mother said.

At one of the bonfires, where Clem — Nicola had heard her called that — was with the farm-stand guy, Nicola had tried to talk to her. As the conversation choked, Nicola couldn't believe she was the same person she'd seen her father goofing with the previous day when Clementine had checked their car's sticker at the beach parking lot.

Her dad could talk — or flirt, if she was being technical — with anyone, another of his gifts, like being able to recite the states in alphabetical order. While most daughters might have been embarrassed by this behavior, Nicola felt proud, as if Ben Silver had his own gravitational force that no woman could resist, even if she was Nicola's camp counselor. Nana was particularly susceptible, though half the time she started it. Her father flirted better than any man her own age.

"I'm impressed that Clementine spoke to you," Nicola said to her mother. "I've never heard her get out a full sentence. Maybe you caught her when she'd taken a Xanax." Nicola regretted that she'd aimed for humor and landed on malice, sounding small.

"I've never had a problem," Luey said. "She's just shy."

Is there anything you can't do? Nicola was tempted to say, but the look on her mother's face — sad and perplexed — stopped her. Nicola switched to the top item on her mind.

"I ran into Michael T. Kim in Boston." Chased after? Slept with? No matter.

"The boy who took you to the prom, that Michael?" Her mother's face is flushed with curiosity.

"The big brain who dumped you?" Luey asked.

"I dumped him." That was how Nicola remembered it.

"What was he doing in Boston?" her

mother and sister asked in nosy harmony.

"Harvard med school —"

"You could have called that one ten years ago," Luey said.

"— and throwing a party."

"Kegger?" Luey asked.

"Catered. With enough profiteroles for a hundred more guests." Already, she was feeling defensive on Michael T's behalf.

"Did you have fun?" Her mother's dependable investigative opener.

Exposing herself in front of Luey was generally an act of masochism, but after a moment's debate, she decided to live on the edge. "I did," she admitted.

"Do you think you'll see him again?" The second question her mother tended to ask, early and often.

I hope so, she thought, while she aimed for insouciance. "I doubt it. He's there and I'm not and med students get no time off."

"Which is why you're blushing," Luey pointed out, though her usual bite wasn't on display. "You like him."

"He's a friend, and after a few even Harvard guys act like horny Boy Scouts," though this didn't apply to Michael T. He was old school, and Nicola's only disappointment was that she'd blown things years ago. When she left — one of his friends

205

drove her back to New York — he promised he'd call. But now Michael T. remained in Cambridge, where more than half of the med students appeared to be not-entirely-unfortunate-looking women eager to compare notes on rotations and matches. Nicola didn't want to push too hard, fearing that he'd see her as a gold digger — as if in this century, marrying a doctor other than a heart surgeon, sports medicine physician, cosmetic dermatologist, or concierge internist was a fast track to anything but debt.

"Your New Year's, how was it?" she asked, looking at Luey. "As eventful as Mother's?"

Her sister took longer than necessary to offer up, "I was . . ." and nothing more until, a bit too eager to change the subject, she added, "That's sweet about Clementine and the condolences."

"Clementine has blond hair down to her butt, right?" Luey says.

"Not anymore," I say, picturing the androgynous sylph I met in my kitchen.

"She parked cars at the beach and worked at the tennis club. I like her."

Luey sucks the tip of a curly tendril of hair and then wanders off. How unhinged have I become to want to ask, Did your father know Clementine, too? Were they ever together — together-together?

Did I imagine the look of shock and upset on Clementine's face when I mentioned Ben's death? No, something that day in the kitchen was off. I am sure of it. Could Ben have seduced this sheltered girl? What was worse, to think of my husband betraying me, or to imagine that he took advantage of a woman who is really a child?

I force myself back on autopilot, as I start cleaning up after our dinner, loading the dishwasher and vigorously wiping the counters, determined to put the same effort into scraping away the foul image I've conjured of Clementine and Ben. I try to see Ben not as a philanderer — or more hideous, a pedophile — his arm around a girl as young as his daughters, but as an ordinary father and husband, watching football until bedtime, Nicola and Luey feigning interest beside him. But today the television is switched off, as is the benign quadrant of my imagination.

"Mother, I'd like an answer." Nicola's voice is shrill.

"Excuse me?" I ask.

"It's time for resolutions," she says. "I asked twice."

New Year's resolutions, a Ben-spawned tradition. Do anything twice and my daughter, ripped from her native land, calls it a family custom, which she will adhere to as strongly as if she were raised in a fascist state. Cola is the child who insists on red velvet cupcakes for her birthday breakfast, decided to hide Valentines like Easter eggs, and wears white lace underwear on first dates. At eleven, when she read that Korean grannies believed you'd grow tall if you cut your hair, she gave herself a Joan of Arc cut. She flatlined at the height of five foot five, and now her hair, as lustrous as enamel, swings below her shoulders.

"If it's all the same to you, I'll pass on the resolutions." I cock my head toward the cupboards. "Chores."

"I'll help you later. This is what we do. Don't be a buzz kill."

"It's my party and I'll be a buzz kill if I want to," I bitch loud enough to be annoying, especially to myself. Nicola tosses the sponge in the sink and leads me by the elbow to the living room couch, where she's arranged pads of paper and three freshly sharpened pencils.

"Luey!" she shouts. "Resolutions!"

Her sister skids into the room more like a sports fan than a person who fourteen hours ago was moaning on a hospital bed. I hold my breath as she seats herself on the couch and leans back, her bare feet propped on the coffee table. They are my mother's feet — impossibly narrow, irritatingly elegant, and impeccably pedicured by her own hand. My own polish-free, peasant-sturdy pair is hidden in cotton socks.

"Who wants to start?" Nicola asks.

"Me, me, me." Luey scribbles quickly. She looks up and recites, "I, Louisa Silver-Waltz, resolve not to watch more than three hours of television a day." With elaborate indifference she lays her paper on the table.

"Unacceptable," Nicola says, since family shtick allows for resolution veto. "You try that every year and it lasts a week." She tears the resolution in half. It's a playful rip, but a rip just the same.

Ben and I weren't the kind of parents who required our daughters to memorize *Maus* or even *Horton Hears a Who*. Luey was devoted to television — *Muppet Babies, Pee-wee's Playhouse* reruns, Civil War documentaries, and police procedurals, all given equal time. That she earned higher grades than her older sister despite rushing through homework during the commercials brought on dependable filial distress. Who could blame Nicola? I would argue with Ben against the girls having TVs in their bedrooms. He'd laugh and offer Luey's grades as a defense. Advantage, Ben.

"Luey, you think," Nicola commands, then turns toward me. "Mother, you start."

The Georgia strategy is to make resolutions too small to fail — doing fifty crunches before bedtime, eating my Omega-3's, learning to make an orchid bloom again and again. These I have mastered. It was Ben who loved his resolutions in high-def. Once, he stopped smoking — cold turkey after two packs a day — and another year, learned Italian well enough to charm waitresses in Venice seven months later. Six years ago he resolved to run a marathon. Given how that turned out, you'd think my daughters would give us all a pass.

"I will go gray," I say. Oh, the money I'll save, and it will be easier than phoning the twenty-four-hour L'Oreal haircolor hotline while I scour stains off my white bathroom tile.

"You will not!" Luey shrieks. "Do better."

"In that case, I will learn a new word every day," I snap back.

"That was two years ago."

She's right. Into daily conversation, I wove *internecine, dyspeptic, concupiscent,* and the word that won the last game of Scrabble that Ben and I played: *mingy.* If only I'd recognized foreshadowing when it met me over a card table.

"Get personal, Mother," Nicola says.

Personal is I will figure out what happened to our family's finances and at least uncover the fate of that storied ring. More personal: I am determined to learn if my husband truly loved me. Most personal: I resolve to discover if there was another woman, a young mother half my age named Clementine, and how Ben could let his feelings for her muck up my and our daughters' lives, and if he's the father of her baby. I'm not sure I can accomplish any of those, so I dial back to, "I resolve to grow up" and wait for the inevitable override. But instead I hear Nicola asking, "How so?"

Indeed. "Every day I'll do at least one thing out of my reach," I say. As I try to reboot, is there a choice?

"Good one," says Nicola, who avoids her sister's eyes and announces, "And I'll do the same." After a dramatic pause she adds, "I resolve to get serious about work." Let it not involve the unaffordable luxury of acquiring another degree she will use no more than the L.L.Bean wardrobe that she abandoned in Iowa a few years ago. I knew those black patent leather clogs would get kicked to the curb.

"Uncle Stephan wants to teach me the business. His assistant is returning, but he says I can stay as long as I want." She looks pleased.

I have learned that my brother's generosity may arrive with hidden tariffs, but I say, "Cola, I'm proud of you" and lean forward to give her a tight, lingering hug.

"Excellent," Luey adds. "Both of you."

"Okay then. We're done. Your turn." Nicola's subtext is, *Top this.*

"I resolve to be an excellent mother."

Nicola laughs, not kindly. "To what?"

"I told you twenty minutes ago. You're going to be an aunt." She raps the wood table three times in Ben's gesture. "In about seven months I'll be big as a yurt."

Nicola rolls her eyes as she did at fourteen and, for that matter, at four. "Go on. Get serious."

"I am." Her words surf on a whitecap of emotion. "Deal with it."

Nicola stares at Luey as if she's blinking green. "Are you certifiable?" she says, but I recognize curiosity embedded in the question.

"Maybe. But don't worry, I might lose the baby. Would that make you happy-clappy?"

"Hey!" I find the voice that has forever defanged arguments between my honey-and-sardines daughters. "Have a little respect. We're talking about a *child,*" who for the first time I am picturing, barely, as a bud on my family tree. I won't suffer sarcasm or bitterness in earshot of this speck of life.

Silence rings like an icy bell and I realize that I, Georgia, have performed my first grown-up act of the year. My daughters' faces show remorse, which triggers a boundless love in me for both of them, for the possibility of a baby, and — before it dissolves like sugar into batter — for Ben, poor man, who is missing all of this. *Ben, I need you to be my partner in parenthood, to help both our daughters finish the job of growing up, to meet our grandchild. Ben, you've been cheated and so have all of us.*

"I'm sorry." Nicola's whisper floats in my direction as she clutches Luey's hand. "Tell me everything," she says. "Is the father —"

Luey wriggles away, puts her finger to her own lips and nods.

More than anything, Nicola wants to be closer to Luey than her younger sister will ever allow, not that Cola has any idea of how to make that happen. And certainly, every part of me needs to know more, wants to know more.

I'd like to say that biology counts for little, something I was sure I believed the moment Nicola was placed in my arms. But I'd be lying if I pretended I haven't been praying that the man who blessed my first grandchild with his DNA was at least a sweet, guileless junior high school biology teacher, not a drifter whom Luey met online or picked up at a NASCAR rally. I can't say I don't hope the father of her baby loves her, and I want him to present himself — the sooner the better — bearing gifts and ardor. I'm afraid, however, to trespass further into Luey's clandestine inner terrain. For now.

"This calls for a toast," to a decision that Luey may still have to make, to a new year, and to the snake dance that is my family's life.

"No alcohol for Luey," Nicola says.

"Now you're the superintendent of pregnancy?" her sister asks.

"Just saying."

I fill three tall glasses of pomegranate juice, two spiked with yesterday's flat champagne, call it a cocktail, and set them down on a tray in front of my daughters.

"To Luey!" I say.

"To you, Ma, and all of us," she answers, clicking her glass to mine and Nicola's.

"To all of us," Cola echoes. "Mother, Luey, baby."

We sip, soundlessly, as my phone rings. I lift it up and squint at the name it flashes.

Chip Sharkey. Real estate can wait; I don't answer. But the mute phone taunts me. Calling Wally has been on my radar. I've waited for him to reach out and when he hasn't, I've thought about him every fifteen minutes and sent him daily emails. Painting a kitchen by myself — the job I've told myself I will start tomorrow — or, say, scaling Kilimanjaro has struck me as infinitely easier than continuing to find the path that might or might not lead us out of Ben's quagmire, and might or might not start with what Wally can discover.

I dial Wally before my bubble of courage bursts. He answers as I am ready to click off on the fifth ring. "Georgia!" he says, as if there is a particular reason to be aloft with joy. The connection is strong and clear.

"Happy New Year," I say.

"To you, too, and the girls." I refuse to fill the long pause that follows. "You've been on my mind," he says, finally.

I'm not sure I believe that. "Because?"

I know he can hear my anticipation, broadcast like reveille. "No news, I'm afraid."

"Are you back soon?" You better be. "I need to get cracking."

"Here's the thing. Not for another week. Sciatica. Doc's orders."

Another week of nothing is a delay I can ill afford is what my mother would sniff, not politely. "Sorry to hear that, Wally, but I can't wait." I am not sure if the voice coming out of me is mine or Camille's, but so it won't disappear, I speak as if I'm running a race — which perhaps I am. "I assume you've got all of Ben's records by now, yes?" I don't wait for the answer. "Tomorrow, have your office send them — credit card bills, phone bills, bank statements" — financial minutia Ben must have kept elsewhere, because I've already looked at what is here.

Dead air hangs between New York and wherever Wally Fleigelman has parked his ample rump. "You there?" I ask.

"I'm losing you," he says.

Perhaps, but I refuse to self-destruct.

"Georgia?"

"Of course I'm here."

"Georgia?"

The connection breaks. I curse the phone, holding it responsible for every hot, exposed wire of anger and frustration.

"Cola?" I say, as I gather my coat, Sadie, and her leash. "You'll be painting the kitchen. You can start in the morning." Paint strips dropped off by Daniel wait in a folder. To my eye they all look rank-and-file beige.

"Luey, no painting for you — but make yourself useful. Start by shoveling out your room." Dear God, the mess.

Luey and Nicola look at me as if I've asked them to capture and dissect a rabid raccoon. When I return to the apartment, however, after a long outing with Sadie, Luey is on her laptop, reading aloud from a DIY Web site. "Listen to this. 'A coat of paint,' " she intones, " 'can rearrange your reality.' "

"What do you think?" Nicola asks as she waves a handful of paint samples. "Stingray or Ionic Column?"

Luey frowns. "Ugh. Too lemony. Looks like piss. This is the one." She holds up a third sample. "Grege Avenue?"

I leave them. Two of the glasses on the tray are empty. I gulp from the one that remains, savoring the sharp taste. I have my own reality to rearrange.

The phone rings again. Chip Sharkey, refusing to give up.

"Chip," I say.

"It's Nat. Nat Ross. I didn't have your number and borrowed Chip's phone. I've been worried about you. How's your friend in the hospital?" The words rat-a-tat-tat in nervous staccato.

It feels as if Nat's party was weeks ago,

not last night, and even if I wanted to explain about Luey, I'm not sure I could.

"False alarm," I say.

"Glad to hear it. Sorry you had to rush out." He pauses. "I'm hoping you'll join me for dinner. One of my customers is the chef as a restaurant I've wanted to try. Some sort of Mexican-Turkish fusion."

Were I a newly minted widower, the brisket brigade would be lined up around the block, and if I were discussing Nat with female friends, they would insist that I give him a rush. Nat's never had kids — no baggage — and been divorced for five years, which puts him safely beyond rebound. He's a recovering stockbroker who owns two bookstores, one in the Village, the other in Park Slope, as charming an occupation as any. But I am no more ready to have a real rom-com date than I am to run for public office.

I wish I could produce a florid, believable lie, worthy of the gentleman Nat Ross appears to be, but all I can offer is, "Thanks, but I'm not up to that right now," as if I am a stroke victim who needs to be retaught how to hold a knife and fork. In my head, Camille prompts me to let down a suitor while magically beguiling him to call again, and shakes her lacquered brown bouffant at my bungled rejection.

"Another time, okay?" I ask. "Please."

"Maybe another time," Nat says. And he is gone.

21.

@notanarcmarc DM @feralkitty *I may take the job.*
@feralkitty DM @notanarcmarc *Y?*
@notanarcmarc DM @feralklitty *U miss 100% of shots U never take*
@feralkitty DM @notanarcmarc *Quoting Life's Little Instruction Book, R U?*
@notanarcmarc DM @feralkitty *Wayne Gretzky, retard*
@feralkitty DM @notanarcmarc *Who u calling retard? I no Wayne is a great golfer*
@notanarcmarc DM @feralkitty *I may take the f-ing job*
@feralkitty DM @notanarcmarc *Heard u the 1st time*
@notanarcmarc to @feralkitty *Well?????*

Luey put down her phone. Since Marc had tweeted her Happy New Year the previous evening, they'd been in constant contact, though she stopped at accepting his Facebook invitation. He didn't need to know she was at Stanford majoring in Comparative Studies in Race and Ethnicity, spoke Mandarin (badly), had 1633 friends, posted quotes from Dr. Seuss ("If you haven't then you should. It is fun and fun is good."), and at high school graduation had hair that matched her royal blue robe. Her FB status remained without an update for the past three weeks, since she realized that if she answered "What's on your mind?" with even 1 percent honesty, she'd be revealing too much. Luey would be deactivating her Facebook account if it didn't remain a way to hear from Buffalo Bob.

At Planned Parenthood, she'd melted into slobber before an employee who may have been an NYU student who'd once played on her fifth-grade soccer team. In Luey's dark heart, as soon as she started her interview, she realized that she'd have been better off if she'd brought someone with her for moral support. The person who came to mind, as she ran down the street, was Nicola.

Is it possible to annul a relationship and begin again, Luey wondered? Would Cola even want to be a real sister-friend? Maybe they both could change. Maybe she'd lose

221

the baby. Many maybes.

@notanarcmarc: *Live dangerously. Take the job.*

22.

"You'll never sell your apartment in this market," Stephan chided, after he approved of Nicola's kitchen paint job, Luey's cleanup, and my considerable efforts to reduce shaggy clutter to Shaker simplicity. I am always eager to believe Stephan may be wrong.

Before a listing hit the broker's Web site, the downstairs neighbors, who now employ Opal for 90 percent of her time, got wind of my plans and bid. The amount falls short of the asking price but nevertheless, I choose to see their offer — all cash, ka-ching; quick closing, ka-ching — as a jackpot. The couple is used to getting their way and wants to move with haste.

"I'm thinking of accepting," I tell Daniel at his gallery, where he is hanging a show.

He stops straightening the art on the wall. "What does your broker say?"

I look past his eyes. "That 'we' can do better. So I've asked her to perform whatever incantations it takes to get these people to sweeten their offer."

The broker checks in at least once a day, always with an idea that tends to involve cleaning or painting. She is a hard worker; I can't say the same for myself. I've filed applications to substitute teach at fourteen schools, but with dusty credentials, the phone isn't ringing. I've applied for dozens of jobs as a fundraiser, but the hundreds of thousands of dollars I've raised for organizations where I've volunteered apparently count for nothing, since I've never written a grant proposal. The only work I've been able to find is helping a handful of high school juniors, harassed by their parents, to rewrite essays for the college applications they won't be filing until next fall.

"How are you doing with selling my art?" I ask.

I'm counting on the proceeds to support three people — soon, possibly four — until when I'm not sure. I have said good-bye to our prize, a minor Andy Warhol, along with an Alex Katz dog litho, a David Hockney print of a swimmer who reminds me of Ben, an early Cindy Sherman — not one of her best — an Irving Penn photo of a grinning Miles Davis, and some oils by artists whose careers have never taken off, old friends all, as well as our first acquisition, an enormous *Gone with the Wind* poster that hung like a benediction over our bed. When we made love, I felt as if Rhett and Scarlett might join us.

"You know it's all on its way to auction. The secondary market isn't having a stellar year. When it's sold, you should see about two to three hundred thousand dollars. Maybe." Daniel strokes his chin. "George, I don't want to criticize but let's get back to selling your apartment."

I am getting ahead of myself. "Sounds like a mistake, right?"

He lifts his shoulders and extends his palms, though not before I catch a glimpse of his hands. I've always wanted to ask if he gets manicures. "If you have to move out fast, where will you live?" Daniel could be talking to a child.

"The beach," I answer. "For now." Spending the late winter and a damp, drab spring near the blustery Atlantic would allow me to see myself as a proud, chapped heroine given to wooly scarves and solitary dog walks. I would fling the word *greed* into the sea and become as self-righteous as a New Age goddess. I'd learn to predict the outcome of cloud formations and cook giant pots of chowder. I stop at picturing fish heads in the soup and making my own soap.

"Did you forget about your daughters?" Daniel brushes aside a black ringlet that escapes over his forehead. I'm sure Stephan must be nagging him to get a trim. I have never known my brother's hair to be anything less than fully disciplined.

"They'd come along."

"Good thinking, Mother Superior. Nicola has a job in the city." Daniel's smile is back.

Despite what she's told me about Stephan's appreciation of her work, knowing my daughter, by the time the apartment sale closes she'll be back in Paris, if she doesn't pick Reykjavik or Sao Paulo instead. Still, I take his point. "I'll help her find a studio if she can't find a place with friends or" — and in a flash of chutzpah midwifed by necessity, say what's on my mind — "you and Stephan, for example, have a big house right over the river."

"I suppose she could stay with us," he mumbles, "assuming Stephan agrees, of course, but —"

"Don't worry, not Luey," I hurry to say. "She'd come with me, wherever, and next semester, hopefully, she'll be back at school" — if I can pay for it.

For the moment, Luey needs me, and if

I'm being truthful, I need her. I miss my husband, my inscrutable husband, and I do not want to be alone. Technically, my daughters might be adults, but all of us know they are caught in a bog. My work as a mother is incomplete, and as long as Nicola remains outsourced to learn a trade with Stephan, it is Luey in the hot seat. Her pregnancy, if it continues, has put a rush on this order, lengthening my job description. Having to be a solo parent in chief is yet another reason to be furious at Ben.

"You'll sort this out," Daniel says, as I sense him rehearsing what he will say to Stephan. "I trust you'll make the right decision."

That is what I need to hear. I am a woman who requires approval like others do potato chips and reality television, and Daniel is a friend I can count on to supply it. I could never expect ovations from my mother, and Stephan was her accomplice, piling on self-improvement suggestions until he became first violin of critics. My father? I believe I was his favorite, but he delegated the task of raising me to Camille.

My husband, I now realize, allowed me to maintain the illusion that I made decisions, but on anything he cared about more than if we ate lamb chops or salmon, he seduced me to his viewpoint as seamlessly as a sorcerer would his apprentice. Being pliable is the sweet fruit of intimacy, I'd tell myself as I fell in line.

I didn't just love Ben. I was — and am, damnit — *in* love, a state that I sensed many of my practical women friends have, like a starter house, left behind without a backward glance. Am I bitter? I am trying not to notice. Despair can anesthetize you into a stupor I can't allow, which is why I'm eager to take action and get rid of the apartment. Not that I'll see real money. By the time I use the proceeds from the art and my jewelry to pay off the mortgages, the brokers, and the lawyer, I'll break even, but at least I won't be on the hook for monthly fees that dig a hole in my dwindling coffers.

I return to the apartment, where Luey meets me at the door and clangs a bell close to my ear. Whenever she closes an eBay deal, she rings Camille's crystal bell, the one my mother jingled, to my horror, to signal her maid to serve the next course. After compulsively organizing and cataloging our possessions, many of which now reside in coffin-sized plastic bins, Luey is selling everything from monogrammed bread and butter plates to my spoon ring collection. I'll see some cash there, too, I hope, even if it's only fairy dust tossed into a dark, looming sky.

"Daddy's antique beer steins?" she says, ringing the bell again. "Goin' to Biloxi." At her feet is a box and bubble-wrap.

"How much for those freaks?" When Nicola began having nightmares about the beer mugs, alive with fiery dragons, I stored them on the highest shelf.

"Seventy-three bucks a piece, times six, and one eighty for the giant tankard."

I give Luey a thumbs-up as I head to the kitchen to hang my coat near the back door and take out Sadie. That's when I see three boxes waiting for me. The return address: Wally's firm. I back away as if they might be bombs left in the subway. *If you see something, say something.* I say, "Holy crap."

The most memorable nugget of advice I can remember my father giving me was to fake courage in a panic. He was convinced that even a counterfeit sentiment could carry you the distance. "I didn't bring you into this world," he'd say, and pause dramatically to puff on his cigar, "so you could be goddamn intimidated, George-a-le."

I stomp to the drawer, find a knife, and gut the bulkiest package as if it were a fish. Out spill tax returns, each year neatly clipped, going back five years. I filet the second box, which yields expense reports and credit card statements. The third contains insurance policies, more cell phone bills, and a phone without a charger, quite dead.

I've already reviewed Ben's stacks of cell phone bills, which showed nothing more untoward than that he called our daughters more than I realized. I take a second look. These records are for an unfamiliar Long Island number. Now it is time to quote my grandmother, who was enamored of all things she considered to be truly American. "Cowabunga," I say, as Luey walks in and asks, "What-cha got there?"

It's hard to deny a roomful of documents. "I'm not sure," I admit. I might simply be looking at the records of a mediocre businessman.

"You need help with that, Ma?"

Luey's face is scrubbed clean. She looks as if she stepped out of a family album from my mother's adolescence. I pull her toward me, wrapping her in my arms. "Keep going with eBay and that's help enough." The last thing I want is my daughter to see anything as stony and disillusioning as irrefutable evidence.

One of the loudest, longest arguments Ben

and I had in our marital history was after he praised another woman's shrewdness. "Are you saying I'm not shrewd?" I asked, as my mother, for instance, never would. Ben howled with laughter as I wriggled away.

"Shrewd?" he said as he followed me, wiping a tear as he vibrated with mirth.

It would be disingenuous of me to call myself stupid. I can recite the periodic table and tell Corinthian from Doric. I don't conflate Liszt and Chopin, and can identify which of Verdi's operas were inspired by Shakespeare. But in the moment of Ben's remark I knew *canny* would never apply. I didn't speak to him until a day later, when he got down on one knee with a bouquet of French tulips and said, "Georgia, shrewdness isn't even a quality I like in a woman. You, darling, have an endless list of far sweeter attributes, and what's more important is that I love you exactly the way you are."

I liked hearing that then, but lacking inborn cunning is like having a Q in Scrabble without a U. I long to make a bold move. As the afternoon progresses and I pore over papers, I keep returning to the cell phone bills. I've been tempted to simply pick up my cell or our ID'd landline to dial the number, but a swell of shrewd-free pride along with confusion stop me — if someone answered, what then, especially if it is Clementine?

Throughout the day I rehearse my interrogation. When, Miss D'Angelo, did you take up with my husband — and why? Where did Ben come on to you, or did you hit on him? How often did you do it and where — in our house? Where you worked? Hidden in the dunes when Ben took Sadie for long strolls at sunset? Did your meetings happen after careful deliberation or after a sudden wham of passion? The voice I imagine on the other end refuses to answer on the grounds that it is none of my business.

I'd like to exorcise the pictures of Ben and Clem enacting every bad movie I've seen, drinking Cabernet in front of the fire or rolling around on our bed, rumpling the sheets and kicking the creamy *matelassé* coverlet to the ground. After they do their X-rated business, which I'm grateful my mind censors, Ben lights a cigarette with a candle he has placed on the nightstand, although smoking is a habit he gave up in 1999. He and his darling Clementine pass a cigarette between them, until he extinguishes it in a saucer he's brought up from the kitchen. It is my grandmother's china.

As my mind wanders to this bleary B-movie, I force myself back to sorting through more records. It takes until mid-afternoon to notice a pattern — gaps in the calls that correspond to our vacations. That Ben ignored Clementine during his absence is no consolation.

At ten p.m. I leash up Sadie for her bedtime constitutional. As we round the corner I find what I'd hoped to see, a relic from another era — a pay phone — and I stop. Even if I'd had the hubris to make a call, the phone has been beheaded, its cord dangling like a noose.

I return home and put myself to bed, but warm milk and an airport novel can't soothe me. I throw the book across the room, as disappointed by fictional love as the real thing, and toss throughout the endless night. When my alarm wakes me, I am flattened like a decal ironed to my sheets, cheated out of the refreshment and common sense you depend on in a new day. At ten, a reasonable hour for an unreasonable act, I call Daniel for counsel.

"Have you tried to look up the number online?" he says, playing his regular role of IT support guy.

"You can do that?" I, the technophobe, ask. I wouldn't be able to explain a Twitter hashtag if I stepped on one and it gave me tetanus.

"Search the number and reverse directories come up. They're kind of spotty, but one might list the owner of the phone."

Who knew you can make such quick work of espionage? I thank him and exercise my credit card on nine different online directories. None yield a result but now I am a woman possessed. I fill my pockets with loose change and four blocks from home I find a functional pay phone, a young woman chatting away on it, oblivious to what is more than the light shower that the morning newscaster described. As I stand a few feet away under Ben's golf umbrella, her conversation continues with whoops of laughter, clickety-clack Spanish, and sweeping gestures, as if her caller could see her. After a few minutes, she puts her hand over the receiver, turns to me, and scowls.

I wait outside this young woman's private office on the corner of Seventh Avenue and Fifty-fifth Street until the gutter fills with water and apparently her coins run out. She sashays away. I approach the phone, hands stiff from the rain, and drop in the required quarters. The phone rings once, twice, three times, four. As I am ready to hang up, I hear a woman's voice. I'm not sure what I hope for; *"Adam and Eve Landscaping,"* perhaps.

"Hello," a woman says.

I try to recall Clem D'Angelo's voice.

"Hello," she repeats.

I can't be sure if this is Clementine.

"Is someone there?" she says again.

I have a thousand questions and ask none. In the background a huskier voice calls out, "Who is it?"

"No one," she says. I hang up, shivering less from the weather than from the electroshock of reality.

Every time I walk Sadie throughout the day — four times more than usual — I pass the phone. It is on the last walk of the evening that I muster the nerve to once again drop coins in the slot. This time the phone obediently answers on the first ring. The voice is robotic. The number, I am informed, is no longer in service.

I slam down the phone so hard that I'm sure I damage the earpiece. One less pay phone for midtown Manhattan.

As I lumber into the apartment, music blares. Luey shouts "Hey!" but she doesn't lift her eyes from her laptop. I collapse on the couch next to her, finish off a pretzel sitting on the coffee table, note the comfort delivered by food with absolutely no value, and think that tomorrow I'll have to lecture

Luey on prenatal nutrition, though pregnancy has graced her in a way that perhaps only a mother would notice. With her hair pulled back to expose every plane and poreless inch of her face, the effect is ethereal. Her skin is the clearest I've seen since she was in seventh grade. As she leans back, lamplight shines on her slightly softer face. My daughter looks ebullient. This is the sort of girl I was myself, the sort that Luey abhors. She'd choke on *wholesome,* but tonight I could imagine Luey leading a group of volunteers building a school in Senegal.

"Where's Cola?" I ask.

"Don't know," Luey says, transfixed by a YouTube video of a performer gyrating in front of a keyboard. "Isn't he amazing?" she asks. I think it is fair to call her expression starry.

My musical taste stalled at K.D. Lang, Sting, and Diana Krall. In my playbook these are singers whose talent qualifies as amazing. "What makes him 'amazing?' " I want to know in the same way I struggle to understand how anyone would willingly pay good money to see movies where characters guzzle blood as if it's tomato juice.

"Everything. The package. The records he picks. His originality. The way he plays guitar to the melodies on the turntable, how he moves his body." Luey sighs and laughs. "Should I go on?"

Now I'm curious. All the camera is showing is the neck-down portion of a thin, pale body with hipbones visibly jutting under snug black jeans. He's wearing a white T-shirt that could have as easily cost a dime at a yard sale as two hundred dollars in a designer shop. His muscles are elongated but defined, although he doesn't look like the sort who'd put in time at the gym. There is a long close-up of fancy footwork that seems to have nothing to do with the music. Maybe he's got a dog's ability to hear sounds in a register I cannot.

The camera pans to the performer's head. I lean forward and squint. He is wearing a brown-and-white hide headdress with cowish eyes and white horns; it covers him from the neck up. I scrunch my face to take a closer look. "Does he always perform in this getup or is it some sort of stunt?" I ask.

Luey beams and I admire her mouthful of small, straight, naturally white teeth. Four years of braces. "He calls himself Buffalo Bob and this is his regular act. Isn't it genius?"

Underneath the headgear he could be Keith Richards or the kid who bags groceries at the supermarket. "How old is this big-headed brute?"

"Twenty-five and his shows are sold out everywhere." I hear pride.

"People pay to watch this?"

"Lots. On college campuses, mostly, but he's toured in Europe and Australia."

I upgrade him from a mole living in his parents' basement to a man in a van filled with unwashed roadies, stubby joints, and blister packs of beef jerky. "So Buffalo Bill is successful?"

"Buffalo *Bob.* He's made two albums."

I elevate the bus to a Hampton's Inn and the food to Taco Bell. The drugs stay. "Has anyone bought them?"

"Two million-plus fans."

I'm seeing a Four Seasons with an in-room masseuse and wonder where irony has left me behind. After people started calling hip-hop poetry but before graphic novels took off, I suspect.

"Has he toured in Palo Alto?"

"Twice — I saw Peter both times."

"Peter?"

"That's his real name. Peter Eisenberg."

I knew a Peter Eisenberg. Peter Eisenbergs join a fraternity and later, a country club, earn a CPA, marry a girl named Nancy, leave her for a younger woman named

Carol, have kids named Josh and Emily, turn Republican, and at the twentieth class reunion brag about their golf handicap and squawk about illegal immigrants. They don't wear buffalo heads while they strut their stuff, which they don't call "their stuff." I feel so ancient I could have shambled out of the Old Testament.

"Have you met Peter?"

Here Luey turns to me and says slowly, "Yeah, I've *met* him — after the show."

My smarty-pants Stanford student is someone who parties with a scruffy musician. I jump to assignations on stained mattresses, documentaries about Ecstasy and STDs. Do I need to dig out the lecture on sobriety and restraint that I thought I'd left behind? I reach for the most obvious remark. "Not to be judgmental, but I'm just saying he looks like the kind of guy who could give a girl something."

Luey shoots me a battle-weary look. "He gave me something, all right."

There are times when being a mother is like passing a kidney stone. My daughter is a pregnant college dropout. The father is a beast from the prairie. What could go wrong? *No. No, no, no. Just, no.* I open my mouth; nothing comes out.

When I haven't been obsessing about how

239

my financial situation may have truly been caused by a betrayal, how I will pay bills six months from now, and, moving down the list, my mother's health and Nicola and Luey's future, I've been tripping on the thought of my daughter's baby's mystery dad. He need not be Luey-smart, I've decided. He doesn't have to be handsome or gifted, but please, God, let him be kind. And let him be earnest. She needs a shot of earnestness, for ballast. Lately I've pictured a war correspondent bearing a remarkable resemblance to a safari-jacketed TV correspondent who consistently puts himself in harm's way, then reports on it with twitchy excitement. Before that, on safer ground, I've imagined an architect who designs spare, shiny houses you see in *Dwell,* and a vet, big animal or small — I wasn't picky. I haven't foreseen a hirsute musical caricature, successful or otherwise, who most likely dropped out of college, if he even enrolled, and obsesses with video games when he isn't impregnating groupies and trying on lewd animal heads.

"Does he know?" I ask, trying to arrange my face, which keeps defaulting to a smoldering shock and anger.

"Why should he?" Luey harrumphs. She has crossed her arms around her chest, pulling herself away from my judgment.

"Don't you think he has a right, for start-ers?"

"I'm making up my mind," my indignant daughter shouts as she stands to leave the room.

What was it like, your time together? I say, only to myself. Has Luey blanked out their hook-up like a failed Italian final, or can she replay the evening, moment by moment, stroke by stroke, word by word, as I can the first time with Ben, because — on the chance that the last few months have been a nightmare from which I will awake — I haven't yet burnt his pictures. A good opinion of Ben simmers on the back burner.

"Mom, some credit, please," she says, no longer shouting. "Get a grip. I can't talk to you when you're like this." This time she makes the first move, sitting back down and embracing me as, yes, an equal. "I will figure this out. For God's sake, you know how competitive I am. I'm not going to let myself fail life!"

My heart is starting to return to a normal rhythm. "Of course you're not." And if she will allow my help, I won't let her.

"I called that ER doctor and he gave me the name of an ob-gyn, and I have an ap-pointment for Friday."

241

"Excellent, Luey. Good job."

"It's still early days, and if I want to, you know . . ."

I raise my hand to silence her. "I've done the math." Then I ask, "Who is he? The doctor."

"She? The name and number are in my room. I'll get it." She runs off, and I can sense that she is as relieved as I am that the air is cleared — for the moment. "Dr. Madeline Casey," Luey reads when she returns. "On the Upper East Side."

"I've heard of her. What time's your appointment?"

"No, you can't come with me. In fact, this subject is now closed." Before I have a chance to object, she adds, "I made four more decent eBay sales, two trips to the post office, and one to Staples for more supplies."

"Thank you."

"And some people called."

The first message is from the city broker: "Very good news in the form of a counteroffer." The second is from a Naomi, no last name, just a number, and the third is from a Susan.

Maybe these are distant cousins on Ben's side of the family whom I've never met yet am supposed to remember — or bill collectors. I've started to hear from their ilk. The fourth, fifth, and sixth messages are Nat Ross. We had a dinner date, for three hours ago.

23.

Her mother was keeping the thermostat low to save money. Nicola threw a robe over her nightgown and knocked on Luey's door. "I come in peace," she said. "Can we talk?"

"Suit yourself," Luey answered, her voice barely audible as she continued to text, not looking up. Nicola entered and breathed in the scent of a burning candle.

Don't do it, Nicola had been thinking for the past hour as she sipped glass after glass of Shiraz. *Stay pregnant.* She sat down on the bed and before she lost her nerve, sidled close to her sister and put her arms around her. Luey stiffened, but put down her phone.

"If you decide to keep the baby, I'll help you," Nicola said. "I'm sure Mother will, too. We'll see you find a way." It was easier to say the words without having to look at her sister's face. Certainly she could learn to give bottles or change diapers. If there was a TED talk about a robot who flies, an expert must podcast this, too.

"I've been thinking of giving up the baby for adoption," Luey said. On television, Luciano Pavarotti and Tracy Chapman, Luey's favorite, were harmonizing on the lyrics to "Baby Can I Hold You" Pavarotti's tenor was so rich and dark it probably had calories.

"That seems like a rash step," Nicola said, though it was exactly what she would do.

"I'm a rash kind of a gal, you know that."

Nicola did. "I don't envy your having to make up your mind about this," she said.

For the next few minutes, both of them cried, as much from fear as affection. Nicola wasn't sure if her own tears were for Luey's bad luck, or because Luey had shared something personal.

"Let's talk in the morning," Luey said, sleepily, after some time passed. Nicola got up to leave. "Thank you, Cola," she added. "I'm so lucky to have you as a sister."

Nicola tightened her robe around her, blowing Luey a kiss. As she scuttled down the hall, she felt happy, as if she had done some good in the world.

She was also immensely glad that it was her sister who was pregnant. Not her.

24.

Nicola kicks off my best pair of faux-alligator heels, rubs her feet, and takes a sip of a martini she's made in a silver shaker that has yet to find its next owner. This is the last of the vermouth.

"Uncle Stephan asked you to call," she adds.

"You don't have to move there, you know," I say, as I did yesterday, and the day before. Once I planted the idea with Daniel and Stephan, it quickly took hold, my brother believing, I'm sure, that if Nicola has full immersion, he can perform a complete Eliza Doolittle. I suspect she sees the move as a gap semester where life will be all Mozart and chiffon, at the end of which she'll have a belated debut. Having Nicola live with Stephan and Daniel seemed ingenious when I first thought of it, but now I worry that if she's naughty and idle or leaves her undies on the floor, she'll be kicked to the drafty room off the kitchen with the skis and the luggage.

I'll miss Cola, and not only because she hasn't asked for money in six weeks. After making her bed, unloading the dishwasher, and walking Sadie, she leaves each morning by eight and arrives home in the evening weary but pleased with herself. She is kindhearted and sympathetic, as she has been all her life. Her bags, however, are packed. She moves tomorrow. Daniel has ordered new bedding with white-on-white embroidery in an obscene thread count and has told me he's stocked the refrigerator with out-of-season raspberries, green tea, and organic everything. Princess food.

My daughter has been getting home from work every night around eight, because only after Stephan's daily inventory and a ceremonial lock-down, does he offer her a one-on-one tutorial, teaching her to find flaws in both gemstones and professional technique.

"Selling is seduction," is his war cry, and since Stephan believes that stage presence counts as much as inventory, courtesy, and refined diction, one of his first tasks was to take Nicola to his tailor. She now rotates three impeccable sleeveless sheaths — black, navy, and taupe — that showcase her hips and arms, skinny as spaghetti but as toned as a fifteen year old boy's. Her hair is swept into a chignon, which in the evening she lets fall to her shoulders. Nicola's once nibbled nails are manicured with scarlet polish. Every morning when Nicola gets to the office he selects one piece of jewelry, never more, for her to display as she works, though the jewels don't leave the shop. The only adornment of her own that my brother allows my daughter are pinpoint diamond studs and a string of sea pearls my mother gave her when she graduated from high school. She fingers them when she is nervous, as she is now.

"I think I'm making a sale," she says. "This man came in looking for a gift for his wife. At least he said it's his wife." Nicola reacts as if I've winced, though I'm sure I have remained impassive. "Sorry, Mother." She bows her head and covers her eyes.

I've never said that I may suspect their father of adultery, but my daughters are not without imagination. "Continue." I wave her on.

"He wanted a topaz pendant that to me looked like the amber Nana brought home from her cruise to St. Petersburg. He'd shown me a picture ripped out of *Town & Country,* but I steered him to a harlequin bracelet, aquamarine and amethysts, from the 1830s."

"Well done," I say. "How?"

"I tried it on. That's all it seemed to take."

One glance at a bracelet on Cola's arm and a man spends thousands? Why did I allow myself to get middle-aged? "Do you think he'll come back for it?"

"We put it aside til next week. Uncle Stephan doesn't require a deposit. Strange, isn't it?"

Requiring no deposit is one of Stephan's courtly twirls. *What a gentleman,* subliminal thought suggests, and usually shoppers return, feeling as if they've been done a special favor by a true merchant prince.

"Whatever." Nicola finishes her cocktail. "How was your date?" she asks.

I was hoping she'd be too caught up with herself to remember. Nat Ross kept calling, and I finally said yes.

"Alarmingly tame. It was a talky movie and dinner at six in a restaurant that was empty except for a couple who were ninety-two."

"Nat Ross has the patience of a golden retriever."

Hardly an endorsement, but just as well, since I am as ready to become intimate with a man as I am to pull my own tooth. "Cola, it's only been three months since your father passed away."

"I thought you might want to put that part of your life on fast forward — considering how messy things are."

You'd hope that the heart would mend faster when it may have been betrayed — you certainly want it to — but logic and desire have nothing do with healing, which moves at its own solemn, out-of-body pace. I am caught between yesterday and tomorrow with barely a scab on my wound. Perhaps I'd be less bruised if I allowed myself to collect a full quota of pity chits, but when friends call to offer tickets to the theater or ballet or suggest dinner or lunch or even simply a walk, I plead "busy," unless the friend is Daniel. Thus, friends have stopped calling. Even when I sat in a movie theater and, later, across a table from Nat, with his calm demeanor and dark brown eyes that never judge — an appealing man in every way — I felt restless and absent. I couldn't shake the sense that to my side was a photographer casting a shadow over the table as he captured the scene. The phantom was Ben, an uninvited ghost scrutinizing me as I tried to make conversation with Nat on trending, impersonal topics. This is harder than it should be.

"We had a good time," I admit. Nat asked the right number of questions, and he didn't reveal so much admiration for his own wit or store of arcane information that I felt as if I was eating with an op-ed column come to life. "It was pleasant."

"Mother, if that's all I reported after an evening out, you'd let me know how 'deeply disappointed' you were in the sketchy detail."

In truth, I remember little, although I like Nat, not least because he didn't know Ben, is less boisterous than Ben, and, with his thinning hair and glasses, looks nothing like Ben.

"You should see the movie," I offer up. "It's the one about the Parisian concierge who was secretly brilliant."

"You can't get to know someone at a movie," Nicola says. "You've always told me that. How was dinner?"

"Excellent. We had sushi — that's what they ate in the movie. We started with edamame. I had the Dancing Eel Roll and Nat tried the Green River Roll."

"You know those aren't the details I want."

"We ended with sorbet and tea. Better?"

"No!"

Nor was that the end. Before I got into a taxi, Nat cupped my face and kissed me, gently. His lips, which I observed with the remove of an anthropologist, felt warm and smooth. I knew the kiss was coming, my first non-Ben kiss since my engagement, discounting a slobbering, overfed husband of a mortified friend at their tenth anniversary party. When Nat's lips left mine, I felt a shadow of a glow, hardly orgasmic, but present nonetheless. It might have been happiness but I'd have to repeat it to know for sure.

Then Nat said the oddest thing. "Happy early Valentine's Day, Georgia."

Is tomorrow February fourteenth? All day? I almost had what every lonely heart older than eleven covets — a Valentine's Day date — and I didn't know it.

"Are you going to see him again?" Nicola asks.

"Up to Nat," I say, although in this century any woman with desire for romance would find a reason to follow the date with an email or text, today's standard siren calls.

"You'll hear from him," Nicola intones like an oracle, as Luey pads through the door, shedding her hat, gloves, and down coat as she heads in our direction. I still can't see her pregnancy, but at this stage I, too, was as tight as a roll of Saran Wrap.

"Six dogs are a lot of dogs," she says,

without preamble, "especially when one's a rotti." Luey has branched into dog walking, a service she established by slapping flyers on lampposts after she discovered that neighbors fork over thirty dollars per walk, all cash. "I don't know how walkers manage seven."

I am enormously proud of my daughter, who once refused to babysit on grounds of terminal boredom and who was fired from her only real job, as a day-camp counselor, for flunking a drug test on account of smoking weed in the infirmary with the waterfront director. She gives us a full accounting of how you manage rowdy pups along with grumpy older dogs, and I think how her charges — Gracie, Nadine, Ruby, Percy, and two Maxes — are better preparation for motherhood than Stanford — assuming she still intends to be a mother.

"Where were you all day, Georgia?" Luey asks. I don't like the first-name business, but I pick my fights.

"Here and there," I lie, surprised that she noticed I was gone. "Another meeting that I hope will end with a job interview." I tell them about yesterday, when through a favor from a friend's cousin I met with a headhunter, who patronized me with a smirk, half listened, suggested how I could beef up my career-deficient résumé and steered me to Web site after Web site filled with terms like *people person.* Maybe, he said, I could become an administrative assistant once I learn to use Excel.

The three of us finish a pint of pistachio ice cream as I enjoy my daughters enjoying each other, and I turn in for the night after a long day, my first as a stalker.

Last week Stephan took it upon himself to hire a detective. In the diamond-and-emerald department, my brother is on the case with renewed, post-holiday vigor. The ring hasn't turned up. But with respect to finding the Silver-Waltz money, he has even less faith in Wally than I do, and once I came clean to him about my Clementine paranoia — at a price paid in ignominy far dearer than any bauble in his velvet-lined trays — he hired a detective. His investigator wears shoes that are as expensive as my brother's. Can you trust an urbane Sam Spade? Apparently not, because all the man has come up with so far are photographs of Clementine shoveling the snow in front of Adam and Eve's office, unloading a Christmas tree at the dump, recycling garbage, and shopping for root vegetables and Preparation H at the IGA. There are no pictures of her pushing a stroller or carrying a baby in a sling, no pilgrimages to lay a wreath at the grave of the unknown soldier of lechery and lust. Beyond evidence that Clem seems as wholesome as a beet, the most I have learned is her address, 321 Hedge Lane in Hampton Bays, a nearby Long Island town I've never visited.

That is where I had driven today. I cruised Hedge Lane several times, then parked in a lot by a church on the next street. Bundled in one of Luey's snowboard hats with strings that dangle like braids, my face eclipsed by the dark, wraparound sunglasses my mother wore after cataract surgery, I felt as foolish as I looked. This village is where hard-working locals live, away from the high rollers of the über-Hamptons on whom their incomes largely depend. The air was raw and bone chilling and carried the scent of fish.

I skulked down the street — there were no sidewalks — and arrived at a redbrick house in the architectural style of the *Three Little Pigs,* solid and snug, defying any wolfish gust off Shinnecock Bay. I tried to stare innocently, as if it's normal to be riveted by a garden-variety wren perched atop a country-style mailbox. Given the family business, the front yard was no calling card. On the door was a tired evergreen wreath with a dangling tartan ribbon, its message falling short of welcome. There were holly bushes but few other perennials. The grandest feature was a blue spruce big enough to be a third-tier contender for Rockefeller Center.

I could not imagine Ben dropping anchor — or drawers — in this house. He was a man who favored expensively cobbled monk strap shoes that would have looked at home in Covent Gardens, a guy who rattled on about transforming our East Hampton roof into an herb garden, and, if he made a mega-score, buying a Bentley. He was a man who employed a driver and rarely accepted the first table offered to him at a restaurant. Until my meeting in December with Wally, none of this bothered me.

My doppelgänger lurched to the door, pressed the bell, and heard it chime. For good measure, she rapped the knocker, shaped like a whale. Real-me was impressed. Where did she find her conviction?

A woman opened the door and peered from behind the security chain. She had an unlined face, thick eyeglass lenses, and a fluff of snowy hair. I put her age north of menopause yet substantially south of assisted living.

"Yes?" she said. Her suspicion came across

as clearly as a wail.

No, I thought. I cannot be on this expedition. I coughed several times, although when I left the house I had been in fine health. "Does Clementine D'Angelo live here?" I asked, after I found my voice.

"Who wants to know?"

"Is she home, please?"

"She ain't here now."

I heard an unmistakable bleating. "Oh, you have a baby," I said.

She grimaced. "The gulls," she said, tilting her head toward the sunless sky. "Those damn flying rats."

While I looked up toward the soundless birds above, I heard a *thud.* I turned around to say good-bye. The door was closed.

I hurried to my car and collapsed on the seat, steadying my hands by gripping the steering wheel. After a few minutes I wound through the empty village streets until I passed by Adam and Eve. The van bearing its name was parked nearby, but I would not be knocking on another door. I had used up today's allotment of courage.

Without a break I drove eighty miles back to Manhattan, exceeding the speed limit as I told myself I must be deranged. Now, as I get in bed, I expect that tonight will be like all other nights, only worse. My mind will churn. Bogeymen will creep from under my bed. I will hear every car alarm, and New York's entire fleet of garbage trucks will grunt down my street, grinding refuse. Yet none of this happens. I shut my eyes and sleep like a block of cement, without a thought in my head. This is not to say that I luxuriated cozily until a decent hour. At five-thirty I opened my eyes to darkness, fumbled for my slippers, and felt compelled to check on each daughter. Luey, looking like a fawn, is curled, fittingly, in a fetal position. Nicola's long black hair sweeps over her shoulders.

While I indulge in a shower long enough to rid myself of yesterday's taint, I am my own judge and jury, evaluating how guilty I should be for yesterday's prying caper by the sea. On a scale of one to ten, I give myself a seven. I'm lost in my ritual cleansing, when I hear the phone ring but miss it. The call is from Daniel and Stephan's home. I towel off and call back. Daniel tells me it was Stephan who phoned, about some photographs, but my brother has gone to an early meeting.

Stephen returns my call at ten. I grab the phone before the end of the first ring.

"What's in the pictures?" is my greeting. "What have you found?"

"Good morning to you, too, sis," he says.

"Please don't keep me in suspense."

"It's a rather fascinating PDF, actually. From Idaho, of all damn places."

Potatoes. A canceled ski trip to Sun Valley. Hemingway. Baby-faced hustlers in a movie starring River Phoenix, poor little addict. What could Idaho have to do with Ben?

"Emmett, Idaho, a grand Gotham in the county of — you're going to love this — Gem. That's where the diamond-and-emerald whopper Ben brought in has turned up. At least someone's got a sense of humor."

I am sure Stephan can sense that my forehead must be blinking *Huh*? "You're sure it's the same one?" I mumble.

Stephan sighs heavily. "The ring I saw was an emerald with two diamonds of the same size, all superb gem quality, exquisite clarity, D color, as white as you get, unusual old cuts from the early 1900's — sharp corners and an open cutlet," Stephan says. "And of course when I saw it, I assumed the chances were good that it would wind up on your finger. Naturally, I kept pictures."

"Could you have made a mistake?"

"Gemstones are like fingerprints — no two alike — though despite what you may think, I am not so arrogant that I couldn't admit to making a mistake. I need to examine the ring to be certain."

"How did the picture make its way to you?"

"We're a small fraternity, practically a barbershop quartet. Not that many of us deal in rare cuts of this size and lucidity."

Stephan started one of his lectures on crown facets and how the cut was a forerunner of modern round brilliants. That it had a line down the center, a cutlet, and the bottom facet looked black. Blah, blah, blah.

"When will you have the ring?" I interrupt.

"It should arrive by courier within forty-eight hours. But Georgia," my brother says, uncharacteristically gentle, "these aren't the most important questions you should be asking."

I know.

25.

Luey would sooner admit that she loved baton twirling than confess that she had an Oprah-esque fascination with aphorisms and homilies. Two hundred years earlier she'd have been happy to tat her favorite bromide du jour on a sampler.

Today she'd taken to looking up what the wise and famous had to say on making decisions. Theodore Roosevelt was no help. "In any moment of decision, the best thing you can do is the right thing, the next best thing is the wrong thing, and the worst thing is nothing." *Thanks a bunch, Teddy-O,* Luey thought. *How do I tell what the best thing is? Why did anyone elect you president — because you could blow the head off a moose?*

Luey had been chewing on Ralph Waldo Emerson's "Once you make a decision, the universe conspires to make it happen" when Nicola knocked on her door. Luey granted her entry, and her sister had flung herself at

Luey, begging her to keep the baby, offering in some abstract way to help. As Nicola crunched her in an embrace, Luey realized in that instant she'd already made up her mind and thought, *Okay, pregnant I will stay.* Yet the minute the words hurtled from her heart to her brain, she wondered how she'd ever be up to the task. Sure, she liked babies; she also liked vacations in Napa but the idea of buying a vineyard was best left to made-for-television movies and venture capitalists. Babies were cute and sometimes interesting. They turned, however, into expensive, demanding, lasting creatures requiring U-Hauls full of tuition, sports equipment, attention, and patience. Luey could feel sweat dripping from her armpits. Babies were best raised by grown-ups.

Why do you want to keep the baby, Ms. Silver-Waltz? She kept hearing the question, as if she were being simultaneously interrogated and smacked on the head by a Supreme Court justice. She was fairly sure it was Justice Ginsburg, identifiable by the dowdy glasses and flouncy lace jabot that looked as if it was ordered from Etsy. Justice Righteous looked down at Luey and asked, *Are you selfish?*

Yes, ma'am, without a doubt.

Are you insane?

Maybe.

Are you a right-to-lifer?

No, no, noooo. Luey didn't feel at all compelled to stay pregnant for religious reasons. Her personal code of ethics aligned with the right to choose.

Do you have a monster ego?

Yes! Now she was getting someplace. Luey really wanted to meet and know her own child. What could be more narcissistic? But before she had time to brood on this point, the justice shouted, *Is your decision because of losing your father so recently?* Justice Righteous morphed into Dr. Heckler, her kiddie shrink. Dr. Heckler and Justice Ginsburg had the same taste in glasses and ponytails.

Do you think your father is being reincarnated in some bizarre way? Dr. Heckler asked, totally reasonable, as if she wondered whether Luey wanted another one of the gummy bears she kept in a bowl on her table.

Luey wanted to say no when the correct answer was *Bingo.* In having a baby, some part of her father would live on. She liked that. She felt that it was not just important but essential. More than that, it was destined. *Beshert,* as Nana would say.

And yet Luey was utterly confused. She

wasn't sure if she believed in heaven or, in any case, if Ben Silver would have made the cut to enter. She did know that wherever her dad was now, he would probably be the last person to suggest that she keep the baby. He'd want to see her back at Stanford, to "make something of herself," not another human being. Her mother was all quiet concern on the other side of an uncharacteristically firm boundary. Luey now recognized that this barbed-wire gauntlet of respectfulness that Georgia refused to cross was one reason she'd been having so much trouble deciding on the right course of action. Her mom wasn't weighing in, as she usually did. Was this because she was up to her ears in her own problems, or because she didn't know what Luey should do?

Both, Luey guessed, and arriving at this realization took no time at all. Now she needed only to determine if she kept the baby, or allowed it to go to another, better, parent.

26

This morning I was in Stephan's office looking at the diamond-and-emerald gewgaw my brother was convinced had to be the ring that Ben had shown him months ago. It fell into the category Stephan called notice-me jewelry, a Cosa Nostra wife's trinket, making Signora the envy of her friends. If the ring could speak, perhaps it would share the secret of how it traveled from Ben to Gem. But it had its own omerta. The dealer in Gem had bought the stone from a jeweler in St. Louis. The St. Louis jeweler bought it from a Chicago jeweler, without a record. That was all Stephan knew. I left his office none the wiser.

An hour later, as I enter the foyer of what will be our home for five more weeks, Luey calls out, "Look who I found lost on our street." I am expecting one of her canine clients until I look up and my stomach does a contortion.

Clementine's hair is now the purple-red of port. She seems even taller than when we first met. Her lightly freckled wrists stick out of her jacket as she perches on the edge of the couch, wearing jeans and boots — black, well-shined city footwear — her legs stretched out in front of her, clumsy and vulnerable at the same time. Even from ten feet away I can see her pale eyelashes are wondrously long. Until now I also hadn't noticed that her eyes are the avocado green of the refrigerator in the first apartment I shared with Ben, the first apartment I shared at all, since I skipped the roommate stage. She takes in my face and appears not to blink. The news crawl marching across the bottom of the image reads: *Georgia Waltz, beware. Two can play this game. Hurricane ahead. Proceed with caution. Deep breath. Do not let drop your paranoia like a bomb. Georgia Waltz . . .*

Luey puts a glass down on the wood table in front of Clementine. This is not the moment to remind my daughter to find a coaster. Having Clem here calls for a fusion of strength, composure, and intimidation. Since I choose not to stand on a chair to be on equal footing with her when she rises, I try to channel Camille, who used to be impossible to dwarf even at five-foot-two.

"Hello there," I say. "I forgot you two know each other." More important than this disingenuous statement, How much do you, Clementine, know? "What brings you to the city?" To my borough, my block and my living room?

Luey is scowling, wondering, *Why so rude?*

"A doctor," Clementine says. She examines her watch in a conspicuous gesture. "I have to leave or I'll be late."

I believe none of this. She stands and, as her jacket flaps open, I see she's as thin as a wire sculpture. Except, of course, for breasts that could entertain a man for hours.

"Thanks for the water, Luey," she says. "Good to see you." The glass is still full.

"If you come to town again, let me know — I'm not in college this semester. We could hang out, see a movie, or I could take you to some of the clubs."

My next thought is how lonely my daughter must be, with her nearby friends caught up with three-ring sideshows at Columbia, NYU, and Sarah Lawrence. When one pal gloated about taking a film seminar with James Franco, Luey threw a plate across the room. One fewer item for eBay.

"This is actually the first time I've ever been in New York City by myself," Clementine says, as if she has made a solo expedition to Saudi Arabia.

When she admits this, my mother-molecules stand at attention. Clementine's honesty and vulnerability, if that's what I'm seeing, make me like her. I don't want to like her.

"Where's your doctor?" I ask. She offers an address on Christopher Street, which makes it twice as odd that she was nearby.

Luey jumps in. "That's easy to get to if you take the subway — I'll give you directions," she says. "But it's tricky after that." The route will require turns through the maze of the Village, and if you attempt a shortcut, you can lose your mind as easily as at Ikea, where you can find yourself buying a new kitchen when you came in for Swedish meatballs. "Shall I go with you?"

Clementine and Luey do not need additional time to bond. "I've got to take out Sadie," I say. "Wait a second and I'll get you headed in the right direction. I'm sure you can find your way at the other end."

And so it comes to pass that Clementine D'Angelo and I are together again. Neither of us speaks and then both of us blurt out, "Why did you come to our house?"

"You first," she says.

I try to steady my voice. "I apologize for

268

dropping in. Did I upset your mother?"

"My grandmother?"

"Grandmother. I thought you and I might talk." I turn toward her. "I sense some unfinished business."

She stares again, holding my eyes, unnerving me. "Mrs. Silver," she says. "I'm very sorry Ben died." *Ben.* "He seemed like a . . ." She grapples for words. "A great guy," is the best she does after she looks across the street for the answer. "But please. Leave me alone. I don't know what you think I know. I have nothing to say to you, nothing, and neither does . . ."

"Does who?"

She shrugs in a gesture common to first graders.

"Who, Clementine?" This time I touch her arm.

"It's been hard enough," she offers, as she shakes me off and her eyes fill with tears she brushes away.

"Please tell me," I urge.

In violation of a red light and good manners, she responds by bolting across the street, dodging cars. I blink and she is gone.

I head home. The two blocks feel like ten. As I pull out my front door key, I — who lately have been so preoccupied that twice I haven't noticed one of my own daughters walking twenty feet ahead — spy the Adam and Eve van rounding the corner. It parks in front of a hydrant, near the next intersection. I run toward it, Sadie barking with the thrill of an adventure, stubby legs flying. In the opposite direction, there is Clementine, sprinting toward the vehicle.

"Clem!" I shout. "Clementine!" Sadie barks loudly. Clementine eyes me and picks up her pace. Someone in the van opens a door. She hops in and tears off. "Damn!" I say, loud enough so that the Ecuadorian flower seller who used to tell me which roses were freshest — when I would buy two dozen every four days — looks up and says, "Missus, you okay?"

"Everything's fine, Alberto!" I shout as I continue to race toward where the van had pulled away. By the time I get there, it is lost in thick traffic.

Until this moment I have not realized to what degree the appeal of my 10019 zip code has faded, with its downtrodden horses, piles of dung, and tourists certain they've spotted a rock legend prancing out of the Ritz Carlton or a Pulitzer Prize–winning novelist cruising for a well-dressed prostitute. Time to move on.

Sadie and I trudge back home and are almost at our front door when I hear the screech of brakes and a thump echoed by a whinny and a smash. Voices begin to yowl with accusation. Now I am running back to where three cars and a horse carriage are locked at an intersection, bumpers and fenders dinged. Their drivers stand outside their vehicles as they curse in several languages and scribble license plate numbers. New York, once my kind of town.

After it is established that the horse is unharmed, and the damage is only to cars, I am ready to go home to a stiff drink and a hot bath, since anesthesia isn't available. Then I do a double take. In the fray, the accident has caused considerable gridlock, and up ahead the Adam and Eve van is stalled between a Lexus and a hansom cab. I run to it faster than I realized I could, Sadie leading the charge.

Clementine, inside the van and focused on the standstill ahead of her, startles as she sees me rap on the door. The window is rolled down an inch. She closes it tight.

The driver of the car, sitting tall behind the wheel, frowns in my direction, all confidence and command. She has a symmetrical beauty-queen face that speaks of time on a sailboat and no use for sunscreen. Her blond hair is pushed back with a head-band, though there's nothing Junior League

271

about her. She'd be the last woman to wear pastels. You'd elect her foreman of the jury or captain of the rugby team. She gestures to Clementine to open the window again, and when she speaks, I'm not surprised that her voice is low and seemingly unfazed by the surrounding chaos.

"Yes?" she says, leaning in my direction and placing her right hand, which is as large and freckled as Clementine's, on the girl's leg in a gesture of protection.

"I'm sorry if I've upset Clementine," I say to whoever this woman may be.

"Apology accepted," she answers, as a policeman comes along and shouts, "Move on now, clear the street" into the car, then turns to me and says, "You, too, lady."

As the van pulls away, I see an empty car seat in the back and the driver sizing me up in the rearview mirror.

27.

"Nicola!" You have to see something." Her uncle motioned her to enter his inner sanctum, its tall windows overlooking Fifth Avenue from the ninth floor. "Sit," he commanded. Nicola settled herself in one of the delicate armchairs and admired its watered gray silk upholstery. "I want your opinion."

Instead of going to the safe, Uncle Stephan unlocked a drawer with a key he kept along with a loupe on an old-fashioned gold watch chain, pulled out a blue satin box, and removed a ring he placed on a black velvet tray. "What do you think?" he asked.

Nicola forced herself not to fidget by crossing her ankles tightly together. She'd learned that emeralds come in many shades, from newly mown grass to the color of string beans that were nearly past their prime. This stone was different. The emerald surrounded by two diamonds looked other-worldly, like the absinthe she'd drunk in Paris.

"I don't know what to say," she admitted, as she smoothed the creases on her high-necked brown jersey sheath. "I'm not sure what period this is from."

"This isn't a test, Nicola," Stephan said, although undeniably, it was. "Tell me whether you like it or not."

She felt cornered. "I don't know the ring's provenance."

"Do you like it or not?" Uncle Stephan sighed.

She didn't like it. The green of the emerald was like nothing she'd ever seen. She thought it might be fake, and that this exercise was a trick. "I could never imagine owning something like this, but a woman who wanted her jewelry to shout would."

"You're equivocating. What else?"

"May I look with your loupe?" Even if a piece was substantial, it needed a gossamer quality, Uncle Stephan had taught her. "This ring has a certain delicacy," she admitted, as she studied the diamonds and emerald. "The stones are big, but," — she looked closely and decided to wing it — "they seem almost to be floating in the setting."

Nicola had seen Stephan smile at Daniel,

over excellent cigars and five-fold Italian silk ties — he once said the choice of a necktie set the tone for the day — but this was the first time, in this office, that he'd shined that beam on her. His teeth were perfect, exactly like her mother's and Nana's.

"A-plus," he said. "This ring, you should know, is extraordinary. One of a kind, from nearly a hundred years ago, when workmanship was done entirely by hand, and standards were higher."

Her job had its moments of pleasure. This was one, though most days were built of drudgery, her uncle endlessly repeating directions in his own homegrown version of ADHD. Most of the tasks, however, if dull, were not hard. Every morning, with appropriate reverence, Nicola was expected to remove items from the vault, review the inventory list, and make certain all was copacetic. Next, she polished the jewels Stephan selected for display, rubbing each treasure with chamois and special potions until it looked air-brushed. Invariably, this lulled her into a trance, remembering how her Grandpa Martin used to simonize his Mustang.

As a child, Nicola was too shy to ask who Simon was, but now, in an effort to be excruciatingly competent, she had been asking plenty of questions, touching Uncle Stephan's hem in the process. *How do you tell a citrine from a topaz?*

A garnet from a ruby? A fake from a real something? Is a sapphire from Ceylon superior to a stone from Madagascar? Who in this century would purchase a ruby, sapphire, and diamond walrus lapel pin? What makes it "witty"? Most important, *How do you decide what to buy from an estate?*

At first Nicola invented questions to feign interest, but gradually her curiosity became genuine. She listened to every answer, and couldn't imagine that she would ever not want to play with jewels, lustfully imagining she owned this or that.

Yesterday she shyly asked Stephan — it had been difficult to get used to dropping *Uncle* if anyone else was in earshot — if a stylist friend could have an appointment in order to scout jewelry that a mysterious client wanted to borrow for the Golden Globes.

"I sell," Uncle Stephan scoffed dryly. "I don't lend." But if Nicola ran the zoo, that's what she'd do. Nicola planned to bide her time and ask again.

It was basic arithmetic that was doing her in, reminding her that the temporary employment could terminate sooner than she'd like. The only numbers she could remember were prices and carats. Every time Uncle Stephan asked Nicola to tally a sum, she made a mistake, even with a calculator. Last night she dreamt that Uncle Stephan left her a phone message. The number included pi, and she woke up gasping, unable to decipher it. On the SATs, her math score of 519 was more than two hundred points below Luey's the following year, making Nicola a shoo-in for the University of South Florida, but, unfortunately, not for any of the schools on her list. It was Luey who suggested her essay be about math anxiety and it was Luey who wrote it. *"Since I was in fourth grade, I've had a lifelong fear of two trains approaching each other at speeds of 60 and 80 mph,"* the essay began . . . and Nicola got into college.

Nicola thought of the ring her uncle had shown her. Two months ago she wouldn't have known how to answer his questions. Today she did. Maybe she'd found her place, even if her answer was utter bullshit.

28.

"Nurse, you're killing that plant," my mother snaps from her armchair. She may no longer recognize a radish or be able to tell a bird from a butterfly, but Camille Waltz hasn't forgotten how to criticize.

At home I have almost two dozen hale and hearty plants ready to relocate. If there's one thing I know how to do, it's keep houseplants alive. Husbands, not so much. "Don't worry, Mother," I say as I water. "This aloe's going to live another day."

"I'm not your" — she air quotes, still remembering how to do that — "mother!"

"Camille." Daniel's voice is a purr. "You're speaking to your daughter, to Georgia." My mother eyes him with the suspicion of a child encouraged to sample liver. "Though she does look like your nurse," he concedes in a flagrant fib. The attendant on duty is taller, ten pounds lighter, and wears cornrows, although yes, we are both middle-aged females.

I am grateful to Daniel for getting me through this overdue visit, just as last week he waited seven hours in the country for the ace installers from my Internet provider, and the day after tomorrow he will help with the move. If I had any money, I'd buy every self-portrait from the beak-nosed, vainglorious painter whose work he hung two weeks ago at his gallery. I know this isn't an advantageous moment for Daniel to also produce the Georgia show, but Nicola can no longer get away during the week, Luey's canine customers await their walks, and I'd rather eat mothballs than visit my mother with Stephan, whom she remembers far more often and clearly than me. Yet here Daniel is, asking, "What do you say we all go out for lunch?"

The local diner is a five-minute drive. Daniel and I split a spinach omelet. Camille polishes off the Bananas Foster French toast as I blurt out, "I wanted you to know I sold the apartment."

She points to a picture of apple pie on the laminated menu and says, "Yum. Whattya think?"

"Mother, did you hear me?"

"What do you think?" She enunciates each word as if I didn't understand the first time.

"A la mode? Why not? You only live once."

"I'm moving in two days. To the house in the country. I — we — sold our apartment. It's a big change in my life."

"That's nice, dear."

Now her fingers wander to the photograph of a cheesecake, rain-slicker yellow. My mother still wears her gold band, marking forty-four years of marriage, and has remarkably youthful hands. Looking at them, I swear I can smell the cherry-scented hand cream she always kept by the sink. I reach out to hold one of her hands. Her skin is as soft and warm as flannel.

"Is Ben retired?" she asks, mild, curious.

Yes, epically. I feel Daniel's eyes on me and choose to believe he is offering approval when I breathe deeply and say, "Ben's decided to practice out on the island instead of the city." I grant myself this pass/fail lie.

My mother looks up and says in her take-no-prisoners tone, "How can that be lucrative, Georgia?" I recognize a flicker of cognition and connection. The jolt makes me sit as straight as if I've been taken to task by the school principal.

"Not necessarily lucrative," I say.

"Honestly, you've made some boners in your day but this is a beaut." She furrows her still-smooth brow. "It's insane to move.

Once a person abandons the city he can never afford to buy back in or start a practice here again and" — here she takes a breath — "you of all people were never meant for country life. Sitting at the beach will make you wrinkle and you're a rotten driver."

I am *that* driver, who still struggles to parallel park and is invariably followed by honking cars because she lags below the speed limit.

"Don't come whining to me when you regret this move," she sniffs.

"Camille, Georgia knows what she's doing," Daniel offers in his unofficial capacity as minister of civility and common sense.

"About what?" she says, looking at him as if they've never met, and I am grateful for the reprieve dementia delivers. My mother can throw a punch, but she can't get to the end of round one. I slump in the booth. After she settles on her pie and gobbles it down, Daniel pays the bill. At Camille's pace we walk back to the car and drive to The Oaks in silence. I escort my mother to her room, and hang her coat. Today I decide not to loop through the pictures on her dresser, filling her in on Nicola and Luey.

"I may not be back for a few weeks," I say. Soon the trip here will take twice as long. I expect to visit less and suffer accordingly, since guilt remains my lymph system.

"Fair enough," she says. At lunch I was shocked when my change of address made an impression on her softening mind, yet not as blown out of the water as when she says, "Ben visited this morning and showed me a ring he plans to give you. Now that is a ring. And that is a son-in-law, a good provider. When you married him, I had my doubts. . . ."

"A ring, Mother? Tell me more about that ring."

But the next words I hear are, "Camille, time for your medicine," as an attendant pushes a cart into the room.

My mother accepts a paper cup containing one red pill and another cup filled with water. "As you wish," she says, and puts the pill behind her tongue. As soon as the attendant leaves, she spits it into the trash. "She was delivering poison to erase my memory," she explains, sotto voce.

"We were talking about a ring."

"What ring?" She yawns and motions for me to come near. When I do, she encloses me in her arms. "Take it from your old mother," she whispers. "Don't do everything your husband says and be sure you keep your own checking account."

I thank her for the excellent advice, only a few decades too late. Her eyes close.

"Let's stay a few more minutes," I say to Daniel. "Maybe she'll remember."

We sit in silence, interrupted by the squeak of sneakers in the oppressively clean hall, the cracking voices of old people, and the sound of a mop sloshing on the linoleum floor until we hear "My *cherie?*"

Morris Blumstein shakes my mother gently. *"Le temps pour le dîner?"* The voice is low and kind. She opens her eyes as he takes a crisp linen handkerchief from his breast pocket to blot the corner of her mouth.

"Papa? *Vous êtes venu pour me sauver?*" she says.

"No, no. *Reveille-toi, ma douce.*"

"Maurice?" she says. "Maurice!"

"*Oui,* Jacqueline." He kisses her on each cheek, extends his arm, and helps Camille rise from the chair. *"Au revoir,"* he says to Daniel and me, as they stroll out of the room, down a corridor hung with poorly executed drawings of sunsets, and head to the dining room. When Camille passes her old friend Vera, she salutes her with a sniff and lifts her chin. Once again, she is the envy of all.

For the return drive, Daniel keeps the

conversation painless — the trip that he and Stephan will take to Bhutan, a country that, he informs me, calibrates success by gross national happiness; a cat they plan to buy of a breed — Tonkinese — known to be chatty, which sounds bloody annoying; and the Austrian Gewürztraminer so fruity, cheap, and great with Chinese food that he stocked a case. I find my eyes closing and when they open, we are pulling up to the address I may continue to call my own — well, my own and the banks' that hold two mortgages — for the next forty-eight hours.

"Want me to come up?" Daniel asks.

"I wouldn't think of it — you've already gone far beyond the call of duty." I mean it. After another set of good-byes, I make my way upstairs.

As I open the door, I am struck by how sad the apartment feels. Dust covers every surface, stirred by the poltergeists of unearthed possessions. The walls, denuded of picture frames, look like maps of a life that is fading more from my memory as each minute passes. Boxes stacked higher than my head crowd every space, clustered by genus and species and, thanks to Luey, identified by colored duct tape — green for the country, red for thrift shop donations, blue for the auction house.

I wend my way through a narrow canyon to my bedroom, the last room I will clear out, stopping first in Luey's room. She is cross-legged on her bed, at her laptop, Sadie wagging at her side.

"How's Nana?" Luey asks, rising to greet me. Pregnancy is sweetening her, I swear. "Mean as ever?"

"She sends her love," I say, wishing it were true, as I bend to kiss my daughter. "What's new with the Barking Lot?"

Luey, wearing one of Ben's old T-shirts and looking only the tiniest bit fuller, has proved herself to be a multitasking virtuoso. One of her customers has convinced her to board dogs in the country and she's been spreading the word, now that her abridged but surprisingly lucrative dog-walking business is ending. A YouTube for her venture, starring Sadie, has gone viral. Louisa Silver-Waltz is her father's daughter. The more she has to do, the more she accomplishes. I could swear she is happy.

After she fills me in on today's eBay haul — my mother's Swarovski owl collection has flown the coop — I escape behind my closed door. The closets and drawers are already empty, and once I've showered off the emotional residue of my maternal torture, I intend to sort what's left in plain sight, a term I use generously, since every surface is swimming with pitifully overdue library books, expired Groupons, pages torn from magazines (including my favorite: "154 Ways to Live on Nothing"), and bits of paper I am tempted to toss without identifying. That's the top layer. Valentines, cards, and love letters, photo albums and my most treasured books, none of which I can bring myself to dump, are already boxed, ready for the country move, as are the Christmas ornaments, including the angel who always topped our tree, which I discovered only two days ago and try to see as an omen. My moonstruck shadow operating under a disclaimer of denial wants these testimonials intact on the remote chance that Wally will call and say, *I just found a Swiss bank account and you, my dear, are an heiress. Your Platinum card will arrive via your new top-of-the-line Mercedes, driven by Fred.*

On top of one of my shorter piles is a message taken today by Luey to call Nat. I dial his number and when he doesn't answer, I feel relief. I don't know what to say to a man so willing to exist in a zone between friendship and romance. The other night, he fed me a forkful of cheesecake, and for a moment we were as intimate as if we were in bed. I pulled away. I'm not ready. Every time we're together — once or twice a week for movies, followed by casual dinners or drinks — I am struck by how Nat is able to wait for me to notice that he has everything a woman should want in a man — decency, humor, a good pair of shoulders, and not just to cry on. He's even two years younger than I am.

I sort the other messages, abusing the bedrock commandment of time management to never touch a piece of paper more than once without filing, recycling, tossing, or fobbing it off on someone else. A few, however, remain mysteries. Who, for example, are Audrey and Renee and Naomi? Are these women I should recognize, or did they leave last names and details that Luey was too rushed to write down? Most likely all three were offering condolences, and my mother would be appalled if she knew I wasn't gracious. Remorse begins to crawl on my skin.

I call Audrey first and reach her voice mail. It's Audrey Pomerantz, moved to Sarasota, who served with me on a Central Park Conservancy benefit committee four years ago and has made a generous contribution in Ben's name, which I should have acknowledged weeks ago in a note. I leave what I hope sounds like a sincere apology and a thanks. Audrey, check.

Renee turns out to be Rene Riviera, Ben's goat of a masseuse. I always told Ben he gave me lascivious looks when his back was turned. We speak, and the lech offers me a free massage. I ask for a rain check, which I will redeem never.

I dial the third number. "Is Naomi there, please?"

"My mother's out," a youngish voice, vaguely familiar, says, and adds, outted by caller ID, "Shall I tell her you called, Mrs. Silver?"

"Certainly, and that I returned her call."

There is a significant pause. "She called you? Really?"

"She did. Please tell her I'm sorry it took me so long to call her back."

"That's weird," she says, which is how I find the reaction of this churlish teenager. "Do you want her to call you back?"

"That won't be necessary," I say, scratching off the last call.

I move on to three soul-satisfying hours of cleaning and packing, working without stopping to order in dinner, since the kitchen is empty and broom-clean for the next owners. It's only a few minutes past nine when I crawl beneath my duvet, weary but rewarded by a sense of accomplishment that only sweaty physical work can bring. I allow myself a nap — I still need to shower — but soon enough my sleep produces a dream in which Ben and I keep getting lost in the canals of Venice. We are no more than thirty and are kissing — long, deep kisses — in what must be a gondola. I savor his tongue in my mouth, as his hands climb toward my breasts and I forage below his belt. In the dream, a phone rings and rings, but I do not want to answer it. I do not want to end the kiss.

I am startled by a loud hammering and I realize the noise is at my door. "Mom, someone keeps calling on your line — if you don't pick up I will," Luey threatens. I force myself awake to answer the phone.

"It's Naomi." Neither the tone nor the hour suggests burbling sympathy, though the green lights of the digital clock announce 9:55, which barely makes the cut of the respectable bewitching hour for courteous conversation. "You called," she says, matter of fact.

"I was returning your call," I say, bleary.

"You seem very determined."

"Excuse me?"

"Coming to my house, pursuing my daughter."

Now I am awake. "Mrs. DeAngelo, please."

"McCann," she says. "Naomi McCann."

"Naomi, I wouldn't have called you if I realized who you were." I immediately regret this candor.

At this, she laughs. "I appreciate your honesty, but it's just as well," she says. "Clementine . . . unfinished business."

I hear a cough while she speaks. "Clementine, is that you?" I ask.

"My daughter is sitting across from me," Naomi says. "Someone's on the line at your end."

"Luey?" I ask, shrill. She clicks off.

"I have nothing to hide," Naomi says. "I'm willing to talk. When will you be out here?"

We pick a time in three days. "Shall I come to your home?" I ask.

"I'll go to yours," she says.

I skip the pretense of asking if she knows where I live.

29.

" 'Good night room,' " Luey says.

" 'Good night moon,' " Nicola continues. " 'Good night cow jumping over the moon.' "

" 'Good night light and the red balloon,' " they sing together as they load the car.

A phase of our moon is ending. I pushed my daughters' strollers across the street, roaming for hours in the park, which I considered our front yard. This apartment is where they learned to balance on two legs, on stilettos, and, to a certain degree, on their own; where I still see my girls in swirly tutus, missing front teeth and sarcasm. Inside the front hall closet Ben recorded their height on every birthday, when I'd start the day with cupcakes for Nicola and pizza for Luey, and ended with a teddy bear cake snowed in coconut to hide icing slapped on far too much in the spirit of Picasso.

The apartment is the only true home my daughters have known. Our house in the country may have sun puddling through floor-to-ceiling windows and whitewashed walls, but it's a destination equally light on family gravitas. Ben and I bought it eleven years ago, when our children were half grown. The two of us visited as much as possible — stealing hunks of July and August and most weekends — but Nicola and Luey spent some of each summer at pampered programs on manicured campuses and do-gooder excursions to beef up college applications, or simply stayed in town so they could sleep with guys I hope were boyfriends.

Home is where I can recite the contents of the pantry and know my neighbors. The country has the kitchen with sour milk, three full jars of stale cumin, and people down the street who are strangers. The beach house is a frill. The city is where Ben paid bills and taxes and thought I paid attention.

New York has always made me feel smart, or at least smarter. I can pass a newsstand and be reminded that the world is a big place with problems that I should help solve. At the beach, my mind never fully wakes up, and the pressing issue of the day becomes whether the lobsters are fresh, how many clams to buy for dinner, and if the deer will dine on the hydrangeas. The dense, crowded city has the grander horizon.

I'm leaving not just my home but abandoning urban life, which I always told myself I needed for its electricity, though it comes with subways clogged by commuters and, every winter, mountains of garbage under snow as dirty as dishwater. I have been willing to overlook flaws of the megalopolis, knowing that whenever I walk outside, even past midnight, I see other dog owners along with hand-in-hand lovers and migrating posses of back-slapping teenagers puffing weed. Most people imagine city life as cold. That's not been my experience. In the city I am never alone.

What will it be like to power walk along empty roads? To wake every day to birdsong? To pass a day without seeing another human being besides Luey? I have given little thought to quotidian country life. Maybe I'll take to it, kibitzing with new pals at the post office, people who manage to be content without coveting thirteen-hundred-dollar red-soled Christian Louboutin suede, fringed ankle boots, which they wouldn't be able to identify if one kicked them in the butt. I could volunteer at the food pantry, sell peach pies by the side of the road, or become the recluse with the chin whiskers whose trees always get toilet-papered at Halloween.

Perhaps Chip Sharkey will sell the house quickly, although so far it's seen less traffic than he predicted, and I'll move on to one of those cities touted as edgy and affordable — Ithaca, Cheyenne, either Portland. Or change my name and go underground like a gangster's girlfriend. I haven't thought of what's ahead as footloose freedom, but between twitches of fury, fear, agita, petulance, testiness, and disbelief I prickle with glimmers of whatever condition proceeds hopefulness.

"Ma, what's left up there?" Luey shouts from the car, as I make yet another trip down to the curb.

"Just a few bags," I say.

The bulk of our belongings departed this morning. What's traveling with us now are artifacts of a once-shared life too intimate to go to the highest bidder or too precious to put in the dark cavern of All the Right Moves' monster truck. There are boxes of books and albums, my grandmother's silver, the Gien china collected plate by plate — a set completed by Ben as a surprise for our ten-year anniversary — and orchids, many orchids. I wave away Nicola and Daniel, who are going ahead in order to meet the movers. Luey and I will take off in a few minutes. Tomorrow Stephan will hand over the keys at the real estate closing. It takes a village to move to one.

In the fridge I've left champagne for the new owners, our neighbors, Mr. and Mrs. Shepard, who, I'm told, will start a massive overhaul next week; the thirty-three-year-old female half of the couple has informed me they will "reengineer" the bathrooms, the plumbing, and the wiring. There will be air conditioning that doesn't cough from window units and music controlled by an iPod in every room. Purloining two precious parking spaces in front of the building on the Fifty-eighth Street side is an empty Dumpster. This is where my glass-fronted antique white kitchen cabinets, custom-built, will wind up along with the Tuscan tile backsplash the color of apricots and the soapstone countertop I drove to Vermont to select.

Good-bye room.

I take a valedictory march through each room, searching behind doors and in every crack and cranny. From the floor of our bedroom closet I confiscate a dry cleaner bag. In the kitchen, a wooden spoon stows away under the stove and the bulletin board is thick with paper. I pull off poison control alerts, a list of the holidays when alternate side of the street parking rules will be suspended — you get a pass on the Chinese lunar new year — and at least a dozen menus, a United Nations of cuisines. Under Plump Dumpling, whose *shu mai* became a family staple, is a small, dog-eared photograph. I gently remove it.

I am carrying Cola in a Snugli, Ben's arm is around me in a gesture of pride and protection as we stand in front of the Guggenheim. We look improbably young, with long hair and giddy smiles, immunized from threats to future happiness. This was the day I discovered I was pregnant with Luey. After years of infertility and dashed hopes, that morning we found out that we could look forward to becoming a family of four.

For three years we'd tried to make a baby, our lovemaking taking on the romance of boot camp. After a year, Ben was tested and declared as good a sperm machine as any. This led to me being poked, prodded, and invaded, which led to a fiesta of injections, which led to nothing but my period every month, whose arrival I met with cascading despair, and Ben's forced cheer failing to mask disappointment.

According to our infertility specialist, I was a fine female specimen. She couldn't explain our failure to conceive and encouraged us to keep trying for at least twelve more months and — worst-case scenario — in the face of no conception, to explore in vitro. Dr. Stork, as we called her, told us all this calmly. She hadn't progressed to a mayday alert.

Patience, however, was never a virtue Ben Silver could claim. One day he arrived home and seemed ready to erupt with news. He'd been talking to adoption agencies — for months — he confessed, and handed me a photograph of a tiny rosebud that couldn't be more than ten months old. Her eyes were chocolate-covered almonds peering out of a round face, and her hair was drawn to the top of her small head in a delicate pompom. She wore a white onesie trimmed with pink that matched her plump cheeks. It was a picture calculated to break a heart and it was working, though part of me felt betrayed by the stealth and complexity of Ben's roadmap.

"There are more babies like this one," he said. "These kids are in foster care. They need homes. They need love. They need families. I want to be a dad, and I see you as a mother." He drew me to him and switched from campaign rhetoric to a whisper. "Think about it, George. We'd be great parents. Mommy and Daddy. What do you say?"

I said, "I feel like you're pushing me over a cliff. It's way too soon for this kind of a huge step. We haven't been trying to have our own baby for that long." With each protest, I shivered and my voice rose. "And we've never discussed adoption."

"We are now."

I recalled then that when Ben asked me to marry him, I didn't feel ready, though every pinpoint within me was in love with the sweet talker whom I met when my roommates and I hit a local bar. My friends, all alpha types, knew who he was and referred to him simply as Handsome. To his face. I was both appalled and in awe of their barefaced flirting. But I, the girl who missed the seminar on becoming a collegiate enchantress, was the one Handsome asked out. When he approached me, I thought someone had put him up to it, but on our first date, an awkward lasagna dinner in an "authentic" — Ben's term — part of Providence I'd never visited, he told me he'd noticed me on campus for months, and he proceeded to rattle off my class schedule. A cynic would have thought *Whoa.* I thought *Wow.*

From our first date on, not a day passed when we weren't together in the eggs-over-easy fashion common to undergrads — studying, sharing meals, walking to class holding hands, going to small movies in hole-in-the-wall theaters, and sleeping at his off-campus apartment, which became all both of us thought about during any of the former. Whenever we were together, we were touching. We were the couple who made others want to retch.

Yet nine months later when Ben proposed, I was as panicked as I'd been when a shark was sighted the previous summer at the shore. He wasn't my first boyfriend, but I felt far too young to consider marriage. I'd fantasized about moving to New York City and sharing an apartment in the Village with my best friend, Betsy, since for both of us returning to the big small-town of inbred Philadelphia was as appealing as eating calcified meatloaf. But Ben Silver was nothing if not persuasive. He always had enough bravado for both of us.

When I told my parents about the proposal, expecting them to echo my instinct to decline it, my dad sold Ben an engagement ring with the friends-and-family discount. Camille booked their country club and we were married the August after we graduated.

Hurtling ahead with adoption was more of the same. We completed forms and arranged for a home visit, but the steps were as removed from parenthood as applying for a loan. I thought the process would take years, as we were warned that it often does. Then one day I returned from teaching to find a phone message saying that a baby was waiting for us in Seoul. We had seventy-two hours in which to decide whether we wanted a particular female infant, three months old, in perfect health. We were told she was abandoned by the unwed university students who were her parents, a brilliant couple passionately in love but with parents who forbade a marriage. There might have been a violin score.

Later, when I met other parents who'd adopted through the same agency, their child's bio was identical. Not that it mattered, for any of us. Once I met Nicola, she became my daughter, no looking back.

We bought the apartment after we learned we were expecting a second child, baptizing every room by making love in it. We adored that it had enough space for a baby swing, a double stroller, and a block corner as good as any that you'd find in a nursery school. Until they became teenagers, and Luey's increasing belligerence started discomfiting her demure older sister, our daughters insisted on sharing a bedroom. They told people they were twins.

The apartment is where we had movie night every Saturday when the girls were small, and where they gathered their friends in gowns and tuxedoes before each prom; where I hosted Thanksgiving and Seders and fund-raising cocktail parties for candidates whose politics we applauded; where . . .

"Ma, chop-chop. You've been here for ten minutes," Luey says. I'd been so deep into the History Channel vortex that I hadn't heard her enter the room. "We've got to get a move on. What's up?"

Nothing. Everything.

She sees the photograph in my hand and takes it from me. "You weren't much older than I am in this picture, were you?" she says, though I was, by a few years. "Did you feel ready to be someone's mother?"

As much trepidation as I had about becoming a mom the first time — for three months I was afraid to give Nicola a bath, a task I left to Ben each evening when he came home — the second time, I never blinked.

"I did, darling," I said. "And if I can do it, anyone can."

"Even me?"

"You, especially." If I say it, maybe she — and I — will believe it.

Luey looks skeptical. "We really need to get cracking, Mom." As if she is leading me away from a crime scene, she takes my hand and starts walking out of the kitchen, through the living room — too big and too empty — toward the front door. Both of us stop to look at the small brass mezuzah, which my parents bought for us in Israel. Luey's research on jewfaq.org told us to leave this religious symbol in place, in case the new owners were Jewish, and with a name like Shepard, how could you tell? Please, let the mezuzah not wind up in the Dumpster.

I pass through the door, turn, and lock it. Downstairs I say one last good-bye to the doormen. The car is packed as if by masters of Tetris. Sadie squeezes between a box of plants and Luey's printer. I'd like to say I got in and didn't look back, but I did until we turned the corner, training my eye on our bedroom window until it was out of sight, and the memory of Ben became a prayer, not a shout.

302

30.

"Do you ever think Daddy might not have been so perfect?" Nicola had asked Luey last night.

As she pulled away from Central Park South, Luey said good-bye to him, once again. Over the last few weeks she'd been so thoroughly busy — not only with the panoramic, all-encompassing mind-fuck of baby making but with dog walking, packing, and eBay selling — that she'd barely had time to think about the aftershocks of her father's death. But when her mind tuned to the Daddy channel, she'd begun to hope — to convince herself — that flaky investment schemes explained the riddle in which her family found itself entwined. Luey would consider no other explanation for why their coffers were as empty as the apartment they were leaving behind. In one of their new heart-to-hearts, Nicola suggested that their father is — *was* — a philanderer; that they're hard up now because he tossed heaps of money at women.

"You mean a lot of women?" Luey had asked. "An assortment?"

"He had a thing for the ladies," Cola said. "You had to notice that. Some fathers make birdhouses. He made —"

"Shut up, Cola," Luey said, which is what she wanted to do when her mother raised the topic as they drove to Long Island. She preferred to stick to the idea that bad luck, or at least schlocky judgment, was her father's dark side of the moon — that, in the words of her Stanford roommate, Mittens Montgomery, a Houston deb, her father was all hat and no cattle. This was far superior to believing he collected girlfriends; it was hard enough for Luey to share him with her mother and Nicola. And so Luey deftly wallowed in denial, thought as little as possible about her father, and allowed herself complete preoccupation with the child growing in her womb.

If I can do it, anyone *can,* Georgia had said of motherhood. Luey realized this disclosure was meant to reassure, but its effect had been the opposite. Luey knew better. If the little cherub inside proved to be anything like her, each day would be a like the raid on Entebbe.

Logic might suggest that having a father who was a flake would make Luey believe a man was unnecessary in helping her raise a child. But since when did logic have anything to do with the heart? Every day she hoped to hear from Buffalo Bob. She'd like to have a partner for at least some of this enormous project she was taking on.

Last night she felt a pull as strong as an alcoholic must feel for a drink. She called.

He didn't answer. Later, however, her phone rang. By the time she found it under a stack of boxes in the hallway, the caller — *the* one — had hung up. She returned the call with a carefully calm statement that went to voice mail. By midnight, Luey was solidly into an REM sleep, dreaming that her baby was a daughter who came out talking in complex critiques of Henry James. That's when her marimba ring tone went off.

"Hey, Stanford girl," the voice said.

In her near narcolepsy it took Luey a moment to realize she was hearing from the person she'd been hoping would call since their high-in-the-clouds night overlooking San Francisco. "Hey, Buffalo Bob," she said, too dopey to remember that he'd asked her to call him Peter.

"Hope it's not too late," he said.

Luey looked at the clock. What woman her age was asleep before midnight? "Of course not!" she said, too heartily. She may as well have been shouting across a gym.

"What's doing?" he asked, his slap happiness hyped by inebriation.

"Not much," Luey responded. Just another down-on-her-luck, pregnant college dropout selling claptrap on eBay, bummed because her dog-walking business came and went in weeks. "You? How's the tour?"

"Sweet. We're in Boston tonight, heading to New York in two days. I'll be back on the West Coast in a few weeks" — and here he downshifted to sultry — "If you're around, I'd like to see you."

Luey's heart began to *thump.*

"A shame you're on the wrong coast," he continued. "I've been thinking about you. But it's been, you know, busy."

"You're heading to New York?"

"Like I said."

"Let's dial back. It's where I live."

"Right. Little private school girl. I'm seeing a kilt, red panties to match."

"*Now,* Peter — that's where I live now."

"Like today?"

"Like yesterday. I'm moving to East Hampton . . . you know, out on the Island."

"What happened to the Harvard of Palo Alto?"

May the God of humility forgive me. "I'm taking a gap year. It's a long story." Short, really.

"Hey! Great. If I left you VIP tickets, could you get to Madison Square Garden on Thursday night? I'd see you backstage afterwards."

"Love to."

"Ask for Gus," he said, and spelled out specifics.

Before he changed his mind, she said, "I'll be the girl with the red panties." No way was she fitting into a kilt.

31.

"Dinner, family!" I shout. If I had a gong, I'd ring it.

I'm thinking of this meal as a feast of the epiphany, honoring the revelation that anything good that will happen in my life is most likely up to me. If I decide to subsist on a diet of bitter herbs and twigs, I'll have no one to blame but myself. Nicola splurged on supermarket tulips, which she arranged with branches gathered from the frozen yard, setting the table as if tonight were a celebration — which I'd like to think it is. Nicola and Daniel grilled steaks UPS'd by Wally, which we — minus an abstaining Luey — consumed with numerous bottles of Pinot Noir brought by Chip Sharkey, he of the unlikely kindness, who joined us for dinner. Chip assured me that the grapes were sustainably grown in a nearby vine-yard. I thanked him, and wished that wor-rying about the origin of red wine could be higher on my list than *money* followed by *job.*

"If you want to know what God thinks of money, look who he gives it to!" Daniel toasted. I clicked my glass with his and the others', but given such philosophy, I wonder, am I obligated to offer up round-the-clock mea culpas for once having had a surplus of income? This is just one topic careening through my brain now as sleep eludes me. My lids stretch tightly over my eyes, which feel like ping-pong balls bulging from my head. I have tossed and turned, failing to find comfort in the raft that is my bed. I cannot bring myself to cross over to Ben's shore.

My conversation with Luey in the car echoes like an annoying jingle. "That woman the other night?" she asked, as I'd been waiting for her to do. "Clem's mom? What did she want?"

"Nothing." I hope my answer was correct.

"I'm not a fool," she said.

We drove another mile until I trusted myself to continue. "I think Clementine might have been involved with your father."

Luey craned her neck in my direction and said, "That's crazy." This translated to: *You're crazy.*

"Sweetheart, your dad wouldn't be the

first guy to fall for a woman as young as his daughter. Don't deify him, please."

We rode past two more exits before Luey said, "I don't see it. Clem is, like, twenty-one going on sixteen." When Luey is upset, she sounds sixteen herself.

I thought of the obligatory premarital counseling session Ben and I suffered through before the rabbi would marry us. "It's sex or money that take down most marriages," he'd lectured. "Sex or money," he repeated for an extra shot of pomposity and fright.

My mother had confided that the man's wife had recently left him for a college sweetheart who owned a chain of A&W drive-ins near Pittsburgh. "Such a *shanda*" — a scandal, she translated for me. When our counseling session ended, I said to Ben, giggling, this rabbi may, with the power vested in him by the State of Pennsylvania, be allowed to unite a couple as husband and wife, but given his track record, what gave this guy the chutzpah to advise us on marital longevity? Lately I've wondered if his pronouncement wasn't a curse.

"I don't buy any kind of Dad and Clementine hookup," Luey said. "You're going off the deep end here."

I didn't try to defend myself and hoped

Luey was right. She futzed until she found NPR and for the following twenty minutes, we played along with "Wait, Wait, Don't Tell Me," egregiously bombing. We've each become so suffocated by the minutia of our insular world, neither of us remembered the name of California's governor.

I turn on my light now and try to read. Nicola has passed along a novella. The author is English. Give me mackintoshes, drinks parties, fine fillies, jumpers, fortnights, and people shouting "Bollocks!" and I'm generally good to go. But in the first chapter, a government wonk agrees to an assignation in the car park with a man she's met on the job one hour earlier. After he rips off her knickers, they do it standing up against a fender. Following this indignity he helps her find a lorry, and semen leaks on her skirt. That's when I pitch the book against the wall. What did the author live through to write it? I'd prefer not to know, and, more to the point, what made Nicola like and recommend this book? I prefer not to know that either.

The wind pounds the window like a bear that wants to get in. I am thoroughly and miserably awake. I get out of bed, tighten a worn robe around my flannel nightgown, slip into my ancient moccasins, and start to roam.

There had been few lookers at this house — as Chip predicted for the winter. I find myself sizing up my property as a prospective buyer might. The coat of Linen White that he insisted on for every wall makes the place feel not only as buffed and fresh as promised but sterile. I could be shambling down the hall of a mental institution. Our family pictures have been replaced by chilly black-and-white photographs of the sea from a collection that Chip rotates for staging. "You want another person to be able to imagine living in the house," he'd advised. What I hadn't realized was that this would mean that I would no longer be able to see myself here.

I don't plan to tell Chip that with Luey's new business visiting dogs will have their run of the place. He'd need a defibrillator if he knew.

Nicola's room is closed but Luey has left her door ajar. I peek inside and listen to the inhalations of her breath and think about how her body is manufacturing my grandchild, cells multiply by the minute. It's a miracle I find impossible to grasp, no different than when I could no longer see my toes beneath my own pregnant belly, needed to wear support hose, and had to pee every twenty minutes. Thanks to an app from *What to Expect When You're Expecting,* at one point Luey informed me that the embryo was the size of a blueberry. I try not to imagine this child too vividly; it's been hard to shake the image of the father's bison head.

From downstairs, I hear a slight rustling. Please, not mice. But bravery in all matters is required, I tell myself. I tiptoe to the kitchen.

The mouse is Nicola, sitting at the wooden farm table, abraded by scratches long before we owned it, a package of graham crackers and a mug of steaming tea in front of her as she reads what looks like a letter. The room is tidy. Only a salad bowl drying next to the sink and the evening's candles, burnt to stubs, reveal that five people ate a meal here hours ago.

"Too much on your mind?" she whispers.

"I could ask you the same." I feel a rush of guilt. I should be charged with motherly infidelity, because since Nicola moved in with Stephan and Daniel, we've hardly seen or spoken to each other.

Like all sisters, when my girls were young, there were taunts of "Mom loves me best." As they got older, the gibes stopped. But along with the devotion that I'd like to believe is a subterranean bond cementing my daughters, I suspect each has moments when she feels the baiting is true.

In my own childhood, it was Waltz boilerplate that my mother preferred my brother. Precisely because of this, I wanted no gaming in my own family. I've tried to mete out love not only lavishly but equally, and hoped that sibling rivalry wouldn't become a blood sport. Yet here I am, feeling I have failed the daughter who was first in my heart.

"How's the job?" I ask, stroking her hand.

"Wonderful," Nicola says, and smiles shyly. "Uncle Stephan thinks I've got panache."

Only Stephan would use that adjective; it must be true. "I completely agree," I say, although I surely haven't mentioned it often enough, and Nicola's never until now been able to express it in a professional setting.

"He thinks I'm a born saleswoman — he wants me to commit full time. And we're talking about having me design jewelry, maybe going to England to take a course."

Amazing, if Stephan is footing the bill. "Congratulations."

"Want to see what got it started?" Nicola lifts a necklace, dreamy and delicate, that she's wearing under her white T-shirt, and points to one of several nearly transparent oval discs surrounded by small, sparkling stones. "These big ones are rock crystals," she says.

Nicola must be gifted indeed to get my Brahman brother to want to make jewelry out of what I suspect is everyday quartz, but all I say is, "Spectacular."

"It was my idea to sell what people my age may be able to buy."

"Smart. Are those little ones diamonds?"

"They are, and the setting is rose gold."

"I'm proud of you," I say.

"But there's more." She sips her tea. "Hey, want a cup? I'll make it. The water in the kettle's still hot."

"You sit, honey." I get up to rummage in the cupboard. "Let me find a tea bag."

"I brought loose tea — it's in a canister over there." No Lipton for my Cola. She points to a small tin. "It's white snowflake tea, hardly any caffeine."

Yet here she is, up at three.

"Supposed to refresh your mind," she says. "Smell it? Chestnuts, right?"

I sniff. Smells like tea. I empty and refill the tea ball in the sink and let it steep in a mug while I rejoin Nicola at the table.

"I also came up with the idea of champagne Saturdays," she says, eager and proud. "I've convinced Uncle Stephan to open the showroom to couples shopping for engagement rings and wedding bands and give them the red carpet treatment."

If Luey ever gets married, she'll probably elope, but Nicola has been planning her wedding since she was in third grade, and has documented it in a scrapbook. Five bridesmaids, because more would be tacky, she declared at eight years old. Sumptuous train, though she wants a ceremony at the beach. Leaving the reception in Stephan's Jag. Guests throwing dollar bills, I suppose, instead of confetti. Decadence I'll never be able to provide even if I haven't always thought that splashy weddings — as I myself had — are corrupt.

As Nicola continues with conversation about bead settings, diamond shanks, and Asscher cuts, I could be sitting at the dinner table with my father. At risk of sounding like a commencement speech, after a few minutes I say, "It sounds as if you've found your passion."

"Maybe," she whispers and sighs.

Here it comes, the disclaimer. Nicola doesn't look me in the eye. No matter how enthusiastic she appears to be about a school, a guy, an apartment, a job, or a continent, there is inevitably a snag. She is in perpetual drift.

"What's it like at home with your uncle and Daniel?" When I've asked how her living arrangement has worked out, Stephan has grunted, "Couldn't be better," not inviting comment. Daniel has amplified the picture by saying only that on most nights Nicola goes out, though once a week she cooks something heavenly from culinary school — to make me feel that that particular two-year investment wasn't a complete wash, I'm guessing. "Are you lonesome?"

"They go their way, I go mine," she says. "It's easy."

I'm not ready to be relieved. "Who are you with when you're out after work?" Once a mother gets to her third question she is officially meddling, but I don't care; I have no idea how Nicola spends her off-hours. She mentions names of girls I remember from high school. "Anyone special in your life?" Why not really push?

To my surprise she says, "Maybe," again.

"That high school friend up in Boston?"

"No, I haven't heard much from him. It's a man from Paris." She glances at the letter on the table.

A man. "Does this person have a name?"

"Emile," she says, drawing out the second syllable. "A chef."

"Sounds romantic." Also geographically undesirable.

"Sometimes."

Once, both daughters turned to me to share what mattered most in their lives — teachers straight from Stephen King novels, four-foot-ten harpies who snubbed them at lunch, and eventually boys who held their happiness in their small, sweaty palms. After one of these young males would get upgraded to boyfriend, I'd know every detail about his braces-flashing smile, his invitations, and his IM'ing. But when the girls left home, the curtain came down. I never got to hear much about men, if that's how they'd characterize their suitors. For that I am sad — and now deeply curious.

"Why only 'sometimes' romantic?" I ask. "Because he's there and you're here?" This must be my twentieth question.

Nicola finishes her tea before she answers. "I thought I'd never hear from him yet now that I have, I feel as if I'm being courted."

She shows me the letter. It's on ivory parchment with flowing cursive in black ink. My French is from junior high school but I'm pretty sure that *"Tu me manques"* means, "I miss you."

"Right, and I miss him. More than I realized."

"What's the problem?"

"I feel pressured."

I don't want to imagine what sexual favor could be left in the twenty-first-century repertoire that would pressure a woman.

"He wants me to move back to Paris."

"But you have a job here, maybe a future." *Possibly a boyfriend, if you give the guy any encouragement,* but even I knew better than to mention Michael T. *And also, I'll miss you if you leave,* another unspoken subject.

"Emile doesn't care about any of that. He wants me to move."

"Isn't that premature?"

"Not after being together for almost a year."

I don't care if the hurt shows in my voice. "That's a long time for you to be together without mentioning it."

"It was off and on," she says, as if that makes a difference. "Plus, Daddy met him when he visited me."

That Ben never mentioned he'd met Nicola's boyfriend would feel like one more treachery were it not consistent with his failing to remember the names and details of either daughter's boyfriends, ever. He always considered these young men to fall far, far short of the mark, the mark being him.

"What did Dad say to you?"

Nicola mimics him as she says, " 'He's way too old.' " She sees my face. "Emile is turning forty."

Forty is the age some women my age date. Nat is forty-eight. "That is a substantial difference, Cola."

She literally pulls back by inches. "One of the things I like best about him is that he's the first guy I've been with who's a man and not a boy."

"Boys grow up, Cola." I married a boy, though maybe he never grew up.

"Emile has plenty of good points." Her defensiveness is so thick she can barely speak. She ticks off an inventory as if she's been keeping a list, which I suspect she has. "He's warm and kind. He has gorgeous green eyes. He's been promoted at the restaurant. He has a wonderful house in Provence with a view of the water — well, it belongs to his mother but he goes there whenever he wants. I love his accent. He thinks I'm beautiful."

"Aha," I say.

"And Estelle is adorable," she adds.

If there is a God, Estelle is a cat, a goat, a canary. I hold my breath.

"His little girl."

Please don't ask me for advice, I think, *because you will hate what I say.*

32.

"Georgia, I'm driving into the city," Luey said. "Where are the car keys?"

She'd fed and exercised this week's boarders. Herb the dachshund had become a weekday regular and owned the place. Al, a skittish collie, swallowed his pills that she'd buried in baby apple-sauce. Gloria, the deaf cockapoo, had bedded down for the night with her stuffed binkies and Piaf, the Coton de Tulear whose owner swore she could sing, and followed Luey into the kitchen along with Sadie, who now barely gave Georgia a nod.

"Excuse me?" her mother said, peering over her glasses and giving her the Look. Georgia was editing — and by editing, she meant rewriting, although her mother wouldn't admit it — an SAT essay for a jumpy high school junior. Word-of-mouth racing through the concierge moms' grapevine had caused a spike in requests for her services since she'd helped the younger brother of Luey's ex-friend, Whitney, polish an essay that their mother was sure would make him irrefutable MIT material. At Luey's insistence, Georgia was charging a thousand dollars an essay. Her mother said she found this shameful, but Luey figured that the richer her fee, the higher the regard and demand for services among the entitled, who assumed that if something cost more, it had greater value. Luey had been right: Georgia was completing one or two essays each week.

"Where are the car keys, *please*?" Luey added.

"We're supposed to get six to ten inches of snow starting before dinner. Have you checked the weather?"

All Luey had checked was her phone at roughly ten-minute intervals to reread the text from Buffalo Bob's manager relaying the information on where Miz Kitty could pick up concert tickets. She wondered why there were two. Did Peter expect her to bring a date? She'd considered inviting Cola, then blew off the idea. Tonight should be a solo sortie.

"You can't trust those reports," Luey said.

Her mother frowned. "It's you I can't trust," she said, and began apologizing as soon as the sentence polluted the air. She hopped up from the kitchen table, reaching out to hug Luey. "I'm so sorry. Oh, honey, what did I say?"

"Plenty."

"I didn't mean it. I worry, that's all." She stepped back to a normal distance, looking Luey up and down, clucking. "I'm really sorry. Worry is in my job description."

Was this supposed to be news? Luey was worrying as well. Prenatal blogs and pregnancy websites could convince any mother that the slightest slipup would cause sideshow babies. Luey did not want to begin to imagine the grisly outcome of, say, absentmindedly eating a cracker spread with Brie. Sushi was the Antichrist, along with cold cuts, caffeine, and alcohol, all of which she'd been dutifully avoiding. Yet even with careful — if belated — precautions observed, Luey felt as if she were a petri dish of emotional bacteria, most of it fear. What if something were wrong with the baby? What if at the end of the pregnancy she couldn't figure out how to raise a child? Or find adoptive parents, if that's what she decided. A relentless game of panic tennis played in her brain. *Whatifwhatifwhat.*

But tonight her plan was to tell Peter. In person. He deserved to know. If after nuking him with the news he chose to have nothing to do with her and their child, Luey hoped this knowledge would help her to put fantasies aside — Peter and Luey, sitting in a tree, k-i-s-s-i-n-g — and propel her to get on with her life.

In the meantime, the question loomed of what to wear. With her height and long, slim waist, if you scrutinized Luey, you might think she'd made one too many visits to the all-you-can-eat buffet, not that she was at the beginning of her sixteenth week. For tonight, she'd swaddled herself in a lacy black tunic over black leggings and tall leather boots, black jacket over tunic, a loopy white scarf to alleviate the effect of gloom, finished by a dangly silver pendant to point Peter toward her ample cleavage. She'd been pleased with the result.

"Okay, go ahead and worry if that's your thing," she told her mother.

"Why don't you take the train or the jitney?"

Because it's uncool enough to be pregnant, Luey thought. She didn't need a smelly commuter conveyance to underscore the point. "I'm not going far." Just all the way to the city.

"What are you doing?" Her mother didn't give her a chance to answer before she added, "Who are you seeing?"

"Harrison," Luey said, the lies coming fast and furious, not unlike the snow she was now noticing through the kitchen window. "He's in town for his grandmother's eightieth birthday. She lives in Huntington and he's meeting me. . . . in Plainview" — a suburb where she'd once stopped to buy bagels. Where was all this coming from? Luey was shocked at how natural it felt for her story to build. Maybe she should write a made-for-television movie.

"Well, bundle up. Wear a hat. Call!"

Luey kissed her mother good-bye and grabbed a knit cap, though she didn't plan to plunk it on top of her freshly washed hair. She started the six-year-old Honda Civic her mother had bought to replace the Audi SUV when its lease ran out. As she backed the car out of the driveway, she imagined that she felt no less brave or scared than Christiane Amanpour might be when heading to war.

Luey drove into town to fill up the tank and handed the cashier a twenty-dollar bill. She no longer had her father's credit card — that account had been canceled months ago — and she knew better than to ask to use the single credit card her mother reserved for emergencies. This was an emergency, but not one she cared to discuss.

"Hope you're headed home," the cashier said, handing back change, which amounted to less than a dollar. Gas was only one of many commodities Luey had discovered were ridiculously expensive. Maple syrup and olive oil? More costly than wine. "I'm closing up early," the cashier said. "It's a cocoa and Netflix kind of night."

"Sounds cozy," Luey said.

Was she nuts? If Miz Kitty didn't turn up, Peter might read her absence as disinterest and surely, if unredeemed, the statute of limitations on his curiosity about her — because that's all she thought she should expect — would expire. She had no idea when he'd be touring again in the area.

This whiteout of an evening was her only shot. She took off, headed for the roads that fed into the Long Island Expressway, and tuned to a news station. "The National Weather Service has issued a winter weather advisory for the entire region, effective eight p.m. this evening through noon tomorrow," a robotic voice warned. "The stage is set for an icy mix, with cold, dry air steadily bleeding into the area. Temperatures are expected in the teens and twenties. In Eastern Long Island, many spots are already below freezing. . . ."

Luey crept along another few miles. It was starting to look like the proverbial white Christmas, a few weeks late and minus the merriment. Her windshield wipers, which were going full blast, began to slow. She'd traveled past only five exits down the expressway when traffic stopped. After a few minutes, Luey got out to get a better look. Cars and trucks were stalled as far as she could see, in front as well as behind her. A driver nearby was standing by his Lexus. "What's going on?" she shouted to him.

"One of those tractor-trailers got into an accident up ahead," he yelled back. "Isn't looking good."

She returned to her car and checked for weather updates. *Apocolyptic storm a'comin,* @Islandgal had tweeted, and @notanac marc was chiming in, too, *Hope u r tucked in tite in jammies — big ole storm comin in yr neck o the wood.*

Five minutes later the ambulance sirens whizzed by along with state highway patrol cars, lights swirling. The troopers directed cars to move to the right. Luey checked her watch. She'd allowed more than sufficient time to get to the city and park, but now a whole hour had evaporated and she was only a few miles from home. The concert was starting in three hours. She fiddled unsuccessfully to find a local radio station that would give her an update on the traffic situation, but reception was garbled.

Minutes later the cavalry arrived in the form of a patrolman who tapped the window of her car, snow thick on his wide-brimmed hat. Military-ish uniforms always stressed her out; sometimes she had even been spooked by her own former doormen. Luey hoped the trooper wouldn't demand to see her registration, because she didn't know if it was in the glove compartment or if her driver's license was even up to date. But what he asked was, "You okay, miss?"

"Fine," Luey said, trying to act that way. She told herself there was no reason to have a meltdown. Under the brim, the patrolman's face looked floury and boyish, round as a pie. "Thanks," she added. "Just waiting for the road to be cleared up ahead."

"That's not going to happen tonight, miss."

"Really?"

"First of all, look around. It hasn't snowed this hard all winter and there's a first-class mess up there, We've got a jackknife, and the driver was rushed to the hospital. Didn't you see the ambulance? We're closing down this section of road and directing drivers to back up and get off at the next ramp. If I

329

were you, from there I'd get on home." He cocked his chin toward the sky and brushed snow off his glasses. "This is only the beginning."

As soon as the patrolman moved on to the next car, Luey texted both Peter and his manager with deep regrets, then reversed her car and began to drive. The trip took an hour and a half. When she arrived, Georgia, Sadie, Herb, Al, and Piaf greeted her as if she'd been gone for a week.

33.

Naomi McCann rings my bell at exactly ten in the morning. Herb, channeling a pit bull, races to the door. Sadie, twice his size, cowers in his foreshortened, master-of-the-universe shadow. Men.

I open the seldom-used front door where every other winter I'd hung a balsam wreath studded with tiny pine cones, sprigs of juniper berries and silvery moss. Wind blows into the entryway crowded with yet another box, this one filled with clothes that Nicola, to augment her humble salary, is reluctantly hoping to resell at local consignment stores. If I were acquiring rather than divesting, I'd shop at any one of them myself.

"May I take your coat?" I ask.

"Thanks," she says, and glances at her boots, sensible laced leather uppers and stout vinyl lowers. The boots drip on the stone floor.

When I woke this morning, a bumpy rash

covered my neck and arms; on my lip, a cold sore is blossoming; I am out of Valtrex and the drugstore that has my prescription is in Manhattan. Bags under my eyes betray my lack of sleep. At least I have clean hair, although I rushed to dry it, and wisps frame my head like a feathered tiara.

Despite blustery weather, Naomi is wearing a skimpy navy jacket. She stuffs her beret and Black Watch scarf into the sleeve and hands me the jacket to hang on a hook. Her hair looks even worse than mine. If she were a friend I would find a moment to gently suggest a different brand of hair color, about which I am now an expert. But she is not a friend.

"Want to sit down and take off your boots?" I make room on a low bench piled high. She carefully sets them next to the front door. To see her wearing only thick red stockings feels far too intimate. Naomi McCann's button-down shirt is tucked into jeans. Her body's a shorter duplicate of Clem's, and the loose shirt fails to disguise an equally substantial chest, breasts cantilevered high.

"The coffee's hot," I say, forcing a smile. I start walking to the kitchen and she follows me down the hall.

Today I am happy that Chip insisted I

remove our family photographs: for this woman to scrutinize my visual history would be an even deeper violation than having her simply under my roof. Then it occurs to me that she may have gotten a play-by-play from Clem. Neither of us speaks as we make our way to the back of the house. I have no small talk for Naomi McCann.

"Please, sit," I say. "How do you take your coffee?" Nicola left early this morning and aside from her rinsed dishes in the sink, the room is neat. I have set out mugs, sugar, and a small pitcher of milk. Fighting my hostess instincts, there are no scones or muffins, not even a Dunkin' Donuts munchkin.

"Black, please," she says. There is a quiver in her raspy voice, which calls to mind Marge Simpson's chain-smoking sisters, whom Nicola and Luey mimic brilliantly and often. I fill each of our mugs. The woman's blue eyes seem to focus on a rabbit in the yard. I can't guess what she's thinking, except that she must dislike both me and this situation. I would want to tackle anyone whom I'd felt had been upsetting Cola or Luey. This meeting is probably no easier for Naomi McCann than it is for me. *Let's get going,* I tell myself, and launch the speech I have rehearsed seven times.

"Naomi," I start.

"It's not *Nigh*-omi," she says. "It's *Nay*-omi."

"Sorry," I say, realizing I've been mispronouncing that name for my entire life. I clear my throat for a do-over. "*Nay*-omi, I can understand if you think I've been harsh with Clementine." The swelling cold sore on my lip is beginning to hurt. I clench my fingers to force myself not to touch it. "I apologize."

The woman's face is motionless, her hands in her lap, one folded over the other. I begrudgingly allow that she has an admirable restraint. Others might take it for elegance, but I am not that generous.

"My husband isn't here to defend himself, and I'm certainly not going to defend him either, just as I won't apologize for him." I feel a tear forming. I wanted to be as cool as, say, Camille. She'd have found a way to have already julienned this guest; Naomi would be trembling. "I have no way to prove anything, but my gut tells me Ben, my husband" — it feels crucial to add that title — "may have taken advantage of your daughter."

Still, no reaction.

"She's young — these things happen," I continue. "If anyone's to blame, it's Ben, not Clem." I don't believe this, but feel the need to say it. "But, well, these last few months haven't been easy — I'm sure you can understand. . . ." I have no evidence for this assumption, but I say that, too. "Maybe I've let my imagination run away with itself, but simply to put my mind at rest . . . woman to woman . . . indulge me, please." I've started babbling. Once again, I clear my throat. "For the sake of closure" — did I really say *closure*? — "I was hoping you might be able to shed some light on what you know — might know — about Ben and Clementine."

This speech drains me. Why didn't I issue myself a gag order?

"Mrs. Silver," Naomi says in that gravely alto that I imagine many men find sultry.

"Call me Georgia," My mother would never say something like this.

"Georgia." I don't care for the way my name sounds in this brittle stranger's mouth. "My daughter has only met your late husband a handful of times. They have never been involved in the way you are insinuating."

Insinuating — was there ever a word more snaky and slimy, *sin* built right into it? Her cease and desist order is loud and clear.

"Keep Clem out of this," she continues.

"I can well understand that you have suspicions about your late husband, but don't look at my daughter."

Her words are a volley of gunshots. It now seems preposterous to ask about the child that I am certain I saw in her SUV and heard cry on Hedge Lane. I will myself to believe that what Naomi says is true, and weigh whether I heard a subliminal suggestion in *well understand.* What does she know about Ben and other women? Concerning my late husband, I've become willing to imagine almost anything.

Naomi has defended her daughter's honor. We have nothing to say to each other and I'd like this woman, with her haughty air, to leave.

She nods toward a tall flowering plant in a terra-cotta pot on the table. "Perfect specimen," she says.

The plant's deep red flowers are close to iridescent, resembling peonies that will bloom here in the late spring. "A double amaryllis," I offer, although I'm sure I'm not teaching the owner of Adam and Eve anything new.

"A Cherry Nymph," she says.

At the name, I stifle a nervous laugh.

A blush crawls up Naomi's face, blotching her freckled skin. "Where did you get it?"

she asks quickly.

"I grew it," I say. "They and paperwhites get me through the winter" — along with jasmine, lavender, holiday cactus, an azalea topiary that I've kept alive for a year, and orchids that I've had longer than most of my bras.

"Unusual." She touches one of the rows of the petals. "I'm impressed."

Is Naomi McCann surprised that a pampered hothouse plant like me can make anything bloom, that my amaryllis wasn't a gift from Madison Avenue?

"Refill?" I ask. Good manners are a knee-jerk reaction.

"No thanks," she answers. "But may I use your powder room?"

I direct her to the bathroom off the kitchen. No, I definitely can't ask about the child, I think as I wash and dry the mugs. When she emerges, she thanks me for coffee and shakes my hand.

I look down. On Naomi's hand is a ring she wasn't wearing before, a whopper emerald — large, square, and as green as chlorophyll — surrounded by diamonds of equal size. She sees me see it.

Message received.

34.

"My granddaughter Louisa is expecting," Camille told her caretaker.

"That's a blessing, ma'am," the woman said. "A baby is always God's gift."

Camille was having what the nurses refer to as a good day. Where was everyone? she wondered — everyone being her family, which included Daniel, the only constituent who counted other than Maurice. Were they staying away because of the weather? Beyond her window it was snowing, which muffled the outside world and provoked contemplation.

"Are you chilly, Mrs. Waltz?" the nurse asked. She offered a mohair blanket, a recent holiday gift, and as she covered Camille's legs, Camille took note of how spindly and mottled her calves had gotten. She detested the ugliness of age, which along with forgetfulness was encroaching like mildew.

Her granddaughters visited yesterday — yesterday for Camille being any time that wasn't now. Louisa had a big announcement. She was going to have a baby. They expected their old granny to be shocked. Do her granddaughters imagine she doesn't keep up with celebrities nowadays, who get married — if ever — years after a child arrives? Do they think she and Martin didn't have Stephan underway before their wedding? It would take a lot more than an out-of-wedlock baby to shock Camille. The young were such innocents, each generation believing they had invented sex. How did they think they got here?

Camille was no less shocked when she found out about Ben and that hussy. Vera Levine stuck it to her with such swollen joy that she thought her old classmate would explode like that poor lady astronaut.

"My Phyllis saw your son-in-law in a compromising situation with another woman," Vera had barked, using her arthritic claws like hooks to put quotes around *compromising situation.* "A hotsy-totsy number. People in the Hamptons are talking."

"Give me a break," Camille lashed back. "Your Phyllis lives in Westhampton. That doesn't even count."

Then she said to Vera . . . what? How did

she swing back? Camille knew it was a choice riposte, one of her best, and that was saying a lot. Stephan would have been proud of her — Ben, too.

What was it? This had been happening lately, fade-outs, as if her batteries were dying.

Goddamnit.

35.

"Stephan," I say, "I saw the ring."

"Impossible." My brother is speaking with all the confidence of a candidate who he Supreme Court has declared President of the United States. "You saw a ring that *resembles* the ring. The real deal is in my vault, or at least it was when I closed up yesterday."

"I saw a ring exactly like the one you showed me," I insist. "Clementine's mother flashed it as if she was mooning me. I was meant to see it." I hear my voice rising with each phrase. I am nearly shrieking.

"And her point is?"

I know my brother is giving me only half of his attention. I am calling him on a Saturday morning when he and Daniel are at Liberty Farm, their house in Bucks County, ninety miles from New York City. I can picture him assembling a cassoulet atop his Aga in the kitchen with its wide-plank flooring and cabinetry from a two-hundred-year-old monastery. Perhaps he's sitting in the heated screened porch that overlooks the forest while he rereads *Swann's Way.* Or he might be puttering in his greenhouse, propagating stem cuttings. Ninety percent of what I know about houseplants I have learned from my mother and brother.

"Listen to me. She wants to show that Ben was with her, not her daughter." I can't stand talking to Stephan and yet I can't stand not to.

"Forget the ring. From what you've told me, this woman couldn't possibly be your hubby's type," he adds. "Ben may have shown her the ring and she's had it copied to throw you off her daughter's scent. And you're buying it. Don't be a fool."

"If you met her — Naomi — you'd get it. Bedroom voice, not the shy, retiring type." And I saw what I saw.

"Rubbish, Miss Marple. What's going on with Fleigelman? That's what you should be concentrating on."

"You and I have gone over this," I say. "Wally's forensic accountant has shown us all the records from stock trades. Ben sold everything off, but Wally and the accountant aren't any closer to knowing where the cash went than I am. No wire transfers into other accounts or deposits to new bank accounts. No thrilling money laundering, at least that anyone can find."

"I'm disappointed our boy Ben wasn't a more complex villain. You're telling me this isn't *The Firm*?"

"There was a private post office box for a while, on Long Island." I toss this out casually.

"Be still my beating heart."

"Feeling better now?"

"What, dear God, was in it?"

"Nothing anymore." After I produced a copy of Ben's death certificate and proof that I was his executor along with Wally, a clerk unceremoniously opened the box. "There were copies of our tax returns, 1099s, and year-end brokerage statements. Nothing we hadn't seen before. Wally, the accountant, and I have gone over everything six ways to Sunday and all we can know is that money disappeared."

"To this Naomi and her daughter, you're thinking?" Stephan asked.

"Yes, especially now."

"Hold still until I'm back in the office Monday and have another look at the ring," Stephan says. "Don't be showing up at her door with the sheriff."

I return to my essays, to helping Luey with

the dogs, to repotting a cattleya that has sprouted a blossom the shade of lobster bisque, to laundry and ironing. I've discovered that I love removing every crumple until our shirts, dish towels, and pillowcases gratify me with smooth perfection. Luey draws the line at my taking a hot iron to jeans. I am also cooking — domesticity has become my ticket to hypnotic escape — because today I have guests coming for a late lunch. Beef barley soup is simmering and I will bake an apple tart. The rest of the morning will fly, and for that I am grateful: when I perform homely tasks, more galling considerations fade as I stir and starch within a bubble of wholesome utopia.

Luey joins me in the kitchen, followed by a maelstrom of barking and wagging.

"Need help?" she asks.

"With gratitude," I say. My daughter has been taciturn since the evening she set out in a snowstorm. I hand her the peeler and nod toward a bowl of apples. "I'll start on the crust."

"Why the fuss?"

"Chip and Nat are coming for lunch." I spread the dough on the counter and begin to roll. "A shame your plans didn't work out the other night," I say, trying to sound sincere, though I am a lifelong failure at teasing Luey out of foul moods. She'll talk when she's ready. I hope. After she's finished with the apples, she sets the kitchen table while I start to assemble the tart.

"Want me to get the salad going?" she asks, making short work of the table. There are few decisions to make when you've sold off most of your possessions.

"It's in the fridge," I say, "but you can do dressing."

"Aye-aye." She gathers vinegar, oil, mustard, herbs, and a lemon to juice.

The weekly opera is playing. Listening to it was my mother's tradition and I've started tuning in every Saturday. This week is *La Traviata,* Camille's favorite.

"A courtesan knows she is dying," I remember her explaining.

"What's a courtesan?" I asked.

"A beautiful woman who men admire," was all she told me. I bragged to friends about my mother being a courtesan until Stephan overheard and corrected me. Violetta and Alfredo are winding down with their duet in the first act when I ask, "Have you felt the baby kick yet?"

Luey turns, her face more animated than I've seen it in days. "I'm not sure. The way the blogs go on, describing a goldfish swimming circles in your belly . . . all I've felt is what I'm pretty sure is gas."

"One day I felt as if corn was popping inside me," I say, remembering the sweet sensation of Luey-baby kicking. "It took awhile to tell with you."

My grown-up baby seems to be ruminating on this benign remark. Did I say something wrong? With Luey, I usually do.

"Ma, I want to run something by you," she says, after a few minutes.

She's backed off from *Georgia*. I brace myself as I slit the pastry. "Of course," I say, as I brush my tart with melted butter. No wonder I have gained five pounds. I am a violin who's turned into a viola and will become a cello if I don't stop eating.

"I'm thinking of giving this baby up for adoption," she says. "I've been reading everything I can find. I want my child to have a good home, to be loved by two parents who are ready for it. To . . ."

She lost me after "my child," because I am thinking of "this baby" as my child, too, my flesh, my blood, my lifeline to Ben.

"I don't need to make a decision right away," she says. "But soon."

"I don't have the right answer." I'd need a machete to bushwhack through my thoughts and emotions. "I'm sorry."

"I didn't ask for your answer." She is back

to sounding like the crank I love. "But I wanted you to know."

I remember how it feels to be a wife who longs to be a mother and cannot have her own child. Then came Cola, my angel infant who, when we met, felt as if she'd always been mine. She may as well have come out of the womb in Korea holding an engraved note that said: *Special Delivery for Benjamin Silver and Georgia Waltz.* Luey could be an envoy of happiness for a couple like us.

In an enigmatic manipulation of fate, has her baby been destined all along to belong to another mother? I see this reasoning and applaud its honor, generosity, and wisdom. Giving up the baby is an act of courage that may make sense for Luey. She could turn the page and return to Stanford, unfettered by motherhood. The memory of the pregnancy would fade like a tan, until it feels like it never was.

Or, giving away the baby might be a decision Louisa Silver-Waltz would regret every day of her life, and as she grows old, she will search the face of every child the same age as hers, wondering.

I feel an attack of zealous love born of possession and connection. I am enough of a peasant spooked by superstition to try not to envision this baby — Ben's long legs, Luey's smile, my father's dimples — but there are moments when imagination overrides better judgment and I do picture the child, my first grandchild. I want to tell Luey to abandon the idea of parting with this child because I'll stay home and care for him or her while she goes back to school, but this isn't my decision to make or even necessarily a good idea, for Luey, for the baby, for me. It would break my heart to part with my grandchild, but all I say is, "Now I know."

"Good," Luey answers, "because our guests are here."

Chip drives too fast, always. His tires crunch my driveway where the gravel needs replenishing, an expense I will leave for the next owner.

He and Nat enter through the back door, like the dear friends they have become. Nat carries bags from a store that started out as a lowly fish market and has morphed into a gourmet shop stocked with overpriced but sublime roast chicken, silky pâtés, and take-away crab cakes better than I could ever prepare myself. "Cheese and nibbles," he says, putting down the bags on the counter. Owning a bookstore is lovely, but God bless his days on Wall Street that make it possible.

Chip places four bottles of wine — two red, two white — on the table. "Good news," he says after kisses and greetings. "We may have something to toast. A couple who looked at the house has made a bid and — shocker — it's not an insult."

36.

"How did you find me?"

"I have my ways."

The last person Nicola expected to see knocking on the glass reception wall of S. Waltz and Company was Michael T. Kim. There was no point in checking the leather-bound appointment book. (Uncle Stephan thought a schedule on a computer was more suited to a podiatrist or veterinarian.) She'd just written in an appointment for Monday and knew the rest of today was a yawning blank.

On Friday afternoons, customers able to afford merchandise sold by Stephan Waltz were either at better city hotels snacking from the minibar or had escaped to country homes. These included clients from South America, all points east, Hollywood, Houston, and Miami; and starting last week, Stephan, too, had headed to his farm. He let Nicola know that since he believed she'd found her "métier," he would grant her the honor of being required to stay until the race between boredom and the clock was declared a tie at six p.m. Only then could she turn on the answering machine, lock up, and leave. For this, Nicola was grateful. If her weekends were demure and chaste, at least they were hers, except for the first Saturday of each month, when Uncle Stephan had allowed her to host her champagne bride-and-groom reception. The first one attracted forty nervous, blushing shoppers.

"Let me in," Michael T. said, grinning and tapping on the glass. Nicola wondered, since she'd last seen him at the New Year's party, was his hair better cut? Had he lost weight? He seemed almost chiseled. She'd considered his looks that of a Korean leprechaun, and had yet to see him scowl. Nicola couldn't say whether his constant good nature was the result of unrelenting optimism, a surplus of confidence, or a facial tic. It certainly wasn't because he was dumb. The type, however, to which she usually gravitated was brooding, perhaps with a cigarette dangling from sensuous lips, exuding earthy romance and God knows what. That type was Emile, and in her life the Emiles had always gotten fullest attention.

Nonetheless, Michael T. was here, with an ear-to-ear smile reminding her that along with Mr. Rochester-like drama, life also needed gumdrops and Tootsie Rolls, at least metaphorically.

Nicola had strict orders to allow no one without an appointment past S. Waltz's gilded threshold. "I can't let you in," she said. But this couldn't apply to friends, could it?

"Please."

"Don't steal anything." She unlocked the door.

Nicola had been deliberately vague with Michael T. about her job, which she couldn't imagine he'd find impressive, so if it ended soon, she'd have nothing to explain. At any rate, it was a moot point because since the weekend they'd shared in Cambridge, their texts had dribbled from daily to weekly.

"How long are you in town?" she asked. She placed a kiss on his cheek, a gesture that promised friendship, nothing more. He smelled faintly of scotch.

"A month," he answered, as he surveyed the small, plush foyer furnished with Queen Anne chairs, glass tables, and a loveseat upholstered in green silk jacquard. "I'm staying with my parents while I study for the boards."

"What kind of doctor do you want to be?"

"A pediatrician."

He's his own man, she thought, more than a little pleased — and surprised — that he'd resisted parental pressure to go with neuro-surgery, or at least cardiology.

"But tonight I'm stealing you away — if you're free."

Nicola considered the coy approach. She could intimate that she had long-standing theater tickets with someone exceptional or plans to go away for the weekend to a destination other than visiting her mother and sister, who were expecting her on the 10:20 train.

"I'm sadly free," she admitted, nervously mirroring Michael T.'s smile.

"And hungry, I hope, because we're going someplace special." He punctuated this news with a thumbs-up. Nicola didn't know if the gesture was earnest or ironic.

"Where?"

"You'll see."

Her mind floated toward the frontrunners on her short-list. If he'd asked, she'd have suggested Il Buco Alimentari, where she was convinced she was eating in the Italian hill country, not an industrial block in down-town Manhattan. Maybe he was splurging on a stars-aplenty spot she'd only read about — Per Se! Daniel! Del Posto!

"Should I go home and change?" Nicola asked, hopeful. She considered her attire. Her dress, which Uncle Stephan described as taupe. Would look even more sadly mouse colored after she would return the diamond chain around her neck to the vault.

"You look perfect."

"Give me ten minutes then," she said. "Have a seat . . . and a magazine." Though she suspected *Town & Country* wouldn't be of interest, Stephan also subscribed to *GQ* and *The Economist.*

"I have plenty to read." He lifted his messenger bag.

She locked up the inventory, saying good night to her current favorites: a chunky onyx pendant from the 1900s, a garnet-circled cameo of Lord Byron, and Goo Goo G'Jobb Goo, the walrus pin that she considered her pet. The sumptuous emerald-and-diamond ring that Uncle Stephan had tried to stump her with was still in its velvet box; what made this curious was that only yesterday a customer had asked specifically for a ring with diamonds or emeralds. "Something old, important, and unique." Her uncle never took it out for even a glance.

Nicola locked the case, retouched her makeup in the back bathroom, sleeked her hair, sprayed on the perfume she stashed in her bag — Stephan forbid her to wear it in the office, claiming it corroded his goods — and slipped into her coat. She fingered the necklace she was still wearing, a simple chain with a diamond heart. She left it on.

"Hoo-boy," Michael T. said, when she walked out to meet him.

It's the perfume, she thought, because frankly, she looked the same as before.

As they left the building onto Fifth Avenue, a taxi was discharging a passenger. "Our lucky day," Nicola shouted. It was six-fifteen, when cabs were all but nonexistent.

"Sorry — too rich for my blood," Michael T. said. "This way." They continued northeast toward Bloomingdale's, six blocks, and downstairs to the subway platform.

"Where are we headed?" she asked.

He bobbed his head toward a sign, his elfish amusement intact. They'd be traveling in a direction that, in all of Nicola's years as a subway rider, she'd never ventured. Queens. Were they eating with his parents, she wondered? *Please, no. Let it at least be a beer garden.* Every time she opened *Time Out New York* they were laying it on thick about outer-borough gastropubs serving homemade pickles, deviled eggs, and craft brews — code, in her book, for cheap date.

The train chugged along. She stood sand-wiched between a backpack attached to a traveler who smelled as if he had last bathed in Belfast and a tall, shaved-head teenager whose piercings marched like ants toward his ear. Michael T. caught her up on his training for a charity triathlon — because medical school apparently wasn't enough to keep him busy — and how his younger sister was debating between Dartmouth and Yale.

"How's your sister?" he asked.

"Barefoot and pregnant," Nicola said, and instantly regretted trash-talking Luey. "We're all behind her, of course," she added.

"Families hang together," he said. "My grandmother raised me so my mom could work."

"What does she do?" Nicola pictured the woman giving pedicures. Few things made her more uncomfortable than going into one of the nail salons on every other block in New York and having an older Korean woman pumice her feet. Once, Nicola had cried.

"She's an ophthalmologist," Michael T. said.

"And your dad?" Perhaps he owned a dry cleaners.

"Anesthesiologist," he said. "You could say I'm going into the family business."

Which made Nicola even more impressed that he'd chosen pediatrics. They moved on to conversation that bounced from the benefits of a gluten-free diet and that their favorite movie was *Jules et Jim,* though they couldn't agree which man the actress preferred, Jules or Jim. Picturing Michael T. examining a newborn baby, Nicola white-knuckled the overhead bar as the train sped, lurched, and finally stopped. He grabbed her by the elbow and led her to the platform. She saw a sign for an exit and pointed. "Here?"

"Not yet, we're transferring!" he yelled over the din. Michael T. needled through the crowd, then squeezed her hand and said, "Here it comes." The train screeched to a halt, discharged a clot of passengers, and the two of them boarded, grabbing empty seats next to each other. "You're right, it is our lucky day," he added. Nicola had a different opinion.

A few stations later, they lumbered upstairs and outside to a commercial street thick with traffic, mom-and-pop shops, and restaurant signs, many in Greek.

"Flushing?" she guessed.

He laughed. "How long have you lived in New York?"

"I love Greek food," she volunteered.

"Me, too," Michael T. said. "Patience, Cola." Only her family used that name. He'd obviously called Luey or her mother to track her down. "And we're here," he said a few minutes later when they rounded a corner and stood facing a small mountain of a building.

Nicola had seen its sign many times when she'd ridden to the airport: KAUFMAN ASTORIA STUDIOS. Were they going to watch a taping? She'd like that. "Is this where they make TV shows and commercials?" she asked, lighting up.

"They do," he said. "And once this was Paramount's studio for silent movies. Lillian Gish, Mary Pickford, Douglas Fairbanks . . . the greats. We're going to eat in their old commissary." Michael T. offered his arm as he pushed opened the wide front door. While they ascended a mahogany staircase, he continued to spew Wikipedia-worthy facts, ending with, "You can be Gloria Swanson and I'll be Groucho! This is where they filmed *Cocoanuts.*"

Yes, their table was ready, the hostess — stylishly imposing with platinum hair and heavy black eye makeup — said, and led them through a crowded dining room to a prime spot, where Michael snapped Nicola's picture again and again until she wanted to nuke the camera. Then he started in on W. C. Fields. While his cinematic enthusiasm appeared to be genuine, Nicola wished, finally, that he'd morph into a silent star himself. As they gobbled oysters Rockefeller washed down by cocktails from Nana's youth, Nicola steered the conversation toward med school. Is it true you draw blood from each other to learn the technique? Remind me of your cadaver's name. How many students snort coke to keep going?

When Nicola ran out of questions, Michael T. was forced to ask, "What do you do at this job of yours?"

She inflated the 10 percent of her tasks that were remotely creative.

"Do you see yourself working there long?" he asked, just as the server inquired, for the third time, if they'd like to order another after-dinner drink. Nicola was relieved to hear Michael T. offer to settle their bill. She noticed that he added an exceedingly generous tip — and that she was blotto. As they stumbled to the street, she had to grab his arm. She was dreading the subway, that instrument of economy whose motion would certainly make her ill.

They wound their arms around each other, for stability as much as affection. He made a turn, then another. They weren't yet at the subway stop, though the route seemed longer than she'd remembered from earlier in the evening. The street was dark and empty, and Nicola was becoming frightened when Michael T. announced, "We're here."

They entered a parking lot and stopped at a shiny blue Prius, whose doors he unlocked. "I know the way to Brooklyn Heights," he said, "although you'll have to direct me when we get near your uncle's house."

Nicola was pleased, relieved, and not too intoxicated to wonder aloud, "Do you think you're in any shape to drive?"

"You'd be surprised at what a med student can do in this condition," he said. In no position to challenge him, Nicola hooked up her seat belt, leaned back, and drew in the matchless aphrodisiac of new leather upholstery.

When she opened her eyes, they were exiting the Brooklyn-Queens Expressway. Five minutes later, he was escorting her to the brownstone's front door. They kissed under the lamplight until she fumbled with the locks and opened the door. As they climbed the stairs to her third-floor bedroom, Nicola gave the evening a seven. Demerits for the R train, points for that thing he just did with his tongue.

Michael T. made reservations and got good haircuts and wore well-shined shoes with laces, not scuffed loafers that needed new soles. He'd decided to be a doctor and, by God, he'd be a doctor. He owned a messenger bag, not a backpack, and somewhere, Nicola knew, there must be matching luggage. He had a little money, which he kept in a wallet. If her father were alive and visited them in the city where they lived, Michael T. wouldn't just fight for the check. He'd have paid in advance, not, as Emile had done, let her father pick up the check at a four-star Parisian restaurant that Emile had selected.

Michael T. was the man.

Taking this into account, the next morning — which ended at one p.m. — she upgraded the evening's score to nine. There was only one problem, which she discovered hours after Michael T. left: the small matter of a missing necklace with a diamond heart.

37.

"Go to bed, honey," I say, rousing Luey. The evening with Chip and Nat is pushing midnight. Cola canceled — her medical student friend made a drive-by appearance — so it was the four of us, laughing during dinner and screaming through *Vertigo,* the first movie in what we have decided will be a continuing Hitchcock film festival. I turn off the television.

"Echhh. I have to give the dogs their last walk," Luey, half asleep, mumbles, rubbing her eyes and drawing a blanket close.

"Absolutely not." Chip gets up and heads toward the back door. "Allow me."

"You're a prince," she says, and yawns extravagantly as she follows him to leash up our squad of snoozing boarders.

That leaves Nat and me in the kitchen. He didn't ask to help but dug right in. Which I like.

Throughout the evening, I felt his glances,

as I have whenever we're together. Tonight my internal GPS recalculated and I felt a crackle of connection. I didn't want to look away. Perhaps it was the full monty of seductive clichés — wine, candlelight, a fire, and a movie that requires you to grab an arm — because I believe nothing essential has changed. I'm happy to hear from Nat, but I don't stare at the phone and will it to ring and for me, obsession has been the only rule I've known.

Not that I feel married. If Ben hadn't left behind a hash, I'd be in a closet, crying into his clothes, but given my financial trouncing, I try not think about him at all. I don't want my confusion to mushroom into hatred. I don't want to unlove Ben.

This has meant that I am finally living in a demilitarized zone denuded of his pictures and possessions, most of which have been reassigned to oblivion or packed away. There is no Church of Dad at which Luey and Cola can worship. Phantom-Ben has, for the most part, deserted my dreams, though his avatar is much on my mind when I am awake. My husband lurks in corners and sails through doors, his spirit in a cool rush. But this evening his back is to me, and I do not hear the echo of his laugh.

I may be ready to move on.

Nat punctures our silence. "I see you're not one of those clean-as-you-go cooks," he says, surveying a mess. He begins to attack a heavy skillet with hot, sudsy water and elbow grease.

"Guilty as charged," I say, grateful for habits that will guarantee at least thirty minutes of side-by-side work.

In my wifely years, I had looked forward to a sociable cleanup, the encore to an evening well spent. Ben and I worked as a team, washing dishes, packing away leftovers, wiping down counters, sweeping, critiquing the cooking, and, if it was one of the better nights, the quips. As couples do, we'd speculate on the stresses and strains of friends' relationships or snipe about how this guest or that could possibly stand his — or her — partner especially with the bombastic political opinions or the drinking. We made bets on which husband and wife were so excessively lovey-dovey that they'd probably announce their separation the following day. This functioned as the equivalent of a postcoital cigarette, our own private prom party.

I am feeling that hum of contentment now with Nat. I survey the breadth and squareness of his shoulders and the sureness of his movements. He is as steady as a train on a track. I like how he sings and sometimes even dances as he works. The small bald spot on the back of his head has begun to remind me of the empty circle on Cola's teddy bear where she loved away his fur.

Nat Ross has become a safety deposit box for confidences. I'm weighing whether he can do the same for my emotions. It's true that Nat doesn't haunt the devil's playground. No roué, he, a man who lacks clear and present danger. Thirty years ago — or even last October — a measure of recklessness felt like required foreplay. Then I remind myself what living on the brink, even unwittingly, has gotten me. So I am ready when Nat turns, takes off his professorial glasses, and pulls me toward him. We kiss.

I have sold him short. The kiss is better than a few weeks ago, a new riff on bliss.

"I've wanted to do that again for some time," he says.

"I've wanted you to," I say, although technically I came to that conclusion only this evening. The second and third kisses are even better, deeper and longer. Eyes open, I pull him toward me and feel as if I am beginning to recall the lines of a poem I once memorized. Nat is solid in my arms and neither of us hurries to stop. But for the fourth kiss, Ben shows up in the form of a shudder, and I break away as Herb and Sadie invade the kitchen, leading the pack. The kisses linger in the air when Chip follows. His quick look around tells me he senses a palpable awkwardness.

Shall I try to signal Nat to stay? Grab his hand? In that moment doing nothing becomes a decision, and within several heartbeats he says, "Thank you — what a wonderful evening, Georgia." The sound of my name rolls out like a term of endearment.

I am a true coward. I should haul this man to bed.

"We'll talk tomorrow after the couple from California comes by again," Chip says. The people who are taken with this house want to see it once again before they fly back to Marin County.

"What are your plans for Sunday?" Nat asks.

"Essays," I say. I have to find a way to tell one overweening scholar why Notre Dame may not be as impressed as he is that his Hail Mary pass single-handedly won the homecoming game, and another that a play-by-play of his summer in Italy spent writing forty pages of a novel isn't going to cut it, either. Henry James, for example, would have found a synonym for *weenie.*

Warming in my bed, I close my eyes and

relive Nat's mouth on mine. Sensations that have gone AWOL flood my body as I drift to sleep, thinking of how I will need a bikini wax.

"I wish the kitchen were newer," Chip's customer complains the following morning.

"We could replace the butcher block with marble," her husband points out. "Or soapstone."

"I like the grounds," she says, referring to what I've never thought of as more than a back yard. "I believe those bushes are lilacs."

White as well as purple, I want to offer from my perch on the stairs.

"It needs hollyhocks and anemones," she adds.

They're there, hibernating with hundreds of tulips and daffodils.

"If we get rid of the patio," the man said, "there's room to expand the garage."

Does this couple own a limousine service?

In the city, I'd been spared the indignity of watching potential buyers scrutinize my home, kvetching about how the bedrooms are dark, its bathrooms cramped, and storage for bikes nonexistent. The neighbor who bought the apartment, flaws intact, wanted only a walk-through that I didn't, fortunately, witness. Here I have the same two choices when Chip brings one of his few customers: leave or hide. Until today, I left.

Chip, I've discovered, says little beyond answering questions. "The pool is heated." "No, you're on your own in taking garbage to the dump — people usually hire a service." "Yes, the owner can vacate by May."

Can she? I should be casting a gris-gris spell and fondling amulets with the hope that this couple will come through. My financial security is still MIA and my hand-to-mouth, pay-as-I-go system has severe limitations, no matter how many dogs Luey boards or essays I rewrite each week. I have to get rid of the house, find a more modest place to live, and figure out a dependable method to produce an income. I could see myself in a studio apartment back in the city, but that's not anything I can explore as long as No Child Left Behind is my operative philosophy. What's ahead looks like a blockade. I'd like a reprieve from selling — for a few more months; I took Chip at his word that it would take forever to unload the house and this is coming too soon. I have not hatched a plan B.

It appears that I do want to live on the brink.

"Thanks, Georgia, I'll call you," Chip says, and leaves with the customers. Minutes later he phones from his car to say they'll stick with the bid. "Great news, huh?" He waits for a hoo-ha of joy.

"Let's see if they'll go higher," I reply.

"I'm confused." I hear him taking a breath. "It's not as if customers have been beating a path to your door, and this is a solid offer. Ten percent below asking price, but better than we thought you'd get, frankly."

"See if they have deeper pockets," I respond.

38.

"Sure, it's a gimmick," one reviewer wrote. "But it works. Boston DJ Peter Eisenberg performs in a preposterous bison head and goes by the name of Buffalo Bob. By creating a persona, he makes Buffalo Bob stand out in the faceless world of electronic music, though the irony is that without the mega-mask that swallows his head, Eisenberg would be as anonymous as his peers."

Untrue! Luey finds Peter's face distinctive — drowsy, heavy-lidded blue eyes; a pointy chin and a strong, slightly aquiline nose; small, milky teeth; and long, loosely curled white-blond hair. Anonymous? Not to her. His features hang together well, like a Rauschenberg. She is hoping her baby resembles a miniature of Peter, minus the schnoz.

"Despite the blizzard outside Madison Square Garden, it was a sold-out crowd where the ladies favored spike heels and miniskirts, with the occasional Lycra body-suit in neon colors," another critic wrote. Luey could picture these women, fashionably tilting toward slutty, swarming the stage and ripping off Peter's clothes after the concert. "Male fans wore artful scruff along with T-shirts that revealed physiques the fans sweated to achieve. The crowd danced in the aisles for a solid five hours . . ."

Five hours!

". . . to a series of electronic artists, culminating in an hour-long set from Buffalo Bob himself, who performed from a tall, tower-like DJ booth that also served as a video screen for projections. He skillfully produced a series of high-pitched bleeps and blorps early in the set. In a robotic voice, Buffalo Bob repeated his lines over a deep, pounding beat. . . ."

Luey snapped her laptop shut. She felt beyond pissed. Under any circumstances she would have liked that concert, but her circumstances were exceptional, and that an apocalyptic snowstorm had thwarted her now made Luey want to fling her laptop across the room. Since the other evening she'd sent tweet after tweet to Peter. It was Sunday and there had been nothing in return. DM @Buffalobob: *Miz Kitty really*

really misses you. Meow, was the last message, hurled into the anonymity of cyber-
space an hour ago though apparently as
unread as a stale tweet from American Express.

Herb chased Sadie into her room, which
reminded Luey that a walk was due. She
dragged herself along the road with the two
of them, returned to the house, and then
leashed up Al, Gloria, and Piaf. The air was
frosty; the sky, cloudless. On nights like this,
Luey used to pick out constellations with
her father and wish on the first star she saw.
Luey wanted him here now. I wish I may, I
wish I might / Have the wish I wish tonight.
"I'd like to talk to my father again," she said
aloud, hoarse and dejected.

She'd trudged about a quarter of a mile
down the road when her pocket rang. The
blast of *The Pink Panther*'s theme song —
bum da-bum, bum da-bum, da-bum da-bum
— rang out like thunder.

Luey was always on the prowl for omens
and portents. If she'd lived in the Victorian
age, she could have been a medium. Her
father adored *The Pink Panther.* Terrified,
she looked at the caller ID — RESTRICTED,
it said — before she answered her phone.
Despite the cold, she began to sweat. Luey
put the phone to her ear.

"Sorry you had to miss the concert." Her father hadn't responded. Peter, however, had. "What happened? I thought you were coming." He sounded as far away as the stars.

Luey began an answer worthy of a meteorologist, which he interrupted. "Where can I see you?" he asked. "And when?"

39.

"Have you looked under the seats?" Nicola had asked Michael T. hours after he left on Saturday. Did she need a Powerpoint presentation to demonstrate the situation's gravity, which was crisis-intervention awful. Her voice had risen, nearing a squeal. "My uncle's going to burn me alive."

"Cola." He'd spoken as if he were talking to the canine obedience class dropout. "My dad has the car now. He's lecturing at U Penn medical school and won't be back for two days. I'm sorry. You'll have to hold tight."

Rats, rats, rats, she thought. "Think back. Do you remember if I was still wearing the necklace in the restaurant?"

Michael T. laughed, which a part — unfortunately, only a sliver — of Nicola recognized as his effort to lighten the mood. "When you saw me drooling, did you think it was because of your accessories?" Nicola ignored the compliment embedded in the question. "Have you searched all over the bedroom? There was a fair amount of action there, if memory serves."

If memory serves. "What should I tell my uncle? I forgot to take off the necklace and an asteroid hit me on the way home?"

"Tell him you lost it and suffer the consequences."

"I can't. I just can't." It would mean admitting that she'd broken two of Uncle Stephan's rules.

"Then tell him you sold it on Friday afternoon."

"Right. The customer paid forty-five hundred in cash and I neglected to write a receipt and lost the money." Nicola groaned.

"I'll give you the money."

"Forty-five hundred dollars? Never. This is my stupidity and my problem."

"Then I'll lend you the money." Michael T.'s exasperation had become evident.

"That's enormously kind — very, very sweet — but I'm going to pass" — and not be beholden to Michael T. in perpetuity, she thought. "When the restaurant opens, I'll call. Maybe they have it."

She said good-bye and paced the town-house stairs — three flights, up and down, five times — then took herself to the Promenade, where she parked on a bench and gazed at Manhattan with equal parts longing and self-loathing until it was late enough in the morning to phone the Astor Room. The hostess switched Nicola to the mistress of lost-and-found who meticulously reported her inventory, the usual assortment of keys, library cards, glasses, BlackBerries, Droids, cigarettes, nasal sprays, wallets, lipsticks, gum, tampons and condoms — unopened, she emphasized — Nooks, Kindles, an iPad, and one actual book, a Bible. No jewelry except an I Love NY lapel pin.

Why did her father have to *die*? He'd have turned the solution to this problem into a caper, thought it was killer funny, and "lend" her the money. Not an hour passed when Nicola didn't think about Ben. Today, looking at Manhattan, a town she always felt he owned, she mourned for her father as if the news of his death was new and raw. She wondered when, and if, she'd ever get used to his absence. She wondered if a daughter could. Her mother might remarry, but she'll have only one father. Well, two, technically, in her case, but one didn't count.

And then she cried.

40.

On Monday, Stephan calls at eight, an hour earlier than he usually arrives. "Good news and bad," he says.

"Good first." It is a new week, after all.

"I'm ninety-five percent sure the ring in my vault is absolutely the one Ben showed me."

"And the ring I saw?"

"You had to be mistaken."

Is my mind sufficiently muddled that I imagined the ring on Naomi's finger? *Cut yourself some slack,* I say to myself. *You're under pressure, girl.* With scant conviction I am willing to admit — only to myself — that perhaps I made a false assumption.

"The bad news?" I ask, though the ring business is bad, or at least strange.

"We're missing a small diamond necklace here, last seen around your daughter's neck."

Classic Stephan, quick to accuse. I bristle.

"I'm sure Nicola simply forgot about it and you'll see the necklace when she arrives at work." Her day starts at 8:45. Stephan rarely arrives this early on a Monday, when he drives from Pennsylvania.

"Let's hope you're right," he says, dialing down his wrath by an atom or two. "And I have some other news."

"Good or bad?"

"You tell me," my brother says. "I checked the calendar and there's a new appointment that must have been scheduled late on Friday. It's your Naomi McCann. She'll be here at four."

41.

When Nicola arrived at the shop a half hour earlier than usual, Stephan said, "Good morning," as she popped her head in to greet him. "How was your weekend, Nicola dear?"

No icy disapproval! "Uneventful," she said, relieved. "Did Daniel get back?"

"He did. Late last night."

As if she were in a Pilates class, Nicola started to unclench, muscle by muscle. She pushed a smile onto her face. "Did he find all sorts of promising painters in Italy?"

Her uncle leaned back in his chair and linked his thin, patrician fingers over his navy pinstripe vest. "Never mind Daniel. Is there something you want to tell me?"

Nicola felt a twinge of panic, but took pride in her recovery. "There is — I made a new appointment at the end of the day. A Mrs. McCann is coming in at four."

"I noticed." Uncle Stephan knit his eyebrows so tightly his face looked like a fist. "Anything else?"

Nicola attempted to keep her voice as neutral as the beige dress she'd worn in an attempt to render herself invisible. Two alternatives had occurred to her. Admitting the truth was one.

"Such as?"

"I'm speaking of the missing necklace." He was speaking of it in an exceptionally imperious tone.

"Really? What necklace?"

He leaned forward in his chair, his fist-face even tighter. "Nicola Silver-Waltz, you're talking to me. The heart adorning your neck on Friday."

"But I put it in the safe before I left." The lie popped out as if her father was a ventriloquist, though Ben Silver would have fabricated a plausible and amusing story by now.

"Show it to me, please." Stephan rose slowly and stood next to Nicola, making her despise the unearned advantage of tall people, able to lord over lesser human beings. "Let's open the safe together."

As they marched to the back room, his keys jangled to the beat of her hammering heart. I've really done it, she thought. This is not an incidental hiccup.

Stephan opened the safe, going straight

for the black leather box in the front, which he snapped open showily to reveal nothing. "May I suggest that we were not robbed?" he said. "That you still had the necklace on when you left the office? That you are prevaricating, right now. This disappoints me. The necklace is either lost or . . ." Mercifully, he didn't complete his sentence and merely shrugged.

Nicola arched her back and lifted her chin, trying to muster the pique her grandmother might demonstrate if accused, even justly. Her uncle glowered. Nicola returned the glare as she soundlessly counted to ten.

"I have given you my trust, which you have abused." Uncle Stephan *tsk-tsk*ed as he nodded. "If you return the necklace, there will be no questions asked. If not, we shall continue this conversation when you care to tell the truth."

He left the room, his pallbearer demeanor intact.

42.

"No, you cannot be here when Mrs. Mc-Cann comes for her appointment." Stephan is emphatic. "That's an inane request."

"I need to know why she wants to see you."

"I imagine the visit is for one of the usual reasons, to buy or to sell, but your daughter — who, by the way, has not as yet come clean about the whereabouts of a certain missing necklace — neglected to ask when she set up the appointment, though frankly it doesn't matter because I'm not without curiosity myself and have more than a prurient interest in this woman." Thanks to years of acting lessons and a brief flirtation with voice-over artistry, Stephan delivers this speech without taking a noticeable breath.

"What if I were out of sight?"

"I won't have my place of business turned into a French farce. You can depend on me to call as soon as the woman leaves, and in the meantime, talk sense into your daughter."

Since no law prevents a customer from perusing magazines in the newsstand of the lobby where S. Waltz makes its home, it takes profound restraint not to drive into the city and swan about like an aging Bond girl while keeping one eye on the people coming and going. Instead, I prevail on Nicola.

"Did Uncle Stephan put you up to calling me?" she hisses into the phone.

"What's this nonsense about a necklace?"

"It's gone missing."

"All on its own?"

"I wore it home and misplaced it." This is the daughter who I considered to be the responsible one.

"Tell your uncle the truth." I try to be gentle. "He deserves that — he's been good to you."

"Mother, how could I make this mistake?"

She is weepy, but all my edges feel rough and, possibly for the first time in my life, I am not in the mood to console another living soul. "Cola, forgive me, but you'll have to solve this problem on your own. I know you can."

"I hear you," she says, contrite.

"And I have a favor to ask, please. Later

on a Mrs. McCann has an appointment, correct?"

"How did you know that?" Curiosity is besting her.

"I recommended Stephan to her." God forgive me for lying. "Will you let me know when she arrives and leaves?"

"What's this customer to you? Am I supposed to say hello from you or something?"

"God, no."

"Mother, you're weirding me out."

"I'll explain later." If there's anything to say. "Don't worry."

The day passes with the illusion of time-lapse photography's crawl. I should be visiting my mother — I haven't seen her for weeks — but I'm too overwrought for that particular persecution, so I move down the food chain of personal pogroms and call Wally.

"No new developments," he says after an incantation of arcane legalese . . . *burden of proof . . . testamentary capacity . . . judgment debtor . . . be it resolved . . .* terms that must mean *I'm clueless.* "I won't be charging you, if that's what you're worried about," he adds, rather sheepishly.

"I didn't think you would" — because you'd know I wouldn't pay you.

On to Daniel. "Amazing trip. In Siena I

ate a dish called *scottiglia* — rabbit, lamb, possibly gophers — cooked with the best olive oil in the world," he says. "I'm bringing you a bottle. And I signed four artists, all brilliant; I'll tell you about them this weekend. And you? Give me a quick download."

"I've figured out if I pretend to be brave, something almost like courage shows up. Does that make me a fake?"

"It makes you a philosopher," he says. "I can't talk now, though — I'll drive out Saturday and you'll fill me in."

I invent a reason to call Nat. "For our next film, how about *Easy Virtue*?" I ask.

"There's a concept I can get behind," he says, sounding pleased enough to hear from me.

"By Noël Coward," I add, but Nat, too, cannot fritter away his workday chatting and says he'll call in the evening.

I'm hitting the low watermark, so I decide to tackle an item festering on my to-do list, to try to create a Facebook page for my college essay writing. Luey insists that this is essential. She calls what I do a business, though I don't want to commit to having become a cog in an inequitable machine — almost everything is despicable about offering privileged students an even greater

385

black-belt edge to get into college — and a business suggests permanence. Never mind that the checks it delivers put food on the table and help pay a mortgage.

Creating this site is, Luey promises, a "just follow the prompts" snap. But none of the directions are transparent for me, possibly the last woman in America to own both a dumb-phone and a hotmail address. I stare at the screen as I have at the dashboard of any car I've ever rented, wondering how the rest of the universe intuits symbols and rank-and-file directions. After two fruitless hours, I find myself defeated, slipping further and further down a cyber-hole.

This is why I had children born in the late 1980s, I remind myself. It's time to enlist Luey. She starts happily tapping away on my keyboard while I peer over her shoulder, pointing. "You're putting it *there*?" I ask. "What are you doing now?" "How did you do *that*?"

After ten minutes, she growls, "Get out of my face, Ma."

I slink away, which restores my screaming meemies, wondering what will happen with Naomi and Stephan. And it's only two-thirty.

I grab my coat and drive to the double-coupon-every-day supermarket. I am fulminating with myself over whether it pays to buy twelve rolls of Scott tissue on sale or use my coupon for an eight-pack of Charmin when my cart gets jostled from behind. "Oh, excuse me. I'm so sorry," I hear.

I swivel around at the familiar voice and find not just Clementine, but a passenger — small, pacifier-sucking, and wearing a red snowsuit and red-and-white polka-dot hat. My mouth says, "Clementine, what a surprise," while my eyes dart to the child.

Clementine flushes and brushes her hair out of her face. "Hi, Mrs. Silver," she says. "How are you?"

Wondering what your mother has in store. "And who have we here?" I ask.

"Theo, say hello, please." She gives the tiny arm a protective pat and the toddler opens and shuts a chubby hand.

My heart goes gooey. My legs tremble. All at once I want to scream and bolt and reach for a tiny, sticky finger so I can touch the child's velvety skin, "Hello, Theo," I say, crouching until we are face-to-face. "I'm so happy to meet you."

Dimpled cheeks, a grin featuring four mini-Chicklet teeth, long-lashed cornflower blue eyes, red-blond curly wisps escaping from the hat, and creamy skin. I search for a resemblance — to Ben, to Luey, to Clem. But the child looks only pleasantly generic, as if ordered from Land's End.

"I'm sorry, but we're rushing. Say good-bye to the nice lady, Theo," Clem instructs. At this, Theo — is that the name I have heard? — removes the pacifier, tosses it a few feet in front of their cart, laughs, and claps his hands. "You little rascal!" Clementine says. Tenderness nests in her voice.

The two of them continue down the aisle to retrieve the pacifier, and after Clementine puts it in her pocket, she removes another — presumably cleaner — pacifier from her bag. "So long," she says, as they turn at the intersection of laundry detergent and macaroni. I stand transfixed, and damn myself for not asking the question I was too stunned to call out, *Is this Ben's child?*

I move on to the dairy section, scoping out the Greek yogurt, and thinking of every kid I know with a gender-neutral name — Alex, Morgan, Rory, Avery, Sasha, Gray, Calder, Harper and Jordan — and I wonder, is Theo a boy or a girl?

When I'm deciding on milk — I will spring for organic — I hear my phone. "The eagle has landed and flew into Uncle Stephan's office," Nicola whispers.

"What did she say?"

"Not much. I offered her water, coffee, and tea. She declined all three. Tell me again how you know this woman?"

It's taken me fifty years to realize life does not require an answer to every question. "Will you be joining Stephan during the appointment?"

"I would if he were speaking to me."

"Call when she leaves, please."

Which Nicola does twenty minutes later, when I am in the middle of preparing chicken that will not be cooked with the thirty-nine-dollar-a-pound porcini mushrooms for which the recipe calls. "She left without even glancing at me." My daughter says, sounding disappointed.

"What did Stephan say about the appointment?"

"Have you not heard me? We aren't speaking."

"Can you blame him?"

"I'll transfer you to your brother."

"I'll get right to it," he says. "The woman was here with a ring she wants to sell."

"*The* ring?"

"I had some deeply disappointing news for our Mrs. McCann." His dramatic understatement is intact. "I explained that what she owns is not inconsequential, but worth a fraction of what she'd hoped."

"The ring isn't the one Ben showed you?"

"Keep up. The ring in my vault trades for upwards of three-quarters of a million, not, say, twenty-five thousand like the bauble on her hand. On close inspection, I could see the stones are flawed and the setting less than fine."

"How did she react?"

"Her skepticism was significant. I rather felt sorry for the woman, so I got out the other ring and the loupe and spent a considerable amount of time comparing the pieces. Ultimately, I believe she was convinced, and terribly taken aback. Sharoosed, if you will."

I'm plenty sharoosed myself. "I'm stunned," I admit.

"Not as aghast as Mrs. McCann, I assure you," Stephan says. "I believe she came here to cash out and was looking forward to a juicy payday. Maybe she'll get it with a fool somewhere, but she won't get it from me."

"So what you're not saying, Stephan, is that the ring that came from Gem was or wasn't the one you saw last fall? You've seemed so sure." Cocksure.

As each second ticks by before my brother responds, I imagine his face flushing until it's the color of a carnelian, one of his favorite semiprecious stones. "Georgia, I have been known to make mistakes," he says with a deep exhale.

The value to me of that admission: priceless. "Who doesn't?" I say.

But he quickly recovers himself. "However, I would swear on Daniel's life that the ring in my vault is the one your husband showed me."

43.

DM @mizkitty: *Diehard NYer now w/car & license. C U soon?*
DM @marcnotanarc: *Luv 2 but leaving 4 Thailand. Later!*

What's a fib between a pregnant lady with a secret and a guy she wants to keep on the back burner? Who tweets the truth anyway? Especially when her baby-daddy would be arriving in a half hour.

Luey tried on all the sweaters and tunics in her mother's closet. Yet despite how voluptuous her boobs had grown, her tummy would now cross the finish line first. Overnight, it seemed to have gone from mango to honeydew melon. Luey saw herself as a very maternal animal in a fat suit but, to her own surprise, not a sexual cipher, which she couldn't have imagined five and a half months ago. Lately, every dream had a porno plot in which she starred. As she painstakingly massaged cocoa butter into her skin, she wished that when Peter showed up, they could go to bed first and talk later.

Luey highjacked an angelic white shirt from Nicola's sparsely populated closet, paired it with maternity leggings from Wal-Mart, and wrapped herself in her mother's most voluminous pashmina. She considered variations on speeches, each with the same punch line: *It's yours.* What would follow, she hadn't worked out. All she knew was that she wasn't fishing for a marriage proposal; Cola was the sister who bought *The Knot* on the sly.

She propped herself up on the window seat by the front door and opened *Olive Kittredge,* which she'd half finished. Olive turned out to be Luey's kind of heroine, a flinty, misunderstood, sharp-tongued shrew with a warm, squishy center. Olive yo-yoed from guile to kindness, and Luey guessed that the author's point was to show how little we know of one another — even ourselves. The woman embodied hope minus sappiness and when Olive caught a break, Luey cried.

"People are never as helpless as they think they are." Luey had underlined that sentence. She'd like to think she had some

Olive in her, that even if Peter would sling some choice words her way when she told him about the pregnancy, she'd carry on, even if that meant accepting interviews with prospective couples who wanted to adopt her child. Luey had been in touch with several agencies and as soon as she mentioned Stanford, their solicitor made her feel like the prize sow at the fair.

Luey didn't expect Peter for at least fifteen minutes. She leaned back and closed her eyes, reliving their one and only tryst, with that bathtub as big as the bed where they played all night. It wasn't the worst scenario, she decided, in which to usher in a new life.

Luey was woken by a pounding, and her mother rushing to the front door. "I'm Peter Eisenberg," a voice said. "Luey's friend. Is she here?"

Even though she'd been playing his music, Luey had forgotten the deep timbre of Peter's spoken voice. His legs looked spindly even in baggy 501 Levi's sitting low on his narrow hips. He'd grown a goatee. Perhaps now he could pass for twenty-six, not twenty-five.

"Peter," Luey said, hopping up, her apricot shawl strategically wrapped and trailing, as if she were an Elizabethan heroine. "How was the drive? Did it take forever?"

"Hey," he said, as he gave her a kiss on the cheek and handed her a wrapped bottle. "If I'd listened to the GPS, I'd be in the ocean now."

"Welcome to our nunnery. This is my mom, Georgia Silver-Waltz. Mother, Peter Eisenberg."

"Your mother?" he said.

Luey hadn't mentioned that she'd returned home, and hoped her mother would take the question as a compliment about her youthful appearance. Regardless, Georgia's curiosity was barely restrained.

So you, Mr. DNA, are Buffalo Bob. Who are you, really? What's your family's health history — maternal and paternal sides both, please? Mental and physical? Your IQ? Did you go to college? Where? Did you graduate? The Buffalo Bob bit? Let's not go there. This is going to take a while, though, so it would be easier if you'd complete this eight-page form. Please don't overlook the essay question: Do you actually recall impregnating my daughter?

Yet Georgia managed the formalities. "We're so happy you could make the trip. Let me take your jacket." He handed over a black peacoat and pale blue scarf. "Now you'll have to excuse me," she had the grace to say. "I have some cooking to finish. You'll be staying for dinner, of course?"

Not just for dinner, Luey hoped.

"I'd love to, thanks," Peter said.

"Sorry I got snowed out of the concert," Luey said, as they walked to the living room, where a fire blazed. She'd been generous with logs. "You have no idea."

"It was a sell-out," Peter said. "I was shocked, if you really want to know. It was nuts."

Luey sat down on the couch and patted the seat next to her. Peter went on about the concert. She tried to nod at regular intervals. Finally, he stopped talking, most likely waiting for her response to a question.

"If you're wondering why I'm out here with my Mom, well . . ." she said.

"Yeah," he said. "What happened to San Francisco?"

"I took a leave of absence from school."

Peter shrugged. "Hey. It happens. Stanford's fucking hard. I dropped out of Yale for a year."

Did he take her for a moron? "I didn't flunk out. My leave is entirely kosher."

His face turned grave. "Please don't tell me you're sick. That would be terrible."

"Oh no, not that," she said. "I'm very well, actually." Blooming. Her planned oratory vanished and she stood, opened the shawl, and pointed to her belly. "Six months."

Peter's face pop-eyed with astonishment. He stared at her bump, back at her face, at her belly again, and then encircled her in a distinctly asexual hug. "Wow. Congratulations! We should toast," he said. "Let's open the bubbly. Right. No, not champagne." He shuffled from one leg to the other, thumbs in his belt loops. "I should have brought a teddy bear! Who's the lucky schmuck?"

She'd have to work up to eye contact. Luey looked at her shoes.

"Hey, that was a rude question," Peter said. "Sorry."

"It's not rude. It's fair." A chill climbed down Luey's spine. She flashed back to the evening they were introduced and felt that fabled click of deep, libidinous attraction, as if arranged by some heavenly Match.com. Luey had never experienced it before. "Here's the thing. That night we spent together?" *We had laughs and sex and we never thought beyond the moment. I left the hotel without expecting to see you again, and if I'd considered it, I'd have imagined you felt the same way.* "Well . . ."

Peter cocked his head like a dog waiting for a command. As he scratched his beard, his voice broke like a Bar Mitzvah boy's.

"What are you saying?"

"What you think I'm saying."

She heard the fire cracking, a creak in the house, the distant, tranquilizing burble of *All Things Considered*, wind whistling and shaking the trees, her own breath.

"What the fuck?" he said.

"It's true." Luey hoped she wasn't slack-jawed, smiling stupidly.

"Shit." Peter sighed.

Fair enough. "My first response exactly."

"But didn't you use something?"

Luey felt herself going bag-lady loony, every emotion set to vibrate. "What's this *'you'? We* did, supposedly. I brought a condom. You wore it." *Dickhead.* "These things happen."

"Christ." Peter stood by the window and stared outside, as if he might find an answer waiting for him behind a shrub. "Jesus H. Christ."

"I wish I believed in him. I really, really do. It would help."

Peter squinched his face as he asked, "Why didn't you get in touch with me sooner?"

"I tried, often," Luey said, though that wasn't true during the stage when she may have ended it all. She waited for him to challenge her as a lawyer for the prosecution.

Peter turned his attention to the flames in the fireplace. "What do you want me to do?" He stabbed the logs with the brass poker.

"Excuse me?"

"Are you looking for money?"

Was he going to have his people call her people and ask where to send a kiss-off check contingent on signing a confidentiality agreement? Did he think she was going to sell her story to *The Star*? "I didn't invite you here to see if you'd pony up. I'm not out to gouge you, if that's what you're worrying about. But I was hoping for some moral support." Luey realized this only when she said it.

"I like you," Peter said after a moment. "We had a pretty great time that night — I haven't forgotten or I wouldn't be here. And you seem like a smart girl. A smart girl who's going to turn into someone even more amazing. But we were together for one night. We don't even know one another. And you're, what, twenty?"

"Twenty-one." She joined him by the fireplace, putting her hand on his arm. She felt as if her father was leading her way. "And yet, you, Peter Eisenberg, a guy who dances around stages with a buffalo head-dress while he makes music that sounds like whales talking," *that I'm not sure I even like,* "are the father of my child. Our baby, who according to the Web site I read every day, can already hear, so you better be careful about what you say." Eye contact ceased to be a problem. "I thought you deserved to know, would want to know. I thought telling you was the right thing." *That's my Luey,* she could hear her father say.

Peter went wan, completely stonewashed. "When are you due?"

"Fourth of July." Independence Day? Not for her.

44.

Before I send off my fiscal effluvia to Wally's accountant for tax prep, I spent all morning attempting to penetrate their hostile world. I scrutinized 1099 forms and shuffled through records of interest and dividends in wee-small type along with a thicket of year-end brokerage statements, surely designed to be cryptic. If I'd been in a plane crash, I could search for a black box that would reveal the naked truth, but trying to marshal evidence leads me only to greater confusion. As an unabridged word girl, it hurts my brain to look at numbers. Digits marched in front of me like artillery, ready to shoot between the eyes.

This much I now know: Ben's earned income has turned out to be fairly high, yet not so flush that he didn't dip into savings. He wrote large checks made out to "cash" from a money market account. There my trail ends. The money's hit the road.

Investigation makes this Nancy Drew ravenous. Fortunately, Daniel has arrived bearing olive oil and pottery handmade by nuns, and is giving me the bona fides of painters he signed on in Italy. There is an eighty-three-year-old, one-eyed woman whose landscapes are entirely in lashings of green and navy; a six-foot, three-hundred-pound miniaturist who paints heartbreakingly delicate metallic religious scenes; and a gondolier-turned-watercolorist whose cloudy shapes mirror a Tequila Sunrise. "But this one, Paulo, is my favorite," he says, showing image after image on his iPad. The artist's work recalls Renoir, if the old master had painted during fever dreams and favored eerie four-legged creatures with human torsos and faces. It's clear that the Picasso in the crowd is Daniel's animal portraitist, whose persona — "a man born knowing how to tango" — he seems to admire as much as his talent.

As Daniel gives the lowdown of why he is magnetized by this work, I find myself wondering if he has a crush and I become happily distracted, able to shake off the morning's cursed numbers as if they were crumbs. "Are you bringing over these painters for shows?" I ask.

"Paulo, I hope, in June."

"Show me," Luey says as she walks in with this weekend's posse of dogs. They heel as she commands and line up like preschoolers waiting for Goldfish crackers. I hope she'll have the same knack with a child.

Daniel moves through his images until he arrives at a leopard with John Lennon's face. "Here's Paulo's work. Tell me what you think." He offers Luey his seat. At the kitchen counter, he helps himself to a panini while she gushes over the art.

"You're looking well," he says to her.

Except for her puffy eyes. Peter left before dawn, and afterward I heard crying behind her closed door. When our trajectories crossed two hours later, Luey's face wore a No Trespassing sign. Yesterday her hair, which hasn't been cut for months, billowed around her shoulders. Today it is pulled into a hurried topknot and she is wearing a pair of Ben's oldest, most cottony pajamas. Luey and I are due for a big talk, and I am counting on a few hours with Daniel to give me the wallop of radiant energy I need to initiate it.

My daughter pats her bump. "I hope I'll be the kind of woman who gives birth in the middle of a field," she says.

Fat chance. She hasn't been in a field since she played soccer. I make a mental note to ask when her next appointment will be with the midwife, and if drugs — many drugs, very strong ones — are an option. This is a girl who fainted before her wisdom teeth were extracted. As did I.

"I see the dog business is thriving," Daniel says.

"I'm turning the hounds away," Luey reports, as she continues to scrutinize Daniel's artists' work. "I can manage four plus Sadie, but I tried a fifth one week and now I totally get 'barking mad.' "

"Has Nicola found that necklace?" Daniel asks. I hear him trying to be casual, but this had to be the subject of Stephan's keynote address as soon as Daniel stepped off the plane from Italy.

Luey looks up from the laptop. "Necklace," she says. "What necklace?"

I was hoping I wouldn't need to tell the tale, but now that I do, I'm careful to salt my account with *maybe* and *misplaced*. Yet there is nothing like a giant scoop of schadenfreude to lift a younger sister's morning.

"Nicola lost a diamond necklace?" Luey asks, incredulous.

"Looks that way," I say.

"Poor Cola," she says, which is not what I expected. She unwinds and twists her hair into an even messier bun than its earlier version.

I am relieved when Daniel begins to report on and debate the merits of gelato with candied orange peel or the sort infused with hot pepper and cinnamon. Will I ever get another stamp on my passport? So caught am I in this spurt of self-pity that I don't notice the rumble of a car in my driveway. "You have a gentleman caller," Daniel says, peering through the slats of the window blinds, "driving a BMW."

Nat? He said he couldn't visit this weekend, yet here he is, I hope, to surprise me. All week, as I've performed workaday tasks, I have been taking our embrace to its logical conclusion. With each round of fantasy we come more clearly into focus. I am writing my own story, sentence by sentence. Ben and I may be yoked by history, but our bond has suffered a mortal rupture, and in that crevasse I have started to recognize a place for Nat, a man who I believe may become precious to me, a flawed, fully-formed adult, not a girl stretching to be a woman.

When I think of Nat, I like where my mind is leading me — away from Ben. I feel certain he would be a lover built from kindness, strength, and everything good. If I get to know him better, will I learn that he, too, has mysteries? Will there be obfuscation and semitruths? These are risks I am willing to take. I have widow-waited long enough.

But the man locking his car, looking purposeful, isn't Nat.

"Decided to revisit the scene of the crime?" I say as I welcome Wally Fleigelman. He is a creature from the black lagoon wearing head-to-toe Prada, the rich man's Gap.

"Love the gallows humor." He thrums with unexpected merriment as he kisses me on the cheek. "I took a chance you'd be home."

"This is a social visit?"

"The price of that answer is a cup of coffee." He removes his cashmere overcoat, which I hang in the front closet. "Two sugars."

This time better not get charged to my ledger. A cuppa is all I am paying for, I think, and lead him toward the kitchen.

"Nice place," Wally says as he eyes an antique church pew lining the wall.

"If you want to bid up the house," I say, "stand in line."

"Got a buyer?"

"So it seems," I answer. The offer still waves in the air like a sock on a line.

"Oh, forgive me," Wally says as we reach the kitchen and Daniel gets up to greet him. "I'm interrupting."

"Not at all," Daniel says, extending his hand for a manly shake. "Daniel Russianoff." I like that he chooses not to add *Georgia's brother's partner* and enjoy watching Wally glance from Daniel to me and do the three's-a-crowd math.

"I'll just stay a few minutes," Wally adds.

I eye his briefcase as I use up the last of the fine coffee Nat brought last week. Tomorrow, Chock Full o' Nuts. After Wally asks about the best route to the ocean — "As long as I'm out here I have to see it" — he quizzes Daniel on his line of work, so he can see if my possible suitor deserves a place on the Fleigelman map of all-that-matters. Wally opens his briefcase.

"For you." He removes an envelope and pushes it toward me on the table. "Perhaps you'll want to open it later," he adds. *In private,* is the message I receive, *when you're not entertaining a one-night stand.*

"Daniel and I have no secrets," I say, and steel myself. I think of how I had to deliver skinny envelope after skinny envelope to Nicola after she'd applied to colleges. In my experience, a thin envelope does not bring good news.

I carefully open the envelope and find a check from Fleigelman, Kelly, Rodriguez and Roth made out to me. The sum is for $100,000, each zero staring at me in bug-eyed shock, which I return.

"So, you've starting to find our money?"

"Not exactly. It appears you have a secret admirer," Wally says, grinning.

"I don't understand."

I expect a story with embellishment, but all Wally says is, "A money order arrived in the office yesterday."

"From where?"

"There was no return address."

My eyes dart to Daniel. If this is his — or Stephan's — way of bailing me out, I am overwhelmed and immensely moved, yet I cannot keep their money. This much I have learned during the past few months: I will earn my own respect only by taking care of myself — self-sufficiency has become my all and everything. But I believe I know Daniel fairly well, and he looks as startled by this check as I must.

"You don't know who sent it?" I ask Wally.

"I couldn't say."

" 'Couldn't say' or won't say?" I ask. Perhaps Wally wrote it himself, overcome by guilt bred from faulty advice. This check might be his prickly ethical payback.

"The money was sent to the estate of Benjamin T. Silver," he informs me. "Your benefactor has gone to a fair amount of trouble to protect his identity, so while I'd like to trace it, there's no way. This donor obviously wants to stay anonymous."

"What the hell?" I didn't intend to say that aloud.

"The philosopher Maimonides is famous for saying anonymity is the highest level of charity," Wally adds.

"*Charity?* I am not a charity case." I drop the check as if it's dusted with Agent Orange. It must be from Stephan, and if he wants to give me money, I'd prefer that he hand it over directly. "What do you suggest that I do with this check?"

"I suggest, Georgia Waltz, that you deposit it. I'm guessing it's from one of Ben's deadbeat clients. Maybe someone grew a conscience."

I sit dumbly for a moment, then stagger along with Wally to the front hall and collect his coat. He kisses me lightly on the cheek. "You have no idea how good it feels to a lawyer who gets to deliver good news," he says, and leaves in a cloud of smugness.

"You've been staring at that check like it's a land mine," Daniel says.

409

He throws his arm around my shoulder and hugs, tight. "Why don't you accept that you've gotten lucky?"

I've always believed the essence of luck is to recognize her when she camps out on your front lawn. Should your streak run sour, if you see that interloper at all, you expect her no to turn around and tell you that she owns the property — and that you owe back rent. Which is why the only luck I wholly trust now is the sort I make myself.

"What do you say we deposit the sucker, like your lawyer suggested?" Daniel adds. "Later on if you find out who your benefactor is and are revolted, you'll give back the money."

I nod in numb agreement, my hands shaking, and Daniel understands that I am in no condition to be behind a wheel, so Sadie and I tumble into Stephan's car. At the ATM I can barely complete the deposit slip, though when I feed the check to the jaws of the bank, I feel a jolt of relief.

From there Daniel and I hit the beach, where Sadie is as oblivious to her improved circumstances as I am mystified and mistrustful of mine. It's chilly, but brisk air is the tonic I need. "It's not enough for me to live on until I'm one hundred, you realize," I say as I toss a stick for Sadie. "I still need to sell the house and find a way to finish paying for Luey's education and support myself" — possibly for more than forty years.

"Think of it as a down payment on your happiness," Daniel says, Hallmark card-ish, "not some bunker of gloom."

"Where did that check come from?" I ask at least four times, as if I am Camille wondering when lunch will be served. I also make a mental note: *Georgia, visit your mother.*

"Like Wally said, maybe it's from one of Ben's clients who got religion and paid a debt." If the money came from Stephan, Daniel is not going to out him.

Daniel and I scuffle along under a shale gray sky until the cold, hunger, and impending nightfall defeat us. On the way home, we buy the makings of a celebratory dinner — steak, the first spring asparagus, and a chocolate cake iced in mocha decadence.

When we get back to the house, Luey and the car are nowhere to be seen. "I won't be home late, don't worry," a note says. She knows I will.

While the steaks marinate, Daniel and I settle down for Scrabble. He is an ace, given to kicking off games by using all seven letters and scoring fifty extra points. He also has an uncanny ability to draw the Z, X, and J, which he plays on premium squares. I begin with *cark*. Given the muzziness of my mind, I'm not half-bad today.

"You made that up," he says. "What's a 'cark?'"

"It means worry," I say. "Trust me, that's a subject on which I am an expert. Want to challenge?"

Daniel backs down, knowing if he loses the challenge, he'll forfeit his turn.

He plays *rowan*.

"That's a name," I say. "No proper nouns."

"Also a tree," he informs me.

Gloating, a few plays later I put down *oryx* on a double-word score.

"Well done," he says. He plays *yahoo*.

I snap back with *dilly*.

On a triple-word score Daniel builds *dilly-dally*.

I carefully put the letters for *napery* on the board. Fifty-point bonus!

"You can't play that," he informs me.

"I most certainly can. It means table linen. You know, napkins, tablecloths. My mother always uses the word." At least she used to.

"I know what it means, but there's only one p. I'm going to challenge," he says.

"Where's the Scrabble dictionary I gave you?"

"Luey's room, probably," I say. "She and Cola were playing a few weeks ago." I go upstairs and begin to search but I can't find it anywhere in the anarchy of her possessions. "We'll have to check online," I inform him.

"Isn't it against the law to live in a house without a dictionary? It's like not having a smoke detector. Next thing you'll tell me you've never registered to vote."

Now that he mentions it, I never did, out here. "You know, there may be a dictionary in the books I brought from the city," I say in my defense. It would be in the box with the first gift Ben gave me, a book of Dylan Thomas poetry.

We go to the basement, which is damp and dim. Ben's wind-surfer fills one corner, a hulking monument to middle-aged denial that Luey plans to sell on Craigslist this summer. A refrigerator and freezer, circa 1985, handed down from my parents' house, stand side-by-side, unplugged. The last time I used either one was for extra drinks and ice cream last summer when we gave our Labor Day barbecue.

Boxes brought from the city are in the corner, two labeled kids' books. I start with one of the other boxes, where I find a complete set of Shakespeare, college art history texts, and many lavish tomes about home decorating and antiques. Daniel searches through a load of potboilers, Harry Potters, and reference books.

"Pay dirt," he shouts, and pulls out a relic whose binding is dried and broken, a leather-bound *American Heritage College Dictionary* embossed in fading gold with the initials BTS, my gift to Ben when he graduated from college. I know its inscription. "To Benjy, with a heart of happiness. Please see page 819. I will love you forever. Georgia." Page 819 features the definition of *love,* which I underlined and circled with a girlish red heart, faded to sienna.

I look over Daniel's shoulder until he finds the page that begins with *nanofabrication* and ends with *narcotic.* When he gets there, a scrap torn from a yellow legal pad flutters to the floor. The paper is filled with handwriting that looks rushed and unmistakably Ben's.

I pick up what appears to be the draft of a letter. "Darling," it begins. But this isn't meant for me. It's filed under the page that includes, "Na-o-mi (ney-*oh*-me,) the mother-in-law of Ruth and the great-grandmother of David, from a Hebrew word meaning 'pleasant.' "

"This is hard to write, but I will try. I realize I have been lying to myself. I despise when I lie," he begins.

"Naomi, love, I thought I could leave Georgia, but I can't. As harsh as this sounds, it doesn't change how I feel about you. I adore you. Every moment we have shared is authentic, and I have felt that way since Hawaii."

His Honolulu marathon was five years ago. I didn't travel there with Ben because Luey was still in high school. I was the parent who remained on duty.

The next paragraph is slashed through, yet legible: "If I'd met you first, things might have been different. I will try to do Right by you — by all of us — but I can't find a way to you, because — there you have it — I am unable to leave my first family."

I trip up at "first family." I have known Ben to be more eloquent. Should I take solace in the banality, or is there another, smoother version of this letter somewhere? Did he even send it? How much of it is true?

"Georgia, Nicola, and Louisa — each one is tender in her own way. I say this not to hurt you or diminish what we have. I wish I could clone myself and be by your side as well as theirs, because you, too, are wrapped

415

around my heart. You need to know and believe that, because it is true."

He has a sense of humor, even in a love letter, because he writes, "I dream every man's fantasy, that we could all live together." It isn't crossed out.

"This is torment, to disappoint you and to deceive Georgia. I don't know what to do with the torture, which grows by the day."

45.

In the Tao of Nicola, a baseline tenet had been to always mistrust her sister. So when Luey spoke in breathy exclamation points, she did not rush to call back.

"I gather this isn't the best time for you, with the necklace and all," Luey said when they spoke. Nicola had been hoping Luey didn't know. "About that . . ." Luey added. "What does it look like?"

"Eighteen-carat gold, pave diamonds — a heart. Why?"

"Do you have a picture?"

"Like, from a Web site? No. I've been telling Uncle Nineteenth Century how much we need one."

"How about the kind of picture lovesick puppies take whenever they're out in public?"

"Possibly," Nicola said.

"Well, if your Michael T. has a picture, send it to me."

"Why?"

"Just send it."

Nicola did. In the picture, the necklace was clearly twinkling though her mouth was agape, mid-admonishment, telling Michael T. to get his phone out of her face.

"Meet me at the Astor Room at six," Luey said when the picture arrived.

Nicola proudly took the subway to Astoria and found Luey at the restaurant, another achievement.

"I'm sorry, we're booked," the hostess informed them. Her sneer said, *It's eight o'clock on a Saturday night. What did you expect, losers?*

Luey stepped forward. Before Nicola's eyes, her pregnant sister transformed into their father, who with winning resolve had not only always been able to articulate his demands but generally enjoyed an 80-percent-and-above success record in having them met to his satisfaction. As Luey shook the hostess's well-manicured hand, she held up Nicola's picture. "We wondered if you'd seen this necklace?" The hostess smoothed her bob, as shiny as wet shoe polish, while Luey continued, "The stones are cubic zirconia and not worth a thing, but our dead father gave it to our mother so it has a lot of sentimental value." Luey's kick in the ankles told Nicola to shut up.

The hostess and Luey sized each other up. "Wait here," she said. "And have a cocktail on us."

"That would be lovely." Nicola did not recall *lovely* being in Luey's standard vocabulary and her tone was all breezy confidence. The hostess led the sisters to the bar and whispered in the bartender's ear before she melted into the dark restaurant.

"I'll have a Pink Lady," Nicola said.

"Cranberry juice and seltzer with a twist," Luey said.

Nicola wondered why her sister was knocking herself out. Was Luey on a mission initiated by their mother, or feeling guilty for being, until recently, a pain in the butt who at least once a month Nicola wanted to upgrade to a more user-friendly model? "This is pretty terrific of you to go to all this effort," Nicola managed to say, "even if the necklace doesn't show up."

"I needed an adventure." As if having a baby alone wasn't adventure enough, Nicola thought.

"How's the job?" Luey asked.

"Great til Uncle Stephan got pissy over . . ." Nicola searched for a word — who could blame him for getting angry? "This carelessness of mine, and decided I must be a thief."

Her cocktail arrived and Nicola was impressed with its pinkness — like a carnation dancing with a salmon. She stirred the swizzler and took a sip. It tasted less demure than its name suggested.

"Tell me, does Michael T. have a chance?" Luey asked. "Seriously, Cola. After speaking to the guy for five minutes, I could tell he was nuts for you."

"I like him, but he's in Boston and my life feels too ragged right now to get serious anyway." She considered how exposed she felt by what she said, every bit of which was true.

"When hasn't your life been like that?" Luey asked.

"Ooh. Harsh," Nicola said, though that was not true of the cocktail, which she decided might become her drink of choice.

"Don't blow it with Michael T., Cola." Luey's voice had turned as uncharacteristically pacifying as elevator music.

Behind her, someone cleared their throat. Nicola turned. There was the hostess, who opened her hand and without ceremony placed the necklace in Nicola's hand.

"What?" Nicola shrieked. "Oh my God! Where did you find it?"

Luey pushed herself off the bar stool, waving away Nicola's question. "Okay, then," she said. The hostess, her back already to them, was moving quickly away despite five-inch heels. "Let's get out of here. I'll drive you home."

"How did you do that?" Nicola asked. "I called and —"

"Did you learn nothing from Daddy? Cola, I greased her palm."

46.

"Mother, I'm sorry it's been so long." I troop into The Oaks dripping guilt and perspiration. All is not right when it's seventy-four degrees in March. My magnolia tree bloomed a month ahead of schedule, and now that I don't employ Adam and Eve, I've been working outside in a T-shirt.

My mother doesn't — or won't — respond. It's been three weeks since I was here, and in that time she seems to have shrunk into a satellite of herself. I rub her arm gently. "It's Georgia," I say. "I'm here." She grits her teeth and shakes off my touch.

"Camille hasn't been talking much," Alice, her favorite caretaker, says, offering her ginger ale, which she pushes away.

"That's what the head nurse told me when I called yesterday, but she didn't know why," I say.

"She might have asked me." Alice sniffs. "Camille's all clammed up and teary because Mr. Blumstein's gone."

"Morris? No! He didn't . . ." I mouth the word *die.*

"Oh no. Moved away last week. Such a shame. He was a grand bit of stuff, that fella. Everyone's favorite."

"My mother must miss him terribly."

Alice clucks in agreement. "Camille here, she was his special bird. He already sent all the girls a big crate of oranges, but Camille got her own box and a letter. When I read it to her, she tore it up and flushed it down the loo. I tried to help her write back, but she refused."

"Was he sick?"

Alice brushes away the thought. "What happens is the children, they get old, too. His daughter retired to Tampa and she didn't want to leave him up north, all alone."

"He wasn't alone — he had me." It's my mother speaking, her head turning stiffly toward us, an animatronic figure coming to life, her voice croaky from disuse.

"Mother, I'm so sorry to hear about Morris leaving," I say. "Maurice, excuse me." Is there anyone else she'll even talk to?

"Men!" she says. "Can't trust the shits, can you?"

I usually second my mother's motions, a

habit I picked up when I realized my father considered this the path of least resistance to four-part Waltz harmony. But now I refuse to let myself become a woman whose knee-jerk response to Camille's question is yes, because for every Ben on his worst day, there was a Ben on a better day. There are Nat and Daniel, always, and much of Stephan, at least lately. I hope I am never done with men.

"Morris moved to be with his family."

"But he had me," she frets, and sticks out her bottom lip. "He didn't even say good-bye."

"Now, Camille, that's not true." Alice's brogue takes the edge off her upbraiding. "He came 'round special for you every dinner hour, and at his going-away tea you were seated by his side like the queen of the May. Your friend was in a tiff about it. She's a mean old biddy, that Vera," she adds, conspiratorially, her voice lowered.

I hope the mention of my mother's loyal opposition will please her, but she frowns. "Maurice took off like a bat out of hell." Her truth and she's sticking to it.

Alice laughs. "Anything more I can do for you ladies?"

"Thanks for everything. We'll see you later."

I sit across from my mother and reach into my bag. Camille Waltz has never failed to light up at the sight of small boxes, silky ribbon, and shiny paper, though it has become difficult to find presents now that she can no longer focus on a book, turn on a CD, and has lost interest in clothes. I bring candy, flowers, or a plant — today it's yellow tulips — as well as a bonus, which she unwraps. It's a photograph.

She leans forward and traces the framed image shown in murky black and grayish white. "Is this modern art?" she asks.

"This is Luey's little baby growing inside her," I explain. "A picture from her ultrasound." A year ago my mother knew the term.

"Why is the head so big? Does it have hydrocephalus?"

I will myself poise and a cool temper. She can remember that term but not what we talked about four minutes ago. "This is what a fetus looks like at six months."

"Ugly?"

"Not to me," I say. "Not to Luey." She drops the photograph. "Would you like to rest?" I ask.

"No," she snaps. "Do you think I'm an old lady who needs to nap?"

I do. Ten minutes feels like ten hours.

"What did Maurice say in the letter Alice mentioned?"

"Who, pray tell, is Alice?"

It will be a long afternoon. "Excuse me for a moment," I say, and leave the room. I return from the lounge with paper cups of tea. Fifteen minutes.

I pull out a copy of Ben's letter. "I'd like your opinion, Mother, on a letter I found." I'd like her to let me know if she believes what Ben has said, and then I will be glad if she will forget our conversation. Perception seems to ignite in her dark brown eyes. Please let that flame stay lit. "It's from my husband," I explain. "To another woman."

"Ben's lady friend? That bitch?"

Did all of The Oaks know? "I'm not sure she's evil. Just another woman."

Someone new, the last thing I could be.

" 'Darling.' That's what he calls her, 'darling.' But her name is Naomi." I read the letter, choking twice . . . "He must have met her when he ran that marathon in Honolulu," I add, and read down the most chilling words. " 'I can't leave my first family.' " I brush away a tear to say, "He calls us his 'first' family. Does that mean the woman has a child? That there's a second family?"

My mother is making eye contact with me,

alert. "Go on."

I read sentence after sentence, stopping at, " 'I dream that we could all live together.' Isn't that rich — 'we could all live together'? I wonder if I'd get to be number-one wife?"

"Keep going. I love this book."

I skip to the bottom. Ben wasn't exactly John Adams. " 'The net net . . .' Can you believe he wrote 'net net' in a love letter?"

"Read!"

" 'I've thought of telling Georgia, of asking for her blessing or even to separate so you and I could be together, but that would break her heart and she's my wife.' "

"He underlines this. See?" I show the letter to my mother. Her eyes have shuttered, but I continue aloud. There is comfort in reading, as if I am a child enjoying a fairy tale, not a horror story about ruination in a marriage. I wonder if Ben recopied and ever sent this letter. My mind goes blank when I try to imagine how Naomi might have felt if and when she got it — or might feel now. I have room for only my feelings, vast and malignant.

There is more, but I stop. I am lulled by mingled accents from the hall — Jamaican, Irish, Puerto Rican, Russian, and the patois of southern New Jersey. Ben's letter has deepened the enigma.

Loyalty is a tight weave, a heathery tweed of which love is only one fiber, but in marriage loyalty can also be two people moving through life on parallel lines, never becoming one. Passion is a rocky EKG, but it's a single line. I wish I knew Ben's devotion to me was built as much on passion, a less dependable fabric than the feathers, angora, and satin of ball gowns and tuxedos. Passion is *Sense and Sensibility* and *A Man and a Woman* and also, I'd like to think, Ben Silver and Georgia Waltz, celebrating their twenty-fifth anniversary fucking and making love and everything in between one entire rainy weekend at Casa Del Mar. We stopped and started and sipped Bellinis and listened to the Pacific knocking on the front door. Loyalty is a stately hymn. Passion is pheromones flying, shouting, *I love you, I love you,* round and round, forever.

I hear footsteps and open my eyes, half-expecting to see Ben. My brother is filling the doorway, wearing concern. "Stephan, I wasn't expecting you," I say.

"Nor I, you," he offers over our mother's snores. Despite her diminutive size, she rumbles like heavy machinery.

"I'm sorry I haven't gotten here much," I say, as I stand to hug. "I've fallen down on the job."

"You have a full plate." I enjoy the brief touch of our cheeks. His heavy beard is shaved to kid leather smoothness, like our father's always was.

"Did you hear everything?"

"Enough." After a minute or two, his voice goes soft. "Do the words make you feel better?" he asks.

"I'd feel better if Ben was alive and I never knew about this. I was happy not knowing."

I'd like to turn back the clock to my own age of innocence. Stephan covers my hand with his. In my fifty years, I never remember a gesture this intimate and openhearted from the brother I wrote off as cold-blooded. This makes me want to cry, but he will be horrified by leaky, womanly emotion, so I shut my eyes tight against the tears.

" 'I sometimes think that God, in creating man, somewhat over-estimated his ability,' " Stephan says, invoking his patron saint.

I smile up at him. "Ben was just a guy, flawed as any."

"More flawed than most. We're not all Bens."

"Do you have any more choice material where that came from?" I have always liked this game Stephan plays.

He thinks a moment and comes up with, " 'In married life, three is company and two is none.' "

"You can't possibly believe that."

"Okay, I have it," he says. " 'I am so clever that sometimes I don't understand a single word of what I say.' "

"That's the most humble remark you've ever made. Too bad it's not original."

"Old Oscar doesn't mind. We're on excellent terms."

I'd like to think Stephan and I might be, too. I take a breath and dare to ask, "Are you my mysterious benefactor?"

Those gray eyes frack into me. "If I were, it would make your life a bit tidier, wouldn't it?"

"I doubt my life will ever be tidy. I'm aiming for content."

"Of course it has occurred to me to give you money," Stephan says, his voice low and measured. "If and when you truly need it, I will. I'm not going to let you starve or make you beg. But you aren't quite at the end of your rope, so no, that check didn't come from me — or Daniel, if that's what you're wondering."

Did my brother say "end of your rope" or "end of your hope"? As I sit in the dwindling light, I realize they are the same and I am not at the end of either.

"You don't have to stick around, now that

I'm here," he offers. "You have the longer drive."

I gather my things, stopping to show Stephan the newest family portrait. "Your great-niece or great-nephew," I say.

"Looks just like Dad," he says.

I kiss my sleeping mother good-bye, and Stephan escorts me to the lobby. "I don't know where or how, but did you hear — Nicola found the necklace?" he says, as he pushes open the front door.

"I did." *Thank God.* "I knew she would."

"I have big plans for that girl," Stephan says, then he kisses me on each cheek and sends me on my way.

I arrive home to an unkempt dog of no breed that the Westminster Kennel Club has ever recognized. He greets me like an intimate, jumping so we are nose to nose. The beast races to Luey and pants until she makes him beg for one of the fancy biscuits she buys in fifteen-pound sacks. I don't want to imagine what part of a wooly sheep "lamb meal" comes from. Even less "chicken meal." Not to be undone, a wagging Sadie shows up and begs for a biscuit, too, years of training undone.

"What happened to 'only dogs under thirty pounds'?" I ask Luey.

"I made an exception for Lester," she says as the dog chomps, scattering crumbs on the kitchen floor. "He's Peter's."

Proceed with caution: parental peril ahead, I warn myself. "I'm glad you and Peter are friends."

"We were never friends," she says, yet her composure tells me something connects them now other than a bridge between disappointment and distrust. "I agreed to take care of my buddy here til Peter gets back from his tour. I couldn't stand to see Lester in a kennel." At hearing his name, the dog attaches himself to Luey's side. When she stops petting him, he starts sniffing Sadie, who graciously returns the favor, happy as any woman around here to have a suitor.

"How's Nana?" she asks.

"She's slipped some. Morris moved to Florida."

"Why would he do that to her?"

"He didn't have a choice. Family loyalty."

"Ah, loyalty," she says.

I see her weighing the good and bad of this notion. I applauded her yesterday when she told me of the derring-do she engineered to find Nicola's necklace. As I heard the tale, I was sure she was as happy about this as Cola. I like who Louisa Silver-Waltz is becoming.

In the living room, she built a fire, using up the last of this winter's supply of wood. Soon I'll have to rustle up some new birch logs for the hearth. But now, I feed Ben's letter to the flames.

47.

"Gridlock on twenty-seven," Nat says from his cell phone. I break a sweat through my own gridlock.

Luey departed early this morning for Brooklyn, as nervous as I've seen her since she took a driving test. Early in the week I asked to accompany her to meet the couple she'd anointed, out of a field of forty-some candidates, as possible parents for the baby. She wisely refused, knowing I'd be wearing every feeling like a blinking emoticon.

I invited Nat to visit and told myself that for the next twenty-four hours I will think only of sex, which has put me in a born-again virgin state, wondering if I'll be able to remember which parts go where. I am counting on my animal alter ego to wake from hibernation, though I'm unable to picture rapture, bodice ripping, or reckless endangerment. I've never been with a man other than my husband and hope my spinsterish equipment is still in working order. Birds do it, bees do it, even folks with old arthritic knees do it. Why not me? I don't want to fall in love, necessarily. I just want to do it. I am afraid of what will happen when Nat and I make love, yet more afraid of what will happen if we don't. I'm far too young for a life sentence of chastity.

"Can't wait to see you," says my knight-errant with his Zipcar steed. I picture my erudite Eros striding through the door armed with a wry grin and *The New York Review of Books.*

I say the same and hope my voice isn't trembling.

I'm setting my expectations low, not vamping it up and answering the door in only a corset UPS'd from Victoria's Secret. There was a sale at Target, however, a store I used to visit to load up only on detergent and paper towels, and I have invested in new underwear. Since the last time I shopped in a lingerie department — excuse me, *intimate apparel,* a term freighted with innuendo — reliable string bikinis have vanished. I wanted to Munch-scream as I hovered in front of the racks, sizing up the alternatives: commodious granny pants my own mother would reject, impermeable "shape-wear" engineered by NASA, thongs only slightly bigger than their hangtags, and lacy boy shorts that would sit jauntily on my hips and leave my belly as exposed as a bowl of rice pudding. Butt or belly, butt or belly — which is the lesser evil? I considered going commando, then hedged my bets by picking one of each of the short-style in ecru and in navy blue. Black was too-too.

I've done all I can to prep my outer self for a man's touch, thanks to a series of ablutions as long as childbirth. I've pedicured my feet in the fetching shade of Tart Deco, moisturized, waxed, exfoliated, and pumiced. Red wine awaits with cheese from the expensive section of the supermarket. Since a fifty-year-old woman is most flattered by male voices who might still think of her as young, I have set the mood by bringing out the sandpapery geezers — Lou Reed, Leonard Cohen, Bob Dylan, Barry White, and Kris Kristofferson. "Help me make it through the night" — or at least the afternoon.

If someone would coerce me into describing sex with Ben, I would have said that seduction improved over time and would pick words like *sensual* and *playful, intuitive* and *tender.* I'm not sure how much of the fulfillment came from him and how much from me. Can I be the same woman with another man? Was he different with Naomi? *Stop that, Georgia,* I tell myself. Today I'm hoping I will become another woman, as able to excite and satisfy as become excited and satisfied. Maybe I'll need some new music.

"There's my Georgia," Nat says as he walks through the door and returns me to reality.

"There's my Nat." I wriggle my hands underneath his winter coat and thick turtle-neck while Sadie and the lot greet him with the same boundless enthusiasm they might display if one of their beloveds returned from a tour in Afghanistan or a drive to the dump.

And then we kiss. "Now that's a greet-ing," he says as he drops his coat on the floor.

"No, this is," I say, and wrap my arm around his waist as I lead him upstairs. Ben always ran first thing in the morning, "before he knew what hit him" and had a chance to change his mind. In this spirit, I've decided to take Nat immediately to my bedroom, and as I thank Ben for the pointer, tell him he can leave now. He's not invited to this party.

"You're like silk," Nat says as he strokes me.

When a lover murmurs a cliché, what woman isn't willing to consider it original and accurate? I have no language to return, or any wish to talk, only a caress here, a thrust there. The bedroom shades are half-drawn for maximal privacy and minimal cellulite exposure. When we start, I am overly aware of awkwardness — new sounds, new smell, new strokes — and I begin to doubt that making love in this bedroom will offer the home-field advantage I thought it might provide. But then I close my eyes and as Nat and I find our rhythm, I realize I am in no hurry to move away from this present perfect tense, our own rough draft of love-making grammar. He's not an unblemished specimen and neither am I and it doesn't matter. He's had a wife — for eighteen years — and I've had a husband, but they are in the past, relegated to photo albums and, at least for me, a lobotomized portion of my brain. When we end, I turn and touch Nat's face, glad to scratch this accomplishment off my list so we can do it again.

"How was your week?" he asks, exactly like a returning boyfriend might, as I fit myself into the V of his shoulder.

I don't need to check the clock. "I'll be hearing from Luey soon, hopefully. She met with a couple who want to adopt her baby."

"I can't imagine any of that — it must be hell — and I have a pretty good imagination." He leers Groucho-like so I recognize the compliment.

I've tried not to lecture Luey on what she should and shouldn't do, but I'm sure I'm about as transparent as a cellophane noodle. "This is almost the last situation in which I ever imagined my family," I say to Nat. The last is Ben's betrayal, because even if he didn't leave me for Naomi, he considered it — and who's to say if he had lived, he wouldn't have changed his mind? And why am I thinking about this now, damnit, when I want to return to the moment of having made love to Nat? Mother trumps tigress, however, and my overriding concern is what Luey will do about her child. I do not want to lose my grandchild. I want her to keep the baby.

"You're strong, Georgia," he says. "One of the top fifty things I love about you."

"Flattery will get you everywhere."

"I'm already there."

I had forgotten about the ancient art of postcoital conversation, where you need to display no wit to elicit a smile. After briefly drowsing under the covers, twined around each other, we begin again, a little less minimalist — classic with an omnivorous twist or two.

After round two, I watch Nat sleep, taking note of how natural he looks sharing my bed, and how unlike Ben, who spread his long arms and legs over three-fourths of the mattress. Nat is compact and pulls me close, as if he wants to make sure I won't leave. I shut my eyes and doze. When I wake, it is past six. Nat is still here, and not just here but comfortably asleep.

I tiptoe downstairs. Luey has come and gone. A note says she's meeting her friend Marc for dinner. I am tempted to call Luey, and am proud as I resist. I will need to wait longer for the big reveal.

The cheese and wine remain where I left them. I pour myself a glass while I sort the mail Luey's brought in and left on the table. Two plant catalogs, gas and electric bills, a Brown alumni bulletin, and a letter from Westchester Hills, the woodland cemetery where Ben is buried a stone's throw from George and Ira Gershwin, Tony Randall, and a mausoleum full of Guggenheims.

"Dear Ms. Silver-Waltz," it begins. "In Jewish tradition it is customary for the grave marker to be put in place and an unveiling ceremony to be held no later than one year after the death. While many families wait until almost the full year has passed, an unveiling may be done sooner. In Israel, the stone is usually placed soon after the first thirty days of mourning. Please let us know your intentions on behalf of Benjamin T. Silver. . . ."

The kind sirs of Westchester Hills go on to suggest a variety of establishments where I, the bereaved consumer, might purchase a tasteful headstone. They suggest that it would be wise to place my order several months in advance of the unveiling and to begin considering an appropriate message.

On that score, Ben had something in mind. We stopped at a cemetery once in Southampton and he was taken by Jack Dempsey's epitaph: *A gentle man and a gentleman.* I'm thinking more along the lines of, *Husband — father — son — philanderer.*

I hear Nat, and stash my macabre mail in one the catalogs.

"Georgia," he says, with a coaxing and ripeness almost like foreplay. He kisses me lightly on the lips and then the top of my head.

"Hey, you." I like his white T-shirt hanging over his jeans, his bare feet, his compact paunch, his rumpled hair. I like everything about Nat and about today.

"Are we cooking?"

"That's the plan."

"No Luey?"

"Only me." We cook and eat and shower and watch half a movie before we're back in bed, the best day and night of my life for almost six months.

48.

Nat leaves earlier than I expect, shortly after ten. "You need time with your daughter," he says.

There's sense and sensitivity in that, which I appreciate, but what's the point of living near the Atlantic and paying fat taxes if you and a lover can't have a briny hike on the shore, fulfilling the requirement of two out of three personal ads? I'd pictured us at the beach. As we stand by his car, I could take him upstairs all over again.

"I'll be at the London book fair next week, but back here the weekend after — if you'll have me," he says.

"Of course I'll have you." *Don't be such a girl,* I tell myself. *This is how things work. Stop imagining the swash is gone from his buckle. Nat's as airborne as you are, but he has two stores to run, a trip to take, and, for all you know — and hope against — other women to see.* "I'm going to stand here until I can't see you anymore."

"I'm going to replay our adult movies, and hope I don't crash."

I wave as he drives off, and when his car turns the corner, I remind myself that this, too, is how it feels to be with a man, to miss the sound of his voice and laugh the minute he is gone. Hello, 1983.

I change into ancient jeans, a tattered sweatshirt, and one of Ben's rattier baseball caps. Now that I've turned into both Adam and Eve, I need to attack the spring cleanup and plantings. Chip has lectured me on the necessity of curb appeal. His California customers liked the house enough to agree to a two-month postponement, which means that in four weeks I either accept their terms and set a closing date or pass up this chance and pray for another buyer.

Every day this week I raked and collected winter debris, and don't my bones and muscles know it, especially after my workout in bed. Cutting grass will be tomorrow's task — the lawn is greening up, and Luey scored a mower at a garage sale. I'd like a day off, but there's a job to be done before a storm hits. I slip on my garden gloves and begin to turn over the earth in preparation for flats of pansies and petunias. The dirt is yielding, like stiff dough. I dig a hole, wiggle a plant from its casing, and pat it in place. I repeat the process again and again, finding peace in the repetition of homey horticulture. Soon two lines of plum pansies curtsy like kindergarteners. I can see why my brother draws the line at these flowers, but I have loved them forever, as I do the complete retinue of old-fashioned blossoms — asters and peonies, hollyhocks and cosmos, wisteria and lilies of the valley.

I am ready to start on the petunias when from across the yard Luey shouts, "Need a hand?" The dogs are off their leashes. They stampede in my direction, tails and limbs aloft, happiness distilled to a blur of reckless energy.

When she saw Nat and me together, Luey strained for blasé, as if every morning a man who wasn't her father sat at her mother's side with his thinning hair dripping from the shower. I imagined her trying to think about anything but what had recently transpired in my bed.

"You're just in time!" I shout, eager for her company. "Why don't you start on the vinca — if you're not too uncomfortable?" Seemingly overnight, like a flower herself, Luey has blossomed. She is carrying her child exactly how she positioned herself in my womb — high, narrow, and vertical, as

445

if she wanted to be introduced to whoever was out there.

Luey kneels on the ground with surprising grace. "It's good to see Nat here," she says, as she grabs the trowel and begins to dig.

"I feel the same way," I say, though I hear my own reluctance. Can I be open to anyone again? Where is my money-back guarantee?

"He's a great guy, Ma. I hope he's more than a practice run."

"My whole life feels ad-lib right now." It's surprisingly fine, I realize, to take each day as it comes. "I'm glad you like him." I plant another pansy. "Does it seem strange to see us together in . . . that way?"

"It does," Luey says. "Good strange. You're special, Ma. You deserve the best."

Like your father? Not like your father? "I appreciate that." I pat a plant in place, divot after divot. "What was that couple like yesterday?" I anchor my eyes to a petunia to tamp down my curiosity, which is acute.

"Pretty much ideal." She praises the food, the house, and the books, details I would care about if she'd gone to a party, not to meet the potential mother and father of her child.

"You can tell this how?"

"They're mature — they must be close to forty — and smart."

If only people got wise simply by having birthdays. "You're smart."

"But they're secure, reliable, prosperous, polished. Want me to go on?" Her usually well-modulated voice goes high. "I felt like a sham next to the wife, like I was wearing a pillow under my shirt for a school play and she was the one with a funky stripe down her belly and a belly button like a third nipple."

Luey is trying — and failing — to laugh. I gather her in my arms, her pregnancy between us like a warm knot tying three generations. She smells both sweet and salty, like she did as a girl after coming in from roller skating in the park.

"It must have been hell," I say, patting her back.

"They want this baby so badly." A tear drops on my neck. "My baby."

When Ben and I adopted Cola, we became a triptych greater than the sum of its parts. "Who can blame them? You could make their world."

Luey doesn't let go. "The whole ride home I started to think, what if the baby I gave away is the next Steve Jobs and when I'm fifty and go looking for him he spits on me? Or she's a girl who publishes a memoir about how her mama abandoned her at birth? I don't want to be the witch who does that to her child."

I have no answers. All I can do is crush my daughter against me.

"I want to be more than an egg donor. Louisa Silver-Waltz, cautionary tale — that story's getting old."

"Listen." I push her away to see her face. "Be whoever you want."

"I want to be a mother, but I'm scared shitless."

"If a pregnant woman says she isn't scared, she's lying."

"The couple from yesterday aren't going to be the parents for my baby," she adds, answering the question no one has asked. "I can't do it. I called them this morning."

"My God, Luey." She has buried the lede. Now I am crying, too. "Honey, what did they say?"

"The wife wouldn't come to the phone. Her husband said I'm the third birth mother — God, I loathe that term, *birth mother,* like you can buy me at The Container Store — who changed her mind, and that he wasn't surprised. When I was quiet during the visit, he thought he could see my gears shifting. He asked if I had a problem with them, begging for advice. I told him they're perfect, that it was all because of me. Ma, it was awful, like I'm a conniving bitch."

I ache for these strangers, but my allegiance is to Luey and her baby, to my family. "I think you owe them a letter. Put your feelings down on paper for them — get it out and send the letter — and then think of your baby, *only* of the baby."

She wipes her tears on a sleeve and leans back, her legs stretched out on the grass.

"I'm proud of you for making this decision," I say, my mind already on knitting a bunting.

"Maybe I'm an idiot."

"Did you discuss all this with Peter?"

"Some." She threw her hands up, as if caught red-handed. "None."

I dare to ask, "Will you tell me now how things stand between you?"

Luey waits a moment before answering, pulling out a blade of grass and examining it. "He knew I was looking into adoption, that it had to be my choice."

"Lu, do you think he'd want to be . . . involved?"

"He's skittish — about me and especially about being with me and a baby — but he might come around, and if he doesn't, so be it," she says defiantly. "I'm making this decision without him. Obviously" — she pats her belly. "I don't have time to wait for him to figure things out. I should call him, though." She takes the trowel and starts to dig. "I thought telling the people from yesterday was going to be hard. . . ."

"It's all going to be hard."

"I have to get this right."

Yes, she has to get this right. Luey plants a vinca behind some pansies. I plant a petunia, then another. "I'm willing to be reprogrammed, inside and out, if that's what it takes. Cola promises she's on board, that she won't go back to Europe, but I'm going to need you, too, Ma. Will you help me?"

I know I will try, day by day, in any wingman role she wants. "Of course. Darling, of course."

I hear her sobs, as she can hear mine, but I can't see her face. We plant flowers, side by side for ten or fifteen minutes. Then she reaches for my hand and puts it on her stomach. "Feel that?" she says. "Buffalo Baby's kicking."

49.

I stand to admire my work. Chip is right. The color scheme is straight from the tween department, but my home now looks as if I give a damn.

Inside, under the letter from Westchester Hills, I find the gardening catalogs that arrived in yesterday's mail. I open one. Plant names call out to me. Eight Mile High Daylily, Red Creeping Thyme, Cranberry Crush Hardy Perennial Hibiscus, and Raspberry Mousse Toad Lily. I want them all, and how can I get a job naming flowers?

I reach for the second catalog. As I open it to consider the 41 percent discount on the Passion Flower collection, the pieces of mail I moved aside yesterday fall loose — bill, bill, bill, letter. I rip open the last and least threatening envelope, handwritten with penmanship of which nuns would approve. No return address.

A check falls out. It is drawn on the account of Naomi DeAngelo McCann for the sum of forty-thousand dollars.

I grab the edge of the kitchen chair to sit as the numbers swim. I feel stunned and light-headed. Have I been Tasered? I look again but there is no mistake. The check is made out to Georgia Waltz.

The memo line is blank. Interest due on the loan of a husband?

I'd been able to convince myself that the six-figure check came from one of Ben's delinquent clients. Anonymity was clean, unencumbered, and required no acknowledgment. I am stuck at the top of a Ferris wheel, afraid to look down.

Shaking, I carry the check upstairs, where I hide it under a book on my nightstand. It sits like a car bomb, waiting to explode the peace of my Jerusalem.

Over the next three days, I accompany Luey to a birthing class, mow the lawn, polish an essay about the tribulations of being a 384-pound high school senior — I thought *my* life had challenges — and plant a bed of lavender. Each night, Nat calls. Our pillow talk reminds me that I am a warm-blooded female who enjoys the attention of a male she wants to know better, yet as I come and go the check is a cryptogram reminding me that Naomi McCann and I have unfinished business.

After tonight's dinner with Luey, I work up the nerve to at least find out what Naomi is thinking. As I dial her number, I feel the cognitive dissonance that a lung cancer victim might feel who knows that a cigarette could kill her but smokes nonetheless. "She ain't here now," says the hag of the Hamptons when I ask for her daughter.

"It's Mrs. Silver," I say, as I never do. "Ben Silver's wife." I recite the number and ask Naomi to please get in touch.

She doesn't call that night, nor the following day, nor the next. I phone again. This time she answers. Even the words, "It's Georgia Waltz," are hard to spit out. Except when I had to let Opal and Fred go, can I remember another time when I have felt this awkward?

"Hello," Naomi says, conveying no surprise.

"The check you sent," I sputter, regretting that I haven't worked up a script, "would you explain it, please?"

"What do you want to know?" I read menace in her answer, but I would even if she were singing "Polly Wolly Doodle."

"Do you feel sorry for me?" I've worked hard not to throw a pity party.

"No sorrier than I feel for myself." It

sounds as if she is choking out her words. "I want to do the right thing." The pause is as long as a semester. "Try to understand. I loved Ben, too."

He was mine to love, mine alone. I don't want to understand. I refuse to try. "If I'd known the first check was from you, I wouldn't have deposited it." Menace is most definitely in my tone.

"Yet you did. You need the money, correct?"

"You can have it back. I haven't spent a cent."

"It's yours." Naomi's voice is controlled, though not cruel. "I'm sure you think I'm a lot of things, but I'm not a thief."

Except when it comes to my husband.

"Cookie?" peeps a small voice at the other end. "I want a cookie."

"What's the magic word?" Naomi asks.

"Please," the child squeaks.

Please let me figure out what's going on. What's the magic word for that?

"You have to wait a minute, Theo," she says. "Be patient, sweetie."

"It sounds like this isn't a good time." Though I'm the one who made the call, I have exhausted my courage and would gratefully postpone our conversation.

"You're right. I'm putting Theo to bed,

and then I'm going out. Can you speak tomorrow?" she asks.

"Sure." I tell myself I want this resolved.

"How's nine?"

"Okay, I'll call you."

"Georgia, it would be better if we'd talk face-to-face."

"Why?" Better for whom? Will it be a duel? Do I get to bring a second?

She says only, "Let's meet at Main Beach. I'll wait near the entrance."

I agree.

The dire occasion for which I've hoarded my last Ambien has arrived. I tell Luey I have a headache and not to wake me, even if Nat calls. Blessing pharmaceutical voo-doo, I set the alarm and swallow.

50.

Seven hours later I wake to fog. At this time of year it doesn't roll in on little cat feet. It arrives like a shroud catapulted from the heavens. By noon the sun may burn through, but now the sky is a dirty windshield. I dress in clothing that is equally drab, with the exception of my wedding ring, which I remove from its hiding place in a wooly sock and put on my finger for the first time since the day I left Wally's office. *Ben, what kind of fool's errand is this?* I think as I drink strong black coffee and mindlessly putter while I wait to leave.

Out of season, even on a Sunday morning, Main Beach is coldly empty, home to a scattering of walkers, often robotically tossing their retrievers a stick. It's devoid of sunbathers who have never heard of melanoma, sandcastle-building children whose parents are convinced they are the next I. M. Pei, and tourists searching for beach glass — beer bottles shrapnel they value like pirate doubloons. I park my car close to the entrance, tighten Ben's worn trench coat against the damp, and pull down my hat as if I am trying to disappear.

"Good morning," Naomi says, waiting at the edge of the parking lot. Her hair is too strawberry blond for her ruddy skin, but she's gone to the trouble of blowing it dry and waves frame her face. In a police lineup, you wouldn't pick her as a perp, though she might look familiar from church or the day care center. She's dressed in a barn jacket exactly like one of Ben's. I wonder if she bought his jacket as a gift, or vice versa. I am glad Ben's jacket now belongs to Fred, along with most of his wardrobe.

"Theo, not so far, honey!" she shouts into the mist.

A child in red trots toward me, a comet with rosy cheeks, and offers me a handful of shells.

"Why, thank you," I say, accepting the gift.

Theo giggles and turns to Naomi, grabbing her hand. "Do you mind this weather?" she says, touching my arm.

I pull away, but answer, "Not at all." Bracing air is what I need. My boots sink into the sand.

"There's so much I want to tell you," she says.

I'm not sure I want to hear it, but I surprise myself by saying, "Start at the beginning."

She takes a deep breath, as if she is going to blow out fifty birthday candles, and says, "Ben and I met in Hawaii." At Theo's pace, the three of us begin to walk down the beach. "It was a flirtation. Period. We didn't ask each other many questions." I look ahead into the nothingness. "I didn't know he was married, only that he was a runner from New York City. After the marathon, I never expected to see Ben Silver again. We didn't exchange numbers or emails and I didn't try to track him down."

Does Naomi McCann want a salute? Moisture is beading on my coat. I feel colder than I did all winter and am glad for Ben's leather gloves that I find in my pockets, though when I slip into them, I imagine Ben wearing them and holding her hand.

"Then we saw one another the following summer on this very beach, when I was out jogging."

I turn to look hard at Naomi's face. I see no softness in this woman. "Had I realized this was holy ground," I say, "I wouldn't have agreed to meet here."

"Please hear me out," she pleads against my sarcasm. I give consent by slogging straight ahead. "Something clicked. I was happier to find Ben again than I ever expected, and he felt the same way."

How can she know that? I refuse to believe she didn't seduce him like one of the leggy, high-heeled working girls I used to see in their fishnet stockings every night going in and out of the hotels lining Central Park South.

"We started seeing one another." Naomi pulls a tissue from her pocket and wipes her eyes. Mine stay dry. "I violated my rule of never dating married men."

A woman of scruples.

Naomi goes on, oblivious to my feelings or my reaction, an emotional bulimic, purging. Like the Ancient Mariner, she needs to get her story out, and as if I am anticipating every soppy detail, like the wedding guest, I listen while I put one foot in front of the other. I am oblivious to stalking seagulls and the detritus washed up by the sea. I can only listen.

"I kept telling myself to end it, and weeks and even months would go by when we'd be apart. Then he'd call or I'd call and it would start up all over again. After every split, we found a way back to one another.

459

He was a drug and I was an addict."

Where was I during all of this? Content and oblivious, trusting my husband; making plans and dinner and love; being a wife and a mother and a daughter and a docent and a dope.

"I was tortured, but it was worse for Ben. He didn't want to hurt you — he never said he didn't love you."

The chop of the water blows and stings. That my husband talked about me to this woman is a violation that slices into my heart. I bark out, "I get it! I've heard enough."

"I think you need to hear more. Please. Ben started suggesting how I could improve Adam and Eve. He thought I was a pretty good businesswoman."

Ben loved to give people gratis legal advice, help kids get into Brown and Columbia, find them jobs, and connect buyers with sellers. I loved that my husband could be generous, without agenda — but not to her.

"And then I got pregnant."

She bends to pick up Theo as I feel myself turn into a shadow that the wind will surely whisk into the sea.

Then she got pregnant.

I want to wail. I want to run back to my

car. I want to stop listening to this treason, which my bullshit detector uncovered long ago, yet all of me denied. Naomi goes on. Does she think if I hear everything, I will forgive her? I wish I could make myself stick my fingers in my ears and scream.

"I missed a few periods and figured, okay, menopause. Forty-two is young but it happens. I was three months gone by the time I saw a doctor. When she said 'pregnant' . . ."

Naomi's sentences drift into the wind.

"I never asked Ben to take care of the baby. I didn't want him to break up his family for me — for us — not that I ever thought he would. Then he had the idea to invest in my business. It wasn't just a way to help me and the baby. . . ."

Ben was expecting a baby. We slept together every night, laughed over dinners and sitcoms and our daughters' foibles, worried about my mother, celebrated holidays and birthdays, planned a trip to Japan, all while he had a child on the way with a woman he loved. And he's not even here for me to kill.

"He expected to get a return on his investment when Adam and Eve became profitable — knock wood."

She says "knock wood" exactly as Ben does.

"A handsome profit."

"Naomi, stop!" I say, standing still. Theo starts to cry at the shrillness of my voice. Naomi scoops him up. "Did you ever wonder where all that investment money came from?" I didn't intend to grab her arm but I did, squeezing tightly.

She flinches. "Ben led me to believe he had deep pockets." She tries to pull away but I hold tight through Theo's wailing.

"That money ate up all of our savings, our investments. Ben took out second mortgages. . . ." To impress this woman?

"I didn't let myself think I'd taken it from you and your daughters."

I am incredulous. We had been comfortable, but not wealthy enough to bankroll a whole business, and even if Ben considered Adam and Eve to be a risk-free venture on which he'd see a significant return, it was *our* money, not his to spend without consulting me.

I am changing dance partners. My anger shifts to Ben, though I recognize this man, who always tried to do right by everyone he loved. This was something I adored, as long as the loved ones were people I loved, too.

"After Theo was born, I moved into my mother's house and with her help and Clem's, I've managed," Naomi is saying. "Clementine and I don't have many friends

— it's fair to call us loners. Most folks think the baby is hers. Out here single moms don't turn a head. No one asks questions."

I take in her story, sordid and ordinary, except that it involves my own husband. I try not think of how the life of Luey's unborn child began, and whether it's any nobler to get impregnated by a single man during a one-night hookup.

"When did Ben give you the ring?" I look at her hands, which are free of gloves, and the jewelry in question.

"Last year on Theo's first birthday. I knew by then Ben would never leave you, so it was instead of an engagement ring. I only wore it a few times, because once he told me how much it was worth —"

"Which was how much?" Is it wrong to ask your husband's mistress such a question? Hell, no.

"Plenty, though a fraction of what Ben thought. He was pissed at your brother's appraisal — that much I know. He wanted to use the ring as collateral for a loan. So he got it appraised by another jeweler who must have been a swindler, swapping out the original ring for another. Of course I didn't know that until last week. But what does it matter? Frankly, I never loved it. Where would I wear something like that?

I'm usually up to my elbows in manure."

"Mommy, I'm cold," Theo says, his teeth chattering.

Naomi holds him close. I stare into the toddler's tiny face to search for Benjamin Theodore Silver. I find innocence and my husband's puckish smile, which almost makes me forgive Ben. But not quite.

"I'm with Theo," I say, sorry for making this little boy suffer. "This is no place for any of us" — the wind slams a wet chill against my face — "and I've heard enough."

We tramp in silence on the hard sand back to the parking lot. I feel dazed and as heavy as wet laundry, when Naomi says, "Now I hope you understand why I sent you whatever money was left in the account. The last check was from selling the ring."

"Restitution?"

"Call it whatever you want — it was less than I expected it to be." She laughs, a short, caustic snicker. "Ben was ripped off. What does it matter? He's dead, poor guy. And I miss him."

I don't, I think, less today than yesterday, as we walk to the parking lot. My life is going forward without him, with its own problems to wrangle and solve. Luey. Her baby. Nicola. My mother. Me. The money from Naomi can buy me time. If I'm frugal,

I could stretch it for two years. But whether I keep it or not, I'm in the same three-penny opera as when I woke up this morning, although now I also need to decide whether to tell Nicola and Luey that they have a stepbrother young enough to be their child. And who am *I* to Ben's son? Perhaps there's a term for it in French.

"Are we done here?" I ask, tired in every way.

"I'm hoping we're not," she says. "I want to show you something. It's not far. We could drive together."

"No," I say. "I'll follow."

She walks to her van, I to my car. Naomi drives slowly, a responsible parent, as we travel roads slick with drizzle turning to ice. The fog is more socked in than before; I was wrong about the sun burning through. I've been wrong about so much.

I consider going back home, but my car is propelling itself. Naomi makes a right turn, then another, and travels down a newly graveled road lined with blue spruce and scrubby pines. At the end is a sprawling gray-shingled building attached to large, empty greenhouses. She slows and stops.

"You can park here," she says, as she gets out and unbuckles Theo from his car seat. He runs to the building's door, Naomi two steps behind. She reaches into her pocket, unlocks the door, and with a smile that turns her tense face pretty, says, "Welcome to the new home of Adam and Eve."

I follow Naomi and Theo into a wide open space and breathe in the clean aroma of sawdust and freshly cut wood. The room is crowded with carpentry equipment and unopened cans of polyurethane. Floor-to-ceiling shelves and deep, glass-fronted refrigerated units that line three walls, waiting for plants and tall, galvanized steel buckets of cut flowers. The ceiling is high, with two industrial fans. Theo runs around the room, his arms spread like wings.

"Terrific, yes?" Naomi says. Before I can answer, she says, "There's more," motioning me to follow through a door. There is pride in her voice as we enter a space with wide casement windows and a view of a large field. "I'll plant sunflowers this summer," she says. "Imagine." She points to another window. "Trees and shrubs and topiaries and garden ornaments will be for sale out front and back here."

White wooden cabinets have already been installed in what is clearly a kitchen. Appliances stand by in large cardboard boxes and a slab of soapstone has been fashioned into a sink. "If you walk through here" — she points to a door — "there's a living room with a wood stove, three bedrooms, and a bathroom. The apartment's not fancy, but what do you think?"

I peek into a room with unpainted wainscotings. I think, this is where my family's security has gone, into hardwood floors, skim-coated walls, and Naomi's dreams. I think, this is agony. I think, that's a God-awful plastic light fixture. I look out the window. I don't see a ripe golden haze on the meadow. I've seen enough.

"It should be done by July. My contractor friend Vince and his crew are working six days a week."

What can I say? You know contractors — good luck with that.

"I was planning to move in with Theo and Clementine, but I've changed my mind."

"Are you going to sell?" Because if you do, those proceeds are mine. Winner takes all.

"It would break my heart to sell. This is everything I've ever wanted," Naomi says.

Did she want Ben — or just what he could buy her?

"Georgia, what I'm saying is, it's yours."

Naomi McCann is insane, conceivably. "Excuse me. You're giving away your business?"

"I haven't made myself entirely clear."

"No, you haven't." I am determined not to like Naomi but in our tug-of-war, she is putting everything into trying to make me believe that inside her lives a fair and almost saintly woman.

"I want you to run the store — there will be a shop here — and start a business selling houseplants. I've seen what you can do, and I've heard more from Ben. He would brag about you a bit. I hated it. . . ." She burbles on about how she would handle the landscaping and I, indoor plants; how we could build the business together; how she's been thinking about this ever since she saw my double amaryllis and how she can continue to live in her *Three Little Pigs* brick house with her mother and Clem.

"Dial back. You're suggesting I live here, too?"

"Why not, for a while? Everyone in town knows your house is on the market. You can stay til you figure things out."

I wonder what it would take for me to see this crackpot offer not as a deal with the devil but as one of two women united by need, pragmatism, and conjoined history, each solving their own problems and possibly building something new, something together.

Naomi McCann is crazy. But in the role of crazier, I, Georgia Waltz, am not saying no.

51.

"Finish up, Theo honey," Naomi says. "We're leaving in five minutes."

She and Clementine have loaded the van with plants to surround Ben's grave before the rest of us arrive. They will pay their respects, then leave Theo with me and his sisters.

Naomi's sea of sunflowers has come and gone. I accepted her olive branch and the two of us are partners, with me living in the back of a store. Most of what Adam and Eve clears we invest in the business — we're far from being in the black — but when I fall asleep, it's with no regrets. I'm taking care of the people I love, and one of them is me. As for my old house, with its vast new garage, dark blue paint, and a second-story renovation that's made history of the widow's walk, the place no longer feels like home. I've stopped circling past it when I travel into town. I have paid my taxes, even those strictly emotional.

To call Naomi a friend would be as disingenuous as a Best Actress contender breathlessly declaring that she slept through the announcement of Oscar nominees. I see us as a team, women who have declared a truce and are too busy to strip-search their souls and indulge in acid flashbacks. I've stopped looking for answers and try to live in the present, sinking myself into running the shop, cultivating hothouse hydrangeas, and scouting hither and yon for garden ornaments. No gnomes need apply. I fix Theo's eggs exactly as he wants them, as yellow as the man in the moon, just as Naomi is an ace at slaying slugs, planning major jobs, and calming Luey's baby by singing "Too Ra, Loo Ra, Luey."

Once, I thought a family was a mother, a father, and their biological progeny. Foolish me. A family is whatever you make it, and mine is a supple infrastructure whose roots grow stronger by the day, as do Theo and my newborn granddaughter, who makes him grin, exactly like his father made all of us grin. She is round with spiky, white-blond hair, a coconut macaroon we pass from arm to welcoming arm. The baby sees her mother on weekends along with her aunt Cola. Clementine is here every day, often with Caleb, the tree EMT. He has that timeless hard-hat-plaid-shirt-Levi's-work-boot-stubble-chainsaw thing going. If I were twenty-three, I wouldn't be able to resist him either.

Stephan and Daniel do drive-bys. For my brother, two tiny children may as well be a pair of barking dingoes. It's Nat who is the secret sauce that makes my life complete. Some weekends he mans the griddle — pancakes for all! — and on others, I escape to his place in Manhattan for cultural pig-outs: MoMA, eel-avocado rolls, art-house movies, and conversation with envoys from the smooth-talking, fast-walking, *New Yorker*-quoting universe who think that eight hundred dollars is what you spend on shoes, not rent. As never before, I notice the city's clamor and grime. By Sunday night I am happy to return to my grassy sanctuary filled with seedlings and second-hand baby gear, grill bluefish freshly caught from Peconic Bay, and settle down with a library book. I'm not sure if I've grown or shrunk and I don't give a damn.

Peter makes his presence known mostly in bank deposits, toys — a stuffed alpaca the size of a collie arrived last week — and, his most generous gift of all, Luey's NYU tuition. He shows up less often than she might like, though that is conjecture. My daughter guards her heart and I try to respect her privacy. Like learning to share, this is a lifelong lesson, because whenever I look at Peter's daughter, I ache for what he and she are missing.

Every day I see more of Ben in Theo — his mojo and, occasionally, his mulishness. Naomi's mother keeps her distance, but from ten to five each day she looks after Theo as well as Luey's baby, whom she appears to like far more than she does me. The woman has her loyalties to her own daughter. This I understand.

Ben is a ghost that Naomi and I do not mention, though some days I feel him hovering, a breeze that could turn to a gale if I allowed it. Then the baby cries or Theo laughs or the bell announces a customer and Ben fades into celestial oblivion.

I look at the clock. "Time to leave, toots," I say as I lift my granddaughter. She is wearing a lavender velvet dress and a striped sweater of which her great-grandmother would approve. I am sure Camille Waltz would ratify little else in my life and — rah, rah, dementia — I haven't had to explain my armistice with Naomi. I am only sorry that my mother is now so far gone, she doesn't realize she has a namesake: Camille

Silver-Waltz. Camille *Prairie-Rose* Silver-Waltz.

Since taking care of one small baby is the hardest job on earth, I am constantly late, as I am today. By the time I arrive at Westchester Hills, Nicola and Luey are standing by a handful of Ben's cousins. Stephan and Daniel are holding Theo's hands. I didn't invite Nat. This isn't a plus-one occasion, though I know he'll expect a full accounting. He calls himself my forever-boyfriend.

"Camy!" Luey rushes to her child and holds her close. "Did you miss Mommy? Where's my kiss? I missed you, baby girl." Luey and her daughter are in love with the force of ten thousand suns.

"Mother," Cola says, and crushes me in a hug. "Did you see what Naomi and Clementine did?"

Until I feel Nicola's tears, I was keeping it together. When I reach Ben's grave, I, too, cry. Naomi and Clementine have surrounded it with boxwood and myrtle and have planted a maple sapling. In years to come, I imagine its scarlet leaves shading his headstone, a final resting place fit for a Broadway supernova. A passerby might say, *Remind me, please — did Ben Silver once co-star with Tony Randall? I don't recall. Who* was *he?*

Good question. Father, husband, lawyer, friend, lover. For Ben's inscription, I considered each honorific, even Stephan's suggestion, "Deceiving others — that is what the world calls a romance." With all due respect to Oscar Wilde, however, I went with, *Benjamin Theodore Silver, an enigma loved by many.* Let generations stand by his grave and think, *Hmmm, interesting.* Ben would like that, my last gift to him.

We make short work of the ceremony. Theo clutches my hand, spellbound by Ben's bearded cousin from Philadelphia chanting kaddish. Nicola recites the twenty-third psalm, and lest this occasion become too macabre, Luey plays "What a Wonderful World" on her iPod while Camille grooves to Louis Armstrong in her arms.

I cannot stop looking at my daughters, whose long girlhoods are ending. Luey is earning A's in both motherhood and economics. Nicola has found a vocation and love, possibly; I hear a lot of Michael this and Michael that — he's been promoted and outgrown his T— and as for the chef in Paris, I've forgotten his name and hope Cola has, too. Michael is hoping for an internship in New York, because my daughter insists she's here to stay. She, too, has a business to grow.

Benjy, where did we go right?

We let Theo pull the netting off the headstone, and one by one we each put a pebble on the grave and whisper private good-byes. I don't forgive Ben. Perhaps I never will. But a woman is fortunate if her dreams overlap even slightly with her reality. I thank my husband for the many years mine did.

I have taught myself how to transplant a new branch onto an old one. I am that branch and I am thriving. The last year has begun to turn into rich compost that nourishes new dreams. Autumn's first leaves are falling, golden priority mail reminding us of beauty, even in death. Mother Nature and Father Time have such a bag of tricks.

I link arms with my daughters. Luey and Camille are on one side, Cola is on the other. I am in the middle, walking into the future, away from anger, from disappointment, and from regret. I refused to be scared, or to believe that my future is a well of endless lament. I am galvanized by possibility.

I am choosing happiness.

ACKNOWLEDGMENTS

Everyday pluck has always fascinated me. *The Widow Waltz* grew from my desire to write about a woman with no history of bravery — in other words, a woman like most of us — who is forced by life to weave a magic carpet of resilience to carry her forward. In writing this book and shepherding it into print, I have received help from many people.

I could not ask for a better publisher than Clare Ferraro of Viking. Thank you for believing in me as a novelist as well as a journalist, and for allowing me to work with Carolyn Carlson, an exceptional editor thanks to her way with words, her guidance in finessing plot points and her bottomless encouragement. I have hit the jackpot to have such wise women in my corner. To Roseanne Serra, great cover! You captured the ultimate optimism of this book while demonstrating that fifty-year-old women can still have great legs. Alissa Amell, your interior design is elegant and timeless. Patricia Nicolescu, you copyedit like an artist. Nancy Sheppard, this book would literally be nowhere without your stellar marketing team. Deep thanks, too, to all of you and to Carolyn Coleburn, a whiz at promotion, and her protegée Langan Kingsley, who keeps thinking of ways to get the word out on this novel. Last, much appreciation to Ramona Demme for her constant kind attention.

For all five of my books, I offer boundless recognition to Christy Fletcher, whose critical eye and excellent taste are matched only by her warm championing. Everyone on her team is top-of-the-line, but I must offer special shout-outs to Melissa Chinchilla, Mink Choi, Kevin Cotter and Rebecca Gradinger.

Special gratitude goes to Paul Hundt, Esq. for his generous research about forensic accounting, a subject with which — happily — I had zero familiarity before I wrote this book. Charles Salzberg, thanks for your friendship and literary gossip and for leading many rollicking workshops where I was able to present the beginning of this book. Vivian Conan, Chaya Deitch, Sally Hoskins and Craig Irvine: you are all exceptional writers; I am grateful for the time you took to offer fastidious feedback on *The Widow Waltz* as it continued to evolve. Thanks, too, to the support of the New York Writers' Workshop; to my book club, whose selections stretch my mind — Salman Rushdie, really? — and to my cyber village on Facebook, Twitter and LinkedIn. You keep me inspired on those long days as I try to charm my laptop into coughing up words.

To the many special book-lovers in my life — especially Anne, Barbsie, Betsy, Dale, Janey, Kimberly, Michele, Rochelle and Vicki — I am truly fortunate to have such warm, funny women in my corner. Thanks, ladies!

To my sons, Jed and Rory, you make me proud in ways that I can never stop counting. I hope you are glad that in *The Widow Waltz* this is your only mention.

Last but always first, thanks to Robert, my husband, who has believed in me since way back when. Your infectious smile and laugh blaze my way.